GORSE

GORSE

SAM K. HORTON

SOLARIS

First published 2024 by Solaris
an imprint of Rebellion Publishing Ltd,
Riverside House, Osney Mead,
Oxford, OX2 0ES, UK

www.solarisbooks.com

ISBN: 978-1-83786-071-5

10 9 8 7 6 5 4 3 2 1

A CIP catalogue record for this book is available
from the British Library.

Cover art and illustrations by Veronica Park

Designed & typeset by Rebellion Publishing

Printed in the United Kingdom

For my grandmother, Rita,
who told me I could do anything.

And for my partner and family,
who had to deal with the consequences.

PART ONE

*"Black chaos comes, and the fettered gods of the earth
say let there be light."*
—Thomas Hardy, *The Return of the Native*

BOG-OAK

The Fellmire, 1781

HE HAS NOT stopped running. As soon as the door of the boat closed behind him, he knew it was for good. *To Hell with him, and the girl. To Hell with all of them.* The books he stole have shown him the way. Besides, he has lived there. He has spent years below. The moor will remember him. He knows it. His arms and chest sting. He hadn't even had a chance to show old one eye the signs he'd carved into them.

He had tried. Every year above, he had tried. He is done failing. Done disappointing everyone he met. His father wouldn't look at him any longer. Had stopped, even, asking him to come to church. He knew he was an embarrassment. Fine! He had never asked to return to this place. It had been a mistake, he knew it, it had to be. He belongs below. They will be so pleased to see him. So happy when he returns! The Fellmire hasn't been easy to find but he remembers the way. He stops at the stump and looks back, just in case. Nobody has followed him, and disappointment, loathed disappointment, singes his chest. I don't need them. I don't need them.

He walks without hesitation into the water, stripping clothes as he goes, naked when he reaches the centre. There is just the sack in his hand with the tools he needs. The book had been clear. He knows the rules. First are the gold candle sticks, the paten and cup he had stolen from the chapel.

9

The cross. Each he drops into the water and watches as the black swallows the gold. *A good offering.* Next, he slips the leather thong around his neck and draws it tight. Taking a knife, he makes a nick in his thigh; he has studied the book, is sure he is right and yet—it is a *lot* of blood—he watches it, running thick and fast across his leg, feels the heat of it. He smiles to see the lights dancing on the bog, pinpricks of brightness at the corners of his vision. *It's you, isn't it? You know I'm coming.* He feels happy, light. Only a few more steps. A bottle filled with the potion he brewed. Each flower measured carefully, only an ounce or two out and he'll be dead before he hits the water, but he knows he mixed it right. It burns his throat.

It's then that he sees them. Their faces peering just as he remembers.

'You came! I knew it. I knew you would.' His voice slurs, and his friends are shifting but he sees them. 'Why do you all look so worried? It's okay, I'm coming home.'

Things are hazier now. He drops to a knee, the cold water mixing with the hot blood that flows more slowly. His mouth feels dry. There is a flurry of panic, though it seems distant, as though it belongs to another, and he reaches out for help.

'My friends, please. I'm not sure I've got this quite right— help me, please.' But the faces don't move closer. Instead, they disappear one by one as he sinks below the water.

I've changed my mind. The thought rises in bubbles around him. It does no good. *Please, someone, help me. I don't want to go.*

The water seeks ingress. It trickles into his mouth, his ears and nose. Fills him up with decay, with rot. He cannot breathe against the weight of it. The potion has robbed him of strength, he cannot lift his arms, lower his feet. There is a dull pulse where he nicked his leg. Too deeply, perhaps. *They will come, him or my father. One of them will notice I am gone and come for me. Surely. They won't let me...*

He cannot think any longer. Cannot recall his name or why he came here. He feels hot, the panic racing across his skin, pressing as close as the water, suffocating him. The world is a red pulse behind his eyes.

He dies alone.

A SHIMMER. A trick of the light. The world turns on a flower head and above becomes below. Two ghosts look up at a boy caught in the sky.

Hello, brother what is this?
A friend in need?
Indeed. Caught on the rocks like eel skin.
Wake up, little changeling. Little left-behind.
We remember you.
Both of us do.
A dulled blade, but we can make you sharp.
Send you back, to finish what you started.
A little pulling on the threads.
A loosening of the weave.
Letting in the nightmares with every dropped stitch.
Sew up that mouth, brother.
Not a word more.

DEVIL'S CLOVER

The High Moor, Cornwall, 1786

THE WIND HOWLS banshee across the barren sweep of the moor. Moonlight catches on the rocks like cow hair on heather and the sky seems empty, even of owls. You'd be forgiven for thinking that nothing sails on this inland sea.

And yet.

Silhouetted against the frosted night sky is the outline of two rocky tors, topped with tumbling boulder stacks that could be sleeping giants, stubby grass covers pulled tight about their ears. In the foothills are scattered outcrops of granite, clustered here and there in the ghostly shape of a home, the last lingering line of a field long fallow. Memories of a Neolithic past that, despite their age have weathered the storms, have lingered long after their inhabitants have gone. Leaving a theatre set, half-struck; understudy sheep wandering aimlessly across the stage.

The best stones have gone, taken to form the cornerstones of farmhouses, the foundation of a church. Old pagan rocks holding the new world on their shoulders. The only ones left are here because they are too big to move, they provide a windbreak for livestock and unwary travellers, their hollows bower-birded with linings of lamb's wool and heather. Cosy spots to freeze in.

The starlight is broken here and there by batwings, and

13

the grass rustles with the scrambling of stoat and weasel, the screech of a fox, whilst hares lie snug in their forms.

The longer grass hides the nests of birds, of plover and pipit and lark. Burying their song-shelled eggs down on the ground. If disturbed birds rise, like sparks from a fire, they draw hungry eyes away from the floor. And distraction is dangerous on such rocky ground, there's more than one traveller killed by the birds.

In the valley, horses, sheep and cows graze, cloven hoofprints amongst patches of reeds where the water is, and sunken men still reach for air though there are no lungs left in their chests.

For there is death here, telling its story. It gives rise to the tangled growth of the boggy marshy mires, iris in the springtime, blackthorn all year round. Most of the dead are old, men and women long gone and nothing, now, but rich black soil.

But sometimes, new tragedies bloom.

In the bottom of this mire, dappled by the shadow of thorns, a boy lies. Moonlit. Stars reflected on open eyes until storm clouds gather for the rain.

COTTON GRASS

IT'S TOO BEAUTIFUL a day for the task at hand, the night's rain frozen into a blanket of ice. Even here on the moor, where all work starts early, there are few about to see the group of men and the cart that trundles over the clapper bridge that spans the ditch surrounding the village. Two pieces of granite, one roughhewn and tall, the other a carved and worn-weathered cross fallen flat. Few around to see the form laid out under a blanket in the back of the cart. The freezing air snaps under the weight of the wheels and it fills with the smells of peat fires, frost, and the ache of lichened branches. Welcome to Mirecoombe.

Watch your feet in the mud.

The party are barely over the boundary when the silence is broken.

'What's this then?' The voice is Luk Calder's, looming from the frost-bitten shadows with an accusatory stare. The men with the cart look up nervously. Luk's voice is loud, and they can feel the village stirring. The cart driver pulls on his reins and slows the horses to a stop.

'What it isn't is something to be discussed here. Go open the long house, Luk, if you've a mind to help, or let us pass without comment.'

Luk's brow furrows into a scowl.

'I'll be the judge of that, Master Wickett. What do you have in the back there?'

Davy Wickett shifts in his seat and plays nervously with the leather reins. At nineteen he's half the age and size of the man in front of him, the man who has moved from his place in the shadows to stand in the road, blocking the way. The men accompanying the wagon are holding their tongues and not one will meet Davy's gaze as he casts about for help.

'Please, Luk, just help me get to the long house quietly and I'll tell you everything there.'

Luk Calder's scowl deepens, and he moves swiftly to the rear of the cart, pulling himself up, heavily. As he reaches for the blanket, Davy reaches out a hand, places it around the other man's wrist and, swallowing his fear, stops him.

'It's Salan Dell, Luk. The boys and I found him in the valley, in the mire. He's dead.'

Wrenching himself free, Luk draws back the blanket revealing the body beneath. The boy lies in the morning sun, his shirt muddied and crumpled from the peat and grass he was found in. Peaceful and pale, he could have been caught sleeping if it wasn't for the livid red handprint that rings his neck, if it wasn't for the loll of his head. Luk Calder takes it in, covers him, then turns to the others. Stepping down with a grunt, feet breaking the ice that cases the mud, Luk turns to face Davy.

'Get him to the longhouse. Then fetch his parents.' Luk looks to the young men standing at either side of the cart. 'Wake the village. I'm going to call the Reverend.'

From a perch on a rooftop, a small face listens then slips away, unseen.

It does not take long for the news to spread. It is not a large village, Mirecoombe. Just a small cluster of houses, each built by lamplight after the day's work was done, that sits uncomfortably on a road that came later, weaving its way past little walled gardens, past the smithy. Here and there, in the stonework, little signs carved into the granite. Some faded with age, and some freshly scratched. Protections. Considering the business of the day people have begun to question their purpose. Theirs and the man who carved them. The villagers crowd about in front of a low, long building. A blackened storm-blasted oak growing from a wall, its eaves studded with ventilation holes. For part of the year, it stores grain, for part it shelters the ponies that wander freely off the moor. When needed, as today, it is a place to lay the dead. This last role once a rarity, now unnervingly common.

Luk stands, arms folded at the doorway, waiting. Out of the shadows, still in the morning sun, it is easier to see him. He is a witless man, Luk Calder, but a cunning one. His eyes, grey and stark, dart from one face in the crowd to the next, so every man woman and child is under no illusion that they are watched. Dark-haired, granite-shouldered, face clean-shaven he is a man capable of hard work who chooses not to do it. His clothes, whilst functional, are fine and though the fabric is tough it is not worn through at the cuffs, at the knees. He is an impressive figure. There is chatter, and the crowd parts to allow two people to walk through. Even Luk's face softens as they approach, and he steps aside.

Hugh and Seren Dell, here to see their son. Hugh Dell pulls the heavy door open; there are markings here too, carved about the jamb. Interlocking circles and a flowerhead, to stop things getting in or out. A hum beneath the flagstones they stand on. A badger heart stuffed with pins is buried underneath, beating.

Hugh and Seren step into the room. It is hard to see at first. The bright light fighting with the darkness until eyes adjust. But there he is. He fills the space, this small and quiet body. There is no room for anyone else.

Salan Dell.

Twenty-two and nice as they come. What would have become of him had he lived? He had a job, stable boy at the house across the moor. He had a beau or two. He would have married, been one of the ones to stay. And now gone. It is a shame to see him lying there, on the slate, eyes closed. His buzzard-brown hair is still glossy in the half-light; a bird's feather, magpie, or jay, still caught in it. His face is pale, fine-boned, the colour drained from it. Though closed now, his eyes were violet. Davy has laid him on the long slate table that runs down the centre of the barn. He has done his best, smoothed Salan's shirt, blue and white stripes running down his body and still neatly buttoned at the front. He has lain Salan's hands across his breast.

Salan's parents move quietly, cautiously to their son's side and reach shaking hands towards him.

'Oh Sal...' Hugh's voice falters but he steadies it just in time to catch his wife as she sinks to her knees, wails filling the cold room. Tears fall from Hugh's eyes too and they hold each other tightly. In the half-light, the red handprint still seems to shine. Salan Dell is the fifth to die with these fingers around his neck and still nobody saw it coming.

Outside the sound of mourning seeps out from between the granite and the crowd gazes sadly at each other. Luk has gone, off up the hill to speak to the Reverend, replaced here by his father, Locryn Calder, who has travelled down from his farm that perches on the valley side. He has heard the news.

'Another, is it?' He announces this question to the crowd, but nobody answers. He is not liked, Locryn Calder. He is his eldest son aged, the same cold eyes, the same powerful shoulders though his bowed with age. Unlike his son, however, his muscles remember a life of arduous work. He took a small farm, made it bigger, and now he manages that and the moor, hands out the jobs. He oversees the turf cutting, the splitting of the stone. There are no lords to take their rents in this valley, no manorial oversight, so he stepped in. He holds the fortunes of the village in his old, gnarled hands and he grips them tight.

'Nobody? I'll answer myself then. It is another. Five! Five dead. Are we still meant to be waiting for help or are we allowed to take things into our own hands now?'

Nothing.

'Has anyone even seen him? Recently. No? What an utterly predictable surprise, and yet still I see you wearing his charms!' He jabs knuckled fingers towards the men stood closest to him, a sprig of blackthorn pinned in most of their lapels. The old man's voice is loud.

'You are a backward lot. And if Pel—'

'Be quiet, Locryn.' A woman has pushed her way from the back of the crowd which parts gratefully before her. Madge Gould, landlady of the Mare's Nest Inn and taker of no nonsense. Calder does as he's told, holds his tongue, though his eyes still sparkle with malice. Madge stares him down. 'I've unlocked the Nest. Pay your respects all of you and then come and drown your sorrows, leave the Dells to grieve alone. All welcome—even you, Calder.' Madge steps into the long house to look in on the dead and the crowd form a line behind her. Calder joins at the back.

Inside the house, Hugh and Seren stand back and allow the mourners to pass. They look at Salan sadly as they do, marvel that the boy they knew is gone. Some lay objects at his side, some say a prayer. Locryn Calder is the last to pass by and looks uncomfortable in such an intimate setting, nodding curtly to the Dells, all three of them, as he goes.

Once all the mourners are gone, Salan Dell lies on a bed of tokens: dried flowerheads and pebbles, knots of red string and stones with holes going through them. There are crosses too, woven from reeds, and glass beads strung on rosaries. Salan's byre shines with belief in one thing or another, and as the door closes on him and his parents, it's hard not to think he'd be glad of it.

ACROSS THE VILLAGE, the frost is almost gone. Only the shining ghosts of shadows, where the sun's moved on, still linger. Back to the Mare's Nest Inn. Forever serving something to somebody. Nestled in the crook of a hill, the arm of a giant, sleeping. It has stood, slant-walled and buttressed with leaning granite for a few hundred years. The old sign swinging in the wind. An unusual name, an unusual place. They build ceilings low in this part of the world, and it's brought lower by the peat smoke that billows from burning turf. From every rafter hangs a trinket. Hunting horns. Mole traps. A thousand shining horse brasses hanging amongst them. A stuffed fox's head, listening.

This was where Black Anne drank, first amongst the highway folk. She sat right there and shot a man through the window, so they say. They say, too, that if you stand outside at midnight, she'll come and offer you a ride. But the cellars aren't deep enough for that much Dutch courage. Nobody's ever taken that cold hand and come back to talk about it.

Everyone passes through here. Locryn Calder has taken his seat at the bar, the same he always takes, and next to him sits Cusk, farm manager, gamekeeper, friend. Trouble both. Next to them, sitting nervously, is Billy Askell. A looker-on. The brewery's man, his delivery made, he'd thought he'd join the lock-in. Now he's trapped in a wake, an interloper in someone else's grief. Serving them at the bar is Madge Gould.

She's been here as long as most can remember. Spry no matter how old she is, and nobody can agree on that, canny too. Long hair tied up with a white ribbon. She keeps all in line. Takes in all news. Doles it out in packets, to those she thinks could use it. Here, away from the reality of a boy now dead, the talk is reverting to gossip.

'Who found him?' That's Cusk, gravel-voiced and not looking up from his glass. Tweed elbows scuffing the bar.

'Davy Wickett.' That's Askell, who ought not to have answered. This chat is not for him.

'What would you know?' A voice from the back but joined by others.

'His magic tricks have told him.'

'Didn't know the real thing came so cheap.' Mirthless laughter. It's true, Billy's waist jangles with charms bought from charlatans he's met on his rounds. He's not from here, Billy. Treats the place like a fairground, thinks it's a case of pick and choose. Those that live here know better. Magic on the moor is life and death, and there's no escaping either.

Madge glares at him as she wipes a tankard clean or thereabouts, and he ducks his head down and stares at his drink.

'He was in yesterday, poor boy.' Madge speaks softly, puts the conversation back on track, and everybody stops to listen. 'Drinking with Mary Fletcher.' Madge sighs, 'He always left a little out for those that wanted feeding. Always very polite when he had something to ask of Them.'

'Aye,' says Calder, not looking up, 'Maybe that was what killed him.'

Like a whippet Madge swings around.

'Oh, out with it, Calder! Get it off your chest why don't you.'
The old farmer turns on his stool, so he faces the room.

'Yes, Madge, I will. Five of our own are dead. Killed out on
the moor. And where is our glorious protector, our "Keeper"?
Where is the man who takes your money? Who gives you
bundles of sticks to pin on your breast? Nowhere! That old
bastard is laughing at us from his house out there. You're
all fools to keep paying him. Nothing in those hills but his
jangling pockets.'

There is a muttering at this. But not from Madge.

'Pel has helped this village a lot more than you have, Calder.'
She does her best to quiet the bar but the mutters have not
stopped. 'He does more than you know. He deals with Them,
for a start. Makes sure They're good to us. Things might not
be what they were, but we'd be a damn sight worse without
him.'

She's not wrong. Once, not long ago, this little empire, this
moor sunk deep between the hills like a book slipped behind
a shelf, ran on the old ways. A belief in things that few could
see but all could sense. A belief in give and take. Many have
wondered how one person could run such a busy little inn
with so very little help, just a boy to fetch and carry and a girl
to make the beds. The answer sleeps on straw downstairs,
below the drinkers' feet. The clientele can't see the footprints
in the spilt beer, can't hear the singing in the cellar, but there's
hidden help here. Pel arranged it, all parties happy. She's one
of the few that still welcome his help. It's a dying art, his.
And people forget.

Things are changing, though, even here. The hills grow
restless, contracts break, these deaths are stirring up trouble.
Half the village already turned to the house on the hill where
God sits and waits for them on Sunday.

Locryn Calder, still not meeting the landlady's eyes, is not done with this. He can feel his friend, Cusk, by his elbow, silently lending support. He knows he's not alone in questioning the way of things.

'All I'm saying Madge is that They aren't what they were. Time was you felt Their help. They don't give as much as They take any longer. Maybe it's time we were done with Them. Besides, the Reverend says They're devils. Always have been. Better to deal with Them as such.'

How long can a thing hold if it's pulled two ways?

A growl from the man to his left, Cusk stands with his friend. With a sigh, Madge runs a hand through her hair, almost all grey but still a seam of gold shot through it.

'Does he?' There is scorn in her voice. She is not one of the converted. 'I remember when he felt differently. When you all did. Funny how things change. It used to be there was room enough for everyone in this valley.'

Calder looks dully at Madge. He is older than her and looks it. His face furrowed and unshaven, bristling with white hairs.

'If Pel had shown his face here once in the past few weeks I'd be more inclined to believe you, Madge. But where is he? Where is our Keeper?'

STICHWORT

WHERE INDEED? WHERE is Lord Pelagius Hunt, Keeper of the High Moor? And, for that matter, Lord of what? Nothing, if he's asked. He's denied the title as long as he's had it—and he's had it awhile. The men and women that work the land don't call him "sir", though they know the castle he's forsaken, know it stands empty and full of ghosts and the sweetest birdsong at dusk. They give no deference, no tip of the hat; he holds no moral or legal sway over any of them. But every now and then one ties a brace of rabbit to his gatepost, replaces a slate on his roof because it's best not to make an enemy of a friend.

He is a Keeper. A person chosen to watch the line, the fragile one that separates us from Them, one from the other. The magic from the man. There is more in this world than many people know, there is plenty in the world we've forgotten. Lie on the ground beneath a tall granite stone and close your eyes, you'll see. Might even feel a small hand take yours. Keepers make sure that the little hands that take don't take too much, or anything that's missed. And in return, they stop unkind men from hurting things they don't understand. A word in a farmer's ear not to plough a field, a house built on a plot suggested as better than the one chosen, a fishing boat delayed for an hour to give another a chance at the catch. There are many Keepers, each with their jurisdictions but they grow fewer, and older, by the year. The job is harder these days.

They help with other things too. With things that wake that ought to stay sleeping, with the dead. He does not live in the village. He never has. It's the edges where he's needed, and it's there that he's stayed. Moored, in every sense, at the base of Echo Tor, the hill that rises sharply above his home. It is an odd house. A ship upturned, keel to the sky as if pegged to the ground by its masts. The caulking in the boards clearly well kept, oakum poking threadbare from the timbers to drive out the rain. There are some on the moor who might remember it arriving, though they would not admit it.

The legend goes that the ship sailed up to the port at Bosmorven and kept on tacking, high above the ground, when a storm beached it here.

Or that Old Pel, then young, built it himself, one plank at a time, from a boat he'd found under the earth.

Others say that Pel heard from a friend about a shipwreck sitting pretty in a cove. That he hired a cart, loaded it with wood and rope, drove it to this spot then went back for another load. On and on 'til done.

Each visitor can decide for themselves which version is correct. History is, after all, what we choose to forget.

He's split the brook, too. It runs from the hill and hits a granite stone, shaped carefully to divide the flow. It branches at the stern and runs two rivers either side of the house, before meeting again at the prow. In his line of work, running water's some help. To enter, guests must step across the rivulets, knock on the door with the heavy iron ring held tight in the mouth of a wolf. The master of the house can't hear, but there are others listening. The door creaks ajar, coal spark eyes always watching for guests, for little hands that open the door.

It's hard to see, at first. Hard to make out a single shape

amongst the dust. It isn't any bigger on the inside, though it's furnished that way. The smell hits first, cedar wood and bitter orange, the smell of twine left damp and coiled.

On a shelf, an egg, cracked in two and empty, of course, but bigger than a puffball. The head of a deer stuffed so long ago there's little left but skull, and the tightly inked label peeling slowly from the mount, too faded now to read. Along the wall to the left, great cases of filigree wings, little shavings of gold dust. A million butterflies pinned to boards and left to twitch. There is small and neat writing beneath each of them as well; he knows the importance of names. On the opposite wall to the butterflies, to the deer, are maps. Of the moor, of an island (two in fact. One small and close, one large and distant, both marked oddly as if he's keeping track of something on each. Red dots moving steadily inland). And books—of course. Hundreds and hundreds of books.

There he is, Old Pel. One-eyed and howling. Sat by the fire playing his fiddle to the woodsmoke. His dress is unusual, certainly. The old, red woollen service coat, rusted now to brown, pulled tight about the shoulders, fingerless gloves letting the old man play. His trousers, black and creased, have pockets bulging with things that rattle. Were he to lay them out, which he often does, he would lay before you an assortment of bones and charms and trinkets. These are not the playthings Billy Askell ties around his waist. These are true, undeniable magic. Each with a purpose. Each with a cause. A favourite is the blackthorn wrapped tight about with blood-red string, each point capped with a dried and rigid sloe, like a blood clot. Or perhaps the polished horn of coral, set in silver and shaped like the tooth of a seal. He has carried that one around his neck since childhood and etched on the setting in the strange, dashed writing of his home are the words that keep him going.

* * *

HE WAS YOUNG when he had lost the other eye. He had heard of a woman who claimed to be midwife to a fairy. He found her, tracked her down, asked her to tell him her story and she did. How a finely dressed gentleman came to the market one day in the search for a nurse for his daughter.

'That's me,' said the midwife, 'I'll be her for you.' He had blindfolded her, taken her with him in his carriage and when he removed the blindfold, she stood in a room filled with things she'd never seen before. With food she'd never tasted, spirits she had never drunk. He had given her a suite of rooms. On the shelf was a bottle that she was to use to bathe the baby's face when the time came. Only the baby, nobody else. When the time had come, she had delivered a son safely to the gentleman's daughter and washed him clean with the water from the bottle.

She had told her story many times and was getting to the best bit when Pel had interrupted.

'Where is the bottle?' he had asked. The old midwife had looked worried then. She had said she no longer had it. But Pel pushed his way past into her run-down house and stood in the dust on the floor. He had taken out a thread with a coach-nail tied to it and had let it hang as he muttered words, pushed the fingers of one hand to his temple. The nail had spun, slowly at first and then faster and faster, before pointing to an alcove, to a shelf high up. There was the bottle. He had splashed the contents over his face before the old midwife could stop him. And then he could see. He could see the spirits sitting ember in the hearth, could see the pisky pickpockets as they worked about the square. He could see little faces everywhere. He had stood in the square and laughed until his sides hurt. He had learnt more than he'd ever dreamt from his books, but this was something new. He had laughed so hard he barely noticed the tall gentleman in the old-fashioned clothes and tricorn hat as he sidled alongside him.

'Funny little creatures aren't they?' the man had asked with a foxtail voice. Smiling, Pel had turned and just begun to agree when the gentleman twisted, pinning Pel against the wall.

'You stole this sight. It wasn't for you. Nor for her.' The man turned, and Pel saw that the midwife was lying dead upon the floor. Devilish creatures pinning her down. Discreetly, Pel had begun to work signs with his fingers, but the strange man's attention had returned to him.

'There is a price to pay, Lord Hunt. And you will pay it.' The gentleman reached back a hand, his long fingers and sharpened nails as clear as a cock's crow before Pel's eyes. He hardly felt a thing as the nails went in, he felt a great deal as his eye came out. Through the pain, he barely saw the man discard his bloody eye onto the floor, but he saw the hand reach back again and with everything he had Pel completed his charm. The gentleman had screamed then, letting Pel go. There was no reckoning nor battle of wits. Pel had run as fast as he could away from the whole sorry scene, the gentleman howling after him. He had his time later on though. The man's hat now sits on Pel's shelf, gathering dust.

THAT WAS A long time ago.

He's as old as he looks, and though he's written no account of it, his life lines the walls. Sleeping soundly, and thoroughly in the way, is the dog, Patroclus. Named as a joke, unfaithful to all but his nose, his chest rising up and down like waves on the sea. He dreams soundly of rabbits that run too slowly and of bird's nests too close to the ground. An English Setter of white and rust, blood in cream, his spotted nose can find his vices in a heartbeat. His bed, an old black velvet dressing gown, all faded brocade and little white hairs now, full of dust and crumbs. He snores and yips and barks in his sleep, but Old Pel plays on.

His hands, moving quickly over bow and strings, are slim and tapered. His nails finely clipped and cared for, except for the right-hand thumb which has a case of jointed silver covering it. They are tattooed, his hands. Lines and shapes snake scrimshaw up his bony wrists and disappear into his coat sleeves. If you watched him undress to sleep, you'd see his whole hollow body is covered with them.

Suddenly, the old man stops playing and smiles, and then... there, a knock at the door, which opens, no waiting for an answer, and in she comes. Nancy Bligh, queen of the moor, a little bit of dawn light trailing in after her. Black hair, green eyes, and magic in between. Just turned twenty-one. She wears a full-skirted dress of yellow and green striped satin, a basket over her arm that smells of home. Fresh bread steaming under cloth.

'I didn't know you baked, Nance.'

'You well know I don't,' Nancy tuts in mock exasperation, setting the basket down. 'It's from Miss Ellers, from the corner house. She says to say she's well. And that what you made leave has stayed gone. For now.' Nancy kneels and makes a fuss of the dog, holding his jowly jaw in her hands and giving him a hard, loving stare. 'How are you, Patroclus, my wonderful lad? You too, Pel.'

'He's not a pet, Nance, leave him be. I'm fine, always fine.' Words once sharply etched worn smooth with repetition.

The old man sets down the fiddle and bow, the gentle echo of fine-tuned wood, the loosening of strings. 'I'm glad Miss Ellers is doing better. A nasty business. It's been a long time since I banished one of what she had.'

'What was it, a—'

'Now now, Nance, no names. You know that.'

Nancy smiles, of course she knows.

NANCY WAS BORN and raised on the moor by her mother, her father dead before she was born. He had made a deal with something he shouldn't have, and it ended badly—her mother never explained what, just repeated, time and again, *don't forget, turn your pockets inside out and don't follow voices in a fog*—it was an embarrassment, a shame, and her mother had used her maiden name since his death.

She'd met Pel first when she was a baby. He had come to help her mother. Something was wrong, she'd said, with her daughter. It was Pel who had seen the truth of it, seen that Ms Bligh's unease with her child, commented on by all the neighbours, talked about by friends, had some reason to it. It was Pel who had marched out, the girl in his arms, onto the moor, up onto the grass and into the ring of standing stones. Pel who'd shouted, 'It's done now!' into the thickening fog. Pel who had placed the baby on a soft grass mound in the centre of the circle, had laid an iron chainmail stole over the little girl's shoulders and watched her writhe. Pel who saw, unsurprised, that as the mist cleared there were two where once had been one. He had taken Nancy's hand then, the original, that is, looked into her eyes and smiled, had carried her home. The screaming of the fairy child left iron-burnt behind them. He had not planned to stay, he never had before, had planned to go back to his boat fee in hand. But something in her eyes as he had lifted her from the circle had stayed with him.

As, in the end, had she.

Nancy gives the dog a final pat before standing.

'There's been another, Pel.'

The old man stops, part way through rebuilding the fire that burnt too low as he played. Setting down the slate axe that he uses to split the logs, he falls back onto his haunches. A frown furrowing across his face.

'I know.'

Nancy pauses at this, searching the old man for an answer she knows he won't give. She lifts a vase of dried flowers and moves them from the table to the windowsill. For a moment, she thinks of biting her tongue, but the words are out before she can act on it.

'How do you know?'

Pel, striking a long phosphorus match, sighs as the fire takes, and stands and walks soft-footed to a horsehair chair.

'One of Them told me, the little one... Rook? No, Jackdaw? The one with the eyes.'

'Jackdaw. Are you going to look into this now, properly I mean?'

Nothing. Pel sinks deeper into his seat and Nancy turns away from the old man sat in the chair. She begins to unpack the loaves.

'Pel, you need to do something. Soon. No more books, no more waiting to be asked.'

In his chair, Pel simmers.

'Five dead. Five dead and still he hasn't come.' Pel looks up as he speaks, his face a mask of incredulity.

'I know, Pel, but you know what he's like, especially since... '

'Five dead and not a call? Not a knock at the door? He knows I could help. He must! I know his son—'

'Don't bring him into this Pel. That's done. He's not the reason you won't help any more than he's the reason you've hobbled me. Sending me to check on elderly women and fetch you bloody bread.'

'It's for your own good!' Pel is on his feet now, thin hands stabbing at the air, flecks of white at his mouth, like a horse pushed too hard. 'You know it as well as I do, Nance. This isn't Their work. I'll not overstep my bounds.' He spits the word. 'The village want my help with this? Then they shall ask for it. If their Reverend cares to step down from that high horse, he'll ask me too. Instead of sitting on that hill stoking up nonsense. More will die, you mark it. One after another until that white collared idiot realises this is not some perversity he can wish away with words. He can't blame this on me and those I work with any more than he could blame me for… well.' Pel loses his nerve. Stands, hands clenched but eyes wide. A storm once the clouds have cleared, he stands blinking in the day. He reaches to lay a hand on Nancy's arm but abandons the manoeuvre at the last moment. Reaches for the vase from the windowsill instead and places it back on the table.

Nancy frowns, but she can see the plea for help nestled amongst the bluster. She watches him, in the corner he's backed himself into, waiting to be calmed. Laying her hand on the old man's shoulder, softly so as not to bruise his pride, Nance sighs. It is exhausting, this cajoling and stroking of his ego.

'Please Pel. Please. Magic or not, you need to look. You need to help. The village needs your help. I know you'll be able to help if you just look. Let's just go out now, he'll be speaking at the chapel. You know how he is; it'll be hours. The moor is quiet, no one dares miss one of his tirades. Let's just see what we can find, you know they won't have been able to see what you can.'

It's worked. Though he grumbles, Nance can see his fingers grabbing items from the room. Notepaper, a pen, little rocks with holes in. The breastbone of a toad. He opens drawers that overflow with rattling, and rummages until he finds his goal. He stuffs items into his pockets each carefully chosen from the mess. She has him, she thinks. There's no stopping him once he starts. Any second now, he'll take it and we'll begin. There he goes, coat buttoned, tasselled tarboosh pulled ragdoll on his head, and bare-knuckled hand on the polished brass head of his cane. A long-snouted beastie shining from years of use. Taps once on the flagstones to wake up the dog and...

'Come on then. Nance, Pat. Let's get to it again.'

VETCH

A BELL CALLS. A beacon to the stream of people flowing up the hill at the centre of the village to the chapel that sits on top. Like the houses, it's built with solid granite blocks held together with lime and earth. Green moss growing where the damp gets in. Simply made, two arched doorways and six windows, a pitched roof with no spire. A small cottage at the rear where the Reverend lives alone now. It's an old place. And though St. Reagan's carved her name above the door each person, as they enter, lightly passes a hand over the little stony face rubbed smooth over the years set into the lintel. There's all manner of things set into the lime. No untangling one belief from another without the whole lot falling down. There's a reason Pel chose this moor to live on, to dock his boat, to make his stand. The age of progress might already be well underway but here, in this valley, they've barely started.

Inside, between the white lime-washed walls, are lines of pews. Creatures carved into the woodwork at the aisle ends, into the stonework, and ivy-mouthed men smile down from the ceiling. Each Sunday they stand half empty, and though it fills (a quarter pew a year) it does so slowly. It is busier today. The villagers chatter as they wait. Gossip, pass well-worn words between them.

'What a thing to lose, a son.'

'The Reverend knows how that is.'

'A strange boy, you remember he had a caul?'

35

'Hedra, God rest her soul, delivered him. Said the boy was trapped in it.'

'Bad omen for a priest, that.'

'For anyone.'

'Pel was there. Back when he was still useful.'

'Back when he helped.'

'Gave the reverend's wife a draught and killed her, dead.'

'Get on. Nothing he could do, he saved the son, didn't he?'

'For all the good it did. Strange boy.'

'Weird lad.'

'You heard what happened when he was—'

Like lapwing on the moor when a fox is near, all heads lift. They can hear the silence coming.

Everything stops, the chatter quiets, children too. Women tell their husbands to stop brushing the limewash from their clothes. And, into the silence comes the stepping of feet, echoing on slate flagstones. At the back of the chapel, behind the altar, a velvet curtain draws back to reveal the Reverend Jacob Cleaver in all his glory.

His eyes sit frostbite in his drawn and pointed face, and though keen and piercing, there is sadness in them. Grey hair scraped back into a tidy thinning cap, threatened into place by his cheekbones. Thin-lipped, he surveys the room, dressed in the buttoned black cassock that he always wears, draped in a white surplice for the occasion, black leather boots peeking from the hemline, and a black fur-lined tippet hangs across his shoulders. At his neck the twin bands of his office, white strips neatly arranged on the black. He is not as old as Pel, though he looks it, and they have some shared experience. Two sides of a coin, balance, of a sort.

His hands, pale pink in the cold of the chapel, whiten as they grip the edges of the lectern. A gilt eagle on which he rests his book. Both bird and man gaze unflinchingly at the congregation.

'Here we are again.' His words are precise, like snowflakes clipped from folded paper. 'Another poor soul dead. I have prayed for him, I have. I pray for you all. But still, you insist on choosing a different way. Here, pulled from his hand. What is this, will anyone say?'

He holds up an object. A key. Old and rusted and tied through with a ribbon. No harm in that, a little extra something to keep a person safe.

'Nobody? A simple charm. Taken from the pockets of Salan Dell. Salan Dell who sat in these pews on Sundays, heard me speak. Heard me warn of the dangers of heathenism, of ignorant, pagan belief. Belief that this,' – he holds up the key, –'would protect him. And where is he now? He lies in the cold room as dead as the last. There is only one path to walk. Take the second and you'll fall. Just as he did. To some monster, yes, but not some ghoulish apparition. To an un-Christian man. A rusted key with a ribbon will not stop him. God's love will.'

Hugh and Seren Dell, Salan's parents, sit weeping in their seats, but the Reverend is not a man easily stopped. He has spoken like this, at what he claims as a memorial, after every one of the five deaths. The village climbing the hill each time for him to bash them over the head with his Bible. A little more gilt from the sermon worn cover sticking to them each time.

'And God is forgiving. Unlike whatever you leave flowers for under stones. I know you do it still. I've seen Salan's bier. I've seen your trinkets. It is not spirits that you work with, it is devils. And those devils do not live under the moor, they do not peek from the long grass or from behind the standing stones. The devils that so many of you still hold dear squat in the hearts of godless men. I have heard some of you talk of these... creatures... being responsible.' Calder sits sheepishly by the silent Cusk. 'You misunderstand me. I do not believe that the world is full of monsters. Salan was not killed by some *pisky*,' he spits the word. 'A man killed him. Out in the bog. And whilst this community still harbours belief, this pestilent and lingering belief, in some old way, some ancient creed, there will be safety in it for killers and degenerates to do what they will under its fluttering black banner. Salan sat where you sit now for seven Sundays past. He knew what was right and still went out into the moor. Conducting some depraved rite in the belief it would help him. And he died for it.'

There is a murmur at this. They do not like it. Though Salan and the others may have sought something from Cleaver and his church, there are few here that have turned their backs completely on the moor. Calder and Cusk are in a small group of those who have converted completely, left the old ways behind. Cleaver's conviction sits uneasily here, in this room.

'Pel will help!' The voice comes from the back, the speaker hiding in the crowd. And well he might, for Cleaver is marching back there now, pushing aside the people as he storms into their midst.

'Who said that?' No flecks of white, no popping eyes. No raised voice. Just quiet steady rage.

'Who dares speak that mountebank's name here, of all places? Lord Hunt cannot help you. He just encourages your heathenism. For his own profit, I would add!'

More murmurs in the crowd. If he is not careful, he will lose them. Can he feel it? He can. He pulls back, walks steadily back to the front of the room, and forces a smile. It's like watching an old wound reopen; you can hear the skin tear. He is no fool, the Reverend. He knows how things stand. The old ways are a fraying cloth, stretched tight across the landscape. Mended here and there by those that care. Held lightly by its weavers. It will, eventually, wear right through. Just tattered scraps of fabric, catching on the gorse. With every passing year the cloth grows more threadbare. With every pew seat filled, with every cart that brings fresh faces. Cleaver sees it clearly, his chance. If Pel has his way, if he wins, the Reverend knows the old cloth will be patched together again. The old and heathen nonsense that his parishioners believed will stay. Fractured and torn and weak but here, still. He could change things. He could lay a new cloth over this godforsaken land. Clean and white and pure. A new start, a clean slate. For everyone.

'Salan rests now. Pulled from the black water and ready to embrace the bright light of the Lord. Let us not bicker amongst ourselves. I know that through belief and prayer, we can all turn from this unpleasantness. You are safe here, with me, under this roof. But please, I ask you, consider it the next time you are placing the needs of some imagined past before your own. Why? What good have these customs ever done for you? Rout the monsters out. Sit in the church every Sunday and be counted until only the wicked remain outside. Rely on hymns and prayers, not spells and rituals. Hold tight to the cross and the prayerbook. Then we will know where our monsters lie. Or they will claim more of you, as they have young Salan. As they did my son. Five years he has been gone and still we've learnt nothing. Please, listen to me, learn from my mistakes. I turned a blind eye to this nonsense when it took my wife, and from the shadows of my neglect, it took Callum.'

The smile falters, something is showing itself beneath. Something uncertain, broken. Around the chapel, heads are bowed. Faces held behind closed eyes, remembered.

'I will not press it. We are all grieving. For young Salan Dell, for the others. For all the others. But please, think about it. These pews will be here every Sunday. Waiting.'

That's it then, shorter than the last. He's learning how far to take it. How hard to push. Or has his own pain caught up with him, forced him to rest? As the congregants file out a young woman pauses, lays a hand on the Reverend's arm, he flinches.

'I'm sorry, Reverend. I knew Callum, called him a friend, even in his troubles. I think of him often.'

On the girl's breast is a pewter badge. An anchor cross haloed with rowan… Pel's crest. Given as protection if protection was asked for. A small charge, to cover costs. Cleaver's face twists into a scowl. A mouth pursed with hate. He reaches out, no thought given to the invasiveness of the action and the girl flinches as his hand approaches.

'Hoping this will protect you?' He plucks the pin from her dress, gently but firmly. Like picking an apple from the tree. 'You think it will keep you safe from reaching hands when you walk across the moor?' He holds it to the light, his face set with a pantomime of concern. He shakes his head. 'Let me tell you. Callum wore one too and look where he is. So deep in the mire ten men couldn't fish him out, denied a proper burial. There's still a chance for you. Don't put your life in that charlatan's hands. Put it in mine.' His expression is a grease paint smear of piety and worry but a cold contempt squats beneath. He reaches into his cassock and withdraws a gold chain, a crucifix spinning at the end. He presses it into the girl's hand.

'Here. To aid your prayers.'

The girl nods nervously and turns quickly away, scurrying

between the pews to the safety of the churchyard. Cleaver stands for a moment, still staring at the badge in his hands. He gives a short, desultory laugh, throws the badge to the floor and he's gone, back behind the curtain.

LOOSESTRIFE

It takes a little while to reach, the lonely bit of bog where Salan was found. At this time of year, the frost sets hard across the landscape and on the moor, unlike in the shelter of the village, it barely thaws by the end of the day. Overhead, clouds of starlings slip their roosts in the trees lining the base of the hills. Billow and pulse a chattering smoke. The moor, at first glance, is an empty place. Bereft of trees, windswept clean and desolate. Take a moment to stand on it, to look, and it's clear that it bursts with uncontrollable life. The smallest pinprick flowers bleed beauty into weather-cropped grass. And sedge. And moss. There is a pit, close by, filled with water. And on a bright day, it dazzles blue, a little Aegean. Fringed with white banks of clay. In its depths, small dragons. Newts with crested backs. Toads and frogs and snakes. Ringed around the edge with moorland ponies, drinking. Their long thick coats blowing in the breeze, their fetlocks like flags, like pennants on a mast. Cattle too, and sheep. Horns on both and cloven-footed, they stomp across the land past plover and lapwing. Past the curving beak of a curlew as it whistles to the wind. Past the wind-dried ricks of turf left to cure in the winter sun. And all around those granite stacks, towering above, sentinel against the skyline. Petrified of change.

Across this landscape come two horses. The first, a dappled blue roan mare with simple tack and a woven blanket across her back. Nancy Bligh sits proud atop her. She rides confidently, well, her hair blowing out behind her. The second is a horse that looks so out of place, so out of this world, that it is difficult to describe. Cream, with rust-red ears and feathered legs, and taller than the broadest hunter, her flanks glistening under elaborate tack. This horse belongs elsewhere. A thick grey sheepskin rug sits under the saddle, which is ornate and dark and stamped in gold. The pommel a shining tusk. Though she does not wear it today, there is armour for her face, finely woven blinkers and ribbons for its mane. The set was given many years ago, a reward for a father found, and it is Pel's pride and joy. He keeps it in an inlaid box stashed deep beneath his bed. The horse was a gift too, led from deep beneath the earth by an ancient king for services freely given.

'Come on, girl, step lively.' Pel's voice rings out as hooves sink into mud. He trusts both horses to know where to put their feet, trouble for all of them if they don't. Pel has lived on the moor for years. It was meant to have been a retirement, of sorts. It is not working out that way. As he rides, he closes his eyes against the strong cold wind that always blows in the lowlands, the smell of mulched earth and spring water.

'How far, Nance?'

'Not long, Pel, below the ridge, at the base of the old stone. Just to the side of the bridge.'

The old man squints against the breeze, eye blazing. Five dead in as many months. Five picked out amongst the accidents, the arguments, the suicides. Each lying prostrate in the bog, necks broken. Hard to get to so deep in the mire. Where the grass billows like a blanket when you step on it. The quaking mires, the sucking peat. No rhyme or reason clearly seen. Some men, some women, some old, some young.

Bodies found by passers-by, farmers with a cart of hay for livestock, a girl picking flowers for a friend. And it bothers him.

Nancy wonders why. Not the sad fact of it all. Pel has fought and lost many wars. He's often counted the death of friends. They have pulled bodies from the mud before.

The way they are left, perhaps. Face down, arms across their breasts as though they fell praying. Maybe. There is certainly something in it, there is ritual there.

Or is it the livid pink mark of a single gripping hand on every body's neck? A hand that burnt, a hand that squeezed.

Old Pel is sharp. You don't do what he does and not spot problems. It had been chance that he was at the Nest when the first body was found. He'd gone with the crowd, or Cleaver would have seen and stopped him. And he'd peered over shoulders at that bright red handprint, at the bright red finger marks. He'd looked up at Nance then. All those weeks ago. He'd elbowed through into the centre of the bar and drawn a circle in the sawdust. He'd offered his help then and there. And perhaps it would have been taken had the Reverend not walked in. Had not stepped into Pel's circle with an amused little look, smudging the edges with his boots. Stood next to Pel and said:

'And what would you do? Magician? There's no pisky work here. Or do these little creatures of yours have man-sized hands, dragging them in the dirt behind them?'

The crowd had sniggered, and some men began to stalk about with their hands dragging behind them as the laughter grew. Proof of what Nancy had long suspected, that the tide was turning. She couldn't blame them. Not really. The Reverend offered some agency. A prayer at least a message sent. A direct line. Not Pel's network of whispers and promises. A coin, a charm, a request lodged. The stream of villagers to the chapel grown stronger than the trickles that went to him.

Another man might have relished the challenge. Won them back, worked with the chapel. Not Lord Hunt. Not her guardian. He'd left that meeting red-cheeked and angry. Nancy had tried to stop him, but he'd stormed into the night with his humiliation. And after every killing he had quietly crept out, investigated alone but would not offer help if the village, if Cleaver, would not ask. And now here they are again.

'Nancy.'

Pel's voice pulls her out of her dreams, and she slows her horse as they reach the stream. Bridged by a row of fallen stones, more solid and steady than the one that leads into Mirecoombe. Built a long time ago, its foundations sunk deep into the sodden earth and laid upon sacks of wool. The long slabs of granite that make up its concourse weathered and whittled by wind and water, gaps between the stone showing the water beneath. It is on the far side that Salan was found. Beneath a tall standing stone, graffitied long after it was raised, hatcheted with lines by ancient hands. They approach and Pel dismounts slowly, pausing as he lands to catch his breath, to lay a hand on his horse's neck and whisper her name.

'Thank you, Eponina. Thank you, girl.'

The mare gives a whinny in reply and nudges him upright. Nance is out of the saddle now too and walking towards him. She offers him an arm. He won't take it.

'No.'

Pel pushes her away and draws from his saddle his brass-topped cane. Edging towards the bog, he curls his lip. This hollow between two hills is sick with water, even under frost. With each step Pel prods the ground, tests its depth; it only takes one mistake to fall through. There are trees here too, in this boggy delta. Haw and blackthorn stunted by the wind; ice-burst sloes ready to be picked.

No birds sing here today, deep in the valley. Odd that. Even in winter, it is usually so full of them, none of the other usual voices either, running silent through the grass. Pel stops, tips his head to listen. Just the impatient shifting of horse's hooves, and Nancy's boots as they crunch through frozen water, the white ice giving way to the black mud beneath.

'Idiots. The mess they have made. Look, Nance, how none of them fell through is a miracle.'

Nancy smiles, rolling her eyes as she kneels beside him. Still, he's not wrong. Beneath the stone and above the stream with its capstone of ice is a circle of muddied black where Davy and his friends recovered Salan's body. Pel stands and Nancy follows behind the old man, lays a hand on his shoulder. Half to reassure herself, half in case he should fall.

'Don't let it worry you, Pel, we're bright enough between us to find something useful, I'm sure.'

And she lets him lead the way down into the mud.

SHE REMEMBERS VERY little of her early years, but it was a story told enough to become something close to memory. How from the moment he'd saved her, he had been a part of things. Had kept an eye, returning every few months to see how she was doing, to see how well she grew. She had loved his visits; he told her that her eyes sparkled. And then, one day, when she was five years old, he had turned to leave, and she had waved to Them. Waved to the little faces poking from the spaces all around him. In his saddlebag, on the back of Patroclus gripping shaggy hair like reigns. Another knocking over pots stacked against the wall. He was so surprised. She'd assumed he'd known. Assumed everyone could see them. He'd knelt beside her, she remembered, his face beaming, and told her that was not true. He'd given his eye to see what she could.

She had spent her days outside, walking the hills, to the top of a granite pile and waiting for the morning mist to clear so she could see the sea. People said that her line is full of witches, stories told in spite. But Bligh is a name to be wary of, in certain parts. And there's power in a name. She had taken to following Pel, asking him about his work. He'd refused her help. A Keeper works alone, he'd said.

And then her mother had died. Not through magic, or misfortune, just through a cruel and swift-working sickness. And Nancy had, once the mourning was done, walked to the boat, and asked for a job. Pel had repeated what he'd said before. A Keeper works alone. But she had ignored him. She ignored his grumbling until it stopped. Until he had forgotten life without her. And she enjoyed the work. She had an affinity for it. He trained her, had been training her, to take his place. Until five years ago, that is.

NANCY SHAKES FREE from the past with an exhalation of breath.

'Here Pel, in this hollow by the running water, this is where he was. Even under the boot marks you can see where his body lay.'

Pel crouches, leather gaiters spattered with black mud, and begins to poke about, tattooed fingers searching. He lifts a caked finger and tastes the dirt.

'He didn't die here. He was brought. Do you see anything?'

Nancy stands too, biting her lip and deep in thought.

'I'm not sure, Pel. Those boys have made a mess, but I have their steps together, I think. I count four sets of boot prints. That makes sense. But there's another's tread here too. And I don't think they belong to Salan, look.' She beckons Pel over, and the two crouch again and peer together at the half-obscured footprints sitting under later steps. Unlike the rest these are of bare feet. Pel looks at the icy steps and shivers.

'Nance, did you bring the flowers?'

Nancy reaches into her saddlebag and withdraws a small, cloth-covered book, spine broken. It did, perhaps, once have words gold-stamped on the front but they're gone now. All that's left is the faint indent of a daisy on the cover.

'Here. Should we not ask Them first?'

She casts her eyes about and looks surprised as she notices the same thing the Keeper had: it is far, far, quieter than it ought to be. Pel snatches the book. He is more impatient than he once was. Less inclined to listen.

'No, Nance. Not yet. I want to know all I can before we bring Them in. You know how They are.'

Pel lays the book open in the mud and reads. Each page filled with pressed flowers. All found on the moor. Little yellow trefoil petals, orchids, foxglove. And filling every other space the tight cobweb of Pel's notes. In Latin, in Greek, in Cuneiform and Ogham. Diagrams too. Horned lines with arrow tails. Circles with a mark inside, a triangle crossed out. They are mnemonics, memory aides. Each flower bound up in his mind with a spell, an incantation. The notes there to remind him of the parts he forgets. He mutters now. And though he speaks so softly not a soul can hear, the short grass twitches in response. The moor listens. He is reaching deep down into the mire, where a century of memories rot.

Stopping just shy of the deepest part. Any deeper and he'd be heard by something he'd rather not disturb for now. Eyes closed, Pel searches the mud. There are the usual echoes of rabbit and sheep, the half-heard voice of a traveller off the path. But nothing else. It's quiet. It shouldn't be. There are memories missing here, as if the mire itself put hands over its ears and didn't listen. Wouldn't. Whatever, whoever did this scares the moor itself. Pel shuts the book with a snap.

'Pel?' Nancy looks worried. Perhaps she ought to be. Pel rises, stiffly from his crouch and looks solemnly at his ward.

'Call Them, Nance. Call Them all. There's something dangerous about.'

EYEBRIGHT

WORDS ON WIND as Nance sings her way upwards.

'Come gather, small children and beasts of the moor,
follow my song to that old rocky tor, tor,
that old rocky tor.'

It is evening when the meeting is called, and a mist rises like
a snowdrift falling upwards, the clouds of vapour erasing the
colours until everything is pale. The air is thin up here, on the
top of the hill, as thin as it comes. It curls around the empty
spaces in the amphitheatre rock. Echo Tor is its name. There,
in the middle, a rock stack taller than the rest. The top stone
cut into a hollow like a chair, like a throne. When the world was
a little younger, when belief in things was strong, gatherings
here were a carnival. On certain days, spread about the year,
when the night was very long or very short the worlds would
collide. The above and below. Flowers and grain were piled
on the stone with the still-beating heart of a bull. The people
that lived here could no more see the spirits than those that
walk today, but they felt them more firmly, knew for a fact they
were here. They looked at the brooks running free over stone,
looked at the pebble piles of granite on the hillside, and saw
their handprints. Heard their laughter. They knew because
they saw that if they left a little gift, raised a tall stone, then
their crops would grow faster, their winters would be short.

Knew too that when they died, they'd be lain in the earth with rocks piled high and grass grown over and that their bodies and their ghost would sink into the mud and the thick black mire. And that even as their bones and their blood disappeared to make the grass grow tall their souls would be welcomed to the place that sat below. The Undermoor. An Elysium of rolling fields and clear water. There they could play, and love, and lie under a puddle moon. Ruled over by Him. The King of the Undermoor, The God of the Mire. Heavy-horned and ash-limbed and older than the stone. He kept an eye, this lord of the dead. As his cousins did under the sea, deep in bedrocked mines, perched on the clouds. And over time once their bodies had drifted piece by piece into the mud and nothing physical remained, he changed them, if they wished it. Turned them into something new and strange, built them new bodies from peat and stone and sent them scrabbling through the hare-runs and out into the day. Their turn now to help the crops grow, lengthen a summer's day. Or, free from mortal morals and constraints they could go above and run amok, lead lost travellers into mud, indulge in any fancy. It meant nothing to Him either way.

On feast days the hillsides had thronged with the spirits and the devils and the sprites. They gambolled like lambs around the legs of early men and sat on the shoulders of the giants that still held up the sky, and from his throne, the God of the Mire sat and watched over it all.

But over time things change, even an afterlife. The men and women above the ground multiplied and spread. And other gods and monsters took up space in their heads. It worked for a while; alliances were formed; there was a sharing of the dead. Then a new god came and laid people out in boxes in ground hot to the touch where souls stayed put. And the world below grew unruly and wild as the scales tipped.

They even built a chapel here, an added insult to the past, with a hermit tending a beacon to guide walkers safely home. A folly on a grand scale if ever there was one. It fell, of course it did, one windy night. The ground itself rose up and shattered it, the hermit dead under a falling stack and the chapel gone, though you can still see the light shine sometimes. That's when the Keepers had arrived. The county split and a portion given to each. To keep the peace, to smooth things over. Only a Keeper calls these summits now. On top of the hills, in sea caves and mineshafts. There are no carnivals, no fairgrounds. Not any longer. Auditoriums have become courtrooms. And the great old thrones stand empty.

'Sit in the rings of the old hermit's church,
warm your hands in the beacon that burns in the earth,
the earth, that burns in the earth.'

An old, forgotten song, lost until one morning Nancy awoke with it in her head. Until then Pel had used a horn to call these gatherings, a hunting horn of brass that rang clarion down the valley. The song works better though. As Nancy and Pel draw closer, the song becomes a melodic hum, like the whistle of birds. They rise out of the fog like bubbles rising through murky water in time to see them arrive.

The Underfolk.

Male and female, though it can be hard to tell them apart, and the difference means little to them. Some earthy-skinned and skipping as they walk, some thick-set and blinking even in this dim light.

First come the smallest of them, the piskies. Lace wings fluttering at their backs. It'll be them Pel's keenest to speak to with their lights out in the bogs. They're the ones that lead men astray in the night-time, keep a husband from a wife. No more reason to it than that they can, no morality here, no motive. It was they who swapped out Nancy as she lay mewling in her crib. They miss her still. Pel keeps them happy, keeps the offerings alive.

Next are the spriggans, small and rocky fronted with quartz running across their backs in veins. Moss growing damp on their shoulders and a diamond in each eye. Creatures to watch closely. As troublesome as the piskies, but with a mean streak to boot. Lost your cows in the marsh? Has your new barn fallen down? Should have been better mannered to the spriggans. Should have known your place.

They help, too, or they do when they're asked. A pisky can lead a man home as easily as astray. A spriggan can split a granite slab into even-sided gateposts. Cut a trough from a stone. All it takes is a little left, a polite word.

The busy household sprites, little red faces like gumdrops, the brownies, are absent. They have hearths to tend, floors to sweep.

There are others missing. This does not concern them. Those that tend the deep mines and waterways, help smugglers land their catch. This far inland there are no sea caves for buccas to abound and this little patch of soggy Eden is too waterlogged for mines, no knockers here. Problems for Keepers with wetter, deeper obligations.

Pel keeps them all in line, keeps them acting as they should. Manages the offerings, makes sure the links in the chain hold firm. They do what he asks out of a sort of fear; he holds sway like a drill sergeant. There is need for this order, especially these days, when the offerings beneath the standing stones are few and far between. Now, if it was only Pel left to persuade the Underfolk that one man's gift repaid would help many who offered nothing—tricky after all to make only a portion of a crop thrive, only part of a building stay standing—then who's to say how long it would last. Until a spriggan or a piskie asked him why one day and the answer or anger didn't suffice? Nancy though. They listen to Nancy. They look out for her. Every spirit under every hill loves Nancy Bligh.

This is the sum of it. The spirits chatter, shift their weight in expectation as the two figures ride into the clearing. They know something is amiss—Keepers don't call a court without reason. Pel and Nancy dismount and walk into this restless, fragile air. There is menace about. The old man climbs stiffly from his horse, resting one hand on Eponina's flank as he does so, breathing hard. He turns, faces the crowd, raises a bony hand, and scratches the socket of his long-gone eye. Nancy knows he envies her, her sight so freely given.

If a traveller were to come upon the scene now, all they'd know was that an old man, a young woman, and a dog had stopped to rest their horses on a hill. They wouldn't see the pointed faces sitting on the banks, the rows of staring eyes and grinning toothy smiles. Not unless one of the Underfolk chose to reveal themselves. It's a gift to see what they see.

Lucky them.

The two horses wander off back down the hill to better grazing, Patroclus barks lazily at the gathering and begins searching for a place to sleep. He has attended many meetings; he knows what he'll be missing. Pel, walking stiffly even with his cane, is making his way towards the centre of the rings, Nancy at his back ready to catch him if he falls. There is a glow on the hill: some of the creatures carry lights, some emit a glow themselves. The tor flickers with them.

'Friends.' A ripple of uncertainty at this. There's more than one spirit present that's met the thin end of Pel's cane. Pel moves to continue, he has the speech down pat, but there is a noise from the darkness that eats at the light. The horses, further down the slope, bridle and Patroclus who had finally found a patch that suited is up, growling at the shadows.

'Pel,' Nancy hisses, and they both start at the sound of laughter.

Stood beside Nancy, Pel tenses. She feels him stand straighter. Sees his knuckles whiten on his cane. He shakes, with rage or fear Nancy does not know and her heart beats faster than it ought to with him at her side. Two rocks stand higher than the rest. Two creatures now crawling to take their seats, one on each tower. The other Underfolk looking up in cowed silence. Sometimes, rarely, the God of the Mire makes a mistake. Just as a coin die presses the same face each time, now and then the die slips, breaks, and a different face peers from the metal. Identical to nothing but themselves. Bedevilled with sharp-edged detail. Nancy has read about them. Pel has told her about them. The jackals of the Undermoor, the scourge of all folk. In shackle to nobody but the god himself and even then, the chains held loosely. Bound by agreements that should keep them down below.

Their presence marks a change. A shifting of power.

On the left stack is a creature that at first glance might be a spriggan. Its small compact body ripples with muscles like a bull terrier, with the eyes of that dog, too. Small and dark and unreadable. It is the smile that gives his malice away. It hacks its way across his mouth like an axe wound. Sharp teeth forcing their way through, begging to be fed. He wears his name lightly though it hangs heavy overhead: Cutty Soames. He should be dead. A curse to all he sees. Bound and trapped in a lead-lined box and thrown into the mire by a long-dead Keeper. Never to be freed, and yet here he squats. It is his cackling that Pel and

Nancy heard. As they watch him take his seat, he drags long, curved claws screeching across the stone, leaving deep white trenches like the wake from a boat. Nancy's chest rises and falls in erratic beats which worsen when she sees that Pel's does the same. She reaches for his hand, but he pulls it away and together they turn to the right-hand stack.

As Cutty could be a spriggan, at a half glance this one could be a pisky. Lithe and long-limbed, she is a creature all aflame with bright blue light, flickering like marsh gas set to burning and her skin blistering beneath it. Her name is Bluecap. As bad as Cutty in her way, she too ought not to be out, above the ground, like this. Pel banished her when he was young, back when he had two good eyes and less sense than he has now. Only young and foolish men go after spirits as bad as this one. He won though, Pel; Bluecap sent back to the world beneath the earth. Deals made, agreements struck, gaolers found. Yet here she squats. Smile beaming bloody from a lighthouse mouth.

'What do we do, Pel?' Nancy speaks low and hurried and struggles to regain her breath. She has followed Pel from crisis to crisis and never once felt like this. Her skin is cold, each hair on her arm bristles and every muscle tenses. Beside her, Pel has calmed himself. He stands firm again though for the first time since she's known him, he looks truly old. Frail against these monsters. His eye waters against the light and the wind, his lips pursed tight. There is a tremor there. Pel does not look at her when he speaks. His eyes stay fixed on the trouble ahead.

'Perhaps you should go home, Nance. Take Pat. Leave this to me.'

Nancy thinks for a moment, looks down towards the earth and shrugs.

'The job is the same. We'll deal with them after. As always. Besides, it could be worse, could be the Hunt.'

Pel frowns at her, though she can see his face flush with pride, and whispers to her.

'Don't even joke about them, Nancy. This, none of this, is anything in comparison to them. Thank you, though. For staying.' He turns to address the crowd.

'Something is wrong here. On the moor. People are dying.'

A murmur, a rumble of discontent and pointed fingers.

'Not us,' comes a voice. Bluecap perhaps (there was some fire in it). Pel grips the head of his cane, and his knuckles whiten.

'I didn't say it was—'

'Can't blame us. It's dangerous at night.' Cutty Soames stirring trouble.

'If you'll just be quiet, let me speak to the others.' Cutty smirks, a tooth nicking his upper lip so the blood stains his mouth.

'So, you do think it's my friends here doing this?' There's noise then, as the whole assembly decries the accusation that any one of them played a part. Pel closes his eye.

'Quiet!' Pel barks it.

'No! Keeper. You'll not silence them. Any of us. You dare come here and speak of death, of things being "wrong"? When you've let this moor slip from your hands through neglect and pig-headed ignorance? No. Our Lord sent Blue and I back, *Pel*.' Cutty spits the Keeper's name. 'To protect those that you can't help, against things you won't stop.' Cutty shifts on his rock and the muscles in his shoulders grind as he does. A boxer loosening up for a fight. 'If you won't remind the folk to leave us a little in return for the lot we give, then *I* will. Blue will. And we'll tear and burn until they remember it well. If they still need a lesson, then I'll blow the horn. Call the Hunt.' The rock ignites with chattering again, Nancy can hear them, the Underfolk, worried but changing sides. Pel shaking now, at her side.

'Quiet!' His shout sounds soft. He's losing them. 'Enough!' Again, no change and the air is thick with noises now. Nancy steps forward and, after catching Pel's eye and exchanging a nod she speaks to the crowd, softly.

'Please.' There's magic in that voice. The noises cease. Small faces still scrunched in simmering rage, but silent.

'I understand you're frustrated. Perhaps we have let things get away from us.' She can see Pel at the corner of her vision and raises a hand to quiet him. He must be shaken because it works. 'I promise we will work harder, to help you. Those here that we know, at least.' She glares at Cutty and Bluecap. 'We just want to know what you saw. You knew Sal Dell; he was kind to you. I know he was.' Some nod at this, but the crowd is unsettled, unfocused. The softer spirits, the piskies and the lamplighters sat bobbing in their glow, are grouping close together, looking worriedly about, their dusty mothwings still.

'Please,' Pel has gathered himself, found his reserves, the cold glint back in his eye. The power in his voice so different to Nancy's. 'I've been to where he died, stood in the mire. Someone killed him. I believe it was a man who did it. Not one of you. But there is a magic to it. To the way it was done. And I don't know what that magic is.'

A silence then. He's never admitted to ignorance before. Nancy examines Pel's face in the half-light. He's given no inkling of this idea to her; he's barely spoken since they examined the bog that morning.

'This can't have happened without a single one of you seeing. Feeling it happen. I know how you are: you have your noses in everything. And not one of you has scampered out to tell tales on who it was. When Coal-Eyes over there was taking sheep straight off the hill, seven of you came in turn and told me about him.' Pel looks to small faces that won't meet his gaze and his patronising tone turns to admonishment. 'Don't give me any nonsense, you've no qualms when it comes to tattle. And this is worse, so much worse, than sheep rustling. The way they were all left, it's... I don't know. I don't know who's responsible. But I'll find out who it was. And if I have to come and find each of you, on your own, and shake the answer out of you one by one I will. Don't think I don't see you all, you at the back.' Pel's tone shifts, like a breeze picking up as a storm approaches, and he turns to Bluecap and Cutty with thunder in his eyes.

'If your master has indeed released you, then He knows something is wrong. He wouldn't send you two to keep the peace. I don't know if he's making a move or protecting Himself, but I will deal with you. I'll deal with the Hunt too, if I must.' Pel slips his free hand into his pocket. It is a small movement that could be merely for comfort but there are things in that pocket. Things that trap and burn. Cutty and Bluecap sit back on their pillars and smile.

'Tell me, friends. How long since you've been paid your due?' Bluecap speaks, not to Pel, but to the others gathered around. 'How long since thanks was given commensurate with your help? How long since you were sought out and brokered with, not through him, but by a man or woman, girl or boy, who wanted your aid? Think about it, friends. All goes through this man. This Keeper. He tells you it's because the village has turned away but who watched them turn? This old man and his whelp.' It is Nancy's turn to bridle, she feels something stirring, but Cutty cuts her off, words carried on Bluecaps hot air.

'The folk are dying, Keeper? So are we. The Undermoor is bletting like a medlar. Rancid with neglect. That chapel yard of theirs swells with bodies and the peat goes unfed. They don't even lay their dogs to rest in the mud these days. Don't give us anything to work with. Life is a circle, you know that. Doesn't work when you break it. And you have broken it, Lord Hunt, you know what you—'

'Enough!' Pel cracks his cane on the stone, and it is enough to break the spirit's rant. Cutty is not done, though. With a snarl at Pel, he turns to Nancy.

'You say you want to help, little girl. Why haven't you? And you, Keeper. Well, best thing you could do is lay down in the mud yourself. Give us all a taste of you, if you're so special. Because from where I sit, it's clear. Can't do what you could do, can you, Pel?'

Silence. Then...

'Can't do what you could do, can you, Pel?' The voice rings out from the back of the circle and laughter babbles round. A spriggan, pointy-eared and mischief-eyed and emboldened by the presence of stronger creatures takes up the call and soon half the audience is chanting:

'Can't do what you could do, can you?'

'Can't do what you could do, can you?'

'Can't do what you could do, can you?'

'Mind yourselves!' Pel is shouting now and behind him, Nancy tries to calm the crowd. Not all spells need the book, Nancy knows. Some are always at the back of the caster's mind. Making a fist with his left hand Pel draws a circle in the grass with his cane. One of the spriggans tries to dance into the ward, showing off to his friends. He screeches as he touches the edge of it and runs away, cursing Pel's name.

There is a rapidity to riots. They come from nowhere.

Cutty Soames laughs hysterically from his stack and leaps to the floor, skewering a pisky on a long claw and by mistake or design the pisky's heart is plucked out as the talon withdraws, then eaten with a belch. Pel, seeing the bloodshed, snarls and from his pocket draws a coloured glass ball like a bauble from a Christmas tree. It rattles as Pel holds it, and Pel hurls it at Cutty as he sits licking blood from his hands. Though it does not strike him, it shatters on the rock and whatever was inside now envelops old Cutty, spreading about him like a sick blue moss, smothering his mouth. He tears at it with his razor claws then runs skittering down the hill. Nancy's training wakes like a bear from the winter. It's been a while since she's fought, cast a spell, but she moves fluidly, at ease next to Pel. Unable to keep the smile from her face as they fight back-to-back, turning in a circle on the tor top. Nancy reaches back at one point and draws a vial from Pel's coat pocket, hurls it out at a spriggan keen to get a jump on them. As he hurls his missiles, she veils the smaller spirits with wards to keep them safe.

Bluecap licks fire at both of them, Pel and Nancy, furious that they do not burn. She would have Nancy pay for that. Bluecap charges, faster than Nancy expects, knocking her down and singeing her skirts. Dazed, Nancy struggles to make the signs she needs, the wards. She pushes the creature back, Bluecap laughing as she does. Nancy looks to Pel, but the old man is fighting battles of his own. Patroclus, deprived of his sleep, is barking at something further down. She is on her own. Nancy feels it then. Something nestled next to the fear. Something that is waking up.

'No, no! Bluecap get back. I'm warning you!' but the spirit still dances in front of her, lapping at Nancy with sparks and fire. Nancy Bligh closes her eyes, clenches her fists, and tries to swallow it down, but she can't. A gift given, a tool she's not learnt to use, the blade too sharp to wield like this. It bursts from her, rattling the hill and shattering the stone beneath Bluecap's feet. The spring beneath erupts, drenching the little sprite, and Bluecap runs steaming from the hill. But Nancy can't stop it now it has started. The hillside convulses, stones are falling, and she is watching helplessly as she does it. It is only Pel's arm on her shoulder that calms her. His voice, soft in her ear, has an edge to it.

'Easy, easy. That's enough.'

Nothing. The hill still shakes, from the stacks huge boulders that have sat for centuries fall and break on the stone beneath.

'Nancy!' Whispered still but sharp and urgent, 'Nancy, stop! It's all right, it's all right. I'm here, it's over.'

It does settle then. The rumbling ceases. She turns, free of the spell she had cast unthinking, and stands to join Pel. The remaining spirits, some paused mid-fight, are all turned to face them, eyes wide and silent. The fog has grown thicker and now hangs about the crowd like a blanket. The air crackles and the hairs on the back of Nancy's neck stand erect and fizzing. There is a tension that ratchets like a bowstring drawing taut, and the hillside waits for the arrow to fly. From the depths of the mist comes a shout and a spriggan comes leaping out like a musket ball from a gun. Patroclus, panting and ragged, bounds forward and cracks broadside into the creature, knocking it to the ground, ribs grinding as it struggles to regain its footing. Patroclus stands snarling in front of his master.

'*Enough.*' Something in Pel's voice has changed. There is an edge to it that sets the hairs on end. The smallest spirits have already fled and the rest stand in disarray. Cutty and Bluecap are nothing but echoes.

'One last chance to tell me what you saw. I can't protect you from it if I don't know what it is.' Those creatures that remain, look, share glances between themselves at this.

'Nothing? Fine. You know where I am if you change your mind. And if you see your master, tell him I'd speak to Him as well.' The old man turns and, as if she knew, Eponina is there, stamping a hoof on the ground as she waits.

'And you creatures that are freed,' he shouts into the mist, 'whoever opened your cells. I will be back for you.' Up on the horse and Pel is gone, back down the hillside.

Nancy looks once more at the gathering, but there's little more to say. She pulls herself onto her horse and follows Pel. Patroclus, still panting and looking accusingly about, trails after them as they leave. It's gone midnight and it's a long ride home.

THE LONG BUILDING in Mirecoombe sits bolted, the mourners gone. Inside the stillness of the cold dark room broken by the fog-filtered moonlight. The lock making no sound as it springs open, the mechanism oiled and well-maintained. The door, though heavy, opens smoothly and easily on its hinges. Footsteps now, as someone passes padfoot over flagstones to the table where he lies. Salan Dell. Around him, on the bier, are the pebbles and stones and pieces of bone. The carefully plaited reed crosses and paper chains that run across the corpse like fetters, or lace. On his breast, placed between his hands, is a folded paper rose. A hand reaches for it, pauses, then rips it from the corpse's grip, crushing the delicate petals to a ball, discarded on the floor. In the soft and silvered light of the moon, the livid mark around Salan's neck shows shadow on his skin. Dropping the broken rose, the hand reaches for the mark and places itself gingerly onto it, feeling for its shape—like a key fumbling in a lock, each finger reaches for its place. But is not a perfect fit, the red mark larger than the hand that lies on top. Outside, an owl screeches into the darkness, and the hand withdraws. Feet step back across the tiles. The door closes. Salan Dell returns to the dark.

MARSH VIOLET

THE MOOR IS a ruin of whispers, the tale quietly told. The story of the hubbub spreads to those who were not there, gossip and rumour flying hard on black-eyed wings.

Those meetings, rarely called, should end better than that. There should be respect. Pel stands in the hallway of the boat shaking out the night sky from his overcoat, stamping out the darkness from his boots. Dawn has broken and already he's sick of it.

Nancy is boiling a kettle on the old, rusted stove kept stoked by the helping hands he employs here, clanking down the kettle and the cups crossly. Patroclus is standing forlornly in the centre of the room wondering what's wrong, rheumy old eyes looking for an answer, asking the question with a slowly wagging tail. Nancy breaks a piece of smoked ham from the hock hanging from the ceiling and throws it to him.

Pel is up and down out of his seat, aching, ageing bones forgotten in his anger and worry knotting up his brow. He's rarely like this. Nancy gives Patroclus another piece of meat and he snaps at her, 'He's fat enough, if you want a dog to spoil get one of your own.'

Nancy kneels and pushes her head close to the dog's.

'He's a silly old bugger, isn't he Pat? Will he talk about it, do you think? Or pretend it didn't happen.' She glares at Pel, but he hasn't noticed. He's pulling books out now. Heavy leather volumes with letter-stamped names. Gold in faded puddles in the recesses.

The old man keeps turning pages in his dusty quest for answers.

'Pel! Stop looking through those bloody books and talk to me. Please. I'm sorry.'

Pel puts the book down.

'You promised you would never use your gifts. I told you; you can't control it.'

'I didn't choose to do it. I never do. If you'd just let me practice, like you used to, if you'd just show me—'

'No!' The sudden outburst rocks the stillness of the boat. It shocks them both. He softens before he speaks again. 'No, Nancy. The type of magic I use, the type I taught you, is safe. It is logical. It takes matter and manipulates it; it is a skill to learn. Like shooting a bow. As I have told you since you were a child, the abilities you were… given, they are different. Dangerous. You cannot practice it. It is not something to get better at. It would consume you. There would be a price and I do not want you paying it.' There is some bitterness in these words. Pel envies Nancy, she's always known it. He has worked hard for his gifts. For his powers. He can call the winds, draw down the moon, but it took him years, and he needs his book to do it. He has studied ancient texts, read long lost scrolls, and memorised half the world but it cost him. Just look at his eye. Yes, Pel worked hard for his gifts. Nancy was given hers. She's been able to see the Underfolk, the fairies, since Pel rescued her from them all those years ago. It's her other gift that scares the old Keeper. Nancy calls it her Murmur. Pel had always explained that it drew on the magic of the Undermoor. That she was summoning help from people she could ill afford a debt to. He gave it no name, but she had seen the starlings, seen them pulse and push the sky. That's how it had felt to her. Something powerful, something changeable. Something that could fly. Pel had told her the name for starlings flocking was a murmuration, but she'd not been able to say the word. The starlings were murm'ring, that's what she'd say. Her gift, her beautiful flighty thing that could grow and shift and move the world. Pel might hate it, but she loved her cloud of birds.

'I didn't mean to. The Murmur just happened. You know how it is.'

'Stop calling it that. You are not six any longer. You know better than to speak like a child and you know better than to give in to that impulse.'

Nancy closes her eyes against entreaties she has heard before, though she permits herself a small smirk. She knows full well Pel hates her saying its name. There's power in a name.

'Fine, Pel.' This is a fight she's lost enough times in the past, no need to lose it again. 'But it doesn't solve our problems. It isn't just the killing; you saw them up there. Why were they there? Cutty and Blue?'

'I'll deal with them.' He does not lift his face from the book, and he holds it so tight it could tear. 'I'll deal with all of them, you leave them to me. Go home. Rest.' Crossing back over to the fire, he kneels in the ash that has piled by the grate. 'Don't worry, they won't be roaming now, not now the dawn light might hit them.'

'Don't worry? You've told me all my life about those two! About how hard Bluecap was to lock away, how much it cost you. And here she is, Cutty Soames himself by her side.' Pausing for a moment, she closes her eyes and sits at the table in the kitchen. 'But if you think I'm running home, you're wrong. I'm worried for you, Pel. I saw you up there, you were shaking.'

'You're mistaken.'

'I'm not. We've talked about this. You can't do this forever, and when you're gone it will fall to me. Let me help. You don't need to worry about me. I can do it.' Pel pauses, hand resting on his book and eye fixed on his ward. Nancy sees the muscles of his iris contract as he focuses his attention on her. She can see her reflection in the glassy surface of his eye as a tear forms. He brushes it away.

'I know you can, Nancy.' A crumb rarely dropped from his table, and she devours it. Hates him for it. 'But please,' he continues, 'I need to do this alone. After I have, I will—we will—begin our studies again. I will even consider allowing you to develop your, gift. I promise. We'll try again.' Nancy moves to sit at the desk beside him, takes his hand in hers. The thin, wiry fingers cold. She rubs them, tries to warm them up, and looks at the books scattered on the desk. In the corner the slim volumes that he bought for her when he taught her Greek and Latin. The big book of folk stories he read to her each night after her mother died. She softens, as his fingers heat, and he grips her hand. He gives it a firm shake then pulls free. The moment passing as the moon dips behind a cloud.

'Cutty and Bluecap shouldn't be free. It's connected to the deaths on the moor, it's too much of a coincidence not to be.' Pel speaks softly, packs away his frailty in a bog-oak box.

'But why? Why kill like that? Even Soames, when he was free before, killed like a beast let loose. No reason, no rhyme. You told me so yourself, it's your account in here.' Nancy taps the spine of the book of folk tales. 'Each of these deaths has been methodical. The way the killer left them, there is a design to this.' He's thinking, she can see it in him, as he paces back and forth. He's mulling it over, her offer of help, she sees the moment he discards it, his face set hard.

'Perhaps, but you'll not help me by dying. I'll put them away alone.'

Nancy closes her eyes, hard, squeezes back the memories of her childhood, furious now. Up and out of her chair sending it skittering across the flagstones. Even the dog moves out of her way, and he moves for no one.

'Why won't you let me help? Is it just because of him? I am not Callum Cleaver, Pel.' Her guardian bristles at the name. 'I can do this'. She holds his gaze. 'I promise, I won't call the Murmur, I won't let it out.'

'That's not a promise you can make. You're right, you can do all those things but whilst that power resides in you, it isn't safe, Nancy. For anyone! You could have brought the hill down tonight. You need to learn how to control yourself. I'll not give power to someone too young to wield it, not again.'

'I'm twenty-one, Pel! I'm not a girl anymore! I remember Callum, you're right, you shouldn't have given him the tools you did—'

'I'm to blame for his mistakes, then? Is that it? You know how he—'

'Enough, Pel! Fine, Callum did what he did. You were blameless. Wonderful. But how is this the solution? Why punish me?' She hates these fights, these well-trod circles, she's tired of them. She looks back to the books, those nights before the Murmur showed itself. She kneels, strokes Patroclus's long coat, rubbing the old dog's belly as he rolls it towards her. He doesn't seem to mind the tears as long as the attention continues. 'I'm sorry, Pel, I didn't mean for the Murmur to fly today, I'm trying.'

Slumping back on his haunches, Pel holds the kindling

loosely in his hands. He reaches over and scratches the dog, too. A shaggy-haired olive branch, drooling on the floor between them.

'Hush, Nance. It's all right.' He closes his eye and sighs. 'Fine. You can help. But I'll deal with those on the moor alone.'

Nancy twitches with the urge to prolong the fight, sure that if it goes on long enough it might finally resolve but she's too tired for that tonight.

'Thank you. I know you're not telling me something though, Pel. I see it in your eye.'

'I have a suspicion. But I'll not share it until I know it's right. I won't put you in more danger than you are now.'

Nancy rises from her chair, but Pel is set, she can see. There is the hardness in his eye that she knows so well, iris like a hag stone with a hole in the middle. So, she sighs, waves him on. Resigned.

'Go to the village and talk to the dead boy's family. Find out what they know. Talk to the others' kin too if you're able. You don't kill like that and not choose carefully.' Pushing fresh wood onto the fire, Pel stares into the flames. 'Things are falling apart, Nance. Whatever this is, whoever is doing it, is just hastening the end. What good is balance if someone can so heavily weigh down the scale?' There is a panic in his old eye. It has shaken him. The hill was fuller than it had been for years, swollen with enemies he thought he'd beaten. Creatures that had long ago laid down to sleep. He'll not lose her. He will manage alone.

Nancy kneels beside Pel in the grey dust, puts an arm around him, lays her head on his shoulder.

'You said you think this is the work of a man, not Them, doing this, who?'

Pel closes his eye, and she waits for the smile, there, lifting the corner of his mouth. He moves to place an arm on her cheek and the smile fades back to worry, though softer than before.

'I... I don't know. Trust me, Nance, help me.'

Both look solemnly into the fire. Feel the heat from the flames. An agreement reached by the light from its embers.

'We'll stop it then. Together.'

'Aye, Nancy. We will. Let's get some rest. It's been a long night.'

Nancy helps him onto his feet and guides him to the camp bed in the corner, pulls faded sheets about his shoulders and strokes his brow. She adores this old man. She is twenty-one and has no idea how old he is. What he's seen. How little of his life he has shared with her, but she loves him. Has been proud to stand by his side and play the part of his "merry little changeling." If he'd just give her a little more trust. Let her stray a little further before he calls her home.

Leaving him, she takes a seat in the horsehair chair and though worried, and fretting, is soon asleep with the frown still on her face. Brownies step from the shadows and little hands draw a blanket up around her. Throw a bundle of lavender into the fire. Pat opens one half-awake eye and watches small footprints pass by to the shadows. Outside, on the moor, dark clouds gather, and it smells like rain.

BELL HEATHER

NANCY WAKES EARLY, steps quietly to the desk where Pel keeps his books and draws one from the shelf. Thick, bound in green leather and stamped in gold: *Drolls of the High Moor by William Sloggett*. She had loved this book when she was little. Pel had told her he'd met Sloggett in Truro, years ago. Told him tales, paid in kind. This was the copy sent in thanks. She flicks through the pages and smiles. Each page adorned with a thicket of marginalia. Nancy's childhood scribbling. She used to sit and paint the borders before she'd learnt to read the stories. Pel hadn't minded, he'd already added notations of his own. Cross little asides where Sloggett had gone off script. She turns to Cutty Soames's page. A pair with Bluecap's. Sloggett had commissioned an engraver to depict his subjects, and Nancy stifles an unbelieving laugh. Both the creatures sit with legs crossed on grassy, mushroom-ringed hummocks. Impish faces grinning from beneath soft Phrygian caps. The paint Nancy had used to colour them faded now with age. She had liked their stories; the quaint way Sloggett wrote, "*There are naughty creatures out there too. Amongst the piskies and the spriggans, like Cutty Soames with his sharp little knives and Bluecap with her fire.*" In between the printed text is Pel's dense hand. "*No no no! These two are barbaric, murderous creatures! Nonsense Sloggett!*"

Nancy had always felt protective of Sloggett, but now,

having met the spirits in question, she was inclined to agree with Pel. Cutty and Blue have rattled her, still, it could be worse. She turns to a page near the end of the book, which falls open readily, the spine used to this particular position. On the left-hand side is an illustration of six horsemen, lined up along a ridgeline. Heads missing. On the right, the legend of the Wild Hunt. They, of all the creatures in the book, had scared Nancy the most. Still, she could never keep away. Had even melted the heads from her little lead cavalry officers so she could play at calling the Hunt herself. She skims the story she knows by heart, Pel's notes scrawled between the words.

Before the Keepers, the Hunt was the closest thing to law the Underfolk had.

They weren't the law. They were brutish, blunt instruments of death and torment. That's why we had to take over. Couldn't trust the Undermoor to police itself!

In life they were hunters of beasts. Driving their hounds across the moorland, tearing down deer and wolf. Bear and badger. The gods below were more vocal than they are now. They played games with men, set wagers. Humans are fickle and easily led. Abundant game each season? Very well, the gods said, you shall have it. But in death you belong to us. And one after another men and women agreed. You'll see their family crests in churches from the Tamar to Land's End. Scrolled stone adorned with harts and boars. Each had thought to outrun their debts. That their new god could outfox the old.

NONSENSE

They could not. They never reached their stone tombs. Each one fell on their last hunt. Thrown into the mire, from horses that bridled at ghosts. Their bodies sinking under bubbles that burst with laughter. Down they went, then up they came. Hunting still. Roaring across the sky on their smoke-maned horses and wish-hound pack. Collecting Underfolk who'd overstepped. Taking the lives of those that transgressed. They cannot be outrun. They cannot be bargained with.

Not strictly true! Supposedly they can be forced below physically, through the earth itself, though I can't imagine the power that would take.

Nancy closes the book and replaces it on the shelf with a shiver, then heads into the day.

LEAVING PEL SLEEPING, Patroclus too, their upturned ship rocking with the windblown morning, Nancy steps lightly across the waking moor. As it did the night Salan died, the rain has stopped, and as the sun rises it shows a world of white set hard in ice. Every surface shining. Every thorn, every blade of grass filigreed in crystal.

She looks for her friends, for the smiling faces and sparkling eyes. No one there. Normally they would be bounding like fox cubs new to spring, across the grass and the heather and the ling. She played with them like feral cats, with a smile and a loving touch but wary of their claws. They had no morality, a stolen apple taken from a basket, a man led deep into the mire. Both the same. Both a game. They'd lived their lives and died, little now to hurt them, few rules left that still applied.

Not like the others that had raised their heads the night before, the two on the stacks the worst of them. Nothing but malice in those old eyes.

She had always helped them, more than Pel. Differently from him. He kept them in line for their own good, as a schoolmaster would. She helped them as a friend. She had never told Pel how much she remembered of her time with them, what they'd shown her. With the sun bright and the frost still hard she chooses to walk, not ride. It isn't a long journey, but after the night she's had it is with relief that she reaches the village. She'll prove to Pel she was capable, could do as he had asked and more. She stops at the fallen-down cross that bridges the boundary of Mirecoombe, old stone speckled with black and green lichen. Taken from somewhere on the moor, no doubt, useful stone. What would Cleaver think of this desecration? Nancy smiles. It doesn't matter how strong the faith is, it's how deep the foundation goes. And nothing pierces bedrock, not on the moor. There is water under the bridge, beneath a slim crust of ice, and Nancy moves across it carefully, so as not to fall.

As she goes, she shoots a glance at the large, jagged boulder resting on the boundary wall to the east. The path of its decent grassed over now, the wound scabbed over. Nancy grins. The result of the last lesson Pel had given her, five years before. He had, once, spent most days teaching her. Up on the crown of Lullaby Tor to the west of the village. Drilling her on spells and charms. Flipping through his book and shouting out the names of flowers. He had even, occasionally, allowed her to practice with the Murmur, though she could always tell it worried him. That last time, she had excelled—as she always did—at his tests and as a treat he had let her call her birds. The same test as always. Try to tip the rocking logan stone, that gave the tor its name, from its perch. She had come close before, but that day, buoyed by success she had been reckless, let herself give in to the joy of it and the stone had tipped right off. Skidded down the hillside towards Mirecoombe stopped only by spells cast by an unusually blue-tongued Pel. She'd never heard him use language like it. Still, both had found it funny once the dust had settled. She missed those lessons. Once Callum had... done what he did, Pel had stopped her education. Clipped her wings.

She steps with a straight back into Mirecoombe and does not give the stone any more of her attention.

People are at work already. From the rolling hills, she can hear the clang, clang, clang of men driving posts into moor stone, splitting gate posts and troughs. At this time of year, it's the only job worth doing. Nancy hopes at least one has remembered to leave a little out for the spriggans. Hopes if they did the spriggans would help the stone to crack. She passes by women letting geese out from their holes in walls, smiles at children playing. The looks she gets back are mostly polite, though cautious. There is suspicion in their faces. Nancy smiles, but it is not returned. She knows they see her as Pel's, but it runs deeper than that. Her mother's cottage, outside the boundaries, always set them apart. Whispers about her family always hissing in the shadows. She kicks herself for still trying to make friends, for wanting to be let in. This frost hasn't thawed in twenty-one years it isn't thawing now. She crosses the green, past the foals at the well, and heads towards the cold store.

The long, cool room seems empty. The stone bier swept and washed and scoured clean of death. Salan Dell shrouded, waiting in his box, ready for the burial later in the day. The door stands open and lets in the daylight, but it's the shadows in which they stand. Hugh and Seren Dell. The grief rises off them like the mist from a river on a spring morning. Arms about each other but still feeling for a third.

Into this comes Nancy, quiet and alone.

The Dells don't see her, not at first. Too busy looking at a ghost. She coughs, softly, and they turn, blinking the sadness from their eyes.

'Nancy,' Seren begins, her voice like a sparrow's wing. 'How are you? Are you coming to the chapel, for the service?'

Nancy looks down, she would like to, she knew Salan.

'No. Sorry, Seren, I can't. He wouldn't want me there, I would distract. It wouldn't be right.' Seren smiles at this, shakes her head.

'I understand. Sal would, too.' The silence hangs awkwardly between them, like a glass dropped in the passing.

'I wanted to talk to you, both of you, if I could. Pel... '

'Don't you dare speak his name here!' Hugh's voice bursts from his chest like a branch breaking from a tree, loud then soft as it crashes to the floor. Nothing left but broken twigs. 'He did nothing! Sal was the fifth, and where was he? Nobody has seen him since the first.' Nancy begins to smile but stops. She thinks better of it, then meets Hugh's eyes.

'I'm sorry. He should have, you know how he is. He didn't think it was his place. Nobody asked.' She doesn't believe it any more than the Dells.

'Nobody asked?' Hugh's face is wet, tears washing salt into his mouth. 'Nobody *asked*? What good is he if he doesn't help! He tells us how he's here for our own good, how he keeps the bad things away! Makes us leave piles of apples in the fields and tells us that keeps us safe. What did this, then? Who did this?'

He quietens now, leans upon the bier, and wipes his tears away.

'I know he does help. My father always had faith in him. He

can do things. I've seen him do them. I saw him change the storm clouds when they gathered over the hay. I saw him bring the Rowe girl back when she fell into the mire!' He stares at Nancy, red-ringed eyes suddenly hopeful. 'Can he bring Sal back?'

'No.' Nancy says with a finality that cuts through even a parent's grief. 'No. He can't do that. Nobody can. Delen wasn't gone. She was leaving, but she was still here. I'm sorry, Hugh, Salan is gone. He can't come back. Pel can do lots of things, wonderful things, but he can't do that. But he does want to help if you'll let him.' Nancy pauses and takes a seat next to Hugh on the stone. Seren sits beside him. 'He doesn't think, nor do I, that it was one of Them. One of the old things. It wasn't the moor. He thinks a person did this.' The Dells look between themselves, unsure of what to say. 'Can you tell me about how Salan spent the last few days, as best you know?' Seren looks at her husband, he nods.

'He spent it as he usually did. Walking to the house a valley over for his work, walking back at dusk. He went to the chapel on the Sunday, he's taken to it, we don't go ourselves. And on Monday he spent the day with a friend. We saw him that morning for breakfast and then… ' Seren stops, drops her head. Nancy lays a hand on her back and thinks.

'He's been going to the chapel… to hear Cleaver?'

Hugh nods, arm about his wife.

'He has, for the last few weeks. We didn't think much of it, we've not often gone. We hang a cross, get on with things, always have. You know how it is here. But he said it made him happy to hear Cleaver speak, so what harm could it do? I didn't like the man myself. But he's been through a lot, I can understand it now. He's been very kind to us. Since he died.'

Nancy stands, walks into the daylight, and turns back to the Dells on their morbid perch.

'I've changed my mind. May I come to the service with you?'

*   *   *

THE THREE OF them walk out into the thin light of the morning. The rain has returned, falling through the sunlight. The world seen through scratched glass, the droplets catching the light as they fall. There is a crowd, the village solemn and quiet in the frost. Even Madge is here. It's only right to see off the dead, so she'll swallow her dislike of the chapel. Hugh Dell and five other men shoulder the coffin; it is a steep walk from the village to the chapel, and they concentrate on the climb. Along the path, quartz is studded to guide the way and halfway up is a slab of stone to rest on. They do not need it today.

The villagers snake out behind them. Some hold flowers, whilst others carry wreaths of rowan and blackthorn. They lay them carefully around the outside of the chapel yard wall. The Reverend does not take kindly to any offering that isn't his. Every member of the congregation, even the pallbearers, touches the lintel stone as they pass. Once inside, Nancy takes a seat at the back and tries to hide in the shadows, avoiding the eyes of the cherubim and green men that peer at her from the rafters. The coffin is laid on a wooden bier and draped in a shroud. The grave stands outside, six feet deep and cold.

When all is still the curtain sweeps aside and the Reverend Cleaver walks in.

He is dressed as he was before, magpied in black and white, his corvid face sharp beaked above. Stood at his golden lectern he scans the crowd, and his eyes stop on Nancy. His lip curls. But he moves on.

'I will not talk today of the crime that brings us here. I said my piece yesterday. We are gathered in this house of God to remember one who loved Him. Salan Dell. He was new to this church, as many of you are. New to visiting every Sunday and sitting in the bright light of our Lord, not expecting him to come out to you in the fields but revering him here. As you should.' Every face is downcast now, as if in prayer. Faces turned to the floor. All except for Nancy at the back who watches Cleaver like a hawk. He holds her eye. Is that the twitch of a smile she sees?

'But, of course, it would be remiss not to speak a little of the terrors that assail us. Of the devils of the moors. For that is what they are. These spirits that you speak of. These creatures you leave food for. They are your sins, manifest. They are not little creatures with hands and feet—they are your demons. Ghosts of a pagan past. The only good spirit lives here, with me. And those that tell you otherwise are liars. I do not know who took Salan from us, who dragged him to the black water Davy found him in, but it was a man. I promise you that. I promise you it will stop. I will stop it. With prayer and your belief, we will end it together. We will step from this darkness into the light together, better, stronger than before. This is a test. I will hold your hand as we pass through the crucible, leave all that is rough and waste behind and emerge pure and shining. These old ways that you cling to end in blood. In death. Let me show you peace. The peace that waits for Salan now the Lord has called him home. Sat with the angels and the cherubim, in that heavenly hall.' The Reverend gazes up to the carved wooden faces in the ceiling, eyes wide and pious. 'Let us sing.'

Nancy rises as the hymn begins and slips out through the door. She sits on the chapel-yard wall and listens to the service as it ends, to the echoed Amens. She hears the congregants file out, hears the coffin lower into the ground and the soil land heavy on the lid. She waits for the mourners to file back down the hill, waits for him.

'Miss Bligh.'

'Reverend.'

The pair view each other with the same measure of disdain, with something close to hate.

'I did not expect to see you in the pews, Miss Bligh. Have you seen the light at last?' The Reverend's voice is clipped, controlled.

'I have my own light, thank you. Reverend.'

'I'm sure you do. Why are you here? Surely you and Lord Hunt should be out in the mud looking for monsters?'

Nancy smiles. She looks down at her buttoned boots, soles wet from the frost.

'We think the monster might live here, Reverend.' Cleaver blanches, his white skin somehow both paler and enflamed at the same time. Nancy frowns. 'That is, we agree with you. We think it is a man. I'm just here to say goodbye to a friend. I was surprised he was yours too.'

Cleaver relaxes and twists his mouth into a smile.

'They all were, each one of the five we've so sadly lost. Salan, of course. Old Tom, Hedra and Bronwen. Young Harvey Gunner too. Each new to my flock and killed for it.' Nancy's eyes widen and Cleaver lets out a short laugh. She curses herself for giving him the satisfaction of surprising her. 'Of course it was a man who did it. But the way they were found—I've read books, too, the Church has writings on this. There was ritual to the way they were left. Ungodly rituals. Have you spoken with them? These creatures you and that doddering old fool claim to speak to?' Nancy cannot tell if she is being mocked. 'Are you so certain it is not connected? This wouldn't be the first time your stories have led to tragedy, would it?' No pretence of civility now, the last few words were spat.

The Reverend Cleaver stares at two gravestones. His wife's on the left, his son's on the right. Only one body lies beneath them.

'Reverend, we tried to help Callum… '

'Don't you dare say his name! He died because of the nonsense you fed him. I trusted you both to help him and you failed. He walked into that water because of what you told him.'

'We tried to help! You called us and we came, but it was too late! If you'd come to us sooner, perhaps.'

'You blame me? How dare you. I loved my son! I loved him more than anything else in this world, I promised his mother I would keep him safe, before Lord Hunt killed her, and yet, in desperation I sent him my boy. I trusted him. Both of you.' His eyes are those of the eagle in the church. Bright, unflinching, and shining. His mouth quivers as he speaks, rage and sorrow shaking the very fabric of him. Nancy stands and turns to the priest, her face darting between anger and pity, and guilt too. But the Reverend will not listen, that much is clear.

'Reverend—'

'Enough. It ends. I have tolerated this blasted "tradition" for too long. My predecessors did too. I will put an end to your heathenism, your magic, your stories, and your lies. I'll not make the mistakes I've made in the past again. I know what I must do. He has shown me how to do it. It all ends. Tell Lord Hunt it's over. His days as a "Keeper" are done.'

Nancy starts to argue, but up over the brow of the hill a man is running, slipping on the ice and mud with terror in his eyes.

'Reverend! Please, come to the village, there's been an attack on the moor.'

BRISTLE BENT

A THUMB-PRICKING, NOSEBLEED wind is raking across the valley now, picking at the slates of the Mare's Nest Inn like a scab. Clearing the last of the frost away, ready for fresh tomorrow.

The bar is full. It often is at this time, as the sun falls away, but not like this. Men and women, standing in the sawdust with their coats drawn tight, sitting round the tables, backs against the settles. Eyes dart with worried looks and no one can stay still. They jump at the door with every new arrival. Madge is handing out hot cups of cider, spiced and heady, into thick bottomed earthenware mugs. To others she pours out beers and double measures in pewter tankards. To all she gives a reassuring smile. Some of the crowd top their mugs up from flasks and Madge pretends not to see. Turf burns in carefully tended grates, flames flickering and guttering in the frigid air that fights its way down the chimney. Children held close under woollen cloaks are told by parents not to play. Even the dogs lie quivering, hackles to the rafters. Under the boards and in the darkest corners the little household spirits hold their tongues. It's dangerous out there.

There is chatter, like murmurous starlings, and it echoes through the bar.

'Did you see it? Ripped apart.'

'Like a storm-torn sail.'

'Like the carcass of a chair with its stuffing pulled out.'

Pel stalks into this confusion with his dog at his heel. Madge sent word. He stamps the cold from his feet, Patroclus pushing past him and taking his place by the fire. Pel gazes coldly into the quietening room. The last crowd he addressed here turned on him, after all. He is wary of another riot. He walks straight to the bar, Madge pouring him a drink from a bottle kept below. His bottle.

'Thank you, Madge,' Pel says and downs the clear liquid with a sharp tilt of his head. His body shakes as the spirit funnels down. Straightening, he turns to face the crowds that press around.

'What's happened?' With two words he breaks the seal of the silence barely held and a torrent rushes forth. A babbling chaos of accusations and fear that deafens. It is the Reverend Cleaver who answers. Stepping from the shadows, his black cassock cut from the same dark cloth, he looms into the bar.

'Ah, Lord Hunt. Too late to be of any use, and no doubt full of dire warnings.' He does not wait for Pel to answer. 'There has been an incident. A calf found on Echo Tor. Eviscerated by some beast. The work of the monster that is killing the people on the moor. If you believe the talk.'

Pel listens quietly, his sharp gaze crossing across the Reverend's features, catching briefly on Cleaver's eyes.

'What do you think, Reverend?' Pel's voice is hard, quiet. Cleaver smiles, not breaking Pel's gaze.

'A dog. Some creature gone wild. Nothing more.' Cleaver is testing the old Keeper. Waiting.

'Ain't no dog did that!' Cusk is on his feet, Calder behind him nodding furiously in agreement. Others are standing too.

'Belly torn apart with one cut! Leg bent back.'

'It's a creature! Pel will know!'

'Ask Pel!'

The Reverend Cleaver is snarling now, thin lips curled over crooked grey teeth, like a line of gravestones.

'It's a dog! You idiots! Salan Dell not two hours buried with his neck broken! Did this calf lie in the same way? Have the same red mark?'

Silence.

'No, I thought not. There is nothing on that moor tonight but animals and their effluence.'

Smiling, Pel steps forwards. Cane tapping on the flagstone. He keeps one hand on its topper and the other in his pocket, turning over polished stones.

'Now, Reverend. There is more out there than that, as well you know. Perhaps I should go and see the poor beast? Cast an eye.'

The crowd shifts at this. They take little comfort in his manner, in his breezy confidence. It has been a long time since he's put on this show, and they haven't missed it as much as they thought they had. Each thinking of a friend lost and a Keeper who was nowhere to be found. Pel thinks of the creatures on the hill. The ones newly returned. He can see Cutty Soames and his sickle-sharp claws. If he closes his eye, he can hear Bluecap laughing. He raises his cane, and the Mare's Nest falls quiet.

'I will look into this.' It has not taken long for the old bravado to come back. All it took was an audience. It's only as he turns that he sees Nancy, quiet at the back, a worried look across her face. 'Nancy and I will go, see what's about. Stay indoors. Keep in groups. Before I go, I'll scratch a ward into your doorframes. I'm sure Madge would like the business so if you'd like, stay here. Drink. I'll join you when I'm done.'

There are turning points in a life. Things best left unspoken.

Pel looks back, a smile on his face still, and stares at Cleaver simmering away.

'Or... ' Pel has the devil in his eye.

Nancy places her arm on the old man's arm.

'Enough, Pel. Let's go.'

Pel glares at the Reverend like a petulant child who knows full well he courts trouble.

'Or, if you'd feel safer. Perhaps you could join the Reverend on the hill and pray.' Pel begins to leave, he is almost to the door when Cleaver speaks. Softly. Mockingly.

'Where do they live?'

Pel turns.

'Pardon?'

'You heard me. Where do they live, these creatures of yours?'

Pel does not answer. He eyes the Reverend warily, a hare caught in the corner of a field, waiting for a chance to bolt, or box.

'In the fields!' Comes a voice. Then several, all at once, keen to show they know their folklore with well-versed catechisms.

'In the heather!'

'On the tors!'

'Between the needles on the gorse!'

Cleaver smiles like the setting of a snare.

'Very well. Cusk, take some men out and dig a ditch, as wide around the gorse as you can manage.'

The men in the bar look to Cusk for guidance, and Cusk looks to Pel. He might be a convert, but old ties hold firm.

'What are you doing, Cleaver?' Pel's voice is bony and hard. 'I'll handle this. I said I would.'

'You will call me by my title, Lord Hunt. As I am courteous enough to do for you. And I *am* helping. What can I do if my parish needs help? I listen. And I give it. So, you say there are creatures on the moor that cause harm. These good people say some of them live in the gorse. Very well. We will burn it.'

Nancy starts to speak, but Pel interrupts before she can attempt a diversion, catch the disaster before it unfolds with a well-placed stitch.

'This is not the season for a gorse fire, Reverend. It's not the way things are done.'

The Reverend walks slowly to the bar, back turned to Pel and Nancy. He lays both hands upon the polished surface, tenses against it and she feels any hope this could have been averted slip away.

'Nonsense. You have presented a problem. I have presented the solution'. Cleaver adopts his mask of plaintive piety again. 'Tell me, everyone, will it set your minds at rest to clear the gorse? To take away the hiding places of these... little people.'

Neighbours turn to neighbour, friend to friend. Under the floor, small feet shuffle nervously. But it is a sore temptation, this offer of direct action. No waiting, no parsing of Pel's proclamations. There are whispers, rising into talk that rings across the bar.

'What's he do for us, really?'

'Never comes for a drink... '

'Takes his coin and waves his hands... '

'I've never seen Them.'

'Never heard Them.'

'What harm, anyway? If They do exist, let's put it up 'em.'

'Show them who's in charge.'

Nancy's eyes flit between the speakers. Panicked, too many voices to speak to anyone directly. He's lost them. Waited too long and now here he is playing the part the Reverend's cast him in: a mountebank, a showman. Busy lives leave no space for make-believe. Nancy will try though.

'Everyone, please! Remember what we, what Pel does for you! What They do! They split the stone they—'

'I split the bloody stone!' Laughter, draped over deeper resentments. Nancy racks her thoughts for anything that might help whilst Pel stands mute.

'Please, I know it must be tempting, to do something, but please leave it to us.'

'Burn the devils!' Calder shouts louder than the other voices with the glint of the righteous in his eyes. He glowers at Madge; no love lost there.

'He's right, Pel.' Cusk now. 'We're dropping like flies as it is. No offence to you, but something must be done, and you've not done it.'

Murmurs of agreement, the shaking of heads. The dropping of sparks on powder leaking from kegs. The fire starts before it's been lit. Hugh Dell stands first.

'You've had your chance to help, Pel. We'll do our part now. Come, Seren, all of you.' The air is full of the sound of chairs scraping back, of drinks being finished and glasses slammed down. Pel looks between the faces already making for the door.

'Don't be rash. Reverend, all of you! The gorse is dry, brittle, even under the frost. It could get out of hand. Let me go and see to it, at least, before you start on this.'

'He's right, Reverend,' Madge speaks firmly from behind the bar and Nancy is thankful for an ally. 'It won't do to burn it now. Wait until the morning, let Pel freeze his ears off if he insists.'

'If you think I'll be lectured to by a conman and a barkeep you are mistaken. Cusk, away with you, now. And all else who'll follow—let's go and burn ourselves a beast.' Nancy moves to block the door, entreating Pel with wide eyes to try again. She isn't sure if she's more scared by the fact she's asking, or the fact that he seems to agree. He takes a step forward, catches Cleaver's eyes with his and reaches for his once-good friend.

'Cleaver. Don't. Remember how it used to be. We could still put this behind us, work together. There's room in the valley for both of us.'

Nancy has never heard the Reverend laugh before. It's unpleasant, an adder shedding skin.

'Together, Lord Hunt? You've no room for a partner. I see how you treat the girl. You're an arrogant old fool. Zounds man, look at you, even your head can only hold the one eye. You're done. Keeper. You've lost them, I will shepherd them now.'

They push past Pel as he stands leaden in the centre of the Nest. Nancy knows he can hear the call of the imps and piskies on the hill.

Can't do what you could do, can you?

They've always listened before, the villagers. Always. It takes Nancy, forcing her way through the throng to shake him out of it.

'Pel! What are you doing? We need to stop this!'

Emerging from his stupor, Pel looks at his ward.

'Run, Nancy. You must get there before them. Stir up everybody you can find, the piskies, the spriggans, all of them. Tell them to run, up to the tor. If any of our newly returned friends cause trouble, tell them to stay and burn. I'm going back to the house to fetch some things, to buy us some time. The fools.'

Nancy looks at the old man. Her jaw set, eyes narrowed, she looks at him with fury.

'You aren't coming?' She glowers at him, but he has turned

his back, 'You did this, Pel. You! You don't always know the best thing to do, aren't always right.' Pel makes no move to follow, lays both hands on his stick and holds her gaze. She can see his lip tremble. 'We're talking once this is done.' And out she goes, into the starlight like a comet trail.

Pel looks down at Patroclus, the dog is eyeing the door and whining.

'Aye, go on. Look after her for me. Go on!'

As Pat's tail disappears into the night, Pel nods curtly to Madge and heads for home.

AHEAD OF THE crowd winding out of the village, torches in hand setting fire to the moonlight, Nancy runs to the moor. The gorse spreads across the hillside in a rough circle, the bushes five feet high in places, the plants tangled together in a maze of spiked branches that spreads over half an acre. A ring of heather stands around its edge like a palisade, fragrant even in the freezing wind that rakes through it, but a fragile barrier to fire. She stands at the edge of the gorse that spreads gilt-needled ahead. Even now, a few tattered yellow flowers still cling to the green like a dusting of stars. She searches the spiked avenues for a familiar face, for the smallest spark of an eye. She hears a rustling and lets out a sigh. She hadn't even noticed she was holding her breath.

There is magic in the gorse. Pel had shown her how to mix its ash into an oil, to spread beneath the eyes to see in half-light. Girls tucked sprigs into bridal bouquets to firmly fix the love. In the springtime the farmers set fires to burn it back and the smoke turned white clouds black. Because, whilst there was magic in it, there was also oil. Gorse burns hot. Nancy shouts into the dense thicket of thorns and shadows.

'I know you're in there. Little reason to stay hid. But I understand, I know things went badly at the tor.' Nancy keeps her voice steady. Keeps the wing beats of worry from it. No reply, though faces do emerge. The piskies first. It pays to be quick to forgiveness if you need to ask for it so often yourself.

'Hello, dearies.' Nance pushes a smile past tense muscles and hopes it looks more authentic than it feels. 'The rest of you too! I need you to listen to me. They're burning the gorse, the villagers, they're on their way now. You all need to go. Head to the tor, or back below. Some of you might be better off staying there.'

Some of the smaller spirits flee, scampering heading up the hill. After the piskies the spriggans come bounding, joints grinding like rockfall as they spring on mossy legs away and over the skyline. There are still frightened faces peering from the gorse though.

'Why are you staying? Please, please, all of you, *run*. I can't help if you stay. Why won't you move?' There, the thick stems of the gorse part and she hears them before they're seen. Nancy's smile, so lightly held, is gone. Like dew from a cobweb. Two heads rear from the furze.

'Because we told them not to. Didn't we, Cutty?' Bluecap spits gaseous flame as she talks, and it licks around the undergrowth hungrily.

'We did, Blue, we did.' Cutty Soames stands tall now, head and shoulders above the gorse. 'We don't believe you. Don't care about him.' The pair of them stand together now, faces grinning from above the sharp and jagged boughs. Nancy puts a hand down and you can see the relief as her hand meets the shaggy coat of Patroclus, resolute at her side.

'You don't need to believe me to burn. They're coming, look, down the valley. You can see the torches. They'll be digging the firebreaks soon.' A few more of the smaller faces baulk at this and make their escape, their footsteps like rain on the hillside. Even Cutty looks worried at the flickering lights growing brighter every moment. But Bluecap stands burning and is not afraid of fire. She is smiling in the cold wind, letting off blustery clouds of eerie steam.

'Let them come.' Cutty picks a tendon from his teeth. 'We didn't eat much of the calf in the end, interrupted, could do with something else to eat. Teach them to forget us.'

The footsteps of the villagers are close now. Nancy turns away and the faces in the gorse disappear, only the faint sound of laughter is left. Cusk, and Calder and his sons are digging deep ditches with earth on either side, and making quick work of it, even in the frost. They're excited, it occurs to Nancy in a wave of disgust, they giggle and joke as though coursing for hare and not for the first time she wonders why she and Pel still try. If they want Cleaver, why not leave them to him? She has been gritting her teeth so hard her jaw aches.

'Enough. Nancy.' Spoken so softly to herself she barely hears it.

The Murmur trembles with her rage, but she stills it. Presses it back down. She made a promise and besides, it won't help her here. Groups of the other villagers make small piles of gorse and heather away from the main crop of it and, laying down their torches, light little beacon fires around the hill to warm themselves on before the inferno begins.

Nancy sees the Reverend arrive soon after. He must have headed back to the rectory to change, for he's wearing his fur-lined overcoat, heavy and black. Always crow-like, the pomp of the evening and the weight of his coat have turned him into a raven, stalking towards the gorse. There is a fervour to him that has been growing all evening and is reaching its pitch.

The ditches have been dug now. The perimeter closest to the Reverend lined with people like spectators at some arena, waiting for blood. Reaching for a still-burning staff lying cinder-bound in one of the smaller fires, the Reverend holds it aloft, the guttering flame burning a hole in the sky where the moon should be. Nancy can hear him, even at the far side of the circle.

'I want to be clear. I do not believe we are burning devils here tonight. It was a dog that killed that animal, a man who killed your friends, and if the foul individual is hiding in this gorse tonight, then he's a fool if he stays. But if this is what it takes to prove to you that we are alone in this world but for the grace of God, then so be it. Watch your folklore burn.'

The torch falls onto the brittle-boned gorse, and it catches like phosphorous. As the fire fizzes across the frosted green, Nancy, at the far edge, sees a hunched figure amble quickly from the undergrowth, passing by the spectators in a shadow of its own.

'You're a craven coward Cutty Soames! I'll send you back myself and it will not be gentle. It will not!' She screams after the spirit but does not follow. She won't leave her friends. She tries once more to call into the gorse, but whoever remains is trapped now. She knows that. No spell or charm will work faster than the fire.

Not one I'm able to cast, a least.

Her chest roils with rage and shame, and it takes all she has to rise above it. She cannot help, but they'll not die alone. Nancy slumps against the cold heather at her back, its frost melted by the blaze, and tears stream down her cheeks. They dry before they reach her mouth. Her mouth that opens in a song remembered from childhood. A song to guide a loved one home.

'Soft, little ones, back to the earth.
Back to the place of your sweet rebirth.
Back to the rest that you earnt each day,
Your friends have been waiting since you went away.'

Her voice cracks. The words turn into sweetly hummed melody and her heart sinks under the weight of smoke and the dying. The song soothes. Their screams quiet into sobs, and then nothing. No sound at all but the crackling of the fire. Nancy closes her eyes against it all. Against the horror of the night. The betrayal of friends. When her eyes open the fire rages, it blots out the black of the sky with a bright yellow flame. The oil in the gorse crackling and popping as it catches. A thick, roiling cloud of black smoke that stinks of burnt coconut and ash has pushed Cleaver and the villagers back but Nancy remains as close as she can bear. She peers into the maelstrom for any hint of a survivor, but all is still. All, that is, apart from places here and there where the fire changes and flames up blue from the yellow. The blue flame licks and creeps from the circle and seems even to climb up on the far side of the ditch, but there is a wind building. And every time a fire-blue hand reaches out to catch a coat or an open hand it is blown back into the maelstrom with a howl. Bluecap is trapped with the rest of them.

Cleaver stands at the edge of the fire and opens a Bible. Though no one, now, can hear what he says through the wind and the fire, what sermon he preaches, all eyes are on him and reflecting the flames. In unison the circle of villagers bow their heads and pray in the fire's glow.

As it burns, the wind grows, and swirls around the boundary of the gorse fire, the fire spins into a vortex, caught in the draft. Nancy looks about but it seems she is the only one who has noticed that the wind now driving the fire is blowing the opposite way to the rest of the storm. That this current blows widdershins against the rest. The centre of the whirlwind grows hotter and hotter until it glows almost white. Right in the middle, at the hottest part of the fire a small skull bursts with a blue-black flame and a wiry-limbed creature curls itself into a ball of pain.

Bluecap burns bright, but Pel's magic burns brighter.

'Good,' Nancy's mouth twists into a sneer, 'but not enough, Pel. Nowhere near enough.' The petty justice of it barely cools her boiling blood. She is glad the demon suffers, that her flame has been snuffed out by a stronger one. But it is bittersweet.

Bluecap is buried under the ash of Nancy's friends.

SEATED ON THE floor of his house, a mile away, Pel sits cross legged, eye rolled back so only the white is showing. In the neighbouring socket, skin drawn tight across the empty hollow a green flame glows. There is acrid smoke billowing from the fire and in his hand is a flint axe head, it's edges grey, and he spins it counterclockwise on his open palm. A deep cut drawn across it, the blood rising and joining the stone in its rotation. He can't stop the flame, but he can make it hot enough that its victims' deaths are swift.

The fire will burn all night now if they let it.

OLD HARRY PASCOE stands well back from the flames, pipe in hand, on the edge of the firelight and the dark. The thick bank of smoke that rolls down the cold hillside hiding him from view. Harry who hangs a bottle in his fireplace full of blood and hair and piss and pins. Harry who sits in the chapel every Sunday. A walking contradiction like the rest of them. He has lived through sixty-eight years, happy as he's able. As he lights the tobacco and draws the smoke through the stem, he thinks. Deep lines furrow on his face.

'No sense in this.' Muttered from under the cloud he has created, the words break through like smoke signals. 'I'm sorry, little ones, if you're in there. I always done my best by you.' Does he remember, when he was young, when the Underfolk were a part of life, not just a story told to hedge your bets? His own grandfather mauled by a wish hound.

A bad end. A good story.

Harry Pascoe does not hear the footsteps in the gorse. The crackling of hard feet on bracken is lost in the snap of the fire. Does not feel, stood behind him, the shadow of a man. He doesn't feel cold breath on the back of his neck, just the heat from the wildfire. But there, Harry's pipe is put down, his free hand reaching for a charm—a little silver acorn—in his pocket, and a fear flares in his old eyes. The flames reflected in them burning his bravery away.

'I know you're there. Whatever you are. The Reverend says we oughtn't be afraid of you. He'll protect us.'

A rasp, like the dragging of stones on a riverbed, muffled by the stream, boiling in the heat.

'I—I am not afraid.' Harry's lie hangs trapped in his pipe smoke. Too quiet to attract help.

In the gorse, burning, are creatures that might have helped. Creatures that, at the very least, would have screeched out in alarm, run for help, as the figure stood behind Harry reaches out an arm and fixes calloused, leather-hard fingers round the old man's throat and grips. There is a heat to this hand that outstrips even the gorse fire. The fire that has driven everything away that could run. Every bird and every spirit. The hand burns its imprint into the old man's throat. Harry dies alone as the outstretched hand jerks to the left and breaks his neck, the man's head lolling and bones pressing hard against skin, blood pooling in the spaces between. Still holding Harry, the figure retreats back deep onto the moor, dragging the corpse behind him like a stoat's quarry.

Through the heat-haze of the gorse fire, under smoke-cloud covered stars, the Reverend Cleaver watches the world burn with a cold, thin smile.

ASPHODEL

It is morning. And if it weren't for the smell, he wouldn't be able to tell the frost from the ash. The moor is a wasteland, at least on this side of the hill, the scorch marks dulled by a scattering of ice. The ring of the fire-break ditch is filled with snow. There is silence on this hillside. No birdsong. The charcoal of the gorse lies charnel under the blanket of ash, tucked up tight and steaming. He can feel it through the soles of his boots. Here and there in the detritus of the blaze are the blackened wings of birds, heads burnt to a point and brittle, like glass blown too thin. The bones of a rabbit, the sooty echo of a stoat that had thought itself safe, the ermine smudge of its tail now indistinguishable from the blackened rest. The skeletons of other things, too.

Pel crunches across this pyre-land with his woollen overcoat tightly buttoned, fingerless gloves each keeping half a hand warm, and hat pulled tight over his ears. His boots and leather gaiters are smoking with a paste of black and grey and white from the grate of the burn site. One hand holding a heavy-lidded bucket, the other grasping tongs. Both made of iron. Both old. Nancy would worry at these dainty, fragile bones. At a skull, half buried, almost like a child's. He loves that in her. Envies it. Her ability to see the beauty and the sorrow. He does not know if he felt that even in youth. He sees each bone as a tally in the wrong column. A debt he now owes. He comes as an auditor, not to mourn.

He walks with purpose, skimming over corpses like a bee does over flowers, searching for his target, one amongst many, all looking much the same. Eventually, he stops. Places the bucket on the ground and lifts the lid, lays it close by and using the tongs he scrapes a layer of ash from something small and round. It reminds him of a sideshow exhibit he once saw. The petrified remains of a monkey stitched to a fish. As the tongs touch it the creature squirms, and from its foetal cramp a head lifts. Deep in empty eye sockets shines the faintest, weakest, flicker of blue.

'Hello, Bluecap.' Pel permits himself a smile. 'A little warm for you, was it? Serves you right. You and I will have a talk later.'

Bluecap starts to say something, some dreadful word that rattles like coal dust down a chimney from deep inside her throat. But Pel drops her in the bucket, lid on, gone. He's heard it all before.

'What on earth are you doing?' The voice is startlingly close. With the hat covering his ears Pel had heard nobody approach, and it is with dismay he recognises Cleaver. The Reverend still stands black-clad in his overcoat and cassock, blue-veined hands going white in the cold. The two men regard each other from ten paces as if in a duel, and the drop in temperature of their meeting causes it to snow.

'What's in the bucket, Pel?'

'Ash, Cleaver, and it's Pel now, is it? Hasn't been Pel for a while.'

The Reverend regards Pel with an expression that is dangerously close to compassion, but it reverts with a snap to disdain.

'Pel,' he says again. 'I'm tired. Can't we take a moment, here, on the battlefield, to talk as old friends? What is it they say, parley?'

Pel purses his lips.

'Parley?' He feels the devil rise in him again, feels a sharp retort, but he can feel the weight of Bluecap in his bucket. He's won one victory. It won't be long before he wins this war. He can afford some magnanimity. Pel walks over to Cleaver and the two men fall into step as they walk up towards the tor. He'll give his opponent a chance to apologise, to admit he cannot win. They are only halfway when Pel stops, leans over, his hand on his boot tops and panting.

'Hold, Jacob. I need to rest.'

'Don't tell me you've gotten old, Pel? You've looked like a ninety-year-old since I've known you. Has it finally happened? Have you caught up to the rest of us?' Cleaver sits down carefully, Pel lowering himself besides him. The cold wind whips up the ash and snow, and in the valley a hare breaks its cover.

'We were friends, Jacob, weren't we?'

'Aye, we were.'

'Did you ever finish your book?' Cleaver looks down at his hands and rubs them together.

'My collection of your tales? No, Pel. I didn't. The joy fell out of it. They were good stories though. Tell me again, Pel, what was it, that one that could read one's mind?'

Pel sits back in the drift and squints. *My. He must be desperate. To travel this far back.* Still, the Keeper will indulge him. If that's what it takes.

'All Seeing Arthyen?' Cleaver nods and motions Pel to continue. Pel smiles. 'Born of a bear, licked into the wrong shape by his mother, Arthyen stood on two legs or four depending on the direction of the wind. The story went that he crept up behind his prey and latched on. Sinking two long teeth into their calf. He hangs there, wrapped around their leg, and suckles from their memories. He stays for as long as he is interested, sifting through their life, until he grows bored and leaves. Though it was said that if he finds a person especially interesting, he may stay. Feeding on their life until the person loses sight of it. Their youth vanishing in a haze, then their adult days. Until they remember nothing but a few moments before the last. That's where I came in.'

'What a tale.' Jacob gives a short laugh and peers into the white. Pel frowns and rubs his calf, the memory of Arthyen's bite sadly still with him. 'Why couldn't you have just told tales, Pel? You could have made money from it. Been happy.'

'Because it would have been a lie, Jacob. A dangerous one.' They lapse into silence and Pel draws a hip flask from his pocket, takes a swig, and passes it to the Reverend who bucks against the taste.

'I'd forgotten this.' Jacob Cleaver hands the flask back to Pel who turns to face his old friend.

'Why are you here, Jacob? Too much water under this bridge, surely.'

'I wanted to give you a chance to stop now, Pel. Before I take it all.' Pel tenses, in his seat of snow. 'Go back to telling your stories, heal people. I know you can do that. Teach Nancy. Give her a chance, she's a smart girl. I know you believe you did your best for my wife, for Elizabeth, I know... I believe you think you do good. I will not stop, though, Pel. You can't see the damage you have wrought but I can. All of this, the deaths, everything, can stop. If you do.' The Reverend Cleaver pauses, Pel can see him scan his face and it riles him.

'You won a battle, Jacob. You won't win the war. What you did last night was reckless. There will be consequences.' The wind picks up and raises an eddy of white powder. Ash and snow.

'Is that a threat?' Cleaver stops, eyes Pel with uncertainty. He knows the old man has talents other than those he claims as "magic," he knows there's a knife in that cane. The fragile, cobweb peace that has hung between them stretches tight.

'No, Jacob. No threat. I can't be doing with revenge. I've too much to do cleaning up your mess. No, it'll be Them that get you.'

The Reverend laughs a snorting, arrogant laugh that echoes down the valley, and a thousand little ears prick up at the sound.

'I don't fear your fairy tales Pel. Only what they do to others. And I'm ending that now. You saw their faces last night, the men and women who came. Over half of Mirecoombe. They have seen the damage your stories can do. They believe in my help, not yours. Your scratched signs did nothing so now they hang crosses on their walls. They sit in my house. Listen to the gospels, to the parables of the Bible—not your foolish stories—and they are healed by me. Give up. Admit that it was your fault he died.'

'Callum?' Pel bellows. 'Is that what all this is about, Callum? Listen Jacob. I am sorry for what he did, but it was no fault of mine. If you'd involved me sooner, I could have helped but as it stood there was nothing I could do.'

The cobweb tears right through.

'What *he* did?' Cleaver roars the words, and though he's fought fiercer Pel flinches at the sound. 'He was a sickly child. He always was. I brought him to you only because he *asked* me to, said he kept seeing things, faces in the trees, and after so long saying nothing at all, just gazing out at this God-forsaken hill, I thought you'd talk sense into him! I knew you believed that rubbish that you peddle but I didn't think you'd let a child... we were friends, Pel! You were his godfather!'

107

Cleaver struggles to his feet, Pel close behind, bucket rattling, cane shoved into the snow for support.

'I'll not stand and listen to this again,' Pel turns and begins down the hill, but he twists his head back, shaking his stick at Cleaver still raging higher up. 'If you'd listened to him, listened to me, he'd be with us still. Not six feet deep in the mire.' Pel knows as he says it, he's gone too far. He tries to remember how to apologise, but Cleaver barrels down the hill, smacks into Pel at speed and puts an end to that. The two men, both older than many, one older than all, fall down the hillside in a tangle of limbs. At the bottom it is Cleaver who finds himself on top, astride Pel like a mongoose on a snake, jabbing where he can as the Keeper tries to strike.

'Do you know what that note said, Pel? Did you ever even read it? I know he sent you one as he did to me.' Cleaver strikes with an open palm, tiring fast. Pel knows this, and lets him exhaust himself, then rolls the Reverend off into the deepening snow. No need to draw a knife, no need to hurt him at all. The two men lie panting now, mad march hares three months too early and all boxed out. On his back, Cleaver stares at the sky.

'He said he was going to find the fairies, Pel. That you'd said they were underground. Why? Why lie to him?'

Pel sits upright, the snow leaving wet spots as it melts against his coat. He checks—the bucket sits upright with the lid still on. Pel sighs with relief.

'I didn't lie, Jacob.' Pel holds up a hand to stop the Reverend interrupting. 'They are, some of them. I know you don't believe me. He knew it too, he could remember them, old friend. He was just trying to find a home. Callum didn't come back and didn't hear the rest. If I'd known his plans, I'd have stopped him. I'd have sent him back to you.'

There are tears in the Reverend's eyes. Pel's too. Melting into the snow.

'We were friends, Pel. How could you? I looked up to you once, you know. I know you can do good; You are an old man and you've learnt things, fine. Why dress it up in make-believe? It ends. The deaths of my parishioners are because of you. And the things you say. Won't you say anything to make them stop?'

Pel stands, picks up his tongs and bucket and offers a hand to Cleaver, still sitting in the snow.

'We were friends, you're right. I thought you understood, this contract we had. There's room in this world for more than one way. Don't do this, don't set me against you. There's a balance and I'll keep it. Don't lean on the scale. I *know* it is a man killing these people, Jacob. Not one of Them. But he's not killing people because of me.' Pel pauses, stares into the eyes of a man that was once a friend. He gets no acknowledgement nor reply. 'Nothing I practice, nothing I've taught or told leads to that. You believed in both our stories, once, Jacob. I meant what I said at the Nest, we could work together again. Let me help you stop the monster behind these attacks. We can put an end to this. Now.'

Cleaver, hoisting himself to his feet, ignores Pel's outstretched hand. Glaring into Pel's eye, tears frozen and brushed from his face, the Reverend Cleaver laughs a thin laugh.

'We'll never work together, Lord Hunt. Not when you refuse to see the damage you do with carelessly delivered words. Callum always misunderstood you. I tried to tell him you were selfish, arrogant, that you'd never give up what he wanted from you. That you'd keep it from him the same way you keep it from Nancy.' The old priest begins to walk away, black shoes burning holes in the snow-covered ash. His parting words smoke, drifting over his shoulder. 'Stay away from the village. I'll deal with this alone.'

'Fine!' Pel shouts at the black cassocked back as it disappears into the snow. 'I've problems enough of my own. Don't I, old friend?'

Pel shakes the iron bucket, and it groans as the Keeper heads home.

THE BOAT ONCE again, steady in its mooring, frozen in the ice. The walls could do with strengthening, so Pel makes a note to remind the brownies of their duties. That girl spoils them, and it shows. Once inside he sits by the fire, toes outstretched and warming. He places the heavy iron bucket on a three-legged stool and hangs another above it in the rafters. Painted red and filled with water. Tied to the handle is a long piece of string and Pel holds it, tightly, in a tattooed hand. Nancy has not been back, not since the night before and Pel eyes the kettle wistfully. He lit the fire himself. The helpers hide in corners, scared to show their faces. They know what happened out on the moor. Heard friends burn. Know too what their master's brought, trapped inside the bucket. And nobody, not even Pel, is sure he's thought this through.

Pat is home, back turned from Pel and coat full of ash and soot. The grey axe head is back inside its box with the others – gold and blue and white and green. Kept for a rainy day. Another drawer has been opened now, a trail of contents from the drawer to its owner. Along the way a box of pins, a dog's tooth, a pouch of softened leather. And in front of Pel, open to a pressed violet, is his book of flowers. The page bent over to keep his place. At his side, in easy reach, the iron tongs. Carefully, like a cat after fish Pel prises the iron bucket open. Nothing, at first. Then the smell of gas before it lights and a pop, as the flame takes. The blue light shining from the bucket top.

'Hold,' says Pel. Hand firmly on the string. 'Look up.' There's a shuffling in the bucket, hear it, claws against the metal. Pel lightly tugs the string and a cupful of water falls, striking the bucket. There is a scream and a hiss and steam billows out.

'Iron filings in the water. Don't make me use them.' Pel goes back to his book, scans the page. Few creatures warrant such brutal work, but he's dealt with Bluecap before. He knows what she can do. Not a risk worth taking.

Slowly from the bucket Bluecap's head appears. Black and smouldering, blue flame licking from her eyes, from her mouth. Her skin cracked like a yule log with the heat shining through like veins.

'What.'

Pel smiles, keeps on reading and, without taking his eye from the page, asks his questions.

TORMENTIL

NANCY ENTERS TO the smell of ash and water and black sooty streaks on the doorframe. In his chair, by the fire, with a whiskey at his side though it's barely past midday, and fiddling a meandering song, is Pel. A face like a sweep and an eyebrow gone.

'Went well, did it?' says Nancy. Eyeing the bucket with a brick on top wedged firmly in the hall. Pel plays on, doesn't answer, and Nancy bends to stroke Pat, rub his chest. Her face is blackened with soot, tear tracks etched into it showing skin beneath.

'Good boy, you kept me safe, didn't you?'

Although he doesn't stop the song, something gives Pel pause.

'You needed protecting, Nance? Was there trouble at the fire?'

Nancy slams the kettle down and turns, steaming.

'There's trouble here, Pel! No, the fire was fine. I dealt with Cutty and Bluecap fine, I dealt with trying to save my friends fine. I listened to some of them die, fine. The only thing not fine here is you. We couldn't have dealt with it worse, Pel. We should have gone quietly to the calf, rounded up the worst of them and continued on our way. Why provoke him, *why?*'

She's too furious to cry. The tears turn to steam on her soot-stained cheeks. Her skin burns red beneath and though she can't see, there is a tear in his eye as well, but he wipes it

113

away with his sleeve as he places down the bow. There was an apology coming, but it's wiped away too.

'He had it coming. There's a balance and I... '

'A balance!' A short laugh, rolling her eyes. 'I know! I've worked with you for eighteen years, sat on your bloody scales. What was that last night? Was that balance? Do you tip one way, and he jumps the other? How many died in the fire? The balance has gone, Pel. Cleaver preaches hellfire in the church and on the moor the Underfolk fight us, joined by Cutty bloody Soames. And in our own home, Bluecap in a bucket! Does she at least have something useful to say? Who let her out? Who else is free?'

Pel rises now, placing the fiddle down, and walks away from Nancy, from her sharp-edged words, into the gloom of his desk and rearranges papers.

'She... I don't know. Perhaps. It's complicated Nancy.' The old man is rattled, and Nancy can't see who is doing the shaking. She stands with the door at her back, hair running ringlets down her face and her brow furrowed in rage. From behind the stove small faces peer in sympathy with their friend though they keep their distance.

'Complicated? Please, let me simplify it for you! People died and we did nothing. They burnt our friends, our *friends*, Pel! And *you* did nothing.' Pel opens his mouth to speak but she shuts it with a look. 'You conjured a wind and killed them quicker. Brilliant, what will the master tactician, the great Magus of the Moor think of next? Perhaps we should trot out and burn the rest? Really make things easy on ourselves? Throw ourselves on the bloody pyre when we're done. How dare you sit there, on whatever secret you've uncovered, and act as though I have no right to it. I am not the moor's Keeper, no. But I love it, more than you I fear, and I could tear it apart if I chose to. I will, Pel. If you'll not give me answers. I'll find my own.' She regrets that, but it is said. No way to take it back so she presses on. 'Tell me Pel. Now. What did Bluecap say because I *know* she said something.'

Pel does not turn, does not lift his bowed head from his work. Nancy rages like the sea onto rocks. She hasn't the centuries to wear him down. Hollow him out.

'Who let her out? Did she say that much at least? You entrusted her to the protection of the crown, didn't you? She was in a cell!'

Still not turning, Pel talks to his books.

'She said there is no crown, not any longer. Things are in disarray.' As he talks, he tidies, arranges his desk. Nancy looks aghast behind him.

'No crown? Who's on the throne then? Who's keeping order? What's happened, what did Bluecap say?'

Pel slams his hand into the dust and turns to face her. Hiding his panic with rage.

'It doesn't matter! The King's lost his grip. It's chaos. All the dark and awful things my predecessors and I put away can come crawling back, up through the rabbit holes and caves and out into the world, and I'm just too old to stop them now. I can't do it. And the last thing I need is to be distracted by the problems of people who don't want my help!'

'Oh of course they want your help!' Her face a picture of exasperation, she's no patience for this today. 'And they asked for it! And you told them no because they laughed at you. One time they laughed at you. These bodies, Salan, how they were found—there is something there, I saw your face when you saw the first. Tell me what you know. Is Cleaver involved? Before the fire, at the church, the way he was talking... did you know they all went to his services, those that died?'

Pel is prowling now across the floor, wiping the soot from his face. He didn't. She can see it on his face, the old taskmaster. Sees a flicker of worry dart across his eye. Can hear his teeth grind this new, unwanted, information to dust before swallowing it down and her heart sinks.

'You did.'

'Cleaver is an idiot. The man isn't capable of this, and how dare you talk to me like I'm some doddering old fool! I'll not have it, Nancy, not from you. I need you for our work.'

'It's our work, now, is it? I am done with this, Pel. It is connected to the chapel, to Cleaver. Whether you want it to be or not. I am not one of your trinkets, to be kept in a pocket until you need me and tucked back away when you're done.'

'That's not what I meant!'

'I know what you meant.'

'I... I do need you, Nancy.' Pel sits, exhausted and picks up his fiddle and bow again. Long fingers worrying at the instrument until his breathing calms. 'I taught Callum what I know, and he killed himself with it. Walked himself into the Fellmire. This job, this life, I was a fool to bring you into it. I—care for you, Nancy, you are my... ' His hand shakes on the fiddleneck. 'I will keep you safe.'

It wrongfoots her, to hear Pel willingly bring Cleaver's son up. Nancy is always the one to mention him first. Callum Cleaver never left. In body, maybe, but his ghost remains. Hanging in the corner like a brace of pheasant on a hook. More rotten by the day but never ready for the pot. She crouches at his side, her anger lost for the moment, trailing up the chimney with the woodsmoke. The fire of it buried under ash.

'I can take care of myself, Pel. I'm not going anywhere. Let me help.' He does not wipe the tear away this time, and the sight of it rolling down his wrinkled cheek extinguishes the last of

Nancy's fire. When he speaks it is slow, measured. Quiet. His eye on the floor at his feet. He's never seemed so old.

'I don't care if the village forgets me. I don't care if they like me. You'd do well to remember that. You won't win them round, Nancy. Stop trying. Your life is here. We don't do this to make them happy we do this to make them safe. There are things below that, if what Bluecap says is true and things below are in disarray, can cause true hurt.

'Like the Hunt?'

'Yes.'

'I was reading Slogget's story of them, whilst you slept after the tor.'

'Slogget was a fool.'

'Is it true, what you wrote? That they could be fought?'

'I'm a fool too and you're another if you believe me. The Hunt is beyond us. I only gave him part of the story. The Hunt are cruel, angry and vindictive. They will never accept their defeat, never rest. They are a rage beyond reason. It doesn't matter what those men and women in the Nest think, or what Cleaver thinks for that matter. If the Hunt was set on them? Nothing would matter. The hounds would find them, the Hunt would catch them and strip them of every title, every crest. Peel their beliefs from them like flaying skin and drag their souls down below.'

'So you couldn't stop them.' Nancy waits for it, the smile, and though it takes longer than it has done it arrives.

'Well. I have some theories. They're Underfolk too, at the end of it. Even a lion can be put back in a cage. It just takes a little more power. Don't worry though, Nancy, I'll keep you safe from the Hunt.' He pauses. 'And anything else that crawls up from below.'

Nancy is a child again, listening to stories by the fire, the warm reassurance that Pel would fix things. That there was nothing that could come he could not send back and for a moment all the horror of the day, the rage of their argument, is lost to her. She remembers him telling her how he had found a man once, bloated in the mire, his belly filled with human teeth. The creature that hauled itself across the moor in search of them. She knows how much that stayed with him, a rare missile in an otherwise empty arsenal. Smiling, Nancy stands, hunches her shoulders, and raises her hands like claws ahead of her. She grimaces, pulls her lips over her teeth in an imitation of empty gums and puts on a reedy voice, tickling Pel as she chants.

'Give me my teeth, give me my teeth!' He pushes her off and she falls down, giggling.

'You cruel thing! Gods but he was a horror.' Pel grimaces and Nancy leans back against him, stares into the fire.

'Let me do something about it, Pel, let me fight,' she cuts him off as he begins to speak, 'I don't mean the Murmur, Pel. Let me do what you trained me to do. You need help, Pel. Surely you see that?'

In his chair, the horsehair poking like grass from every burst seam, he sets his fiddle down and strokes Pat. Nancy kneels by him, grips the arm of his chair.

'I am not Callum Cleaver. He wasn't well, you are right, you shouldn't have taught him what you did. But I am not him. Listen, come with me, I know you don't believe he's involved but if we just talk to the Reverend we can—'

'I spoke to Cleaver. On the moor, this morning.'

Nancy sits on the stool, still by the fire, and stares at the old Keeper. Waiting. 'And what did he say?'

Pel pauses, brushes ash from the cover of a book. 'He won't help us. Won't help me. His feelings, since Callum died, he'll not see it clearly. He just won't.'

'Callum wasn't… '

'You're right, I know it wasn't my fault, but Cleaver won't see.'

'That's not what I said. Callum wasn't easy, Pel. He was angry, confused.'

Nancy has no great love for Callum Cleaver. Callum had been sent to them by Cleaver when she was four or five. Pel had been tasked with stopping his nightmares. It hadn't worked. Though he was one of very few children she'd had much contact with once her mother died, he was not the playmate she had hoped for. She had found him intense. Prying. His presence had made her almost queasy. She had been glad when the rift between Pel and Callum's father had widened far enough to prevent further visits. Furious, later, when Callum bridged the gap. She can still remember the day he returned. She was thirteen, he was three years older, and he set the wards on the boat to crackling. A thing that ought not to have been possible—wards were an either-or thing, no room for maybes. He had roamed about, searching for Pel, never settling. Like a dragonfly resting on a lily whilst it hunts, its wings never still. Pel had entered with a hand outstretched, a spell crackling at his fingertips. He did not shake it away when he'd seen who waited for him. She'd been sent away then. Pel had never spoken about what they'd discussed.

'He had a right to be. His father should have called me sooner. As your mother did.'

Nancy turns. A piece falls into place. She feels something close to jealousy. That Callum could have had what she has. That their lives had overlapped.

'He was the same as me, then. He was taken?'

Pel sits quiet and stares deep into the fire. The firedogs hold a half-burnt log of bog-oak like a sacrifice. His face softens, staring not in anger but sad solemnity. An ember, not a flame.

'Aye, Nance. He was. Though not quite like you. You're special.'

The old man turns to her and smiles. The corners of his eyes fold up like an accordion. Nancy smiles back and reaches for his hand, but he pulls it away. Holds it with its partner in his lap, balled up as if protecting something. The truth. A story.

'Callum was taken, I suspect, when very small. A baby, newly born. His mother, Cleaver's wife, Elizabeth. She died giving birth.' Pel stops. Tongue tied. He's never been able to speak about Cleaver without rage and regret taking over. Choking his words. Nancy resigns herself to another brush off, but he has a look in his eye she's not seen before.

'You won't remember when he was returned. You were only small. It was the summer, he would be four or five, I suppose.'

'He'd been with the spriggans for five years?' Nancy asks. Pel nods and sits back, reaching for a drink that has magically appeared at his side, the hidden butler already back in the shadows. He drinks deep. Nancy stares at him. Pel won't meet her eyes.

'The piskies took you because they thought you beautiful, a plaything. They swapped you as a child might swap one toy with another. The spriggans took Callum because they could see what he could be worth. He was never meant to return. They left in his crib a clumsy changeling. Mewling, red-faced and angry all the time. I don't know why they sent him back. Locryn Calder found him, wandering the moor. Too much bother, I suspect. Too hard to care for. When he returned, he needed help adjusting. Help Cleaver couldn't give.'

'And you couldn't have given it, Pel? Just done what was needed, ignored Cleaver? Shown him what to do rather than lecture him? You'd been so close.'

'I had other things to worry about.' Pel pauses for a moment, his mouth set in a grim line, and *now* he stares at Nancy. Makes sure she understands. And Nancy stays quiet, holds her tongue. 'I was there soon after he returned, the first time he woke. He babbled about monsters, then stayed virtually mute for years. Did not go to school, lay on his sickbed in Cleaver's cottage, covered in sheepskins and quiet as a grave. Then, on his tenth birthday began to speak. Quite suddenly in the middle of the night, startling his father awake. Talk of fairies and monsters and tunnels underground. Of the Undermoor, even though he can't have been there. Of the God of the Mire. Cleaver had called me then.'

'That's when the visits began.' Nancy lowers herself to the floor, head tipped by the realisation. 'Callum's visits. Cleaver wanted him fixed.' Pel nods. 'Why did you never tell me? All those visits. All those trips and I never knew. I used to show off to him! Tell him I talked to spriggans, daily! Told him they were friends to me! No wonder he hated me.'

Pel pauses in his story. Closes his eye.

'He was obsessed, Nancy. He could still see them, the fairies, the Underfolk. Though not as you can, not clearly. I think they flickered about him. Like pictures in a zoetrope, half-finished scenes. They haunted him. He was not your burden to bear, he was mine. I'm sorry I kept it from you.'

Pel's face creases, his eye opened, focused on the ash in the grate and the memories that burnt there.

'It doesn't matter anymore. It didn't work. His father stopped the visits before I could get through. By the time he returned, in the years before he died, it was too late. The damage was done.'

Nancy sits, shakes her head.

'I remember when he came back. You sent me away, what

did you say to him Pel?' Pel sits back in his chair and strokes the remains of an eyebrow. Sighs deeply.

'I told him he was broken. That he couldn't learn magic. You know as well as I do, Nancy, it takes a clear head. We both know what happens when power's wielded without focus.' Nancy bites back on her anger, puts the dig away for later.

'He wanted to go back to them, didn't he? Thought he had let them down and that is why they'd abandoned him, just as his father had. That's why he stole your books.'

Pel squints, shakes his head.

'Perhaps. They were books about the lands of the dead, about the fairy-world. The bridges between there and here.'

Pel's face is fretful. He rubs his stubbled chin with tattooed fingers, grips the arms of the chair, picks up and sets down his drink. Nancy's face, too, is worried. She has not heard the whole of this before… If she'd known, things could have been different.

'You should have told me this, Pel. All of it, from the start. I hated those visits. Hated him. When he came back, when he was older, I could feel him staring, every time he came it was worse. The way he looked at me, towards the end. I thought it was me he wanted. But it wasn't, was it? He wanted my life.'

Pel turns his face towards the fire, uncomfortable.

'I used to dread seeing his horse tethered outside, I used to turn and walk home if it was there. I could have helped him; we could have helped him.'

'I tried!' Short and loud Pel's face snaps round as he admonishes her. 'I tried. He left me no choice. The night it happened,' Pel continues, 'the night he died, he visited me. He asked me again to take him back. I refused and he grew angry, began throwing things about. Accused me of giving you your abilities. Told me he would take them from you if he had to. I threw him out, Nancy, I threw him out then cast a ward on the door so he couldn't return. I was angry too! Angry that he'd taken the books, angry that he felt entitled to what I knew! But more than that, Nancy, he took my friend! He took his father from me, and I'll be damned if I were to let him take you too.'

Pel stands now, walks to the fireplace and leans over the flames.

'You're right. I wasn't there for him, as I should have been. I wasn't there as he walked down to the Fellmire. I let him walk there alone, I let him step into the quaking mire, feet tearing through the turf into the peat, into the water. I let him sink. Alone.'

The silence sits between them like a stone. Even the fire's gone quiet.

'Cleaver always blamed me. For filling his head with my stories. That friendship will never mend. After that, after Callum died, Cleaver became, well... You know the man.'

The spell of the story broken, Pel downs the last of his drink. His lips, still wet with the fire of it, quiver but hold. He's never told her that tale in full. She's not sure how to feel about her place in it. Nancy sits, staring at the floor. Thinks of a secret never told. A letter sent. Pel had shown her the note written to him by Callum, the night he died. Delivered after he had gone. Full of anger and apologies. A desperate howl of a thing. She had never told Pel he had sent her one too. Hers was a promise. A vow to see a debt repaid and the memory of it chills her.

'Pel, is it not—could it not be—that Callum has found his way back?' Pel pauses just long enough to worry her.

'Don't be stupid, girl. The boy was flailing at answers. He was barely competent enough to kill himself with magic, he couldn't possibly achieve that. *I* couldn't achieve that.'

'Just consider for a moment—'

'No. Nancy. It is not possible.' He's up now, any hope of humility buried under a rockfall of pride and misplaced confidence, but his eye betrays him. He'd like a way back from this, but he's walked himself to a ledge, and he'll not back down so off he goes, into the darkness.

'I was not to blame. Cleaver did not want my help then; I'll not help him now. The moors, the things we hold the line against, are not dangerous. It is men like him that cause the trouble. Same as the one causing it now.'

'Seems to me that if you'd stepped in sooner even though you weren't asked, you'd have skirted a world of pain. For you and Cleaver both. Same as now. I've seen you scry for lost stock more than once, have I not? If you can find a lost sheep, then you can find the killer, whoever it may be.'

Pell sits mute, eyes fixed on the fire.

'I'll not see my community damned because Lord Pelagius Hunt feels slighted. I won't, Pel. Get up, do something. You don't believe me, fine, but what harm to talk to Cleaver again? Visit the chapel? Only the Underfolk can't enter, Pel, you won't burn on holy ground.' She kicks at his leg to rouse him, but he doesn't move. Patroclus, one eye opening to see if he should intervene, decides he shouldn't and closes it again. 'Get up, Pel! Fine, there are two of us, I'll sort the killer and you sort the moor, or the other way round but either way we'll sort it, or what are we for?'

The old man sits in his chair and simmers. She's known him like this before. He's a stubborn old coot and she's fed up with him. Reaching for a book she slams it open on his desk.

'Here, scrying for lost persons. I'll do it if you won't, where's your ink?'

Pel's hand slams the book shut—she didn't hear him rise, and his face is there before hers spitting out the words.

'Put that back! You're not ready for it. I do not need your help tonight. You're tired.'

She tries to give him a moment to think about it, knows he'll regret this. But he doesn't take it.

'Sit down and help me do what actually needs to be done or leave. If, after I have shut whatever door's been opened, after I have sent all these buggers back, after I am satisfied the job's been done, they still haven't caught whoever's killing in the bog then maybe, maybe I will let you help. But I'll not stand for you getting ideas above your station. You wanted to help me, I never did, don't make me regret it now!'

He turns, panting, into the empty room. He did not hear her leave. He runs long fingers through his tousled grey hair and leans back against his desk. Patroclus glares at him from across the room.

'What?' Pel barks, and Patroclus rises and slinks off into the gloom. The dog gone, Pel sits down heavily again in his seat by the fire. He picks up his fiddle and tries to draw out a tune but he's not the heart for it. He tosses the instrument into the corner.

'You fool, Pel. You bloody fool.'

He sits like this for an hour. Eyes staring glassily at the fire. His glass refills when he needs it to; the little helpers under the boards don't want to risk his ire. And he knocks back the whiskey like water. After a time, bleary eyed he rises and heads to his desk, sitting in the spinning captain's chair, it's wooden strutted back stopping him falling out of it. He steadies himself on the desk. He pulls the old book of folktales from the shelf and opens it at the start of a story. He smiles, traces the green ink lines where Nancy has coloured the pictures in, illustrated the margins. Remembers how angry he was at the time. How silly he was. He opens a drawer, pulls out the little mail cloth that had brought her to him, each metal link flattened so it moved like snakeskin. He puts it back in the drawer, nestled between the flint arrowhead she had found and given him. A glove she had long since outgrown.

'My girl.' He closes his eyes, the memories come unbidden, the last time he saw Callum, how Callum tore through the boat in search of answers, and finding none, fled with his armful of stolen treasure and Nancy's name a curse on his tongue. Pel has never told Nancy how he had crept out that night, sat outside her cottage and stood guard in case the boy came. Waiting until the sun rose and she was safe. Another memory, Nancy standing frozen as the rock calved from Lullaby Tor, rattling furiously towards her and the village. He had never used that spell, had no idea if it would hold. He has a piece of that stone on his desk. He can feel the energy her Murmur left. A nonsense word for more power than one girl should hold. Still, a smile licks at the corner of his mouth when he thinks of that last lesson. He looks across at Patroclus, who still has his back turned, 'I made her too much like me, Pat. Didn't I?'

He stretches out his arm, waits for the dog to look up, but instead Patroclus huffs and hunches away. Pel leaves his hand lingering in the air for a moment before snatching it back.

'Fine. I'll do it. Cleaning up messes that aren't my fault. It isn't my fault. It isn't.' He says this to the shadows and draws out a slim volume from his shelves. It is an odd-looking book, the cover some animal leather though cracked and torn, dried out with age. The pages, bound vellum, are inked carefully with intricate words, the tail of each letter intertwining with the next and the first letter of each page picked out in gloried illumination. It is both an instruction manual and a travel guide, and following it can be fatal. Pel starts at the beginning and reads.

SHEEP'S BIT

MIRECOOMBE STANDS QUIET in the snow. No smoke curls from the chimneys, not a soul has got the heart for a fire today. There will be more snow later, the heavy grey clouds poke their heads from the horizon like an army waiting to advance, but they keep their cover. The chapel watches from the hill, keeping an eye on the morning from its hilltop perch. The village seems cowed by its gaze. High above, the tors shake their boulder-heads in the wind. The only sound the cracking of ice on the pond as it warms in the afternoon sun. There are no ponies clustered around the well; they have nosed open the door of the long house, coarse haired flanks scratching against the mortuary table, leaving tufts behind, and have warmed it with their presence so that out of all the white roofed buildings clustered in the valley it is the only one whose slates are still grey. Steam rises from it, like a smokehouse.

The Mare's Nest Inn is full, but muted, and although it is early in the day none of the patrons have slept, so keep drinking away. All drink in silence, still smelling of smoke. Some things don't wash out in a hurry. In her apron, at the bar, Madge polishes rarely used wine glasses with a careworn look. She didn't go to the fire, but still she's burnt by it. The helpers under the floorboards are nowhere to be heard, just an empty nest of horsehair and straw in the crook of a beam. Each booth, each settle, is full. The firelighters and the sappers from the night before sit shoulder to shoulder, faces hidden in soot and shadow. Sat at the bar, in a line, are Calder and Cusk and Billy Askell. Next to them Hugh Dell who feels no better than he did, his wife back at home sweeping her grief into the corners.

It is Madge who breaks the silence. Hanging the last cleaned tankard on the brass rail that is fixed above her head she places both hands on the bar and eyes her congregation.

'You shouldn't have done it. And you know it, not one person's eyes have met another's since you all started drinking.'

Throughout the pub comes a mumbled dissent, but it's silenced by a glare from the bar.

'The Reverend has turned your heads. Those little folk on the hill have never done us any harm. Never killed. Not once. How many did you burn?'

'There's no little folk,' Calder says, not looking at Madge. 'The Reverend was helping us, showing us what we needed to see.' Calder's voice is quiet but gains a murmuring assent from his fellow drinkers. Madge laughs.

'Was he? And what did you see? I don't see any of you up on the hill, raking through the ash. Digging up the blackened bones of murderers and rabid dogs. So, what did you see, what did he prove? I'm asking again because as I see it, all you did was make a mess of things.'

Scraping back his stool and making lines in the sawdust, Hugh Dell stands. He sways slightly. The words bubble out of him slowly; you can almost see them making their way from his gullet like he's throwing up pebbles.

'You're right, Madge. We aren't on that hill. Because all we burnt were birds and gorse. Nothing ran out, nothing died in there. Not whatever killed that calf. Not whoever killed my Sal. It's done us no good, but it was needed. He showed us the truth.'

'He showed you his, you mean. There's more than one way to look at a thing. Hugh, I've seen you put out a basket of apples when the harvest comes in. Salan too! Go and talk to Pel. We should have had his help long ago. I've said it from the start.'

Hugh staggers back from the bar, drunker than he looks, and swirls like a weathervane in the sawdust, arm outstretched.

'Pel? Why, Madge? He's done nothing. Nothing when Jacob lost his son, or when Delen's mother went. Nothing for Bronwen or Tom and nothing for Salan. He sat and sulked because the Reverend showed him up, just as he did last night. So, you'll forgive me not crawling back to him now. Whoever killed Sal, well, you saw his neck. You all heard how he was found. Just like the rest. Reverend Cleaver says it's ritual. Heathen. That's why Pel won't do anything, he's probably involved.'

Madge places the shining glass down on the bar so hard it cracks.

'Who else thinks that? That Pel is involved? Because if you do then you've a shorter memory than I. Butler, you look me in the eye and tell me there was nothing in your woodshed, gathering scraps of wool, building a nest. Tell me Pel didn't help. Remfry Doble! I see you in the darkness. What sat on your chest in the night for a month before Pel helped? Before he turned it into a moth and caught it fluttering in a bottle? I'm sure he'd be happy to give it back. James Asley! You'd still be wandering after marsh lights if Nancy hadn't called you home and you know it. All of you, you've all been helped by Pel, by Nance. And now suddenly you're scared, and they mean nothing. Everything you knew means nothing.'

The room stagnates in silence. Memories of monsters long buried rise up and poke their heads up through the froth of men's pints. There's sense in what she says, but no one's keen to see it. There are dark looks passed between the drinkers, gazes meet at last.

Howel Jennings, who's always held firm, makes a stand. 'She's right. He helps. Stopped whatever was souring the milk.'

Locryn Calder turns on his stool as he drains his cup. 'That was a decade ago, Howel. What's he done since? He's been no real use since the Reverend's lad died. The bastard knows he had a hand in addling the lad's head. *I* know it. I found the boy, remember.' A groan, the drinkers have heard this before. Locryn Calder speaks on undimmed. 'Five years old, wandering the moor bare arsed and muttering about spriggans. He was piskey-led, that's for certain, though young for it. I should have taken him to his father, but this was before I saw sense. Took him to Pel.'

'Right thing to do.' Howel Jennings nods sagely as Calder scowls.

'Aye, so I thought, back then. That boy had been a mute since the day he was born and now he couldn't stop babbling. Pel set to pinching the boy with the fire tongs, a child!' There are dark murmurings rippling through the bar and Madge tenses against the tide. 'I should never have left him there when I fetched the Reverend. Boy was raving when we got back, the old goat had filled him up with nonsense. He was never the same, after that.' Madge sets to sweeping the sawdust around the floor.

'You don't know that story well enough to tell it, Locryn.'

'Don't need to know more than I know, Madge, to know which way the wind blows.'

'We've chosen our faith, Madge,' says James Asley.

'We're sure of the way,' says Butler.

Billy Askell says nothing. He was not at the fire, but he is staring wide eyed at the conversation, drinking it in. Once again, a tourist. Madge chews her lip, thinking, then walks around the bar, sits on a stool next to the drinking men and leans back on the bar.

Hugh Dell steadies himself on the beams that hold the roof. 'The Reverend tells us he can help, and I believe him. He knows how it feels to lose a child. I'll see you all in church tomorrow. It is Sunday after all.' And he's out into the sunlight, a little snow drift tumbling in as he goes. Madge frowns at the closing door and turns back to the room. She's known them all for a long time, some since they were small.

'I understand. I'm scared too. But not of Pel. Somebody out there, in here perhaps, is killing people. But we'll need all our faith to survive it.'

It is Calder who stands now. More steadily than Hugh Dell. From the back, where they've been drinking, his three sons rise as well. Luk a stack of granite, Jan a bank of slate, and Little Yestin, a broken piece of tin.

'Who are you accusing, then, Madge? You tell us it's one of us after a pretty speech about community. Fine, then. Who is it you don't trust? Me? My boys? These other fine men? The Reverend trusts us. He says so. Chose us special to light the fire. So we'll not sit here and be made fools of, made to feel like we've done wrong. You're right, we've all left a parcel out, my father taught me to, as his taught him. But you can't just go on doing a thing because you think you ought to, wasting apples and corn on things you can't see.'

'Happy to pray to something you can't though? What makes his ghosts better than our own? Tell me that.'

From the darkness, Remfry Doble, thirty-six and fat as a bear, comes tumbling. Madge riled him up with her talk of moths. He still can't sleep without a candle burning.

'What if we are? His don't scare us. If there are things out there, things living in the earth, then they're devils! I've read my Bible. Cleaver will protect us from them, not trap them in jars and place them on a shelf. Pel's time is through. Even if he isn't doing the killing, he's probably sheltering the beast! More than likely it's escaped from another bottle.'

Madge stands, places her hands on her hips, and laughs loud and deep at the swaying man.

'You think Pel has them all chained up do you? All the dreadful things, all the nightmares? He sends them packing, as well you know. That moth he took from you was tucked back deep into the earth and you thanked him for it. It's not his fault you're still scared of the dark.'

The large man rushes towards her, but Madge has done this dance before, and she steps back behind a low hanging beam hung heavy with old tankards. Remfry Doble cracks forehead first into the wood and pewter and stumbles back bleeding.

'On your way, Remfry. You're a fool.'

He totters out of the front door, picking up followers behind him. Left in the inn are Calder and his sons, all still standing, and Cusk still sitting at the bar. Billy Askell is still sat at the bar, mouth hanging open. Madge glares at him, and he's up and gone with the rest. She can hear him fall as someone pushes him into the mud. Can hear the others asking why his charms didn't protect him and whilst the jokes are nothing new, the razor blades sewn into them are.

'What about the rest of you, you'll turn your back on it all, will you? Take your seats on the hill tomorrow morning and pray tradition away?'

No one answers, no one meets her eye. Old Madge Gould sets her lips firm and frowns.

'Time, then, gentlemen. Time.'

One by one they file out into the snow and leave Madge stood alone in the sawdust. She slumps onto the furthest stool and looks to the rafters with a tear in her eye. But she's no time for this. Dipping her head, she pulls back the tears and begins to collect tankards from the tables. Under each tabletop there is a mark carved, over the doorway too. Peace and prosperity, he'd said they'd bring. She smirks, then wipes away the pools of spilt beer and rum.

OUTSIDE, FAR FROM the village, in a snow-filled dell, a figure kneels half buried in the cold. At a distance it could be a tree trunk, or a gorse bush twisted out of shape. They must be freezing in the snow. There is a sadness that can be felt even from here, the loneliness and the pain of it, their head raised as they look about. There is nobody here, no animal, no sheep or cow or pony walking in the snow. The figure rises, as the cold winter light hangs with a pale fire in the sky and for a moment they stand, picked out on the horizon, their long limbs burnt to matchsticks by the setting of the sun.

SPEEDWELL

Up the hill to the chapel. Unlike the crooked, tousled slopes of the valley, with their rockfall granite and bursting springs that keep the hillsides wet and reedy even under summer sun, the hill on which the chapel is set is almost a perfect mound. A bump between the tors and the scree side. There are legends, of course, about how the chapel hill came to be, about a king long dead that lies under tonnes of earth with a complement of horses prancing up into the ground. How the top was crowned, once, with a grove of trees. How a priest of some old persuasion hid in the boughs with a knife against challengers, pretenders, or undevout pilgrims. How the trees were felled by a lightning strike. The hill stands tall above Mirecoombe, though the tors stand tall over it. The very old watching the old watching the new. At the summit are the low sunk chapel wall, the wooden gate with its carved spiked top, and its curled and heavy iron furnishings. The hinges shaped like pike tops that grasp the wood, the heavy iron ring that lifts the latch. Under the lych gate with its coffin-resting stone and down the steps into the chapelyard are flowers that thrive on corpses lie dormant under grass, roots tangled in bone trapping souls in the loam. There is a path that skirts the chapel's entrance, that heads round the back of the old stone church, past the crooked stones with the dead carved deep in scrolling, flourished words. Past a half-sunk, grass-sucked square granite slab—on the other side, a carving of a woman pressed breast first into the earth, chiselled from the church by a priest who didn't like what she did to him—to the little stone cottage where the Reverend Cleaver lives. It stands tumbledown at the back of the chapel, connected to the church by a weatherboarded, slate-capped throughway that shivers when it rains. It is known as 'the rectory' though it has no proper name and there's a story that says it was built before the chapel was. That it housed another god. If it did, they lie uncomfortably now under the weight of Cleaver's belief. There is a single small window that looks out onto the moor from lead-lined, diamond panes, the top row stained blood red. And on the opposite wall stands a door that is battered black and blue, decades of paint stripped bare, its strata revealed by the wind. It has few visitors, this place. The Reverend meets parishioners next door if there's need for it though he prefers to visit them at home; his chapel is a quiet place, why trouble it with sound? When the wind is up as it always is it whistles round the walls like a kestrel, circling the hill.

He did not always live here. When he had arrived, fresh from the seminary with his wife Elizabeth at his side, he had a cottage in the valley, though not in Mirecoombe itself. It still stands, a little way onto the moor, though nobody lives there now. This single-roomed tomb was his study before. A place to entertain friends, read his books, prepare his sermons. Pel used to sit in that chair by the fire, Cleaver on the daybed, and they'd talk until the stars went out, under clouds up past their bedtimes. Arguing amiably over who was right, who was wrong, the spaces in between. Pel would tell Cleaver stories over glasses half drunk, and the Reverend would smile and shake his head then totter home to Elizabeth. Before Callum was born. Before she died.

Cleaver had enjoyed Mirecoombe, so different from his Sussex upbringing. Enjoyed talking to the farmers of piskies threshing corn, talking to the old men about the riders on the hill, about the Underfolk below it. He had begun, even, a little book about the folklore of the county. It would not be finished. He saw it for what it was now. It wasn't just a pastoral whimsy, a hangover from the past. It was a dangerous distraction from the message of the Lord. Callum had blinded him to it, he saw that now. And Pel. He hadn't seen it coming, that betrayal or that the very landscape he had grown to love would turn on him, take his son away.

After that, after Callum vanished in the bog, he'd withdrawn. The small cottage had been left empty; furniture sold. Now he spends every evening hunched over piles of books and paper, candlelight burning shadows on the lime-washed walls. He is still in his cassock; he would sleep in it, if he could, but he worries it will crease. His shelves and Pel's are not so different. The heaving libraries of men with curious dispositions. Books on anatomy, on religion, on the mind. And smaller volumes of poetry and rhetoric. But all stand in service to the one open before him. Heavy, leather bound, and gilt across the edges, his Bible squats on the table like a toad. He marks passages, copying them out in the lined journal at his side without looking as he writes in a sure and steady shorthand of his own devising. His codebooks, Pel had called them, indecipherable to all but their author.

It had taken two hours to walk back from the moor, from the burn site, the snow slowing his gait. On his desk sits a stick of charcoal he had taken from the blaze, and he sets it there, in front of him, as a reminder of his victory. As he stares at it, shifting in the candlelight, it could well be a bone. It was worth it. Even for vestments that stank of smoke, boots caked in ashy mud. The community had turned a corner, him at its head, onto a better path. Away from devils that would fool them, away from Pel. He finishes writing. The Bible is covered in its execution-cap cloth, dull black in the half-light and placed in an alcove in the wall.

Standing, Cleaver moves to the window. The sun is almost gone now, snow falling again in flurries as the clouds cover the sky. The last of the cold light shines on his face in a bright red stripe and he closes tired eyes against the colour, the brightness of it. He can just make out the moor smouldering in the distance, see the village cower in the shadow of the snow clouds, and he prays. The words are low, almost mouthed silently—but they are spoken, sound comes out. And as he finishes, bows his head, he turns and lifts another book from a high shelf above the door. The paper-bound volume is battered and torn, the pages thin, densely written in his shorthand scrawl. It is a diary of sorts, kept for many years. He places it in the space made by the Bible and lifts again his brass-nibbed pen, dipping it into a ceramic well, and begins to write his entry for the day, hiding the pages with his turned back. Behind him is a cot, low to the floor, a mattress stuffed with straw. His woollen blankets carefully made, and the feather pillow plumped. It is sat back in an alcove that may have once held a rack for hay, or a manger. Or an altar. On the wall above the pillow is a gorse wood cross, carved by his son and presented to him as a gift, long ago. It is worn smooth by handling, the needle-knots in the wood shining like eyes, peering through cracks. Opposite is a mirror so he can see the cross from his bed. There is a stove here, too, with a kettle on top, and the remains of a meal of bread and cheese. A bottle of weak beer. He is no ascetic; he lives well, if within his means.

He's finished writing, the tattered book is closed again and back in its hole in the wall. As he turns to the bed—he is tired, it has been a long night—he is startled. Something draws him to the window with hurried, panicked steps and he looks into the snow. His breathing quickens, his pallor deepens and there, out in the cold it is almost as though a figure stands staggered in the whiteout. Half erased by the falling snow and gone as soon as he looks at it. Cleaver rushes to the door and pulls it open. There is nothing but white on the pale grey sky and the black specks of clustering birds. He looks down. On the slate step is a shining silver acorn. He kneels to pick it up and turns it over in his hands. Returns inside and places it on a shelf next to a little brass horse, a white feather. He goes back to the window and watches the birds. They leave him to it, let him be. He can deal with his ghosts on his own.

FOXGLOVE

THE BOAT CREAKS in the cold. He closes the books, one by one and lifts them from the dusty table, leaving squares of clean wood underneath. It is dangerous, what he will do. He must say goodbye. Each volume, as he places it back on a heaving shelf, is handled lightly, Pel's hands lingering as the book slides into place, the embossed lettering on the spine caressed. His life, and those that came before him. All she'll have left of him if he fails. His mouth purses, and he moves on. He opens drawers one by one, takes out what he might need. He lifts a signet ring with a trefoil flower in relief in the gold and slips it over a bony finger. It rattles around the joint and he sighs as he thinks of the father he stole it from. Others too, some simple gold bands, others more elaborate with signs engraved. He checks that his folding knife is in his pocket, the handle made of bone worn smooth from years of use. The blade, though pockmarked with dark spots and rust, still cuts like a scythe. It is there, in the top pocket of his waistcoat as it always is. He still pats the pocket to make sure. He places pouches of herbs in the folds of his thick and heavy coat. Chamomile, lavender, rue. Hellebore too, and wolfsbane. And last, the petals of a flower that grows in only one spot in the lee of a hill. Sheltered by the wind with one flower blooming on a single black stem. He had found it signposted by the dead sheep that lay next to it, black wool turned white.

He runs his hand through his own white hair.

Most of the herbs are loose in their compartmentalised drawer, cedarwood boxes neatly slotted into place. But the dried petals of that plant are in their own little case, lead-lined and covered in velvet like a ring box. He places it gingerly next to the rest. Once his pockets are filled, he shakes his coat to redistribute the weight and hangs it on a peg. He winds his shirt sleeves up his long thin arms, showing the black ink beneath. Each mark, each letter, each Latinate phrase is there for a reason. This one stops him burning, this one keeps him warm. Some are single symbols drawn from very old books. Here, this sign means moon, this one sky, this one air. Important all three. He takes his knife out again, opens the blade, and carefully, deliberately, draws it through three lines of verse. Three single words, three symbols. It stings as the blade passes through but as each tattooed mark is severed, he feels a jolt run the length of his spine. His blood flows across the knife, the hungry metal drinking it in. The cut marks boil, the ink heating and turning to gas that vents from his skin leaving blistering welts where the tattoos once sat. He clenches his jaw against the pain. When he is through, he folds the knife, still bloody, away. He winces, withdrawing a stoppered glass jar from a shelf, rubs a liniment in to clot the wounds. It burns more than the cut itself and he grimaces like a gargoyle at the pain. There. Some protections removed, some strengthened.

One last task. He holds up his hand, turns it so the silver case over his thumb is facing him and unscrews the end. He smiles. Some secrets he has always kept. Within the hollow of the covering are the scrimshawed bones of a saint, traded long ago for his own. The silver case a prosthetic as well as a reliquary. Kept mobile with magic and hard won gifts. He takes out each bone. Distal phalanx, proximal phalanx and metacarpal, then places them in a dish on the table. Screws the top back onto his thumb. The last thing he needs is help from that quarter. He is surprised to find he feels their absence. A glow, taken for granted, has faded to black.

As he works, he mutters words beneath his breath and far underground, chains rattle. A corpse laughs. And an old head capped with a crown of silver birch covered in bronze lifts up from its sleep.

Pel picks up the iron bucket with smoke creeping from the lid and shakes it. He doesn't need any distractions. No escape attempts tonight. His desk tidied, he places a dried rose, taken from a jar of them, into the centre of the table and draws an 'N' in the dust. She'll understand. He turns back to his boat-hold room with jaw set. The moistness at the corner of his eye his only concession to the severity of the task. There are faces watching from the shadows. He pauses. A larger part of him than he is happy with wants to kneel, take their faces in his hands, and say goodbye. But though, in truth, it's the weaker force, his head overrules his heart. He nods curtly at the darkness and puts the brownies from his mind. His fiddle is where he left it, leant against his chair and though the fire burns low, it is warm in the boat. Patroclus lifts his old shaggy head and whines; he wants to know if his master needs him or if he can stay asleep.

'Don't worry, boy,' says Pel, his gaze catching on the dog, snagging, not wanting to pass. 'You stay. I'll be home again, soon.' Pat whines again, something is wrong, but he trusts Pel. He believes him. And the tired old dog goes back to sleep, stretches out and kicks long, old legs against the grass that he runs across in his dreams. Pel smiles and starts to say something but leaves his friend asleep. It is only after he's collected his cane, as the door closes behind him, when he is back out on the moor and the wind will carry his words away that he says it.

'Good boy.'

And he is alone. Alone with the wind that sweeps like a foxhunt across the moor. Alone with the cotton grass, with the cold and the moonlight. Those faces that watch him pass do so warily; they see he's in no mood to talk. No small hand will tug at a coat hem and ask for help with this or that.

He walks steadily and surely across the moor. Up the small hillock covered in iron age homes that still rise from the earth. Past the long-fallen menhir that once pointed at the stars, now a capstone for the tomb of a stillborn foal born with one too many heads. Past the turf ricks and the pits of fresh dug peat. Past the serrated faces of moor stone cut for gateposts.

He is not rushing this walk. He is in no hurry for the end. Pel has done many things in a very long life but never this. Under his feet he can feel it. The earth rumbles, plates shift. He remembers when he came here. When he first hauled his boat out of the sea. He had followed the scent of the magic, tasted the earth. Watched a few small houses become Mirecoombe. Made deals with villager and moor-sprite alike to keep the houses up, to let the ponies graze. It was here, stood on moon-polished rock he had talked the last giant back into the earth. Seven foot six and tired as time, the old creature had been ready for it. Over there, under the rocking stone on Lullaby Tor he had struck accords with the moorland witches. Signed their contract with blood and watched them sail away into starlight, with staves of ragwort between their legs and laughter trailing back into the sky. He'd not seen them for many years now; a part of him regrets sending them away.

'What changed?' he asks the bucket, still swinging at his thigh. The wrong question and he knows it. He reaches the mire at midnight, the moon high overhead and beaming a worried face down on him. The ground here is dangerous, doubly so under the snow, and as he walks, he tests how solid his path is with his cane. When he feels the earth move, when it rolls like the sea from the black water beneath, he stops. He stabs his cane deep, so it stands upright in the mud, polished top facing away. He won't be overlooked. He unfolds his knife, his own blood now dried and flaking on the blade and with the clasp locked he pushes it deep into the stump of a hawthorn rotting by his side. An anchor point, a way back. Powerful thing, lost iron. It can call a man home. His return mapped, Pel stands above a murky lake where the water has pooled in a tear in the grass and lays the bucket down. He needs both hands. Rocking unsteadily on the quaking mire, he removes his rings. No ferryman here, but a price must still be paid. As he drops them, one by one, into the black water they are sucked under, replaced by popping bubbles on the scrying mirror surface. He speaks low words as he offers them to the water, announcing his arrival with respect to the one he seeks. Next, he removes his old wool coat, taking the lead-lined box from a pocket, and folds it, laying it neatly on the grass. His boots and socks follow and then picking up the bucket and standing shaking in the church-bell wind in his shirtsleeves and woollen waistcoat and his trousers, he steps into the pool.

He gasps at the cold, at the sucking mud and though it's slow, he is sinking. The black ooze is at his waist, and it takes effort to turn, to lift his legs. The water is thick and full of peat and mud and with his weight spread he lies as if on a funeral pyre, arms crossed over the bucket on his chest. His eyes close and he recites a prayer in a language these bare hills haven't heard since they were woodland, since the piles of stones were homes and the world went as far as the horizon, no further. They are the oldest words he knows. As he finishes, with a granite 'Amen,' bubbles rise around him. In silence he opens the box, takes the dried black flowerhead and places it on his tongue, closing his mouth around it. The water boils and steams and he sinks, slowly, like a coffin lowered on ropes.

Down into the grave he goes. The black and viscous mire wraps around his chest, around his legs, until nothing but a death mask of his face is left, and then even that is gone. Just the sound of death under moonlight. Across the moor word spreads, and small faces look nervously about them. Creatures that haven't dared to leave their homes for three decades come slithering into the night. As the last bubble bursts and the pool grows still, there's a thunderclap that echoes from a cloudless sky and miles away, in an upturned boat, a dog howls.

NANCY COMES LATE to the boat. She hears Patroclus whining even before she's crossed the brook and she pushes the door open with a panicked shove. Though the fire still burns it is untended, the house spirits cowering under the stove. Something has happened, she knows it. Pat runs to her and wraps himself about her legs and she stumbles across the room to the desk, to the rose.

'You idiot.' The words come out like curdled cream. She rushes out with the dog at her heels and is out into the cold, the door of the boathouse hammering in the wind. She knows where he will be, he's shown her the place before. A legend, a story. No Keeper has crossed that line before but that's where they'd do it. If they could.

Where Callum died.

'You arrogant, stupid man,' she mutters as she runs, because if she stays cross with him, perhaps he'll still be there. He wouldn't do this. Not alone. Her feet slip on the snow-covered grass, black mud scarring the white in a harrow line behind her. Patroclus runs faster than he has for years but he's too slow, and besides, he doesn't want to go. He knows where this journey ends, he can feel it in his bones, so he stands on a flat stone in a bracken nest and howls again, a soulful cry into the snow.

She runs alone, though she's watched by little faces from under brambles, under stones. Turning to each other with worried looks and shrugs, then burrowing below. Nancy runs on. She breaks into the clearing where the mire-pool is as the moon comes out from behind clouds. She walks slowly to the edge of the pool, sees the neatly folded clothes and is reaching for the handle of the knife stuck in the stump when she stops herself. A man always returns for lost iron.

'Come back, Pel, please.'

She sits on the bank. Grass stretched tight over stone. There are comfier seats. Then she sees it, the cane, standing like a moon-dial stuck deep into the mud. She reaches for it, but as her fingertips brush the top she stops, closes her eyes, and weeps. That polished brass head, always in a hand or kept warming by the stove, is cold.

PART TWO

"Jack-the-lantern, Joan-the-Wad,
That tickled the maid and made her mad,
Light me home, the weather's bad."
—*Traditional*

VERVAIN

NANCY SLEPT IN the boat last night, at least for the few hours that remained of it before dawn. She had sat on the bank for a long time. Cold and alone, eyes fixed on the water, on the blanket of grass that rippled in the wind. It was nearly dawn when she had left. What more could she do? Pel had left her. With no warning or goodbye, and done the most foolish thing she could think of. What good was sitting? She had a job to do, just like him. She had left the knife in the wood, hilt deep in rotting hawthorn. Hoped it would do its duty and bring him back to her. She had collected his coat though, and his cane. He'd want them when he was back, they'd only grow damp in the mud.

The walk to the boat had been slow and lonely. The friendlier spirits had gone to ground below. Things were already unstable. Without Pel's protection, the moor would be a dangerous place. For everyone. Those left had no use for her, or worse, had plans for later. But even they knew when to leave well alone. Patroclus was waiting at the door, and she had considered continuing home. She had lived with Pel in the boat before, once her mother had died. But as she'd grown older, she had wanted space. A home of her own. She had returned to the house she had shared with her family, years ago, in the lee of the hills to the west of Mirecoombe. But once she stepped inside, laid a hand on the old dog's head, she knew she'd stay. Tonight, she needed Pel, and without him, the dog and the boat would have to do. The door had been left open, or rather, something had opened it for her. It was dark and warm in the boat, the rose still sat in the dust at the table and the smell of the fire still hung in the air. She noticed then the spots of blood on the floor, where Pel had cut himself, scored into himself a key to the Undermoor. She had laid the cane against the range, in its usual spot, draped the heavy wool coat over a chair. Walking slowly to the bed in the corner, unmade, unslept in, she had lain down on the wool and the cotton, the old dog slumping protectively on the floor beside her, and both had fallen asleep.

She dreams herself a mirror. The silvered glass spotted with black, her reflection tarnished so she cannot see her own reflection. Just the shadow of a figure staring back it twitches, this opposite, jerks like a marionette cut free from its strings. Nancy sits still. In the reflection, as the puppet's spasms increase, another shape emerges in the mottled glass. Tall and thin. It lays a hand on the twitching figure's shoulder and the puppet stills. For a second, the glass clears, then Nancy screams herself awake at the squeeze of a hand on her own right shoulder and the sound of starlings chattering her name.

IT IS BARELY morning. She lies there, in the half-light of the morning as the boat rocks in the building wind. She hears the boards creak and lift, feels the cut of the breeze as it finds its way in. Closes her eyes against the light, beaming pistol shot from knot holes in the walls. The fire burns, the hearth is lit. The house spirits, the brownies, did not leave with the rest, not when Nancy still needs them. She calls them now, these creatures of the ashy grate. Her voice is small, tired but her hand is stretched out towards them.

'Here, here all of you.'

There is movement, in the darkness, then the shadows part to let them through. There are six in total that crew the boat. All identical, male and female and some in between. They creep forwards across bare boards, their stout bodies covered in downy fur like a mouse's, though it thins across their elfin faces where rosy skin glows through. Small eyes shine within, like garnets, like coal bricks glowing. Under these a small flat nose in line with the face, nostrils like those of an otter or seal, easily closed against dust. And beneath that their small mouths, soft and cleft-lipped with rows of shining teeth hidden within. They run the world behind the skirting, woe-betide any pest that wanders in. A creature has to eat, has to defend its home, after all. They can tear a house to the ground if they're pushed to.

'Hello, dearies.'

Nancy is tired, dark circles running rings around her eyes. Her movement is slow and sluggish, but the brownies kindle something in her. A warmth that spreads, a flickering flame in a forgotten grate. As the spirits reach her, they nudge and wriggle into her outstretched hand like kittens.

'What will we do now then? He's gone, darlings.'

The creatures look to each other, then worried faces turn to Nancy. She hadn't expected a reply as, unlike the larger spirits, the brownies do not speak. She'll find the answers herself.

She spends a day here, unable to focus. It isn't the icy wind that keeps her here, and though the night spent on that cold, dark ground as the snow fell hasn't helped her mood, she can't lay the blame there either. It's something deeper, colder.

An absence of warmth where his face should be. Sat there, in the chair, by the fire. She wishes it hadn't ended on a fight. Though they have enough of those it was always a likely end. She could always feel his affection, his love, underneath the shouts and admonishments. Nancy places a hand on her shoulder, where he often did, a soft squeeze an impression of an apology. She never apologised either. The two of them always rocking on a see-saw of sorry, since Callum died, at least.

The brownies spend the day busying themselves with the boat. They race up the walls to stuff cracks with fresh oakum that they've picked apart from lengths of old rope. They keep the fire lit and the hearth on, sparing no fuel for their hollowed-out guest. Nancy slips between restless sleep and harried wakefulness, a pebble on a shore never let be by the tide.

The next morning, she wakes hungry but listless still. She cannot focus. She knows she must work, Pel expects it, or he would not have left her behind. People are still dead. Could still die and she has her suspicions as to where to turn her search. Better be sure though, before she walks that path. She needs to get up, but lying on his old cot, wrapped up in blankets that smell of him, she can't see her way to begin. It is Patroclus that helps. The old dog stands and barks at her from the corner, deep and resonant and loud enough to break a spell. Nancy looks at him, his shaggy coat shining in the firelight, old eyes full of love and worry. For the first time in days, since before the fire, she smiles. It is a small thing, a spark. Pat barks again, the wag of his great tail sending brownies flying, and it kindles the smile on Nancy's face. Strengthens and nourishes a flagging soul, and with tears in her eyes, she is back. Or at least, on her way.

'Nothing gained by lying here, hey, boy.' And she's up, legs swinging onto floorboards. Patroclus, bounding like a puppy, leaps to her side and drags her to her feet. She manages a smile again and though still weak, still unsure, lets the dog lead the way. The brownies race ahead as the pair make their way to the kitchen, eager hands dragging the kettle to the stove, reheating porridge made the night before in readiness for their guest. Nancy is tired, she eats a few spoonfuls from the pan then scrapes the rest into Patroclus's bowl, chipped white enamel with a gun-grey rim, where it is eaten eagerly. Nancy moves to the desk. She pulls back the chair, Pel's chair, its strutted back strange and ill-fitted to her shape. To anyone's, she suspects. Just like him to choose a chair out of contrariness, to sit in discomfort when he worked. She lays her hands splayed fingers on the desk, pressing hard into the dusty wood, turning pink fingertips white. Her eyes closing, she breathes deeply and sits, just so, for a full minute, thinking. Then, eyes open she takes the rose from the desk and moves it onto the shelf above, sweeping clear the ghosted 'N' from the dust.

'Come now, Nancy. You can do this.'

But she is not sure. She has worked with Pel for fifteen years, has learnt a lot from him. But he was always there, watching. Helping. Keeping her in check. How could she do this alone, until he returned? What would he do? She turns to his books, pausing when she sees the volume of folktales still on the desk. She drags her fingers across the cover, the gilt piskie drawn there, and a knot forms in her stomach. Replacing it, she pulls a slim, odd volume from its place on the shelf and reads, just as Pel had the night before, the path a person could take to the Undermoor. She reads of the signs and the sigils and the words and the spells, of the dangers. The author, whoever that person had been, had never followed his own instructions. Had never lain down in the cold dark water and drifted into the ink. His work was cobbled piecemeal from things he'd learnt from friends lost to the bogs and the mires. Would Pel be lost? She pushes the thought down and another surfaces, floating like a rat fallen into a trough. She thinks of Joan.

She had not known it was Joan-the-Wad when they met. Then it was just another bit of magic in a world that seemed to contain an unending supply of it. It had been during one of Callum's visits. Pel and Cleaver were arguing outside the boat, and she had been sent to keep Callum occupied, out of the way. She had been showing off. Her dislike for Callum had grown over the few years he had been visiting; she barely attempted to disguise it now. She had led him up the banked hill of the moor to a peat pool she had seen frogspawn in. As they walked, she had listed her friends to her wide-eyed companion.

'There's Turfcutter, of course. She's a spriggan but quite nice, really, when she stops throwing stones. And Leat, he's a pisky and I think the funniest.'

Callum's eyes had darted around, staring first at Nancy, then between every blade of grass.

'Are they here, Nancy? Now?'

She had scoffed, rolled her eyes. 'No, of course not. Why would I be talking to you if they were here?'

Nancy winces at the memory. She had run off, then. Left him behind. She had reached the pool and was counting the frog eggs when Callum had called.

'Nancy! I've found some fish!' She turned and saw him further down, at a different pool. She ran towards him, there couldn't be fish. These pools were transitory, they dried too unpredictably. No time for fish. No place for them to come from. She reached Callum and knelt down next to him.

A flash in the water.

'See?' Callum had been jubilant. In three years of visits, not once had he shown Nancy anything she'd not already known. The two children stared into the water. Whatever it was flashed again, catching the sun. Then the face appeared and both children gasped.

'You see her too?' Nancy was furious when Callum nodded. The sight was *her* gift.

'Yes, but why is she flickering? Why won't she stay still?'

'She is still, you just aren't allowed to see it.' Callum's face had fallen, and Nancy had revelled in it. It swam higher, the thing in the water. And she had gasped when she saw its face, just like hers, it seemed. Though its eyes were larger, its skin a silvery blue. It had been hard to see any deeper under the water. As the surface rippled, it seemed at first the creature had legs, then a tail, then a horrid tangle of seething things that floated like kelp in the water. The silver a reflection from the ball of green-blue fire it held in its palm. Holding her gaze. The flickering light all she could see. She had leant closer, over the water and she would have been gone, deep within the peaty tunnels if Joan hadn't laughed. Hadn't sent bubbles rising up that burst on the surface with the rank and sour scent of death and rot and moor-gas. Of the bloated belly of a drowned sheep pierced on a bullrush. And deep within her something snapped, and she was back in the world and terrified. She had leant back just as Joan leapt from the water, knocking Callum aside. It had happened without a single thought. Nancy's arms had twisted and with a wrenching crack, the moor side had split, the pool Joan had leapt from emptied in a moment and in its place a jagged granite fissure, soil and water trickling from the grassy wound at its mouth.

In another moment, with another sweep of her arms the hole was closed, and Nancy was left alone with Joan and Callum. Joan had screamed, seeing her retreat cut off and had swiped a clawed hand at Nancy, but Callum had grabbed her by her scaly wrist. He had tumbled backwards with the creature onto the scorched summer grass and held it tight, this howling thing, a monster scared to death.

That was the turning point. When she had stopped finding Callum irritating and begun to fear him. She could see Joan drying in the sun, her face pleading, her light dying. Callum staring at it with eyes filled with fury. Blame. Nancy had pulled Joan from his grip, let the creature go and for a second it met her gaze with ancient, hateful eyes. Then Joan-the-Wad, who had never lost a fight, never missed a meal, had raced down the hill, diving into the brook that ran at the base. Pel had run up, then she had beamed at him, sure that he was proud of what she'd done. That she'd shown him she could handle herself. But he'd grabbed her by the shoulders and shaken her, and for the first time since Nancy had known him looked utterly, completely terrified. That had been the first time she had affected the world so dramatically. Shaped the earth. Cleaver had stormed up too, roughly taken Callum's hand and scolded him for talking nonsense as he tried to explain. Callum had fallen silent and turned his stare to her. His eyes hungry, envious. She had pressed her face into Pel's shoulder, but the image of Callum's face remains. She'd learnt not to give in to it, her Murmur. To listen to Pel.

He has always been there, since then. To guide her hand, to stop it. And now she is alone, for as long as it takes him to come back to her.

She shakes the thoughts from her head.

'Come Nancy. How would he start?' she says aloud, then breathing deeply she takes three books from the shelf. Just as she's seen the old man do a thousand times. So confident all the answers lay neatly on his shelves. She opens the heavy book on the top of her pile, a book on ritual and sacrifice. Let Pel deal with the trouble below, she'd start on the problems up here.

These are not the sort of books that can be flicked through idly, they require an active read. It is midday before Nancy finds anything of use. Buried in the dense text is a description that fits. Of bodies left face down in the mud with their hands across their chests. Nancy notes it in a blank journal taken from the shelf. They were punishments, not sacrifices, the acts described here. Recriminations for unknown sins. She reads on, but the book gives no more answers. Nor the next. She is weary now. She's never liked the reading, the endless texts.

The sun is arcing back towards the horizon; she has spent the day here, at this desk. She notices for the first time the plates of food, untouched at her elbows and she thanks the house spirits watching with concern from their corners.

'Soon,' she says, 'I'll stop soon.' There is only one book left in her pile and she has been dreading it. She skims through the Latin. Not expecting answers here. It is the inserted section she is interested in. The section she cannot read.

Pel never spoke of his home, the true one, though she knows one of the maps on the wall show it. He stole this library from it when he left, this book one of the many he picked from the hoard. The island, for it is an island he ran from, has its own peculiar script of dashed marks and lines that few can read. Even Pel struggled. She reaches for a journal much like the one she writes in, the one she cannot help but feel pride at starting, the first she can call her own. The volume she pulls from the shelf is filled with Pel's neat writing spidering across the page. It is a dictionary, a translation tool, constructed carefully over many years, entries here and there scratched out with a single confident line where Pel thought better of something, was proven wrong. Nancy turns the old book's pages until she reaches the vellum at its heart, carefully inserted into the binding. She opens the dictionary and arranges both around her blank pages and begins to write, very slowly, a word at a time. The book gives up its secrets reluctantly. A sentence translated negated by the next.

It is midnight when she is done, and in front of her squirm pages of dense text, difficult to parse, and she still does not have what she needs. Words swim in front of her, of long dead men pushed deep into bogs, wicker hurdles pressing them down. Of whole sunken fields filled with rusted iron, buckled swords. But nothing that helps her here, helps her now. There is something, tangled in the black ink of the page in front of her, useful somewhere. She is sure of it. The insert, its old pages brittle and cracking as they turn, seems to be instructional, steps taken to prove innocence, or the lack of it. But translated as best as she's able the words don't make sense. Whatever it is ends with some prayer, though benediction or anathema she doesn't know.

"*Left on the dark shore, let black water or white light take you, to torment or to rest.*"

And she shivers as she reads what she has written. It has rung a distant bell. She does not know how to answer it.

'Pel would know,' she thinks. And he might. But he's too far down to tell her, no way of knowing when he might rise. She falls asleep in the chair, and the brownies leave her where she sits, though they place a cushion beneath her head, draw a shawl over her shoulders. Nancy sleeps, and the night shatters under the weight of the morning sun.

SUNDEW

Pel can feel the moor working its way in. It is worse than he had expected. The deep and cloying earth a symphony of rot, ages of bone and blood and flesh transmuted into peat, into soil. It fills and clogs his nostrils, his ears and with every fibre of his being he tries not to resist, not to open his mouth and scream at the horror of it. The words he spoke on the shoreline are already taking effect. As he sinks, quick then slow as the water gives way to the peat, his old body grinds almost to a halt. Pel's old heart, that's worked so hard, is finally slowing to rest. It feels as though he is half asleep, at that point where dreams invade the room and stop a mind from sleeping. He cannot decide if his eyes are open or closed. The darkness feels wet, his eyes move frantically against it. He feels the pressure of earth breaking ribs, water in his ears. Panic. The sound of Nancy's footsteps above him, the *thud, thud, thud* of her run. Feels her sit on the bank. Salt tears mingling with the mineral earth. He reaches for her, cannot move his arm against the weight of the world above him. He has sunk too deep to turn back.

He focuses on his breathing, on stilling his chest. The powders he took, that flower still sat on his tongue, are working with his charms. He does not know how long he will have but it will be enough, he is sure of it. Lord Pelagius Hunt has rarely lacked certainty, he'll not start doubting now. The iron bucket sits heavy on his chest, its prisoner silent, quiet, and scared for the first time in an age.

The mire gives way to him coyly, admits his shape into its depths with a sticky-fingered resistance that folds at his touch. It wants him there, he knows it. He is waiting for the tipping point, the gravity shift. The moment that the pull from above gives way to the one from below. He is not sure how deep that axis lies, how far underground. He distracts himself with anticipation of reaching the Undermoor. He's spoken to piskies about it, spriggans too. A perfect inversion of the moor above. More verdant, more alive. Where the moorland grass is stubby and coarse, the Undermoor's hills are a flood of long green stems. The stone above is beautiful, yes, the granite flecked with tourmaline and quartz, below, the rock is a rainbow. The lodes of copper and silver and gold shining on its surface. The rocks stained blue and green from oxidising metals. And the moon. He cannot wait to see the moon.

He is aware of the presence of others. The bodies of animals, slowly decaying husks of things long dead, the skin still clinging like leather to the bone. He focuses on them to distract from the pain, the panic that rises from the fact he is not breathing. Their presence helps. They have been through this already. He does not need to see them to know they're there.

Callum must be here, he thinks, *lying alongside me.*

How long does a body last?

His life flashes past and he bristles at the cliché. Memories long buried rise like counterweights to his body. How many years has it been? He remembers his boyhood, his ancestral seat. Remembers the queen who gave it to his father such a long time ago. Remembers why he fled.

Enough. He resists it, this avenue of time. He is not dying. He pushes his mind to the academic. This is not the time for his stories to come back to him, he is a Keeper. He will learn from the pain. He considers his position. Considers to the exclusion of all else. The process he has set in motion is so close to death it is understandable there would be similarities. His pulse quickens briefly from its slow steady drip. If he is wrong, if he has miscalculated, he will not know, he will just go quietly into the black and not wake up.

No use to those thoughts. Instead, he thinks of Nancy. A worry he can still do something about. His past is done, he cannot change it. Nancy is still here. He will learn from his mistakes. He regrets it, the way he spoke to her. His love, his worry always a stone's throw from anger. He is scared for her. His ward. He is scared for himself if he loses her. Again, the panic flares, blooms like blood in water. Though he knows she is strong and capable and wise, he has still left her with the monsters, and the men. He pushes down the feeling and steels himself. He has a job to do.

The water and the peat hold the history of the moor, bound up in the moss and the silt. An archive of the dead. Enmeshed in its layers are the ghosts of bears, of wolves, and the men who killed them. The pollen of flowers grown under a fresh-faced sun. It strips away everything, all flesh and bone until only a ghost remains. Memories free to head below without the weight of life to bind them, their bodies left to feed the earth. It collects these fragments, these pieces of life. It is the price it takes for its gift, for its acts of transmutation. Pel risks a lot refusing the charge.

The pressure is greater now. The blackness heavier. The panic undimmed. It is an odd sensation this, Pel thinks, breath stilled but heart still beating its infrequent thud, sending ripples through the dark. He can no longer feel Nancy above him, though she sits there still. The ink in the marks on his arms stings in the dark water, the signs he pulled the blade through burning the worst. He can feel the knife, too. Blade stuck deep in the rotting stump, calling him home.

Through the darkness memories swim, again. When she was ten, during one of Callum's visits, Nancy had been playing with the boy on the hills behind the boat. He and Cleaver engaged in the argument they had each time they met. He had been so focused on the fight he'd not given a second thought to the children. Either of them. The first he had known of it was the cracking sound of earth breaking.

He still remembered the sick feeling he had when Nancy had emptied the pool, split the hill. He had never seen Joan out of the water. She led people into the bog with dancing lights and a smile. She was a thing to be put back, she was not meant to be out, not any longer, her time was done. In fact, Pel had thought she had left. Yet here she was, one of the old terrors. But she was not as frightening as the ease with which Nancy performed her gift. Her Murmur, as she insisted on calling it. It was the first time he had seen the extent of it. He remembered how he had felt then, frozen to the spot as the little girl he cherished so fully stood in the sun with death, Joan's dark, blue skin drying scaly in the day. She had saved that monster. From Callum. His stomach knots as he remembers it, Callum had been able to hold Joan in his hands, he had seen her, could Nancy be right? No. It was impossible. Callum was dead. It had been Nancy who had caused the events of that day, he is sure of it. He had known Nancy was special but that... it gave him pause to think of that afternoon. Cleaver had thought it a quake, a geological event that though rare, was utterly explainable. When the Reverend had taken Callum away, the boy's eyes that day had stayed with Pel, he had taken Nancy to one side. He had made her promise not to use that gift without him present. Had told her that she had been given it below, when the piskies took her. Had explained that gifts were rarely freely given. And she had given him her word. He had allowed her to practice, under his direction, as an occasional treat. Practical, too. A venting of something that ought not build. Perhaps he had been rash to stop her training when Callum… no. He was right. Knows he was right. His thoughts turn to the night on the hill, but that was an exception, surely? Extreme stress. And she had stopped when asked, had looked scared, had listened. No, she would keep her promise. She would be fine without him whilst he was away. He trusts her.

A change.

He sinks faster now. It is as though a chasm has opened up, and he is falling deadweight down it to some cathedral space below. But he can still feel the water pressing in. Still feel the seeking fingers of moss and peat working their way into his ears, prising up the corners of his mouth.

Then it happens. Like an overcoat snagging, caught on the gorse, he pulls free of his body. It is a moment of such immense pain that the world flashes white before him. He feels his spirit tear free as though peeled from his body like a rabbit from its skin after a hunt. Feels nerves spring from tissue like harp strings cut. His head rings with the sound of it. He tastes blood and his whole form feels raw, he is glad he cannot see, he is terrified that should he look down, his very core would be exposed, muscles and organs open to the world unbound by skin and tearing in a thousand tiny lesions. When his vision clears, when the pain has retreated into a dull persistent ache, he looks up. He can see it, his body, hanging above him in the darkness, swaying softly in the undertow and he is separate from it. He realises with a start that his eye is open, his mouth too but no water rushes in. The panic from before is gone.

He still doesn't breathe, but it no longer seems important. He floats in the darkness, a ghost ripped from its machine. And one by one lights appear in the dark. He is taken aback. His level head knocked off kilter by the madness of this place. He is drunk on a heady mix of pain and sheer impossibility, bursts of flaming colour, a night's sky of shining stars, the spirits of creatures taken by the bog, of sheep and cattle and horses. He feels each as clearly as if they were sat before him. Of birds, of frogs and toads. Men and women, travellers who didn't watch their step. There are faces he knows. He can see himself, too, shining in the darkness. Can see the light as it passes through his shadow hands, the shapes of his protections cast in gold on his arms, shining molten veins replacing the ink. This pathway he has chosen is not the only one. But it is the only one that would have admitted him, and only like this. The warrens and rat runs that the Underfolk move through are too narrow and winding for him to drag his body through. And by the stars not as beautiful. Nowhere near as beautiful. So enraptured by the sights of this transition he hasn't noticed, for a moment, that he can move.

Tentatively he pushes off, swimming in the dark water, moving like an otter in a stream, spinning and twirling. There is sound here too, the muffled roar of an ocean trapped, the sound of birdsong, plucked. And the scent of the place has changed. Gone the heavy dirt weight of peat with its ground up bones and leaves and moss. The whole weird chamber smells like a storm, like the air after rain and lightning.

'My word.'

His voice a shadow in an ill-lit world and echoing in the darkness.

'My gods.'

There is movement, there, to his left. Like a stone skimming on a lake, like a fish moving upstream, a blue light, flickering. It is Bluecap, her spirit at least, untethered from her body just like Pel, but she is scrambling to get back to it. Pel can see the bucket still held firmly in his arms, high above. And something is pulling at Bluecap, she swims against the current, against a force that pulls them down. Pel feels it too. He follows the devil's trajectory down, to a light glowing deep below him. It is different to the rest. It does not twinkle or shimmer like quartz in sunlit rock, it thrums like thunder, breaking like sunrise. It is not giving him a choice; whatever force is pulling at him does so expectantly. It knows it will win. Pel does not fight it. He is here for a reason, after all. Bluecap is racing towards it now, the draw greater on her than Pel, he can see her panicked strokes as she strikes in vain for the surface and then, like flotsam on a stream into an underground cave she is gone. Into the light. Pel treading water above it.

Something comes up, too. A crowd of lights, burning with black fire, tearing past him in a horde of flame the sound of galloping hooves echoing around the chamber. The sound of dogs barking. A hunting horn blowing out a call. A bell rings deep in Pel's mind but it is hard to focus here, hard to keep hold of a thought.

It goes deeper than he thinks, this sunless sea. The space around holds him like water but with a different threat. It does not feel safe, but Pel feels he could stay here forever if he wished. He does not. He pushes on towards the glow, past the shining lights, past confused spirits that skim past him in the twilight. Pel had not known what he would find under the moor, but it was not this. This is beautiful in a way he had not expected the journey to be, not expected anything to be. He wishes he had more time, but his mission remains, and it presses on him as urgently as the soaking peat presses his body high above. He is at the light now, almost, its glow obliterating the darkness. Its pull is stronger now, a physical draw like a rope lashed tight about him, reeling him in. Nothing for it. Pel tucks himself into a ball, pushing his old head between his knees and wrapping his arms tight about his body. Holding the thought of the paradise he's about to enter in his mind. He leaves one hand free to form a bent knuckle shape and he's out and through into the brightness.

STONECROP

Black water in a pool at her feet. Her own face staring back. A hand reaching from deep within it. Withered and dried, the bones show themselves as ridges under the cold dead leather. There are faces, too. Her mother. Pel. Salan Dell. She leans over the water, something else rises. The water explodes in a geyser of foetid black ichor, covering her in its tarry weight. As she falls backwards, she hears the thundering of hooves, smells the hot wet breath of a dog and the scent of horsehair burning. When the torrent has abated, she is left in a muddy patch of grass, trampled to a bog in a matt of horseshoe prints and the paws of giant dogs.

The day is a storm. Nancy wakes to mortar fire rain, heavy drops beating against the window and the whole boat shaking in the wind. She is stiff and cold from a night at the desk, the papers splayed under folded arms, the notes from the night before still alien to her.

'Keep your secrets,' she mutters, and stretches tired limbs. Her back aches, her head too but she sighs, gathers the papers neatly, as if apologising for speaking to them roughly and looks again at the final line:

"Left on the dark shore, let black water or white light take you."

If the dark suspicion those words have stirred is right, there is a dangerous road ahead. She needs to be sure, and she has no way of checking her work, her translation. 'Pel

169

will know,' she thinks, though she knows as she does how unsteady her faith is. It's written on her face. It's only been a day or two and already it's her mantra. Pel will know. The smell of coffee, brewed by brownies now in bed, drifts across the room and pulls her to her feet. Rising stiffly out of the chair, she trips over Patroclus curled beside her and the old dog opens an eye in sleepy reproach. Nancy smiles and crouches beside him. She's not forgotten his help, at her lowest. She strokes his head, takes his jowly snout in her hands, and looks him in the eyes.

'We'll hold the fort, you and I.' The old dog wags his tail, licks her hand, and goes back to sleep.

Nancy sits at the kitchen table and sips the coffee with her eyes closed, scrunched tight against the looming day. He could be back any moment, she thinks, eyes open now and darting to the door. Or in a day, or two. The uncertainty binds her. She thinks back again to their last meeting, hers and Pels. It's painful, the memory of it, of the words spoken. She hopes he'll have a chance to set it right. She knows he didn't mean it. No good fretting over a fight unfinished. She casts back further, to the time before, and settles happily there. Memories of him teaching her to ride. The pony he'd "tamed" from the moor who she'd named Teasy, who tittuped every time she got on, sidestepping back and forth until she rubbed his neck the way he liked, and he settled. Remembered Patroclus, younger then, running alongside her as Pel shouted from the boat to slow down. Remembered him teaching her that first spell. The one that placed a ward around the caster. Pel had stood and flicked stones at her until she got it right, not hard, but not gently, either. She had always loved that he'd taken her seriously. Never softened a lesson. From the moment he let her in she'd always known he cared.

Even if he'd never said so.

Even if she'd never told him, either.

She shakes the past from her head. There are things to do. She had told Pel she would speak to the families, the bereaved, and she had barely started the task, the fire had put paid to that. Her dream rankles though. It reminds her of a story that she couldn't put a finger on. The sound of hooves still echoes in her head.

Turning the page in her notebook, the cryptic lines banished under fresh white pages, she makes a list. It invigorates her, this new purpose. When she has finished, she closes the book neatly and reaches for her satchel, untouched since the night at the Fellmire. She places the book inside, with a pencil stub, and looks about. She can see him, pacing. His long legs striding as he opens drawers and she stands, set to mimicry. Opening the first drawer she scans the contents, mentally evaluating and discarding most of the trinkets inside. She takes a set of dice, a string of rowan berries stuck with pins, and two small bottles tightly stoppered with cork and wax, and places them carefully in the bag. Next, as an afterthought, she moves to the other side of the boat, under the deer's head, and pulls a small silver case from beneath a folded shawl, opening it briefly to check the contents. A small cloud of black dust eddies in the pale light. Lastly, she returns to the desk and takes Pel's book from its space. The soft indented daisy on the cover, the corners well worn by her adoptive father's old hands. She holds it for a moment before slipping it alongside the rest of her kit, closing the flap and carefully twisting the brass catch, checking the bag is secured. It cheers her, this pantomime, this following in footsteps. And she is smiling as she makes her way to the door, as she catches sight of herself in an old, silvered mirror, meets her own tired eyes in its reflection. The green light in them still dimmed with worry but growing brighter with the day.

'Looking rough, girl,' she laughs, running a hand through unbrushed hair. 'Besides, can't go out in weather like this dressed like that.'

The rain still rakes across the heather, tearing the flowers from the gorse. Her dress is crumpled from being slept in; the green fabric creased. Not that it matters; she's never been one to worry about appearances, but she'd rather not get wet. She has her cloak with her, but it was brought to protect against the cold, not a storm. Her eyes alight on Pel's coat, still folded neatly over the chair. She moves quietly to it, like a child stealing up on a deer, almost fearful. She lays a hand on the coarse wool, runs fingers along the lapel.

'He would not mind, would he?' She looks at Pat whose indifference is read as assent. She lifts it from the chair and swirls the heavy coat around her shoulders, onto her arms, and it envelops her. For a moment she is overcome, it smells so much of Pel that she is intoxicated, confused, it is as if he is here, as if they share the same space. She laughs, great gulps of laughter escaping her, uncontrolled. She spins, taken with the momentum of the coat, surrendering to it, comforted by it, its heavy wool wrapping about her in the echo of an embrace. For a moment she feels like a child again, playing dress-up with the old man's things. She is giddy with it, and such is the energy that for the first time in years, old Patroclus is on his feet and bounding, yapping like a puppy, happy just that she is smiling again.

'Here we go, Pat!' Nancy almost sings it, 'Out again!' The brownies poke their faces out, happy, though nervous with it, there is a mania here. Nancy does sing now, old rhymes, songs her mother taught her.

'See-saw, Margery Daw,
Sold her bed and lay on the straw.
Sold her bed and lay upon hay.
And Pisky came and carried her away.'

And then laughter again, coming out loud and uncontrollable as she remembers other verses she's only heard at the Nest, at the tail end of a night. She can see so clearly Pel's face screwed up with mock disapproval as the verses grew ruder. She wheels and dances about the boat, the pockets of the greatcoat jangling, and her face is wet with tears. She reaches out in a spin, the coat hem flying out dervish around her and she grabs the brass-topped cane from its rest by the range and shouts:

'Come on then, Nance, Pat! Let's get to it again.'

And taps the cane three times on the floor. On the third strike she falters, and the laughter stops. Patroclus stands mouth wide and tail wagging, but he moves to her now, nudges a heavy head under her arm and the two of them sit quiet on the floor. Nancy buries her face in his coat and cries into it, her shoulders racked with sobs.

'We'll hold the fort, boy,' she says through tears, 'he'll be back soon.' She wills herself to believe it. 'We'll hold the fort.' Standing with the help of the dog she places the cane carefully back against the range. The moment has passed. Red-eyed, Nance smiles at Patroclus. 'He'll need that, won't he? Best not mess with it.' And though her gaze lingers on the polished brass, the worn wood, she leaves the cane be. The coat she keeps tied tight about her, and she draws it up around her throat as she opens the door and steps into the wind and the rain, Patroclus trailing faithfully after.

*   *   *

IT HOWLS AT her, the moor. The wind tears over rocks and hurls rain at her like pitch. The landscape rages and rends itself before her, great ragged turf edges fluttering, hanging over black peat, rivers of melted snow whirling in the holloways. She walks head down to the linhay where Pel stables his horse, the open fronted barn set with its back against the weather. Though the walk from the boat is short Nancy breathes a sigh of relief as she turns the corner, steps into the barn. The wind suddenly gone, its absence briefly deafening, she's brought back to the world by the smell. Warm hay, the smell of straw and horses. The comforting stench of a stable. There are three bays separated by low walls of wood and stone, the back granite wall inset with a long trough that runs the length of it, passing through each section in turn and stuffed with hay. Nancy smiles. In the nearest bay stands her own blue roan mare, left stabled since the night Pel sank. The horse eyes her reproachfully from its stall, the racks of hay almost gone.

'Hello, Selkie,' Nance speaks softly, apologetically. The animal was named after a story in one of Pel's books; Nancy had always thought her mottled grey hide looked like sealskin. 'I'm sorry, girl.' By the entryway is a sack of windfall apples, collected the previous year and stored, carefully. Even so the green skins are marked with black spots, the flesh bletted and brown on the verge of rot but at their sweetest. Nancy takes one and feeds it to her horse on an outstretched palm. There is a snort, the sound of scuffling in the darkness at the other end of the linhay.

Eponina stands in the furthest stall, deep in shadow and stamping at the ground. Nancy has never ridden her. She is not sure the horse would let her. Eponina's pale cream flanks stand out even in the gloom, her rusted red ears pressed back to her head and bleeding freckles into her neck and mane. A miracle of a horse.

'There, girl,' says Nancy, softly. 'I know, something's up, isn't it?' She has walked to the rail in front of the horse, reaches out tentatively with a hand and lays it on Eponina's velvet nose. The horse's lip curls, as if thinking of biting but she settles, accepts the stroke.

'He'll be back soon, don't fret.' Nancy checks the horse has water, takes an apple from the bag by the door and places the black spotted windfall on the floor. As she turns away, she can hear Eponina bend to eat, hears the crunch. She pauses at the middle stall, Teasey's stall, empty now, and fetches another apple. Lays it on the floor for his ghost. She saddles Selkie with a practiced hand and is soon astride her, Pel's coat hanging over the horse's rump like a riding cloak. Nancy places her boots into the stirrups and lightly flicks Selkie's neck with the reins.

'On then, girl.' And the horse moves reluctantly into the rain.

It is not a long ride from the boat to Mirecoombe. Nancy has made it a thousand times, but the moor is disruptive today, argumentative. The ground thaws under the deluge and slips under the horse's hooves, under Patroclus' paws. Selkie's mane, Nance's hair plastered to their faces and necks. They climb up and above the boat, away from the valley floor where the marshes are rapidly expanding. The hillsides run with water, rain cascading off granite caps, bubbling up from hidden channels and springs. The moss and worts that lace amongst the grass are spongy underfoot and the hillside stinks of rain. As she rides, Nancy turns to look at the gorse patch, the snow and ash washing away leaving a cemetery of twisted black wood. Pulling the horse to a stop, Nancy glowers at it.

'Bastards.'

Nancy spits as she says it. From below comes a thin howl, Patroclus's face looking up at her in the rain. Nancy clicks with her tongue and the group moves on. Across the hillside and down towards Mirecoombe, smoke curling from squat chimneys, the smell of damp peat burning. As they descend the ground grows wetter, grass tips poke out of waterlogged pools and the horse struggles to see the bridge. The fallen cross and granite slab still ripple underwater, still bridging the ditch, and it is with cautious steps that they cross into the mud. In weather like this, the banked walls of the ditch that runs around Mirecoombe are supposed to keep the water pouring from the hillside out. Not today. The old leats and culverts that should divert the flow are blocked with muck and mire; Nancy shakes her head.

'That's what they get, Pat, for driving Them away. Who did they think kept the channels clear? Idiots.' The whole village looks as though it is floating, houses merging with their reflections. The long-house door is closed again, against the weather and the rain, and nobody is out in this torrent. The ramifications from the fire are evident inside the village, too, the stone arch linking the smithy to the smith's cottage has come down, the mortar washed away. Nancy knows the spriggan who maintained it, watched him burn. Without the Underfolk's help and protection the village has the air of decay. A fresh corpse. No outward signs of rot but the eyes already dull.

There is something else, too. Nancy keeps looking up, to the dark clouds above her though she's not sure what she expects to see. The clouds are knots of grey and black, like the wool of hill sheep. There is a weight to them that discomforts. As though they hold more than rain. Nancy is soaked to the bone and cold with it, and before she sets to work, she needs to see a friendly face.

Steadily she guides Selkie to the Nest. It stands firm. Madge had no part in the mess on the hill, the Underfolk know that, know her. The Nest will hold. Even if the rest doesn't. Passing the front door, Nancy ducks under an archway. It opens on a yard and, dismounting, Nancy leads the horse into an old chall barn, neglected and leaning through lack of use, but dry enough for now. Patroclus sticks close to Nancy's heels and, leaving Selkie to shake off the water, the pair wade to the back door of the Mare's Nest Inn. Nancy's firm raps are rewarded quickly, and the door opens outwards.

'Come in then, the pair of you,' Madge says smiling, and the two bedraggled creatures trail in out of the cold.

The backrooms at the Nest are low-ceilinged and comforting. Just as the boat creaks under the weight of Pel, so too the Nest shouts Madge's name at every turn. This inn has been with her family since it opened; it knows her well. The walls are lined with pictures, their frames butting up against each other so the wall beneath disappears. They show maps of the valley, of the moors, old drawings of the village. One shows the chapel hill covered in a grove of trees, painted in watercolour, years before. Some are gifts from Pel, framed butterflies and beetles, dried and pressed flowers mounted over red-ink signs. He used to joke that if she wanted him, she need only break the glass. She's never held him to his word, but she'd believed him. Nancy traces the edges with a finger as they pass. The entrance hall narrows, branches off, and into one of these rooms the trio go.

'Don't worry,' Madge whispers, 'no one will see you here.' The room is a private bar, of sorts, velvet chairs placed around three tables, a brass bell with a rope. The room is immaculate, the oak polished, the floor swept, but despite this Nancy knows it has not been used in a very long time. The landlady sits next to Nancy on a settle bench and pulls her into a hug. Nancy can count them on one hand, these hugs: when her mother died, when her pony Teasy had grown sick. When she lost him, too. It was never acknowledged, not to Nancy at least, but Pel and Madge were both her guardians in their way. Hard and soft. Madge the mortar that filled the gaps between Pel's stone. Both important, when it came to keeping the weather out. Nancy lets herself sink into the old woman's shoulder, dampening her apron with her tears. Madge gives her a pat, a squeeze and a shake then stands and moves to the bar. There are pewter tankards hanging from hooks along the polished rail. Nancy notices the initials on the first, 'P.H.' Pel. Madge notices her looking. 'Aye, it's his. The second is the Reverend's. The rest, well, long gone.'

Nancy reaches and lifts Pel's tankard from its hook. It's heavy in her hand. She lifts it and sees the glass bottom, an anchor cross etched into the base. She lifts Cleavers's and is shocked to see the same. She's only ever seen Pel wear that sign.

'It's hard to imagine them being close.'

'Aye, thick as thieves once. A Reverend and a Keeper had a lot to chat about. A lot of overlap in their notes. A sad day when that friendship ended. Sit down, Nancy.' Madge motions to one of the tables. 'I'll light the fire and fetch something warm and you can tell me what you're doing here, soaked through. Don't think I don't see your red eyes, girl.'

Nancy replaces the tankards and sits, still in the heavy wet coat, on a velvet seat. Patroclus is pawing at the rug in front of the fire, rucking it up until it suits him, then down he lies. The fire lights, suddenly, to the surprise of Nancy if not the dog, and she smiles as she sees a brownie race back behind the grate.

'They came back, didn't they, Nance? My good little people?' Madge has returned and places a steaming bowl in front of Nancy, and a hot glass, too, the scent of whiskey and ginger wine intoxicating even at a distance.

'Yes, Madge,' Nancy says, 'I see them. They came home.'

'I was so worried, after the fire.' Madge pauses, the smile fixed on her face. 'I'm so glad they came back. Now, tell me Nancy. What's happened, where's Pel?'

WITCHES BUTTER

'Now, brother, look *at that.*'

'*A rare sight indeed.*'

'*A ghost not dead.*'

'*No invitation sent.*'

'*Running with the Underfolk on see through legs.*'

'*It's been an age since we've had his kind visit.*'

'*Since He let one in.*'

'*Trouble, that.*'

'*For someone.*'

'*Hush then. He's waking.*'

'*Bleary as the dawn.*'

'*One eye open, the other...*'

'Will you two be quiet.'

Pel groans wearily as he rises to his feet, pulls himself from the mire he has emerged from. He can feel the ground beneath him; does not remember falling, so he must have climbed up. He has no memory of the light, of what passed between then and now. He surveys the shallow bog, the dark shale shore on which he's run aground, and two old spirits clamp hands to their mouths. Pel stands, straightens, takes a look at the view before him and pales in the glory of the Undermoor.

It is not what he had expected.

It rolls out before him, a strange reflection of the moor he knows, the tors and stacks as above though tinted. As if seen through stained glass of fuchsia, teal and indigo. The veins of metal dulled, the stained rock souring. There are no rolling fields of green grass. The earth dark and foetid beneath it, though there are flowers breaking out. Plants and flowers that the world has lost, seeds that sank through peat and time and mire and landed here, layers of them, over the millennia. Finding rest in fertile ground and blooming around the dead.

The hills seem familiar. At the crest of one is a pile of rocks that seem a reflection of Echo Tor. Pel sees too the Queen's Rocks, high on the wrong side of the valley and at the centre, in the distance, the smaller hill that ought to hold the chapel. At its crest here is a small grove of tall trees, a darkness penned within.

At the edges of his vision things move, running quickly through grasses, diving into pools. He catches glimpses, long limbs and faces that never stay still long enough to identify. He can guess, though. He recognises the backs of spriggans, the fluttering wingbeat of piskies. The salt-spray laugh of buccas, too. The hallucinatory experience of the journey has faded. He feels his usual self return. Across distant hillsides he sees rockfalls move and he stiffens, fingers curling into a spell, and he crouches for a fight. It is only then he relaxes, though he does not feel safe; it has been a long time since he's seen a giant full height and striding.

As he follows the creatures' path, he sees just how astounding the Undermoor still is, despite its decay. It stretches on forever, a fever dream of land, and at the farthest reaches, distant hills merge purple with the sky. So engaged with this is Pel, this old man, this Keeper distracted by the earth, he almost doesn't notice the sky. It glows from the light of a huge round moon, hanging heavy at its centre, and clouds roll past in silvered banks. But though there is a clarity to it, something is off, and Pel smiles when it happens. This, at least, is as magical as he had hoped. A wind blows, gusting through the grass and reeds and high above the sky ripples. Waves roll across the moon.

She would love to see this.

Turning his attention to himself, Pel raises his hands before his face. For a moment, they are as they looked in the space between, pale, ghostly, and veined with gold. But in an eyeblink they are corporeal again. The familiar wrinkled flesh, the black bleeding ink of the tattoos. His spells have worked. He nods, satisfied. He feels grounded, less in danger of floating.

Pel turns to face the shapes on the bank. Two hazy creatures that crackle, like the ground after a lightning strike and he straightens his back to address them.

'I have questions, you'll give me answers.'

'He's speaking to us, brother.'

'He can hear us.'

'He can see us.'

'Yes,' says Pel, 'I can. What are you? I don't recognise your voices. I've not seen you above.' He glowers at them, the look he reserves for all impertinent sprits, and the two shapes shrink from him.

'We've not been above for... oh, how long?'

'An age or two, how does a person measure these things?'

'Were we always two? Have we once been one?'

'Hard to say, brother, hard to say.'

Pel tuts impatiently. He has little time for the vagaries of Underfolk at the best of times, and he has things to do.

'It does not matter. We are nothing now but our selves.'

'Each our own.'

'Together.'

Pel reaches out a hand, and surprise flashes across his face as he grasps for his cane. It has been many years since he's been without it.

'Did something come before me? When I fell?'

He looks back towards the mire he crawled from and then up at the watery sky, his wet clothes. Did he fall? He doesn't remember. But he must have, he was heading down...

The two spirits don't notice his confusion.

'*The little lucifer?*'

'*Fiery blue?*'

'*Yes, she's here too, but hiding now.*'

'*From you.*'

'*From Him.*'

'*He doesn't like gifts squandered; she'll have to pay a price.*'

Pel thinks for a moment. Scowls. The longer he stands on this bilious shore the more uncomfortable he feels.

'What's happened here? This—this is not how the Undermoor should look.'

The two spirits stand with Pel and survey the earth around them. The colours, though vivid, are those of decay. The purples and blues of a bruise, the red and pinks of open wounds. The two spirits look to each other and shrug.

'*A storm. We were hit by a storm.*'

'*A storm on two legs.*'

'And the king? Where is he?' In unison two arms are raised and point towards the chapel hill, to the grove at its crown.

'*Though he's not what he was.*'

'*Lightning-struck, a hollow crown.*'

'*It's a free for all.*'

'*For those who are free.*'

'*Trouble for the rest of us.*'

'*We can feel it in our bones.*'

Pel looks at the two spirits again, harder than before. Something about them unsettles him, he knows a lie when he hears it, however well it's told. They shimmer in and out of focus, unlike any of the folk he deals with in his work. They seem diminished. Confused. It's hard to pick out the sense from their words.

'Can you not tell me straight what has happened here? I need to see your master. We have something to discuss.'

The two spirits look askance at the old Keeper and though it's hard to see their features, it seems they are smiling at him.

'*Oh, we know, Keeper.*'

'*We know.*'

Pel ignores this.

'Will you lead me to Him?'

'*Others will.*'

'*For a little in return.*'

The shapes drift further into the mire. Pel does not trust them, instincts sending itches down his spine.

'Fine. What are your names then, give me that at least?'

'*Our names, he says!*'

'*And nothing in return.*'

'*Shall we, brother? Tell him?*'

'*What harm can it do, we're all dead here.*'

'*Long past troublemaking.*'

'*Long past strife.*'

Pel steps back onto the unnatural grass and watches the shapes twist together and grow, until they tower above, their twin heads raking bow waves in the sky. Then two words, spoken at once as if to be one.

'*Gog, Magog.*'

And they're gone. Pel shields his face from the vapour that falls as they vanish into air; it smells of rust and iron. He knows those names. There's trouble in them. A great deal of trouble. He folds thoughts away, to be considered later. No time for more riddles here. It occurs to him however, with a shiver, that they might have been right, those two. They could all be dead; he could be dead. But if the ritual had worked or hadn't, wouldn't the end be the same? He is stood here and that's the end of it. He shakes it off, this fleabite thought. It makes no difference; he'll get the audience he seeks. Dead or not, he's coming.

ON A DISTANT hill, between trees not seen on the surface for a thousand years, a tomb stands, a temple. From inside its stone walls, bound with ivy and thick with moss, long limbs stretch from a granite throne. Ancient limbs creak like woodland in a storm, and a hollow chest rattles with a long-buried laugh.

High above, in a different world, the moorland shivers.

SWEET GALE

THUNDER ROLLS ACROSS the valley, shakes the Nest.

Madge has listened quietly to Nancy, leaving only now and then to see to the bar, to serve drinks to the few old men not put off by the weather. She sits now with Nancy's hand in hers, Patroclus dozing by the fire, Selkie in the barn eating fresh-brought hay. Thunder has begun to roll around the valley like a cavalry charge, the lightning the flash of sun on swords.

'It's a dreadful thing he's done, Nancy. Arrogant, stupid. But that's what will bring him back. I've always said he's too pig-headed for death. You don't get to his age and die readily.' She smiles at Nancy, who is not yet ready to return it.

'I need to speak with them, Madge. The ones left.' Nancy ignores Pel, his ghost sitting in the corner of her head. There's work to do. He can wait. 'To Delen. To Kenwyn. The Dells won't speak to me now, not any longer.'

Madge sighs. She's seen Nancy grow up, knew her mother, her grandmother too. She had offered, once, to take Nance in, when her mother went. But Pel had insisted. She thinks often of how things could have been. Nancy sits before her, but her shadow is Pel's; her eyes have the same quick, calculating glare to them. Though they are kinder than the Keeper's.

'Be careful Nancy. There's trouble in questions, especially now. Would you not be better waiting for Pel?'

'No, Madge. I shouldn't have waited this long as it is. He's wrong this time. I know he is, there is a link. He'll see, he'll find something down there and when he comes back, I'll be ready to help. I'll have answers for him.' Her eyes burn with the conviction she's spent the last few days searching for. This is what she can do. This is how she'll help. Madge leans back in her chair.

'Fine. Go see Delen. She'll be home. Neither Bronwen nor Tom left anyone behind who can help, but Kenwyn? He's been doing work for Calder, up at the farm. I'll send the boy to fetch him here.'

'Thank you, Madge. I'll be back when I'm through.'

'Nancy, before you go. Seeing you in that coat. Hearing you.' Madge pauses, turning over words like pebbles, worried what might be underneath. Nancy stands impatiently, halfway to out into the hall.

'If you've something to say Madge, say it. I've things to do.'

'You aren't him, Nancy. Remember that.'

Nancy stares, brow furrowed, and her jaw tenses with a rebuke, with a defence but she decides against it. Instead, she turns and is off, barely dried out and into the rain again, Patroclus trailing reluctantly after her. Alone in the bar, Madge looks to the tankards hanging on their hooks, and shakes her head.

DELEN'S COTTAGE SQUATS low in the village. Roof thatched, reeds kept on by turves of peat, pinned on in strips. The walls are granite, of course. Stacked blocks held firm with lime and here and there, in the cracks, objects stuffed: a horseshoe, the broken blade of a knife. At the doorway is a small pile of similar items crusted with lime, recently pulled from the structure. Nancy wades into the yard, stoops to inspect them. Protections discarded; help refused. A goose honks and she leaps out of her skin, darting a savage look at Patroclus who saw it coming. The goose, its job done, races back into the hollow built into the yard wall, a large, rounded slab of granite drawn aside, to be shut again at bedtime. The door opens, and Delen appears.

She is younger than Nancy, her dark chestnut hair falling ragged round her shoulders, catching on a yellow dress. She's as close as Nancy's gotten to a friend. In memories of her childhood, Delen is always there. Callum's company was forced on her. Delen was the only child who played with her when she crossed into the village, the others scattering when they saw her, shouting names and laughing. Delen's father had been good with tools and had built two rocking horses from a fallen ash. He would set them up in the goose yard and Delen and Nancy would sit on them, side by side, and ride all morning. Nancy would make up stories based on Pel's books and together they'd fight monsters, ride with the Wild Hunt, go adventuring. As they'd grown up, the friendship had stayed, though they didn't ride together anymore. Nancy visited less than she should but her friend was always there. Though Nancy had not seen her friend since Delen's mother had died. Had been killed. Now, faced with her, she is braced to be sent on her way. Delen looks out from the doorway. Her eyes, sunken from lack of sleep, take in her visitor slowly, carefully, before breaking into a grin and sighing.

'Mother's doing,' she says wearily, nodding her head at the pile by Nancy's feet. 'Though she stopped halfway, "something's better than nothing," she said. She never could see anything through.' She looks up to the chapel hill, the top obscured by rain. 'She should have left them in. Or taken them all out, I suppose. You'd best come in.' She withdraws into the dark doorway and placing a lime caked coin back on the step

Nancy smiles, wildly grateful this door has not been closed and follows her friend inside, Patroclus left whining on the porch.

Nancy takes a breath as she steps inside.

The air is thick with smoke, acrid and sweet, the tang of the peat sticks in the throat, the turf burning thick under root-tangled skimmies. Above, in the large open hearth, hangs an iron kettle, base blackened with smoke and singing softly. It is in front of this that Nancy sits, directed by Delen. The chairs are low, a vain attempt to keep heads below the smoke line and Nancy sits uncomfortably, coughing in the smog. She's grown used to Pel's house, to the luxury of burning wood. Delen bustles behind her, in no hurry to sit and talk, busy shaping a loaf. When she is done, she opens a small clay hatch, built into the side of the fireplace, and places the bread inside. She sits.

'Pel sent you, did he? Finally doing something to help?'

Nancy bristles.

'No, I've come alone. Pel is,' she pauses, 'away, up country.'

Delen scoffs and rakes back the turf on the fire, exposing glowing embers.

'We're friends, Nancy, this hasn't changed that but you must see why folk are angry.'

The kettle's low song rises to a whistle, and she unhooks it, makes them tea. Nancy sips, then breaks the silence.

'I'm sorry about your mother, Delen. But I need to ask you about her. Do you know why she was... chosen?' Nancy picks her words with care, blackberries from the brambles.

Ignoring the unanswered question, Delen replaces the kettle, places damp peat over the embers, and sits back in her chair. She doesn't look at Nancy, focusing her eyes on the fire.

'No, Nance. I don't. I don't know why she was out there, even. She never went onto the moor. Terrified of the moor, mum was since Dad went. Scared of snakes. You know that.'

Nancy remembered Delen's father, Robert, brought to Pel with the bite. An adder, dozing in morning sun and not expecting a turf cutter's spade to fall so close. In the shock of it, Robert had driven his spade through the snake's neck, but the damage was done. Nancy remembers skinning the snake, passing the still-warm scales to Pel to wrap around the wound, but it had been too late.

'I'm sorry, Delen. How had she been since Robert passed?'

'As fine as is proper. She was glad to have me, I think. And she had the Reverend.'

At the mention of Cleaver, Nancy lifts her head. She'd known Hedra Rowe, Delen's mother a little. She'd not struck her as one of his.

'Aye, I know. I'd not have guessed it either,' Delen laughs, 'but after Dad, she found something there, up on the hill. She'd been going each week. I didn't hold much truck with it, but it made her happy. Didn't do her any good in the end though.'

Nancy frowns at her cup, the dark tea almost gone, leaves swirling in the bowl.

'Did you know Callum, Delen? Were you friends?'

Delen frowns. Sips her tea.

'Was anyone friends with Callum, Nancy? No, I had little to do with him. Always staring, that one. Mother used to say he put the wind up her, sitting at the lych gate watching her come and go. She looked after him when he was a boy. She was there when Pel cut the caul from him, the night Cleaver's wife died.'

Nancy nods, as much to herself as Delen, and moves to set down her tea.

'Is there nothing else you can think of that was odd about your mother's death? Aside from the obvious.'

Delen looks down, thinking.

'Only one thing, when the Reverend spoke. Not at the funeral, but after she'd been brought back from the bog. He said she'd been found with a charm. Here.'

Delen stands and heads to the rear of the smoky dark room. When she returns, it's with a small black velvet pouch tied with red string. Delen motions to Nancy to hold out her hand and into it she tips a pile of tiny bones, and a snake skull.

'He said it was protection, from snakebite. But she was terrified of them. I don't think she'd have had even a part of one on her. She had charms, of course, never could stick to one thing. That little brass horse Pel gave her for her back, sure. This though? I can't see it. The Reverend went on something awful about it, took it very personally indeed.'

Nancy examines the little heap, bones jumbled in her palm. It doesn't feel right. Pel made things like this sometimes, when asked. But this wasn't his work: it was clumsy, ill-made, like the nonsense sold by mountebanks in towns, toys for credulous tourists.

'Can I keep this, Delen?' The girl nods. 'Thank you, if I can help ever, or Pel, when he's back, please do ask.' Nancy stands, remembering at the last moment to bow her head, to avoid the beams. Delen stands too and opens the door, smoke billowing out into the rain, still falling heavily. At the far side of the yard, from the goose hole in the wall Patroclus rises and yawns, the evicted goose honking furiously beside him.

'You don't need an excuse, Nancy. Just come and see me. The old horses are still in the shed—we can go riding. Or you can buy us a round at the Nest. Whichever.' Delen stands in the doorway arms crossed against the cold and she smiles, it fades in the face of Nancy's own strained face. Sighing she pulls Nancy into a hug. 'Be Safe, Nance. I miss you. Go steady on the moor.' She pulls away and steps back into the doorway.

'The Reverend's right: it's dangerous. I'd not like to hear you'd come to trouble. Are you heading home now?'

'No, I'm off to speak to Kenwyn. He's waiting at the Nest.'

'Wish him well from me. He's the only other now, isn't he? Tom and Bronwen gone. It's funny, I know they're gone, but I can see them so clearly. The two of them and mother, sat pretending to read their Bibles by the fire. I wonder if the Reverend knew they couldn't read when he gave them?'

Nancy stops halfway across the yard, ripples radiating across the submerged mud and stone.

'The Reverend told me they'd been up there. Can't imagine a stranger trio!'

Delen laughs.

'The picture of piety! Those two old heathens! It's enough to tempt you up there on a Sunday, just to see what the fuss is.'

Nancy looks to the pile of objects sat waterlogged at the door. Every home has them, charms bound right into the stone.

'Will you put them back?' she tilts her head towards them and Delen frowns.

'Do you think I should? There's plenty left in there. Mum wanted them out, didn't think Cleaver approved.'

Nancy bites her cheek, worried.

'I don't know, Delen. I think perhaps you should leave it for now. Stay off the moor.'

'I will, Nance, don't worry about me. Maybe it's time for a change after all. I've been thinking of going to the services. The Reverend thinks I'd benefit.'

'Just stay at home. For now. Please.'

Delen looks quizzically at Nancy and goes inside, shutting out the questions with the rain. Nancy is so deep in thought that as she walks out of the yard, she doesn't see Calder's youngest son Yestin stood before her and walks right into his oilskin coat, into the stink of sweat and lanolin. He jumps and, cross with himself, turns embarrassment to anger.

'Mind yourself, Miss Bligh.' The man is not the force his brothers are, this hat fits poorly, and when Patroclus growls low and fierce the farmer's son puts up his hands in surrender. Nancy moves laughing from his path when both dart their eyes upwards at a roll of thunder. Nancy catches the youngest Calder's eye.

'You're better than this, Yestin.' She forces a smile and leads the dog away. As she walks back to the Nest, she can hear him knocking, hears Delen open the door. The rain takes the rest of the conversation away.

SHE DOES NOT knock at the back door of the inn but pushes straight through. She finds them sitting in the back bar. At the largest table are three men. At the centre, Kenwyn Gunner, looking older than his sixty years. Closely flanked by Calder's older sons Jan and Luk; it was their brother she had met outside. Little redemption in Yestin's siblings. Luk, the oldest, sits to the right. Jan, his brother's shadow and just as dark, on the left. The two brothers sit close to Kenwyn, pressing him between their huge shoulders like a cider apple waiting to be crushed. At the bar, Madge looks on nervously, apologetically.

'We heard you wanted a word,' says Luk. His brother stays silent. Nancy takes a step forward, her hand resting on Patroclus's head, the old dog tensed and ready.

'With Kenwyn, yes. Not with you.'

The brothers look at each other.

'Mr Gunner is a hard worker. Dad wanted us to look out for him. Make sure he wasn't upset.'

Kenwyn Gunner starts to speak, but as soon as his mouth opens both brothers straighten, their broad frames squeezing the breath from the old man's lungs. Nancy sits opposite them, carefully arranges her hands, and turns to Madge.

'Will you fetch some drinks, Madge, please?'

The landlady starts to object, but meeting Nancy's eye she withdraws, a glace over her shoulder as she goes. Nancy does her best to avoid the mocking eyes of the Calders, and keeps her gaze firmly fixed on the old man trapped between them.

'Kenwyn, I just wanted to ask about your son, about Harvey.' Kenwyn glances at his guards nervously, but Nancy continues. It will take more than this to stop her. 'I've been speaking to Delen, she told me about Hedra, about Bronwen and Tom too. Harvey had been going to the chapel too, hadn't he?'

'Yes, he—'

'And what if he was?' Luk interrupts, leaning forward. 'Kenwyn should be proud to have a God-fearing son. To have a boy with the sense to turn away from your fairytales, from your devils in the bogs.'

Jan, caught up in the pantomime, chimes in. 'Should have turned further!'

Luk glares at his younger brother, who does not speak again. Nancy takes a deep breath. She has dealt with these two before. Many times. Unwelcome hands and stupid mouths. It takes resolve not to hurt them.

'Kenwyn. Was there anything found with him, with Harvey?' She pulls the velvet pouch from a coat pocket, places it on the table. 'This was with Hedra. According to Cleaver.'

'A pin! A lead rose! Weren't his though, he'd gone to Pel for something or other, but it was a feather he gave him I... ' In his eagerness to speak, the old man has leant forwards, a mistake. In a pincer movement the brothers shift their seats, crushing the old man's waist between them. He heaves out a grunt, there is pain in his eyes.

'A shame, that,' says Luk. It is not clear if he means Kenwyn's actions or his own. Reaching into her pocket, Nancy takes hold of the little silver case and bites back a smile. *So nearly not brought.* She opens the lid. She can feel its inmate scuttle out and over her hand, and out of her pocket.

'A dreadful shame,' Jan smiles. 'If only he'd been a little more devout, he might still be with us.' At this, Luk jabs a fist into his brother's ribs and glares ferociously at him. Jan drops his head and mutters something Nancy can't hear. There is a silence and then the brothers rise together, Kenwyn Gunner pinned between them. The beetle, resident of Nancy's silver case, its iridescent shell glinting green in the light, scurries across the floor. Patroclus watches it with interest as it climbs up Jan Calder's trouser leg and into his pocket.

'Be careful on your way home Miss Bligh. The moors are dangerous these days.' Luk does not show any sign of emotion as he speaks. Jan dips his head, he doesn't look at her, and the three of them move back out into the storm. Nancy follows, stands in the doorway and watches as they load Kenwyn into an uncovered cart, brought round by Yestin sat holding the reins. There is a muttering between the brothers and Nancy catches Delen's name amongst the whispers and hopes they won't punish the girl for speaking to her.

As they drive off, water cascading from the feet of the horses, from the wheels of the cart, Nancy waves at Kenwyn. The old man smiles thinly back, and they're gone. Nancy watches the cart roll off and out of the village, watches with a smile at the sound of an axle snapping and the cart tipping Jan out into the morass of mud and water. Nancy watches long enough to see Yestin help old Kenwyn down and into the shelter of a barn before helping his brothers repair the cart.

Pel wouldn't approve, she thinks. The bad-luck beetle wouldn't cause any real harm, and it would move on from Jan eventually. Ideally onto each of his brothers. Nancy allows herself a smile before patting Patroclus and sitting back down at the table.

Madge walks back into the room, places a small glass with amber liquid clinging to its sides. Pel's drink. Nancy takes it like a draught, coughing at the harshness of the liquor.

'Thanks, Madge. Calder's done a job raising those three hasn't he?'

'Aye Nance. He's a cruel streak of clever in him, old Calder, though it seems the clever didn't pass to the sons. Don't let them shake you. How was Delen?'

Nancy places the empty glass on the tabletop, the warmth of the drink running through her, blooming in her chest.

'Well, Madge, she was well.' She's certain she can trust Madge, but something in her knows it's best to keep some thoughts to herself. 'Madge, you were the last to see Sal, weren't you?'

The old landlady shifts in her seat, eyes filled with tears.

'Yes, Nance. He was in, the night it happened. Sat in the corner seat with Mary. I know what you're asking, there was nothing about him, no sign. He seemed as happy as he always was.'

'And when he left, he went with Mary?'

Madge lowers her head.

'No, Nance. He went alone. Before Mary. It's funny, he'd not had all that much to drink but he came over dour suddenly. Seemed keen to get home. I wish I'd stopped him, but how was I to know?'

Nancy reaches across the table and places her hand over her friend's.

'You did nothing wrong. Whatever this is, I'm beginning to think none of us could have stopped it. Not at the start. The key, the charm, the one the Reverend found. Had you seen him with it?'

Madge furrows her brow in thought.

'No, he was a good boy, Sal. I know he went to chapel, but he'd not forgotten the folk, still left a little out for them, asked their help. But I'd not seen the key before. Not one of Pel's, was it?'

'No, Madge. It wasn't.'

Nance rises, shakes off a thought and calls Patroclus from his nap. Before leaving she walks into the main bar. Most of the men drinking there don't look up when she enters, won't notice when she leaves. Billy Askell back again and who by now should know better, smiles and raises a hand to her.

'Nancy! Good to see you.'

Nancy sighs. She has no time for Billy today. He is a sweet boy, but his interest in her and Pel has always been grating. Always with a new charm to show her, bought in town and protecting him against nothing but good sense.

'And you, Billy. I don't have time to stop I—'

'Oh, I know, Nancy, I've heard all about it.' He gestures to the bar and Nancy wonders who he has been talking to, as not one man in here gives him so much as a glance. 'Don't let me stop you, and don't worry, I'm taking care of myself!' he holds up a string of rowan berries he must have made himself and looped around his neck. 'Perhaps, once you're done, you could let me buy you something to drink?'

Nancy closes her eyes and breathes before answering.

'Thank you, Billy, that's a kind offer but I'm very busy. Perhaps another time.'

Billy smiles and turns back to his drink. Remfry Doble lifts his head to speak to Billy.

'Wrong tree to bark up, lad. She's an odd one, our Miss Bligh. Though I can't deny a man would sort her out, I don't see you being the one to do it. A firmer hand than you've got on you needed there. Ideas above her station.'

There is a growl of assent from the other drinkers. Mumbled statements met with laughter. Billy smiles along with them, though his eyes have missed the joke.

Nancy pays them no mind, returns to her investigation. She looks at the corner seat, sees the bullseye glass in the window next to it. The world beyond is warped like a roiling sea, and she can barely make out the twisted blackthorn visible through it.

'What did you see, Sal?' Nancy mutters under her breath.

OUTSIDE, NANCY MOUNTS Selkie once again, guiding the horse out of the warmth of the stable. The rain falls as heavily as it did when she arrived, and Nancy shields her face to see Madge standing at the door, watching.

'Do be careful, Nancy,' Madge shouts, the rain beating loud on the slate. 'I don't like this, none of it.'

Nancy smiles at her and waves. The sun breaks from behind the clouds and Nancy rears Selkie up, rain beating a bright halo around them before hooves crash down, and they are away. Horse, girl, and dog racing into a gold-grey storm.

They are almost home when it happens. The upturned hull of the boat floats on the horizon. The ground wetter than before, they ride in the valley through the remaining unburnt gorse. Nancy feels it before she sees it. The air prickles, her skin feels like nettle leaves have been raked across it. She hears him then, his voice weaving between raindrops, carried on the wind.

'Old Pel's gone, little Nancy, he's left you here with me.'

Nancy sets her jaw. Swallows rising terror.

'Go away, Cutty.' She closes her eyes, imagines Pel, channels him. 'I've no time for you now, you'll be dealt with later.'

Laughter crackles.

'Poor little Nancy, I'll be quick, don't worry! I'll send you to see him, I know where he is. Besides, can't you feel it, in the storm? My master's let the Hunt out. Better me than them, I promise you that.'

Nancy shivers. *He's lying,* she thinks. *He wouldn't send the Hunt. It's madness.* A lead weight across her shoulders. *As mad as releasing Bluecap, as mad as releasing Cutty.* She sees Cutty then, running low to the ground through a warren of gorse, following her. She has a decision to make, she knows it. She can't cast spells and stick to the road; she can't fight and keep running. She could use her gifts. She can feel them like tremors, rising through her. But she promised Pel, and the boat is so close she can smell the smoke rising from the chimney. She looks down at Patroclus. The dog hears him, too. She can tell.

'With me, boy, stay with me.' Pat looks up at her voice, he's unused to hearing a tremor in it and then puts his head down, keeping pace. She decides. She won't use the Murmur; she will do what she can without. Reaching again into her pocket she draws out the rowan berries and drops them in the road behind her, muttering a short phrase. She can't cast spells and ride, but these trinkets are like spring-traps, the magic already set. Activated by fresh water, they burst into a tangle of mountain ash. She hears the sprite curse as he is enmeshed between them. It will not hold him for long. She does not look round, but her head fills with the shape of him: his sickle claws, his powerful muscles. She takes a deep breath to try and steady her racing pulse, the flush of fear that is spreading across her chest. One hill between them, one final push. Selkie's ears are flat against her head, foam flecks at her mouth.

'Good girl, nearly home, nearly home.' Nancy tries so hard to ignore the fleetfoot shape reappearing at the corner of her eye.

Then the horse is gone from under her and she's falling.

She lands hard, but somehow, amazingly, she has landed well and rolls to a stop in a foot of water. Her head whips around and her heart is beating so loudly she can't, for a moment, make sense of anything she sees. Every shape, every movement the death of her. Every glint of sun on rain a razor coming for her throat. She forces the panic down, presses hard against it as though it was a physical barrier. Stows it deep within. She sees the horse struggling to right herself a few feet away, a crimson gash across her left flank. With a last kick, Selkie is up and racing, bloodied and frantic over the hill to home. Patroclus has braced, his shaggy wet head looking quickly about him, searching for the source of the laughter that has somehow drowned out the rain.

Pushing herself to her feet, Nancy tries to clear her mind, to make the shapes with her hands that might save her. She has barely formed a defensive spell when he charges, his curlew claws raking against her cheek. She tastes blood. But the spell holds; with a crack of static, she sees him fly from the path, rolling into the undergrowth with a splash. Panting now, she looks back to the boat. The rain grows heavier with every passing second, the thunderclaps louder and she swears she can hear the blowing of a horn. She calls to Pat, barking in the downpour.

'Come on boy, home!' He is racing to her when Cutty is back on them, leaping onto the old dog, digging curved claws into his coat like the spurs of an infernal jockey. Patroclus howls and gnaws furiously at his shoulder, twisting and falling. Cutty Soames leaps before teeth meet flesh and he's lost again in the gorse, a forest of it at the path side.

'Get up, Pat!' Nancy screams through the water and the old dog lifts himself and limps to her side. She puts her hand on his sides, frantically searching for the wound, but in the rain her hands just froth the blood into a foam that matts into the dog's coat. Her breaths are loud and shallow in her ears, the panic so high now that she is barely able to move. Her muscles locking as she thinks of it. She can hear Cutty running, hears the gorse wood breaking. Pel's heavy woollen coat is all soaked through, weighing her down.

'Would you like to see your master, dearie?' The imp cackles as he runs and the sound of his laughter is enough to drive her upwards, forcing through the fear that stopped her moving.

Nancy pulls Patroclus along by his collar, willing him to move just a little faster. The boat is so close, they can make it.

Another sound. Something else is here and gaining fast.

Nancy runs through images in her mind, was Cutty telling the truth? Is it the Hunt? No. She's read the stories—those aren't hoof beats. *So then, who is it? Who else is free?* A childhood reading the diaries of Keepers, of Pel, has led to no shortage of horrors to choose from. The Sea-Queens? Howling Jenny? Jack of the Nails or Pick-up-sticks? She can barely cope with Cutty, she can't take another.

'Who's there?' Cutty's heard them too. 'She's mine, damn your eyes! Stay back, I'll have you next!' She can hear fear in the devil's voice. He shouldn't be scared of anything from below.

Head down, Nancy, keep running. She sees Cutty from the corner of her eye, his talons slicing through raindrops but his head keeps darting back. *He's scared*, she thinks, and images of rats backed into corners fill her mind. *Oh, Nance, don't you dare die here.* She laughs suddenly.

'Oh Gods, Pel, I'm sorry.' She throws off the coat and it lands heavily, wetly in the mud. But without it she's a little faster, her dress sticking to her, boots full of water as she runs. Her sweat runs cold under the rain and yet she feels her whole body burning. She hears the scampering tread of Cutty approach until he's alongside her, tenses herself for a fight, then he's running past. Not a look over his shoulder, not a word not a sneer. Nancy almost trips her body shakes so much. She can hear the running steps of a man. Gaining on them both. The muscles in her neck are locked, she cannot turn round to see, so she focuses on the shape of Cutty, a silhouette in the downpour and then, as the rain reaches a tempest peak— he's gone, Cutty is gone. Snatched from between the raindrops. There is no sound, nothing following just the clatter of rain. Nancy stops, listens.

Nothing.

Raindrops hitting puddles. That is all.

She is dazed, the moment only broken by a whimper from Pat, his white coat running red where it oughtn't do.

'Oh, boy, I'm sorry, come on we're almost home.'

A splash as she turns and she's screaming. Landing heavy at her feet and still jerking, the last dying electric twitch still skittering through nerves, is Cutty Soames, the terror of the moor. Dead. His body, that had terrified her seconds before, that tight, balled up rock of muscle is now a husk smouldering in the rain, burnt from the inside out and the back of his head is gone. As though whatever bile filled him had heated to such astounding temperature it had to vent. On his chest, still white hot though cooling fast, the precise imprint of a hand.

Nancy's mouth feels dry, even in the rainstorm. She cannot move, again her muscles have locked beneath her. Dread fills her body, wraps her in a heavy cloak and it is with difficulty that she turns. She can barely see it through the rain, but there is a shape stood in the gorse. The broken shape of a man, his right hand sizzling as the rain hits it. She can't make out his face but something, deep within her, curdles at the sight of him. She feels sick.

'Who's there?' Nancy forces out a shout, no reply. The figure, the man, takes a step forward. Patroclus whines again, whimpers like a puppy.

'Answer me!' Her voice cracks.

Still the figure marches on.

'I'm not afraid.' Her voice is so quiet, the raindrops wash away the lie.

Nancy squints, but the rain is so heavy now she can barely keep her eyes open. The thunderstorm must be directly above her. The crash of it is deafening, the flashes coming quicker than she's seen before. The sky itself feels low, the black clouds within reach. The fear she felt for Cutty has nothing on this. Every atom of her itches for freedom, as though, were she to let it happen, her whole being would tear itself apart rather than face what's coming.

She feels the Murmur. It tugs within and offers its help, but she stills its voice. Something in the way the figure moves towards her is familiar. Hungry. She'll not see it fed.

Quietly, urgently, she holds Patroclus, walks him steadily back towards the boat, always with the figure in view. She almost cries with relief when she steps into the brook that runs rings around Pel's home, feels behind herself for the slatted board sides of the boat.

The figure stops at the edge of the stream and screams into

the wind. It breaks her, that scream, and she turns, bundling the dog before her through the door and into the boat. She spends the night clutching Patroclus in the centre of the floor. Outside, she can hear it, pacing. At some point, she does not know when, there is a thud. The front door shakes and then there is silence. The rain that has beaten down all day stops suddenly, the wind drops. The thunder erupts with a final crash. Nancy collapses exhausted where she sits and there's nothing more 'til morning.

FROM THE BARROW at the base of Lullaby Tor, the tomb forgotten, covered in soil and grass, they burst. An eruption of black fire. The storm the herald of their arrival. Blown through the Undermoor and up into the world above. The horn call lost on the wind, but the scent picked up. The hounds sent out.

The Wild Hunt rides again.

SULPHUR TUFT

A SOUND ABOVE like nails on a chalkboard. The sky is a patchwork of ripples, circles within circles as raindrops strike it from the moor above.

Pel watches, turns, then walks steadily across the Undermoor. Time slips through him; he loses track of days, and the hill seems no closer than it did when he started. As he walks, he sees more clearly the decay and rot of the landscape. Sees the ragged leaves on the plants, on the trees, sees the dark mires that bubble up between stems of burnt grass. The colours, those purples, pinks, and reds, echoes of a putrefying wound. Flesh rotting in the sun. There is a stench to it. There's something wrong, too, about the creatures that scamper out of his way. He has not seen a single one stand still, but he's seen their ragged limbs disappearing into undergrowth, their bruised backs and torn wings. He had expected some to talk to him, to recognise him from above. But nothing seems keen to be out in the open. He's not seen the two that met him here again either. Though he can hear them now and then and suspects they never wander far.

'This is not my fault.' He mutters it mostly for his own benefit but can't help shooting accusatory looks to any creature about to challenge him on it. The words of the two spirits, jumbled though they were still stick in his head. 'A storm,' they'd said, and certainly this place looked windswept, broken.

As they have done since he arrived, his hands reach out for comfort, for a cane, for a dog. Each time meeting empty air.

'You're not so old yet, Keeper,' Pel growls to himself, eyes darting, but his frailty is showing. He sets his jaw, steels himself and walks. Confidence has got him this far. It can take him to the end. He is on a plain now, wide and rolling. The grass short and cropped, small white flowers snaking through.

'Watch your step, Pel!'

The voice in his ear startles him and distracted, head twisting to see the speaker, he does not see the cow. Its flank black and shining with sweat. The calm day he walked through gone, it is a torrent now, a wind-driven fine rain that soaks him. Twisting to avoid the creature, he falls.

'You tried, brother.'

'Did my best.'

'You have the devil of a smile, brother.'

'You and me both.'

Ignoring Gog and Magog, whose shadows he can now make out in the downpour, Pel sits in the waterlogged grass and peers through half closed eyes at the emerging shapes. More cattle, raindrops bouncing off their flanks as they pass into the downpour then gone. He gets steadily to his feet and looks about. There are hundreds of cows now. Huge, broad shoulders with tree trunk necks and horns that stretch an oar-span either side of their heads. Their hooves and horns gilded, shining under the moonlight and a ring through every nose. The herd binds Pel in their spell. The beasts move with indifference past him, golden hooves sinking into the sodden ground. As the herd passes, the enchantment fades and Pel shrinks back. On closer inspection some of the cattle are emaciated, nothing but skin stretched tight over bone. To the rear of the herd not even that—skeletal beasts, their bright horns glowing against the white of their skulls, rain running through eye sockets, dripping from ribs. They are lowing now, mournful, and strong, filing either side of Pel as the rain grows heavier, striking the ground and the backs of the cattle and exploding into a mist.

A shape appears.

'Out of the way, Keeper.'

The voice comes from high up, and Pel scans about for a hill, for some perch the speaker must sit on. And there, look. A shadow looming, a moving tower, and with a hard and driving squelch, a tree is pressed into the ground next to Pel, knocking him back.

'Out of my way, I said.'

Pel looks up and through the vapour, the tower squats, two anthracite eyes in a boulder head, long arms leaning on the beech tree staff. Pel knows this face. Gow. Last of the old giants. Man-eaters. Not like the old fellows he had last laid down to sleep. A rush of adrenaline runs through him, the ghost of his younger self. The felling of Gow his last great deed. Years ago, he had crowed about it. He remembers how it felt. Gow had killed young Kit Green, his body—what was left—washed up in the silt of the tinnery, eaten away by fishes. But there had been tooth marks on the bones.

'Gow,' Pel glowers through the downpour, a smile playing on his lips. 'A cowherd now, are you?'

The giant grimaces, lips parting like a mudslide.

'Yes, Keeper. And I was happy with it. But seeing you? Well, old habits rise.' Gow's hand reaches towards Pel, fingers outstretched. Pel crouches. He does not know his limits here.

Quietly Pel forms a shape, and a light breeze blows through the rain. The sky ripples. 'Fine,' he thinks, 'good.' He reaches down with his left hand and digs his fingers into the odd, pink grass, digs nails into purple ground. He digs his right thumb into his temple and flicks upwards, hard, as if it were a match striking and the sky erupts with thunder. Keeper and Giant stop, withdraw their hands. Neither did this. Gow looks up at the sky eddying above them, and there is fear in his eyes.

'You are lucky, little man. You are here under His sufferance. I would take payment for what you've done. For what you failed to stop.' Gow looks sadly at the corpse-cows filing by. At their ragged flanks.

'What do you mean, Gow?'

The giant's coal-dusted eyes turn towards Pel. It is hard to tell in the falling rain but some of the drops hold salted water, squeezed from stony eyes.

'You had one job, the only job a Keeper has. And you failed. Balance, Pel. What happened to balance? Now, out of my way. Pray we don't meet again.'

Pel looks up at the giant, as he straightens his back, the Keeper barely abreast with his shin. This will not stand.

'Gow, you coward, don't you walk away! How do I reach the grove? Gow!'

But the giant is standing now, adjusting his staff. Pel balls a fist, wishes he had his cane. He might not need it to walk down here but it had other uses.

'Gow! Answer me!'

From high above, Gow spits out a reply.

'Just keep walking, Pel. You'll be seen when he allows it. And then get gone. You've caused enough damage here. The Hunt rides again, to fix what you couldn't with beatings and blood. You're no use to us, old man.' And the giant strides over the Keeper, his steps and the strike of his staff shaking the ground as he goes, disappearing into the mist and the rain.

'Gow! What do you mean? The Hunt are free? Speak you monster!'

Pel stands alone, bone-soaked and howling at the wind.

COLT'S FOOT

Nancy dreams of starlings. They ball and pulse above the moor. A thousand. A million. And she is at their centre. They swarm with one ear cocked. Listening for her song. It is beautiful, it is powerful, she sweeps them across the grass and tor tops, twisting the murmuration into intricate shapes. A sailing ship. A beating heart. Mirecoombe appears on the horizon, and she swoops down to see. But one by one the birds turn away. Close themselves off from her instruction. And they hit the village like a scourge. Birds shattering through windows, breaking slates, the sheer weight of bodies pulling down walls and grinding hills flat. When the flock has passed by, she is left. Sitting alone. In a patch of moor scrubbed clean of life. The grass and rocks covered in the dust of houses, sand from windows ground down. All bound together with a paste of blood and bone. Across the mulch six horsemen come riding. A pack of dogs at their heels.

Wind howls down the chimney, rippling the ash. Waking with a start, Nancy gasps in the morning air. She is tired. The sleep she has woken from was one of necessity, not rest, her body recovering from its flight. Looking across the room she sees Patroclus sat bolt upright and staring at the door, ears flat against his shaggy head, matted blood dried to a crust in his coat. She'd never woken and not found him asleep. Rising, she shrugs off the still damp dress she has slept in and shivers, though it is warmer out of it, and rummages through

Pel's drawers, finding a pair of regimental trousers – dark blue with a red stripe down the leg, and a shirt that when tucked into the high waist of the trousers fits well enough, red suspenders in an 'x' across her back. Rolling up the sleeves, she crosses to the dog.

'Oh, my love, you poor brave boy.' Patroclus turns his head from the door with an effort. He does not want to leave his post, but Nancy's ministrations appeal to his deep love of attention and he folds at last, nuzzling his head into her lap. Nancy carefully peers through his coat, gently assesses the cuts beneath with her hands and draws in a gasp.

'Well now, you've been in the wars. Let's sort you out, Pat.' It is a forced practicality she draws on. Her tears a blink away. She turns to find help, but a bowl of water and a jar of salve are already waiting in reach. Mouthing a 'thank you' to the shadows, Nancy administers to the wounds on the dog. Packing the cuts with salve, sewing up each ragged hole.

'I'm sorry boy, I'm sorry.' Patroclus pushes his heavy head into her side, forgiveness, she hopes. Pel would have kept his dog safe. She grips the dogs coat, pulls him close taking care not to press on his side.

When she is done, Patroclus's coat washed free of blood, Nancy stands and approaches the door. Her muscles stiffen, and it takes everything to keep moving. Whatever was with her in the storm, she knows it killed Salan. Killed all of them. Patroclus whines as she approaches the handle and as the door opens, he's up and barking at the empty space revealed. There is nothing there but moorland stretching empty with the day. A clean winter sun burning the water from the ground, low-lying mist rising up from moist soil. A curlew calls and Nancy jumps. It is a beautiful, menacing morning. She takes a step out but stops short as her bare feet touch something thick and furry and damp. Pel's coat lies crumpled on the doorstep, the wet stain on the wood of the door still marking its impact.

Gingerly Nancy lifts it by the collar, shakes it out. When the still, cold body of Cutty Soames tumbles out, she isn't surprised. Something is playing with her. With all of them.

Patroclus lies down heavily on his bed, old legs giving out, exhausted, after his vigil. Nancy lays Cutty's body on the table, then drapes Pel's coat to dry in front of the fire. She checks the pockets, the contents still there but something else, too: a bundle of gorse sticks wrapped with string. She throws it onto the fire with a shiver where it crackles and spits, the gorse oils catching and burning with black smoke, then the whole cursed thing is gone. A reminder of the fire, perhaps? Or a warning of another.

'What do we do with him, Pat?' Cutty seems small laid out on the desk, eyes closed, curlew bill claws blunted in death. His body is fragile to the touch. Whatever burnt him did a fine job of it. Where the hand touched is now a hole, perfectly shaped, the flesh beneath turned to ash and blown away. The rest of his body a black carbonised shell. Nancy lays her right hand over the imprint, her long fingers lost in the size of it. Her left hand she lays on the cheek of Cutty Soames's burnt face. He is the size of a child, and with his cruel face, his pointed ears and crooked smile burnt away that is how he looks now. Neither spriggan nor pixie, Cutty was one of the creatures that were entirely their own. A special kind of monster. But he was a man once. A child, once.

'Who scares a nightmare, little Cutty?' The answer scratches at the base of her spine and no matter how hard she tries to brush it away the shivers keep on coming.

She's still shaking when the brownies emerge from the shadows, gesturing towards the corpse.

'You want to take him?'

The spirits nod, reach for Cutty. Nancy looks to the dog for answers he's unable to give and turns away from the table. She hears the body as it slides into the brownies' arms, hears them scuttle away. When she turns back, he's gone. The fear however, remains.

'Enough of this.' Nancy presses the fear into diamond anger. 'Cutty was a monster, but we should have handled him. Sent him back below. He didn't need to die, nobody needed to die.' She reaches for a large book, towards the rear of the shelf, and opens it at a point halfway through. She lays it on a raised stand, kept at the back of the desk, and lifts the copper clips over its pages, keeping her place. She's seen Pel do this before, but she needs to be certain, so she'll follow the steps.

From a drawer she takes a brass ink stand, shaped like an ewer but without a spout, its little brass lid held fast with a hinge and clasp. On the side, symbols and complex lines of verse in Greek and Latin are etched. She lifts the lid and looks inside; it is full, the mirror-black surface of the ink shining in the morning light. Good. Pel always did like to keep things ready.

Next, she crosses to the stern of the boat, where an old map cabinet holds myriad goods. In a wide, flat drawer she finds sticks of incense, heady even when unlit, and a holder made from ivory and shaped like a small capuchin monkey. The ivory's creamy white blackened by years of smoke, small ruby eyes shining from its face. She had always loved this, had pestered Pel as a child to play with it. He had never let her. Placing the incense next to the inkwell she sits, thinks, looks at the small paws of the monkey as it clutches the cedar sticks.

Patroclus slumps at her side, lending silent and sleepy support.

'We need to know who he is, boy, the figure we saw yesterday, the man who killed Sal. Keep watch for me whilst I'm gone.' Patroclus yawns, but his eyes stay open.

Nancy lights the incense, and a heady, thick fog of smoke fills the boat. The smell is familiar to her, a blend Pel makes from wildflowers and a paste of bog-oak shavings, bound with gorse oil. It smells like the moor, burning. The smoke blots out the sunlight, draws the world close about her until all she knows is the desk in front of her and even Pat is lost at her feet. She has heard Pel, shrouded in this same smoke, speak the words needed. But she's never done this herself.

'Spirits, Masters of truth and deniers of falsehoods, hear me. Children of gorse, of peat and decay. Tor-spillers, cave dwellers. In this ink the world's reflection, in its darkness the abyss. Show me answers.'

The smoke thickens. The boat rattles and shakes as if caught in some great storm, rolling on a sea. Nancy can hear the waves break against the windows. She repeats her verse, holds her question in her mind: 'Who am I searching for. Who killed Salan Dell? Hedra Rowe? Cutty Soames?'

In a haze Nancy lifts her arm, heavy and sluggish, and she can barely move it to the task at hand. But she manages. She knocks the inkpot over, spilling the black liquid across the surface of the desk. After impact, the liquid does not run off, does not spill from the wood, but like mercury coalesces into a perfect circle. A reflective disc of darkness. Nancy stares into it, and the disc stares back. She concentrates, furrows her brow, and focuses on the shape she saw the day before, in the rain. Willing it to come into a greater clarity, for its face to be revealed.

The boat still shakes, in the kitchen pans fall from hooks.

The fire gutters in the grate and the smoke from the incense billows ever thicker. On the wall behind her, safe behind glass the wings of pinned butterflies twitch, strain against their mounts. Nancy stares deeper into the ink, sees a face.

'No, that's impossible.'

She shakes her head, tries again but the face remains. Jenkins, dead in the bog two months now, drowned following a calf. Did she and Pel miss something? Was he a victim? She tries to clear her mind, focus again, she does not want the dead, she wants the killer. But Jenkins remains, the boat shakes more violently, and she can hear a window break. Behind her the wings of the butterflies are beating harder now, the frames rattle on the walls and in the pool, Jenkins is joined by another.

'No! Please, show me the killer, show me who followed me!'

Nancy grips the desk with hands turned white with the effort. Next to Jenkins is Caleb Setch, killed by a corner post breaking free of a rope, the seven-foot pillar of granite pinning the boy into the mire. Dead the same month as Jenkins.

The butterflies flap wildly now, wings breaking on the glass of the case, bodies tearing from pins and bouncing around the frame, desperate for release. The smoke impenetrable, the only thing Nancy sees is the disc of black and the two faces in it, no—three—another emerges.

Hocken Darrow. Hocken Darrow who at eighty-three fell down dead walking back from the fields. Six people saw him fall. Eight weeks ago.

'Enough of this! Show me who I seek, spirit, show me!' Nancy is shouting now, the boat feels like it will lift, and objects are falling from shelves, glass bottles break and spill herbs and liquids across the floor.

'Show me!' Nancy screams it into the smog and another face begins to rise from the pool. It shifts and shakes, blurred and torn its mouth a gaping maw that seems to swallow the others, Jenkins, Caleb, and Hocken. The boat shudders as if broadsided by some giant frigate, the boards creaking, cracking with the weight of some unseen pressure. Shaking, Nancy stares into the pool, desperate to make sense of the shape. There is a flash, a crack of thunder that rolls around the boat as if the storm is inside now. Nancy hears herself screaming but cannot stop it. The butterflies, fevered and wild, beat themselves into dust that piles in iridescent heaps in the corner of the frames. There is a final crack, and behind Nancy the back window of the boat loses a diamond pane. The smoke clears through the gap. The ink, released from the spell, pours in rivulets onto the floor, and Nancy slides sideways from the chair. Exhausted, she looks at the devastation. Patroclus emerges from beneath the desk where he was hiding, coat matted with ink. Brownies stand in broken glass and wring their hands in the dust.

'Well, that never happened when Pel did this.' Nancy is dazed, laughing in the aftermath. Happy that she has some direction, something to work on. Something to hold over Pel, he'd never let her perform this ceremony before. 'Jenkins, Caleb, and Hocken. Whoever the other face belongs to, they have some part in this. I'm sorry, loves,' she smiles towards the brownies sweeping flagstones clear of glass, 'to leave such a mess. But we've work to do.' Crunching through the boat Nancy and Patroclus head out of the door.

THE JOURNEY ACROSS the moor is quiet. Nancy can't shake the faces from her mind. The three dead men. They had all died before the first of the murders. Before Delen's mother had been found six weeks ago.

The moor was a dangerous place, people died. There had been no inquest, no further thought given to the deaths than was warranted. Each buried, each mourned, each gone.

She did not relish what must come next.

Caleb and Jenkins were buried at the chapel; each turned to Cleaver before their end. But Hocken, he had never wavered. He sat with the rest in the pews at the holidays, at the feast day, but his faith stayed on the moor. When he had died, Cleaver had refused his body entry to the chapel yard. A pit had been dug to the west of Mirecoombe, into the peat banks at the base of the Queen's Rocks. A standing stone had been raised. That is where Nancy heads now.

The day is still dry, even a cold sun can wring the wet from the earth and though in patches water still seeps from the ground there is a warmth in the air. She sees the stone, rising from the peat, from across the valley. Pel had held the ceremony, had spoken the words. The flowers laid are faded now, the gorse wreaths dry and brittle. The ground beneath the stone still untouched by encroaching grass.

Dismounting from Selkie, Nancy draws a blanket, brought from the ship, about her shoulders. Pel's coat is still steaming by the fire. As she approaches the grave something breaks underfoot, not a stick or twig but something sturdier. Crouching, Nancy sees it is a pipe. White clay with a long stem and a bowl shaped like an acorn cup. Hocken's pipe. They had laid it on the grave after they'd interred him. There are other signs of disturbance, muddy marks in the grass, a wreath crushed underfoot.

'With me, Pat.' The dog sticks close to his mistress, nose down, hackles up. Nancy looks about, at the gorse bushes and thickets of blackthorn. Hocken had been a good friend to the moor. One of the last to remain faithful to it. He'd still have some watchers; she was sure of it. And she needs them.

'Out with you, please. I know you're there. It's for Hocken.'

A rustle, and two stony heads showing parapet from the bushes. Two spriggans, coal-dust eyes blinking at the girl and her dog. Nancy smiles broadly at them.

'Hello, you two,' Nancy knows these spirits, Clitter and Moorstone. 'I need your help if you'll give it.'

The pair look to one another and reply in unison, voices like rocks on a riverbed, like distant thunder.

'Why.'

Nancy pauses. No spirit has questioned her before, she's unused to the pushback.

'I know what you lost. What the fire took. I'm sorry. But I need you to bring him up. It's important.'

There is a muttered discussion between the two creatures and though Nancy cannot hear it, she gets the gist.

'I know dears, I know it's not right, but I need to see him.'

Clitter speaks, turning his rockfall head towards her.

'Once buried, shouldn't bring back. He's already on his way.'

'I know, I know. But I only need him for a moment then you can tuck him back in.'

Her thoughts turn to Pel. To the journey he's made. Moorstone speaks now, softer than his friend. Softer than before.

'Why?'

'Because I'm not certain he's dead.'

The pair look to each other and begin to dig. They are built for this, large hands scooping away the peat, sharp nails cutting like a turf spade. They burrow into the soft dark earth and disappear, the faint sound of digging rising out of the soil.

Smiling again, Nancy kneels, she has work to do too. From a saddlebag she draws out Pel's book, still damp but usable and turns to a page with violets pressed between it. Bleeding into the paper like blackberry stains. She loves Pel's book, his flowers. Each flower bound to a spell or ritual, the spidery writing around each a lock to their key. Violets are for protection. The task at hand is grim, unpleasant, and there are spirits loose that would be drawn to it like moths to a flame. Nancy traces fingers across the tissue paper petals and mouths an invocation. As she does a breeze blows and there is a pulse, beating slowly as if for a moment the world has a heartbeat, then it fades. Leaving the book open, Nancy turns back to the disturbed earth and steels herself for what comes next.

A spriggan on either side of him, Hocken Darrow rises from his grave.

Though only dead a few weeks, his face is sunken, the skin hanging off in rags. Eyelids closed, beneath them squirms maggots eating through what's left of his eyes. Nancy retches, and even Patroclus baulks at a closer inspection. Neither Clitter nor Moorstone will meet her eyes. This man is as dead as any corpse ever was. Swallowing hard, Nancy turns back to the body. His shroud, a white muslin now stained black with rot, hangs open across his front. Carefully she runs her hands over him, feeling gently his chest, his stomach.

'Why did I see you, Hocken?'

She mutters to herself as she searches. There must have been a reason. The ink had never led Pel astray. From her trouser pocket she pulls a silver chain with a weasel skull hanging from it, the chain running through the creature's empty eyes. Closing hers, Nancy holds the charm over the body.

'What do you see, little Galanthis, what am I missing?'

Eyes still shut, Nancy can feel it as the chain pulls taut. Feels it circle and tug. When the strain is at its strongest Nancy opens her eyes. The little skull, white teeth shining in bone, is pointing to the side of the body's abdomen, high on the left, beneath the ribs. Folding the charm away Nancy lays a hand on the skin, presses, feels about. The flesh, cold and fragile, feels wrong. There's something pressing against it that should not be there. With an effort, Nancy turns the body over, gasping as it rolls and hoping that nothing bursts, that the bones barely holding will not give way, will not give vent to the gases building inside. Hocken's back is as putrid as the front. The skin torn here and there. Nancy can see the spine poking through like skerries from the sea. But her attention is focused on the neat line of stiches closing a wound in the body's back. The edges pale and jagged though held neatly together with catgut threads.

Pel has been teaching Nancy anatomy since she was eight years old. This interests her. Hocken was dead when he hit the ground. People saw him fall. And this cut was made after the old man died, she is sure of it. The edges of the gash like raw chicken, bloodless, no thick black clots of blood, no stain on the skin.

Clitter and Moorstone draw closer now. Lean in. Watch as Nancy takes the knife from her pocket and opens the blade, cuts through the stiches one, two, three then the rest and prizes the flesh open.

'Straw.' She pulls it out in tufts, fresh enough though beginning to rot. Once the cavity is empty, she searches again. For an absence, for a loss. She holds in her head the diagrams in Pel's books, feels for the lungs, for the heart, for the kidneys for the... for the spleen. There is no spleen. The gap where it sat packed out with straw so no hollow would show. Sewn in to keep it in place. Sitting back on her folded legs Nancy wipes the rancid ichor from her fingers onto the grass.

'He is incomplete?'

Clitter speaks, tentatively, worriedly.

'Yes, he is. Someone has taken a part of him.' Nancy speaks quietly, eyes not leaving the body, and Clitter and Moorstone hang their heads. They know what it means to go below with a piece missing. What a person might become.

'We'll take him back,' the spriggans offer, 'we'll stay with him and keep him safe. Keep him away from danger. He was a friend.'

Nancy nods her assent, and the pair of spirits begin to agitate the soil, the vibrations admitting Hocken Darrow back to the mire, to the dark peaty soil. They pause in their work, frozen, eyes cast upwards. Nancy turns and follows their gaze. Her body locks. She can't move. The sky has lowered again. The dark clouds have returned but they are churning in a tight vortex of vapour and through it come galloping hooves. Between the wisps of cloud Nancy sees the muscular flanks of war horses, the legs of armoured riders who clash swords against shields. The clouds do not clear enough for her to see their heads, but she knows if they did, they would not be there. She can hear a hound pack baying higher in the sky. Cutty was right.

It is the Wild Hunt.

Nancy does not know what to do. The Hunt has not ridden out for centuries. Even Pel has never faced them. Their time is done. Her heart sinks.

'Who are you here for!' She shouts at the sky. They are a hunt after all. They have quarry. The familiar thunder begins again, the clatter of hooves. Through the clouds, trailing the soft wisps of the heavens with them, ten huge dogs fall and land heavily on the moor. The wish hounds. She can feel the ground shake with every paw. They are the size of small ponies. Their bodies lean and sharp like wolfhounds their coats thick and black and matted with grease and blood. Their necks are ringed with heavy, plate metal collars inscribed with cuneiform texts, each has a name tag with the writing scratched out. Their heads are heavy with teeth, their eyes alight with black flame that flickers blue in the sunlight.

Nancy does not move as the largest pads towards her. Sniffs at her and breathes hot, rancid breath on her face. Her heart beats furiously in her chest. Even the Murmur is cowed. The hound throws its head back and howls, the others in the pack follow suit and they bound into the landscape. Once they have gone, the clouds lift and their masters retreat. The dogs released, their job done, for now. Their warning, their announcement made. Clitter and Moorstone resume the burial, Moorstone shooting one last request as they disappear.

'Find the piece taken from him, Almost-Keeper, bury it. Give him rest.'

And the moor is quiet again, Nancy and Patroclus alone beneath the standing stone casting a shadow overhead. There is panic in Nancy's eyes, in her chest. This is getting beyond her. Beneath her arm pushes the warm nose of Patroclus, and she breathes a little easier again.

Focus on the job. Pel will help when he returns.

'Come on, boy. We need to see the others. We need to speak to Cleaver.'

HEMLOCK

THE SKY RIPPLES as Pel strides on, the landscape stinking of wet dog after the rain. Though he keeps the chapel hill and its grove of trees in his sight, always, the path keeps changing. Creatures appear and fade before him, hard to keep track of them all. And there are shapes in the shadows. There is rustling in the grass. He thinks of Gow. Remembers laying him low, dismembering his colossal limbs and dragging the pieces into the bog, watching them sink. No other way. Gow was a monster. A remnant of an early age too savage for the future. His shin bone hangs in the rafters of the boat. Pel had found it washed up on the mire shore years later. A souvenir.

As he walks the rot reveals more of itself, the ground belching sulphurous gas as he steps across it and seeping like a wound. He makes notes, mentally, for when he returns. He is the first Keeper to travel here, it will be important to record it for the next. For her.

Nancy is on his mind. He knows she thinks he should be in the village, grubbing in the mud for answers, but she'll see, when he returns, when he's fixed things here. The rest will settle down. She has a lot to learn before he's ready to pass the torch. He won't let her get burnt.

'She'll be fine, in the boat.' He talks out loud, it's a kind of spell. Built of hope and confidence.

'So sure, so foolish.'

Pel stops, he has had enough of voices appearing in his head.

'Who's there? At least do me the courtesy of talking to my face.'

'Down here, Keeper.'

Pel looks towards the sound and sees them. There is a pool, as black and peaty as the next, its surface slick with rainbows, like oil has been spilt. There are objects floating in it. Three of them. Pel steps closer and recoils at the sight, three eyeless heads, bobbing like apples. As he looks on, the centre head, its eyeless sockets peering above the waterline, rolls back and its mouth gurgles up out of the slime.

'Tell me, Keeper, have we met? Was it you who sent me here or another?'

'I... ' Pel starts but the head stops him.

'No matter. You're all one to us. Sisters! Wake now, girls.'

With an effort the two remaining heads roll back, the rancid flesh hanging off skulls black and shiny from the mire.

'A Keeper? Here? Well now. What to do?'

'If he's here, He'll know. Careful how we tread.'

'What is your name, Keeper? Tell us.'

Pel sets his mouth in a hard line and says nothing. He does not know these three and names should never be bandied about.

'Clever boy. No matter. You can have ours if you like, we've nothing to fear anymore. I am Kensa, sister to Nessa, sister to Tressa. We rode on stems of ragwort when Eluid reigned. Does his kingship hold?'

Pel smiles.

'No, sisters. It does not. A hundred have ruled since his flesh decayed. You have been here a long while.'

The heads grimace at this, rolling back and forth and setting the puddle boiling.

'Tell me sisters, how do I reach the throne?'

The head in the centre, Kensa, spits out her reply.

'You reach the throne when he sees fit to receive you. Our King.'

The last word carries extra spite, and the head rolls down again as if keen to wash out the taste. Pel crouches, leans close.

'Listen, sisters. I will speak with your King, God of this place, and I will do so soon. Help me. Perhaps I can help you. Why have you not been given bodies, like the others who pass through here? I've met witches above, long dead, returned to the world as piskies, as spriggans. Why do you rot here, in this swamp?'

The third head, Tressa, takes her turn, rolling back to look the Keeper in his eye with cold and empty sockets.

'We have no bodies, Keeper. A man like you cut them from us, tossed our heads in the mire and burnt them. There's nothing left to remake us, just ash in wind.'

Pel scowls. He has some sympathy for these three. There is a history of violence in his predecessors. A belief in suppression, of short-tempered control. And yet, something worries him.

'And what did you do, to deserve such treatment?'

All three, in unison, roll back and smile.

'Nothing, Keeper. Gathered herbs.'

Something still twitches in the back of Pel's mind. He has read the ledgers. They go back a long way, though not so long as these beings' deaths. They watch him from their puddle, eyeless though they are, lips quivering. He scans through innumerable pages read, then stops. Freezes. Does not take his eye from the hungry faces roiling in the swamp. He is careful now, steady and measured. His fingers curl into familiar shapes and he bows, slightly, as if presented at court.

227

'My apologies, sisters. For the transgressions of the past. I name and apologise to you each in turn, to you Derowen, to you Elowen, to you Kerdhinen. Sisters Of the Grove, I name you.'

As he speaks each name a howl issues from blackened lips. He feels it then, the presence at his back, and turning slowly, stands to inspect the three headless bodies now stood behind him, hands outstretched to push him deep into the mire. Frozen mid-reach. Each slender body draped with sodden folds of fabric, black ooze seeping from the weave.

'I know you, fiends.' Pel has turned back to face the heads. 'You have a history. I know what you did, and how many died because of it. You should have chosen better names to hide behind, better lies.'

The three sisters still writhe in anger in their pool, their bodies still held transfixed by whatever Pel cast on them.

'I will speak to the King. I've seen what he's let out already, I'll not risk him freeing you. Tell me how to reach him, quickly. I have lost patience with this dallying.'

The heads roll under one by one, faces submerged and silent. Pel has none of it. Reaching in, he grabs each by the hair that hangs threadbare from their skulls, and holding all together ties them up into a tree, out of reach of their headless forms stood hopeless below.

'I said tell me how to reach him, directly, no roundabout way but swiftly. Or I will leave you hanging here until the skin finally rots from your skulls and you fall back into your swamp.'

The sisters confer, quietly, an accord reached.

'Fine, Keeper. When presented with a choice take the left-hand path. It will lead you to him, however contrary it seems. Now let us down.'

Pel regards the creatures, eye flitting between each.

'When I have concluded my business, I will be back for you.'

And turning on his heels he leaves. Three heads scream after him as arms strain uselessly below.

Pel's feet splash in the dark water as he walks through the grove. He follows the sisters' advice, takes each left turn, and soon the chapel hill with its black grove is close ahead. Nearer now, he makes out a structure amongst the shadows and branches, a ruin, large bricks locking together carved with circles and lines. A necropolis, a crypt. Pel is so focused on the ruin he trips over the root that juts out across the path and tumbles face first into the mire.

'Damn.'

He lifts himself up, brushes wet mud from his front and stands in a clearing. There are three paths ahead of him. The leftmost hung with blue-petalled dog rose, the scent so sweet as to be unpleasant. And the path behind it curving back on itself, disappearing from view into a tangle of flowers. The central path leads straight on. The doorframe free of vines or clutter. The stone bright and new. The path to the right, it seems, leading direct to his goal, stretching beyond to the base of the hill he's set to climbing. He can feel Him, the Lord of the Undermoor, the God of the Mire. Sat on his throne and staring.

The sisters have not led him wrong so far, he pushes through the fragrant blue blooms and onto the path beyond.

Behind him, the creeping tendrils of thorns recede, and a new path is revealed, the leftmost of the four.

If he stopped to listen, he'd hear it howling.

The path Pel has chosen is different to the rest. The arc of the trees on either side converges above him, blocking out the moon. The path itself is sunken and rocky. This holloway echoes with Pel's steps, drives him onwards. Through the thicket of blackthorn, a flower grows, pushing and twisting itself through the dense wood. The blooms are like honeysuckle, though black and shining, and their scent is sweeter. Stronger. Pel has read of flowers that rarely bloom. That sit quiet and green and wait. He has read that when they blossom, when the green opens wide and the flower unfurls, they stink of death. This tunnel stinks of death. The flowers, sweet though they are, are rank with it. But Pel pushes on. Without even the moon to guide him, his sense of time has deserted him completely. He walks on through the holloway with a grim determination. Wherever this path leads, it will not be pleasant. *For so it goes*, Pel thinks, grimly, as he strides on.

Pel is tired. This was not part of the deal he had made with himself. A life of fighting, of adventure and regret had led him to the moor, a desire for peace. He had cleared it, years ago, of the last of the giants, the witches, the beasts. Until nothing remained but the Underfolk and their troubles. An easy life. A training ground for Nancy. He had seen how many in his life? Six? No, seven kings, come and go. Three queens. The 'Lord Protector' and his son. Had fought in most of their wars on one side or another. He had hoped never to journey to a court again and yet here he was. Off to bend the knee, a supplicant. Still, decayed though it may be, the Undermoor is a novelty. Even to him.

'One to cross off the list,' Pel thinks and smiles. 'Few enough of us foolish enough to do this.' The smile does not last. The tunnel ends, and Pel steps hotfoot into a wide-open space, the floor covered in bones, bones of the Underfolk, bones of giants. The smell of death is strongest here, the air a miasma of decay. The charnel crunches under Pel's light steps and there is movement, straight ahead. Pel pales, takes a step back. His hands work furiously a tangle of signs and shapes wreathing him in the semblance of protection.

Padding out into the clearing is the largest dog he's ever seen.

It stands as tall as the Keeper, at its shoulder, the heavy head lifted high above. Its tangled, matted black hair still wet with blood shines with the patina of a raven's wing; there is green and blue in the black, under the red. Built like a wolf, though it does not have that creature's head. Its snout short and snub-nosed, wide nostrils breathing clouds of steam into the air. Pointed ears tip forwards, listening, and beneath black brows glisten two eyes burning with blue fire. Its jaw hangs open, panting, a great pink tongue lolling out like a corpse from the gibbet-cage of teeth that line its jaw. Pel knows this creature. By reputation only, though he's suspected its presence above a time or two. There are books written about it, this fiend. About how it straddles the worlds, how it comes and goes as it pleases, feasting on human and spirit alike. It is old. As old as the Undermoor, as the King Himself. As old, even, as His Queen. Yes, Pel knows this monster. It is Bal Dhu. The beast of Bodmin Moor. Pel scowls.

'You're supposed to be a cat.'

Pel walks in circles around the pit, the beast keeping pace across from him. The creature makes the first move, running swiftly across the bones and leaping with a growl that cuts a jagged gash in the air. As it hits Pel's wards, blue fire meets green and the dog slams to the ground, skidding to a halt on its side and adding burning hair to the already pungent space. It is on its feet in a moment, shaking its body and scattering the viscera from the floor as Patroclus would shake off the rain. It stands and stares at the Keeper, unused to a fight lasting more than one bite. Panting with the effort of the spell, the old man catches his breath. Staggers on the uneven, broken bone ground. Pel knows he can't risk a bite. This monster preys on spirits and men, and the Keeper, at this moment, is both. This needs to end quickly.

Kneeling, grabbing a handful of bone and blood from the floor Pel speaks a charm under his breath. A mark on his leg, the black ink tattoo of a chalice, burns and the handful of remains catches fire. Pel winces as he feels his skin blister beneath it. The spell was magical. The fire is real. The old Keeper hurls it at the beast, still getting to its feet and the burning clod hits with a sizzle against the huge dog's neck. The fire spreads across the creature's body, as if it's covered in pitch, and the beast howls. It drops to the floor and douses the flames, rolling in the slurry of flesh carpeting the pit, and rising as a smouldering stinking mess.

Pel is winded; it has been many years since the Keeper's been in a fight he might not win. He tries to shake off the fear like a boxer throws off a punch. His mind scrambles for attacks. He has one, he thinks, but before he can form the shapes, speak the words, the beast is on him, the great jaws snapping, finding purchase on his wrist. Pel lets out a howl and curses the animal. By some miracle, the maw gripped him towards its rear, between the molars meant to grind, not cut, his arm well clear of the knife sharp canines, the teeth that rip and tear. Still, Pel cries out with the pain of it, the crushing, bone breaking force of the creature's jaws. Pel places the thumb of his free hand between his index and middle finger, speaks the words, and punches the beast hard in the side of the jaw. The bones in his hand come close to shattering, but the spell holds, and the beast releases his arm, reeling backwards, trying to shake off the pain one eye closed against the blow. There is little left in Pel. He does not know what to do. In desperation, he runs beneath a giant's ribcage, left from some awful feast, and regains his breath beneath the bone, his chest rising and falling in short sharp bursts. The peace does not last. The beast is on the ribs, gnawing and ripping shards of bone—they will not hold. Pel can hear them crack, the noise echoing off the sides of the ribcage. Pel nurses his torn arm and closes his eye.

If I die here, she'll think me a failure. She'll be ashamed of me.

'I'm sorry Nance. I'm sorry.'

He can hear the bones shattering above him, feel the hot breath, smell burnt fur and blood.

'Now then Keeper. Chin up.'

'A little help offered if you'll take it.'

Pel opens his eye. The two shapes shimmer, their bodies overlapping, merging.

'You can help?'

'We can, Lord Hunt.'

'We might.'

'But a helping hand given needs a gift in return.'

'A favour to ask.'

'A promise to keep.'

Pel is no fool. But nor has he the luxury of time. Frantically he weighs up the risks, of accepting help despite everything he knows of the creatures that offer it.

'What do you want. No riddles, no rhyme. Tell me. Now.'

Above the beast still tears. If he has seen the two interlopers, he has no interest in them, attention fixed on Pel.

'Well then. Simply said.'

'Re-joined.'

'Returned.'

'Reunited.'

'*Make us one again.*'

'*When you're able.*'

'*See us whole.*'

'*In return we set you free.*'

Pel closes his eye again. Tries to block out the sounds. Reunification. It could be worse. Details for later.

'Agreed!'

'*Yes.*'

'*Agreed.*'

'*Together but trapped.*'

'*But still, together is freed.*'

'Enough of your prattle! What do I do, how do I stop him?'

'*You don't, Keeper.*'

'*The Beast is forever.*'

'*The creature remains.*'

Pel blanches, his bone cage shakes as the dog hauls its way on top, one of the ribs cracks under its weight and gives way, the dog sinking down half a foot closer, the creak of the other bones barely holding.

'Then what do I do?'

'*Over there, under the roses, a hole.*'

'*An escape.*'

'*A path back to the one you should have taken.*'

'*The sisters didn't lie. You were misled.*'

Pel looks across the pit, sees the blue roses clustered across from him. The beast has almost broken the bars now, two more ribs have given way, and death is hot and wet above him.

'I'll never make it! He'll see me.'

'*So, stop him seeing, Keeper.*'

'*Put out his eyes.*'

'*Douse the fire.*'

'*Quell the sparks.*'
'*We'll see you soon.*'
'*Take Heart.*'

And they're gone. Droplets in the air. Pel is breathing hard, Trying to piece together the nonsense those two have fed him.

'Put out his eyes, douse the fire.'

He has it. His eye focused again. Staring at the beast as it pushes on in its quest for meat. There is a spell. He does not use it often; it reminds him of home, of the island of his birth. And it takes a lot from him. Closing his eye, he holds an image in his mind of a gorse-covered rock thirty miles from the coast. On his chest, inscribed above his heart is the anchor cross of Eythin, and it burns for him. The spell has no words, it is a birth right, and he moves as though underwater. Reaching up towards the fragile cage that protects him, his hands reach its bounds as the last bone breaks. And as the great head of that infernal beast lowers, Pel, Lord Pelagius Hunt, Keeper of the High Moor, lost Lord of Eythin Island, pushes his thumbs into its eyes. Still focusing on the island, Pel pushes harder, his thumbs burning in the blue heat of the sockets, ears echoing with the deafening scream of the injured beast. But still it drives on.

From the cuticles of Pel's thumbs, trickles of sea water flow. The salt making the pain from his burns blossom into a fiery wrench of hurt. But the trickles increase, the water flows, and he can hear the hiss as the blue flame of the old dog's eyes begins to dim. Pel does not let up, does not waver, and as the fires hiss, he can feel the coal hard eyes under his hand, still hot to the touch. He knows if he stops now, they will burst into flame like marsh gas again. He needs them to be out. The beast, its eyes useless and cold in its head, makes a desperate lunge, but Pel is free of him now. As he backs towards the hole, ringed with roses, the beast tears around, biting at air, howling to the wind.

When he is against the exit, body wracked with fear and sweat and the hallucinatory, blooming relief that he has escaped, Pel shouts back at the beast in a poor attempt at confidence.

'I gave you a choice. Do not return to the moor above, dog. I will drown you.'

The dog is still blind, though Pel can hear the popping sound of a flame trying to take and the steady flicker of a pilot light in each eye socket. Once Pel has finished speaking it stamps across the charnel floor towards the noise, raises its head and howls, the bones and stone shaking. It howls so loudly in the sky above waves tear across the sky. Then it turns its attention back to the Keeper, both eyes bursting into flame. Pel jumps, turns, and drags himself through the hole just as the creature's head crashes against it.

Shaking, Pel walks unsteadily through a tangle of blackthorn and the same blue roses that led him to the dog. When he returns to the chamber he began in, the fourth door now revealed, he sinks down. His torn arm aches, his soul drained from spells cast, from magic spent. *A sorry state to meet a king.* Pel allows himself a moment to breathe. Looking down there is no sign of the injuries he has sustained, but he can feel the dull ache spreading down his arms, across his hands. High above in its suspension in the mud, his body smoulders. His thumbs and hand blistered, his bones broken. When he returns to it there'll be some mending needed.

Standing, he recomposes himself, shakes the worry off and steps through the archway to the left. This path is short, bright. The moon in the night sky-sea shines on it, on the too-bright grass, on the ground. The path rises steadily and

Pel can barely contain his relief when he sees he is at the base of the chapel hill. As he climbs, he looks back across the Undermoor. He sees the pool he emerged from, sees the plains and trees laid out before him. Gow still strides across the landscape, driving his desiccated cattle ahead of him. It's clear now, from above. The land is rotten. The rivers and pools look like lesions in torn, sick skin. The pinks and blues and purples of this world less of a novelty now, Pel sees it for what it is. A cancer.

High to his left, the Queen's Rocks stand. Pel can almost make out a shape at the top, a throne. To his right, the echo of Echo Tor, another throne. The chapel hill at the centre. He sees, now that he is closer, that the trees surrounding the necropolis, the tomb, are not just sickly. They're dead.

YELLOW RATTLE

With Hocken Darrow back below, and the noisome fury of the riders buzzing in her skull, Nancy climbs the Queen's Rocks, Patroclus following steadily behind. From the top, she sees the whole valley laid out before her, its rough-edged magic smoothed from a distance, its folds and rises pitching like a circus tent. Unlike Echo Tor, across the valley, this hill is a ragged assortment of stone. Echo Tor's clitter of tumbled stones cluster around the peak, leaving the lower slopes bare except for large hunks of moor stone breaking the skin of the grass. But on the Queen's Rocks, the climb is a hard and angular scurry up bracken-tufted rock, startled sheep bolting from hidden fissures, the clamour of underground springs. If the climb is harder, the reward is worth it. Higher than any other hill in the county, it is the only point in Mirecoombe parish where a person can see the sea. The water hangs in a grey line on the horizon, a dim division of earth and sky. As Nancy climbs, past the three blackened hawthorn trees in their soggy pool, she shivers. Looks towards the stone circle that stands on a patch of rocky grass between the hills. She thinks, for a moment, she sees a dog there. Pacing the perimeter. No. A trick of the light. She continues up the tor.

The stacks at the top here, like on its twin across the valley, hold the semblance of a court. The coin stack of rocks that stands highest has the same cuplike hollow at its crown, an abandoned throne for clouds to sit on. The centre of the

239

hilltop has never held a chapel, or a hut. And Nancy does not remember Pel ever visiting. It is always barren too of Underfolk. The Queen it takes its name from older than the King, older than the stone. She is safe here from the Hunt. There is room to breathe. And yet Nancy does not feel alone here. She never has. She can't see Pel's boat, or Mirecoombe, or her cottage from here, but she can feel each one of them. This is the hill she climbed when young. When her mother died. When Pel had taken her in, it had been overwhelming. Each day a clamour of piskies asking her to dance, of spriggans asking for aid. This is where she came to find peace. Away from the noise of the valley. She needs that peace, that quiet, now. The exhumation of Hocken, the arrival of the Hunt has scared her beyond belief. But the thought of visiting Cleaver is terrifying. She isn't scared of the old priest, he's harmless, but speaking to him would mean revealing herself, her ideas. Without Pel to shield her, she feels exposed. She turns to the dog for comfort.

'Just an old priest, Pat, nothing to worry about.'

At her side Patroclus raises an ear, still exhausted from the climb. Nancy sits next to him, places her hand on the ground. Idly she focuses on the breeze, on the earth, and a feather shakes free from its resting place beneath a stone. She tries to think of the earth beneath her as a friend. An ally, and slowly the ground yields, shudders apart and from the fissure it creates pushes a small piece of quartz up and onto the grass.

Pel's magic is complicated. It needs practice, it needs words, the signs drawn on his skin. It needs his book. Nancy has studied it for years and still needs it by her at times. It's powerful, but it takes work. This, this quiet magic, this Murmur, this is hers. To tease apart the soil comes as easily as breathing. She has been able to do it since she was a child.

A game to play. She used to lie on the grass and push up treasure. Quartz like the piece she's found today, but other things too. Bones, coins with the heads of dead kings and ragged at the edges. Once she pushed up a gleaming torc of metal. She wears it still, pushed up to the top of her arm, beneath her shirt. She has never known why it scares Pel so much. He's seen so many things you'd think a little more magic wouldn't bother him. But it does. She has learnt, over the years, to hide it from him.

This hill is where she practices. Just a little at a time, working the magic loose from her mind. She used to stride about the tor top, acting Keeper, an old coat swirled over her shoulders and a stick in her hand. She commanded unseen spirits, fought witches and giants, with an old hobby horse between her legs and its moth-eaten woollen mane threadbare but cherished. Recently, when she has visited, she has been testing her gift. Seeing what the Murmur can do. She has never managed to crack the ground as she did with Joan, or on the hill with Bluecap. That was reflexive, born of fear and she still aches from the effort of it. No, to move the ground more than a little, to do more than part the way for a stone with any sense of direction or purpose has been— difficult. Though she has, on occasion, knocked a stone from the stacks.

A noise interrupts her reverie. She starts, and the earth settles. Nancy looks round and up to the cupped seat in the rock. A cloud of starlings whips around it, the soft thud of the wings as the murmuration changes direction, the whisper of the birds as they pass in closed beak silence. The birds pass up, around the tor and sweep down into the valley. Pulsing and writhing as they go. They form a ball, a feathered sloe, that bursts with birds when it breaks. The starlings land and begin to chatter. A deafening chorus. Then stop, all at once, as they rise. If it is a sign, she does not know its meaning.

'Come on Pat, let's go down.' She looks towards the little chapel-capped mound in the valley, dim in the mist but a glow shining through the windows, the red stained glass making the light bleed. Cleaver is home.

The walk down is faster, if more precarious, and even Nancy's practiced steps falter once or twice. Patroclus, against his better judgement, takes the rocks in bounds, landing with a thud after each leap, his wide paws splaying as he lands. At the bottom, breathing out clouds into the mist, the pair start towards the village. They reach it from the rear, taking the narrow and winding sheep trails through cobwebbed grass. They pass a group of men, Nancy recognises Remfry Doble amongst them, splitting a piece of granite moor stone. Trying to, at least. An iron tripod, set up around the rock, holds a heavy spike at its centre. Remfry, thick arms straining, pulls a rope and the spike rises, drops, rises drops. Slowly working a hole in the stone. Six others already drilled with iron splitting stakes inserted. Nancy watches as they remove the apparatus, and another man, Remfry's son, takes up a great hammer and cracks it against each stake. Even Nancy can see the line where the stone should break, clean and straight. A gatepost cleaved from the monolith. Instead, as the hammer comes down time and again, nothing happens. The stakes get stuck. Six rods of iron lost, and the stone won't budge. On the final swing the hammer's handle snaps as it's raised, the iron head landing with a crack at Remfry's feet.

'What are you looking at, girl?' the man glowers at Nancy. 'I've no need of your advice, or help, never have, so move along.' He's right, Remfry has never been one for charms and trinkets. His deliverance from his devil a last resort he still resents. Nancy holds her tongue. Says nothing about the fire. About the Underfolk burnt who helped stone break. She turns away and heads to the far end of the village. From this side, without the wide coffin-path cutting into the hill, it is a scramble over grass and stone, the remnants of old walls and buildings long since fallow. The chapel rises above enshrined in mist; eerie, alone. Reaching the top, Nancy and Patroclus climb the lowest point of the wall, next to the entrance to Cleaver's room.

'There he is, Pat, pacing about.' She can see his shadow crossing the glass. 'What a busy little man.'

Steeling herself, she goes to knock but the door opens before her and Cleaver stumbles into the day. If he is surprised to see her, he buries it immediately beneath irritation, a sneer curling his lip.

'Miss Bligh. I'm afraid I'm on my way out, I'm needed in the village.'

He moves to push past her, but Patroclus has lain down across the path, passivity his best offence. Nancy takes the opportunity the dog has given her, stepping inside before the Reverend can close the door.

'This will only take a moment, Reverend.' His title used. Unlike Pel, she sees the value of flattery. And it has worked, a little, for Cleaver has turned, relaxed.

'Very well, but a moment only. And the dog stays outside.' Pushing past Nancy back into his home the Reverend Cleaver shuts the door on the mist. Patroclus closes two tired eyes and sleeps in the chapelyard, warming his body on the dead.

It is cold inside the Reverend's quarters. Despite the temperature outside he has lit no fire today, though the bitter tang of candle smoke still hangs in the air. On his desk, Nancy sees stacks of books, hastily moved, sheafs of papers tidied. He was not expecting company and she reads with interest the titles embossed on the spines. Books on the moor, books on the dead. She sees, too, the little line of charms on the stone fireplace. She has seen that acorn before, she's sure of it. More questions to add to her list. Nancy can feel Cleaver's impatience radiating from his cassock and turns to face him.

'Well, Miss Bligh? I said a moment and yet here you stand mute. More interested in my décor than my time. What is it?'

Nancy lets a moment pass, keeps the preacher's gaze.

'Your décor, Reverend, your library too. We have some shared interests it seems.'

Cleaver moves to the desk and tidies the books, placing them back on the shelves and hiding the papers.

'I believe, as you know, whoever is killing my flock is doing so under the misapprehension they are performing magic. I was merely researching their madness.'

Nancy smiles but makes a note. These are books a man might use to cause trouble.

'I was attacked, Reverend, on the moor. I believe it was by the man we're both searching for.'

Perhaps it is the cold light, but Nancy swears the Reverend blanches at this. But it passes, his thin lips tight again. He continues tidying, clearing away. She watches him sweep the line of fireplace charms into a desk drawer and the silver acorn stirs her memory again.

'I'm sorry to hear that, Miss Bligh. I'm glad to see you well. Did your charms not help you? Pel?'

Even in the half-light Nancy can see him smile.

'Pel is, away, Reverend. And the attack interrupted another.'

'My, aren't you unpopular. Who was the first?'

'A spirit called Soames. The other attacker killed him.'

'Ah,' Cleaver turns back to Nancy, 'I see. And this creature, where is he now?'

'The house spirits took him, buried him.'

'How convenient. Look, Miss Bligh, I have no patience for this at the best of times and I really am needed elsewhere, so if that is all—'

'No,' Nancy is determined to speak to him. He needs to hear this. 'I went to Hocken Darrow's grave.' If there was doubt at Cleaver's reaction before there is not any longer. His face has drained. His hand, on the latch of the door, firmly shuts it. She has his full attention now.

'And why did you do that, Miss Bligh? Hocken died of heart failure, of age. Several people saw him fall. Or are you suggesting this attacker is as invisible as your friends?'

'No, I think he died as you say. But I, I saw him. And others. I performed a ritual and... '

Cleaver slams his palm on the desk.

'Enough! I have had enough, Nancy! This nonsense must end. Leave the dead alone. What could you possibly have discovered at that old pagan's grave? Nothing. Wilted flowers and silence.'

'I raised him, Cleaver, I had his body raised.'

Silence. Cleaver is still. His eyes search her face, twitching, darting.

'You did what?'

Nancy starts to speak but Cleaver stops her.

'He may not have been mine, but he has earnt his rest. What you've done is blasphemy. Against my religion and, frankly, against his. I've nothing more to say. Leave, Miss Bligh. Now.'

'But Reverend, I found something. Someone had taken a part of him, his spleen. Stuffed the body with straw to hide it.'

Cleaver turns and places his hands on the desk.

'God forgive us. Nancy, I hope, I pray, that you see the connection? A man is buried a pagan and he is plundered for parts.' Cleaver raises his eyes to the rafters, to a higher roof beyond. 'The consequences of a heathen life. Alas.'

Nancy ignores him, she'll not be derailed.

'There were two others, Cleaver, two of yours. Jenkins and Caleb. I need to see their bodies; we need to bring them up.'

Cleaver spins round, face contorted in incredulity.

'Bring them up? Are you mad? This is hallowed ground! Neither you nor anyone else will lay eyes on them again. They are at rest, Nancy. I do not care what fever dream brought you here. Without Lord Hunt to moderate you, it's clear you're inclined towards hysteria. I suggest you go home and wait until he returns. Even he, and I have seen that man do a great many sinful things, would not suggest that to me. I want you to listen, very closely. I forbid you to disturb a single grave. I forbid it. You'll find nothing of interest in Christian graves.'

'Reverend, please, I'm just trying to help!'

'Help? For God's sake woman, if you meant that then you would be heading down to the village with me, not trying to dig around in holy ground. Harry Pascoe is missing. They fear the worst and they have asked me to minister as they search. If you don't go home, then I suggest you join us. Good day.'

Pushing Nancy in front of him, Cleaver is gone in a sweep of black, the faint trace of carbolic soap and incense and Nancy is alone in the chapelyard, the mist holding her and Patroclus close. As the Reverend's steps disappear, the silver acorn finally falls into place.

'That was Hocken's charm, Pat. Why did he have it?' She looks back at the graveyard, at the slate stones, Cleaver's garden. She crouches, pulls her dog close to stroke him. For her comfort as much as his. 'I fear I'm seeing a thing too late, Pat. I have to know.' Nancy looks towards the village where the sound of the search rises up to meet her. 'Forgive me, everyone, if I'm wrong.'

NANCY KNOWS WHERE the grave is. She was here when it was dug. It's a short walk across the chapelyard. When she reaches Caleb's stone she closes her eyes, steadies herself against the task ahead. Then she kneels and begins to dig. Weeks of snow and ice have compacted the earth and it breaks and chips her nails. The mist has grown thicker, drawing a veil over the exhumation, as if it knows this ought to remain secret. Nancy wishes she could ask for help, ask some passing spirit to rally around and dig for her, but none would set foot in the chapelyard. Even the hounds are staying away. Pel had explained it, once.

'An incompatibility of magic,' he'd said, but wouldn't be drawn further. No, she was alone in this, even Patroclus had turned his back on her. She has been digging for what feels like an hour and is barely a foot down.

'I just need to see, Pat, just the one. I need to know.' Tears of frustration roll down freckled cheeks and she pounds the dirt with her fist. A tremble. A shake.

Nancy sits back. She had not meant to do that. She shouldn't have been able to do that, not here. It crackles in the air and passes.

Pel had asked her not to use her magic, but he'd left her alone, defenceless. If not now, when? It was her duty to help, wasn't it? Come what may? She has not used the Murmur like this before. She has controlled it, yes, to knock over a pebble, to rob the ground of coins. And it has leapt from her accidentally, outbursts like the night on the tor. This would take something else, something she has never managed. Control.

Closing her eyes she reaches for it, tries to get a sense of it, something to hold on to, but it is faint. It pulses. Like the swarm of starlings that she named it for she can feel it expanding and contracting, beating with her heart. Holding it like this without letting it out is draining. She struggles against the pull of it. It does not want to be held. Nancy focuses on her breathing, allows the Murmur to explore the chapel hill, lets it approach and lap at the wall like a wave against a beach. It licks at the edges and Nancy opens her eyes, the Murmur surges over the wall like the sound of birdsong in a storm and as it crashes again and again over the stone she grabs it, takes it into herself and it fills her. Like a guest returning home. She gasps, raises her eyes, and feels her body fill with the heat of it, spreading across her chest and out through her open hands. She has never let it in like this before. It is exquisite. Her breath rushes out in staggers and the ground trembles.

This is not Pel's magic.

She has made no sign, spoken no words. This power comes from the moor itself, flowing through her like a conduit, and the whole chapel yard shakes, tiles falling with a crash from the church roof.

'Pat!' Nancy cries out. The dog is cowering under the lych gate, whining, and pawing at the ground. There is a low rumble of thunder and the air smells of bitter orange. The Hunt is near. She tries to put them from her mind and turns to the task at hand. Draws the Murmur back to herself, holds it in her. She looks down half expecting to see her clothes rise and fall under the pressure of it, she feels it beating inside, waiting for a way out. Nancy lays her hands on the ground beneath the fresh cut tombstone, Caleb Setch's name chiselled into the slate, which begins to heave and retch. From across the yard Nancy sees another stone topple, Jenkins' name shattering as his tombstone falls. Nancy lifts her hands sharply from the earth, tries to sever the connection, but whatever moves through her is too strong.

'No, no, not like this. I just needed to see one... please.'

But now it has been set in motion the Murmur will not be stopped. Not until its job is done. Simultaneously from the two graves, the earth-spattered coffins break the surface like breaching whales, landing with a thud on the mud and dirt.

Nancy feels the Murmur leave her, the flock of birds scatters, and she is left with nothing but a heart beating too fast and a prickling of her fingertips. Exhausted, but painfully awake, Nancy falls back, and the echo of the last roll of thunder recedes. Her whole body shivers and she realises with a start there's a smile on her face. She wipes it away with a darting look around the chapel yard but nobody has seen. She can feel the corners of her mouth lift and she presses them back down. Still. It is done. No changing that now. And it did feel good. Cautiously, she creeps to Caleb's box. The lid has been prised open in its rise and the stench of the newly dead seeps from the cracks, overwhelming her excitement at the Murmur. Pushing the lid free, Nancy blanches at the contents and is relieved to feel Patroclus' snout push under her arm, apologetically.

'I'm sorry Pat, I'm sorry.' Nancy is shaking as she looks into the box. 'We'll be done soon, boy.' Caleb lies quiet in front of her, pallid and cold. Delicately, Nancy pushes his shirt front open and presses lightly on his chest as a doctor might, looking for the source of a cough. Beneath his crushed ribcage, on the right side of his chest, she feels the prickle of straw through his skin, where his liver should be. Scrambling to her feet, Nancy races across the yard. Jenkins' coffin has fared worse, and his body lies prostrate on the ground. Pulling his shirt up, Nancy finds the cut quickly, the catgut already rotting, the edges of the wound decayed, and the straw spilling out green and damp packed tight in the hole where his heart once beat.

Nancy is so focused on her task that she does not hear the shouting from the valley. It takes Patroclus' barking to pull her back, to regain perspective. Nancy looks at the chapel yard, at the devastation she has caused.

She feels drunk, struggling to focus as the echo of her magic sloshes around her in the desecrated churchyard, a libertine revelling in the aftermath of a party. Desperately, she tries to summon back the magic that had surged through her, to catch even the faintest spark of the Murmur. But it has left her, for the moment, and she feels bereft, angry. She had trusted it. Given it free rein and it had betrayed her, left her high and dry. Nancy brushes the bronze torc on her arm absentmindedly, lets her fingers press the metal into her arm beneath the cotton of her shirt. Despite that, she knows the truth, it showed her what she was seeking. She longs for it to return so she can let it run wild again. It is only as this feeling subsides that the panic takes over.

'I'm sorry,' she breathes and tries to lift Jenkins back into his box. The coffins had been driven up from below with force, the ground mashed and rattled as they rose. There is no hole now to lay them back down in and Nancy has no shovel, no means to dig.

'Come, Pat, we need to see Cleaver. We... ' a gulped sob escapes her; it isn't the Reverend she needs now. It isn't

Cleaver she wants. But he'll have to do. Leaving the ruined chapel yard behind her, she leaves through the lych gate and stumbles and slides down the hill, Patroclus at her heels.

THE VILLAGE IS in turmoil. Men and women are running through the houses, heading for the moor. Some of the men carry burning torches, peat spades and scythes. Nancy grabs a girl as she passes.

'Annie, where is the Reverend? I need to speak to him.'

'Out on the moor, with the rest, looking for Harry.'

And she's gone, moving with swift purpose towards the milky-white mist that still clings to the air. Nancy looks to the Nest, for Madge's smiling face, but the door is closed, and the lights are off. Billy Askell stands staring from the darkness outside; Nancy does not have time for him now. She is still nerve-achingly alive from the chapel yard.

'We'd best join the hunt then, Pat.' Nancy looks worriedly to the dog at her side, strokes his broad head. And they are out into the fog.

THE MOOR RUMBLES with echoing voices. Through the mist, like embers, torches move. The search has been going for hours. Old Harry Pascoe, who lived alone, has not been missed since the night of the fire. It had been Madge who had raised the alarm. That many days without a visit to the Nest had been rare for the old man. When she had reached his cottage, finding it still and cold and his geese clamouring to be fed, she had stirred up the villagers and started the hunt. Though a few voices called for reason, for the search to be delayed until the mists had cleared, they had been ignored.

The community could not bear another death. Harry must be found. And so, every able-bodied woman and man had fanned out across the moor, through the bogs, steps placed carefully on the treacherous ground.

Nancy can hear them, shouting to each other. Discussing evidence found. But she has a different quarry. She thinks she sees him a few times, Cleaver, her eyes catching on lean black shapes, but it is never him. The villagers she accosts, mistaken for the Reverend, look at her with wild, desperate eyes. None she speaks to have seen him, though all say they know he is there. It is hard to believe that the day is still strong, that there is any sun above the mist, that there is light. As Nancy moves deeper onto the moor, she realises the searchers are not alone. The stench of bloody fur, matted with dirt and peaty water reaches her before she sees them. The wish hounds are padding unseen through the crowd, sniffing each person before moving on, searching for their master's quarry. Nancy steels herself, forms a ward, and stands in the path of the nearest. It does not even raise its head, just walks around her and into the mist. Nancy lets out a rasping breath, as at her side Patroclus howls, the sound echoing across the hidden valley's sides.

'Where are you, Pel?' Nancy speaks into the fog. 'What should I do?'

There is a shout from further down. Nancy has still not shaken free of the Murmur's stupefaction, intensified by the swirling fog, the light from searching torches. She is barely aware that she is walking, and she struggles to locate the source of the sounds. The mist dulls the voices, and they seem to come from every direction. Nancy stumbles, trips over a dropped torch and picks it up. It is still burning. She steps into water, her feet sink into boggy ground, and she jumps back, gasping at the cold, onto solid earth. The shock has wiped a little of her grogginess away and she sees things more clearly. A wind has picked up, and it swirls tufts of mist like clouds about her, revealing the shape of gorse brush, the twisted lines of thorn trees. And then, stood in a copse of blackthorn, the Reverend. Alone and staring at her.

'Cleaver!' Nancy shouts and starts towards him, but something in his expression stops her. The old preacher's face is white, his eyes wide and filled with tears and his mouth set hard in a grim line. Silently he draws his hand up to his chest and making the sign of the cross he mutters a prayer. Nancy only catches the end.

'... to torment or to rest.'

And then he's gone, vanished into the fog.

'Cleaver!' Nancy shouts again. 'Go boy, stop him!' And Patroclus, always faithful, bounds into the mist after the vanishing shape. Nancy starts after them, but stops, frozen. She raises her own hand to her throat, to the anchor cross Pel gave her and turns, slowly, to face a new figure emerging from the fog.

'Pat... ' what is meant as a shout comes out as a whisper and the dog is too far to hear.

Moving slowly, jerkily, like a shadow puppet moved by subterranean sticks, Callum Cleaver lurches out of the fog. His body is drawn, dark and shrivelled. The skin taut across his skull, sinking into the sockets where two black eyes sit and drawn back across a lipless mouth, across his teeth. Nancy can hear his leather-hard body creak as he moves. She feels as she did the night Cutty was killed. Frozen, limb locked. Sick. After the delirium of the last few hours, she has nothing left. The Murmur nothing now but a whisper.

Lowering her hands, she tries to form a ward, some protection, but her fingers fumble the shapes. Callum moves steadily towards her standing statue in the mud. As he draws closer, she sees he is naked, the peat and mire he drowned in preserving his body as a mummified husk, the echo of a man. She sees too the suture marks, one in his chest, two at his sides, can see the pulse of lividity through cardboard flesh.

'Callum, it's me, Nancy, do you remember?' She races through a thousand possibilities, but her thoughts are muddled. She cannot see a way through.

The creature continues steadily, a low rasping rattle forced through dust-filled lungs and from one eye socket an ember glow. The voice, when it comes, sounds like it hurts.

'Nancy.'

'Callum, stop, please. I'm sorry. I didn't know, what you must have been through—'

Callum's voice is halting. He stops to gather himself before every word, and the corners of his mouth crack as he speaks, tearing a ragged smile across the leather, bone showing white beneath.

'Slave. I. Was. A. slave. And you,'—he stops here, claws at his throat as though it might ease his words—'You. Were given. Everything.'

Nancy searches for something to say, but what could make this better? And though she wills herself to cast a spell, to do something, she cannot. It is as though the magic has gone, as though Callum has absorbed it. For an instant there is the flicker of the Murmur, but it holds back. She can feel it recoil from Callum, and she does not push it. He is a leech, she can feel it, can feel him pulling at the Murmur as he pulled at the spells she had tried to work. She does not want to lose the Murmur to him, so she lets it leave. She is alone here with him. When he stands before her, she closes her eyes, feels the rank breath that whistles out from between his teeth.

'I'm sorry, Callum. Truly.'

The wight raises an arm and his outstretched hand bursts into a blue flame. Nancy can feel his stolen magic. It strains against a leash, tethered to the figure before her. Staring into his black eyes Nancy sees colour there, a pulsating thrum of energy that beats deep inside Callum, caged. When he places his hand around her throat it feels like the case of a mermaid's purse, the fire cool, and she swallows hard against his palm. There is the flicker of hope: from the fog, the hounds emerge. And behind them, their masters, their headless necks towering over the scene. Nancy waits for them to help her, at least to hurt him, but they do not. Callum, it seems, is not who they are seeking tonight, and the Hunt turns to leave. She turns her gaze back to the corpse that holds her.

'Please, Callum...'

If he can hear her, he gives no sign.

Across the moor, an old dog howls.

ADDERSPIT

PEL IS TIRED. The grass at his feet has changed as he climbed, the pinkish blue giving way to black. There are no leaves on the branches, the ash limbs silver and burnished by time. The trees rotted to their bones. There is nothing hiding in the undergrowth here, no fleeting sightings. He is alone. Ahead of him the carved stone wall of the building stands. At its centre, a door flanked by two monoliths, a capstone across them. The architecture the remnant of a distant past. Pel recognises the stonework from ruins on the moor, from the shapes of the ghost houses.

As he climbs the last few feet of the hill, the inverse of the one the chapel stands on, Pel looks up. The sky, until now a calm sea, rocks with waves. It is a strange sight indeed to see the breaking foam crashing above, obliterating the puddle moon, the sky. He thinks he hears birdsong, in between the waves, the beating of hooves. He pushes on. The violence in the sky above builds as he climbs. By the time he has reached the door it is a maelstrom and then, silence. The sky is a millpond.

A cold wind blows out from the door in front of him, and Pel steps into the cold, stone room with a sure and steady gait, leaving the arcing dead canopy, the wave wracked skies, behind him. It takes a moment for his eye to adjust, for things to coalesce. He takes the chamber in with a cold precision. Files it away. Along either side of the room, braziers burn.

A thick and heady smoke billows out from them above the flickering of the flames. The unsteady light throws the carved stone walls into relief, panel after panel of the Undermoor's life, of its history, pictured as Pel had imagined it. Dancing piskies and spriggans, wish hounds sleeping by a fire. Long-horned cattle in herds in the hundreds. The pools and trees healthy and full. There are spirits passing back and forth, from the ground to the sky, with bundles of goods in their arms. Giants climbing up the tors into the clouds and into the rippling firmament, their torsos disappearing into the concentric rings of the disturbed water.

The ceiling is painted with a peeling, cracking fresco of the moor above, of his home. The image painted as if seen from some vantage point below. The edges the painted green of the earth, the centre the sky with Echo Tor picked out rising to the middle, its stony throne at the centre. Around it fly witches astride their ragwort stems, beetle-winged spirits and demons that resemble Cutty and Bluecap. From fissures in the rocks, giants force themselves into the world, smaller spirits swarming around their waists. Some humans flee from the colossal figures, others lay offerings of fruit and wine at a giant's feet, heads bowed to the floor. The paint is most faded at the centre, on the figure on the throne. It is as if some hand has reached up to touch the paint, to caress it, endlessly over millennia so that the seated figure can barely be seen, their long limbs and horns just visible, long robes falling golden around them picked out with embroidered stars.

Pel is transfixed. In the painting, at the base of the throne, a man kneels. His face hidden, one hand curled into a shape Pel recognises, he has made it many times. It is a protection.

'Do you recognise your predecessor?'

The voice is deep and violent, a tree trunk hollowed out by

lightning, and it pulls Pel back to earth. At the far end of the room a carved stone throne echoes the one painted above. At either side stands a Huntsman, mount-less, in their hands thick leashes with a tugging wish hound at the end. And on the throne sits the King of the Undermoor, the God of the Mire.

A pale unsteady spectre of his portrait. His arms and legs are long and sinewed, the knotted limbs of an ash tree. He is draped in the same raiment that is depicted above but the threadbare shift that hangs on him bears little resemblance to its glorious past. Though a few shining diamonds mark the stars sewn onto it, most are missing. The red thread that picked out the lines between them, mapping the constellations, is frayed and torn. Huge auroch horns, bone white even in the firelight and dipped in fading gold, the leaf falling from it like dead skin spread like a cancer from the crown beneath. It shines in the firelight. Panels of silver birch veneer, tiger-striped and glowing are wrapped around a headband. Each panel with a thin leaf of hammered gold, delicate scenes embossed into the metal and pinned carefully to the wood with studs. Hanging from the crown and covering the imposing figure's face is a pieced mask, made from carved bone. Built in segments connected with silver rings it follows the contours of the face beneath, fine high cheekbones under heavy brows, the grain and patina of the bone polished into a high gloss. Eyebrows and a thick moustache and beard, gilded and carved with deep lines. From beneath it the voice comes again, and Pel sees a glimmer from deep in one of the mask's eyes.

Bow to Him. Pel feels the instruction press on him.

'It is the first of you. The first Keeper, not just of the High Moor. The All-Keeper of Dumnonia, as it was, then. Kneeling before his God. Why do *you* not kneel, Lord Hunt?'

The voice has power over him, Pel can feel it. The voice of a god. It takes a lot to remain standing, knees buckling, but the old Keeper does not kneel. There is a ceremony to this, Pel knows it. But he knows his place within it, will not enter this negotiation prostrate on the floor. Still, some respect is due.

'Your Grace.'

Pel bows, sweeping a hand before him before rising to his feet. It has been many years, but he remembers his statecraft. 'Thank you for the audience.'

There is a rumble, like a cliff falling, and it takes a moment for Pel to recognise it as laughter.

'You are welcome, Keeper. It has been a very long time since I was visited by one of your order.'

Pel looks up. He had thought himself the first. The King sees his confusion.

'You're such arrogant creatures. No, you are not the first, Lord Hunt, but please, do not let that diminish your achievement. It is still quite the feat. It has been a very, very long time since I entertained the last of your kind. I warn you, however, I do not care for it. Your predecessor did not leave. Your fate is uncertain. Be assured it sits here, in the palm of my hand.'

From the folds of the cloak an arm emerges and a huge, strong, hand curls itself into a fist.

'But enough of this posturing. We both have power here. And I suspect it is a different breach that you have come to discuss. Have you not?'

Pel looks into the black hollows of the mask, tries to pierce the veil to the face beneath. But he feels nothing but emptiness from the void.

'I have. I have come to discuss the release of Underfolk I had thought bound. I am sure I do not need to tell you that our arrangement rests on the understanding that these creatures stay below.'

The King leans forwards and Pel takes a step back. He had not fully comprehended the god's size before. Looming towards him now, Pel sees he must be ten feet tall, his horns protruding seven feet either side. The masked face draws a few feet from Pel's own, and the Keeper feels the ripples of the King's breath as he speaks. It smells of orchids.

'Our agreement is void, Lord Hunt. The terms broken. Stop with these games. You know what you did. Who you sent.'

A cloud passes over Pel's face. This link broken means the end of the chains. All manner of things will be loose.

'I would ask you to reconsider. I know that times have been harder than in the past, but I have done my best! You cannot ask me to stop the world turning. Things change.'

On his throne the masked god sits and stares.

'I would never ask you to, Lord Hunt. I am a pragmatist. I have been weathering my decline with stoicism. With grace. But there is a breaking point. I am fully aware things are not as they were. Men are no longer laid in the mire, seeking my embrace. I have armouries full of broken swords bequeathed to me, sunk into the mud with a request and a promise. Rusted now. I used to hold court with a pantheon. All forgotten. With a queen. Until she left. Their thrones sat empty until new gods came. Gods whose faces stayed as their names changed, Greek to Roman. We sat and feasted and shared out the world. They had no qualms. They understood the way of it. Their priests laid sacrifices under hazel-rod hurdles and pressed them into the bogs, gave their bodies and souls to me. When the one-eyed thunderer came in the heads of the Danes I sat with him, here, and broke bread, shared stories, shared the dead.'

As the King speaks, the light in the room dims, the flames die back in their baskets, and the two guardsmen shift uncomfortably on weary feet. The voice comes clearly through the mask. Pel can feel the words hit the base of his skull, and in the absence of eyes he looks at the glint of the bone.

'And then He came. The God that now sits on my hill. It was mine, before. I suspect you knew that. The chapel that stands there now was built on the foundations of my temple. The raised earthen banks topped with your little stone wall. And I waited for Him to visit me. To ask me to dine. But he never came. Instead, he bewitched his stolen hill, bound my magic from it. Stole my dead. Fine. So be it, there were enough. Men and women may have sat in his house, listened to his priest, but they still asked me for help. Were still—now and then—laid in the dark water when their time was at an end.

'Did you know you've been waited on by kings? That your house spirits, the spriggans and piskies, all of them, count in their numbers the dead kings and dukes of the past? Henuinus, Cloten, Tenuantius, and Dianotus. All have passed through here, sought my gifts. And then suddenly, none! Only peasants and paupers reached these shores. The high and the mighty too good for me. Fine!'

He is leaning forward again, the orchid breath flecked with spit as his anger rages, a simmering pot of oil that crackles and hisses. Spitting out warnings. Pel doesn't care if he is burnt.

'I offer an eternity of tangible, touchable existence. What does He offer? Vague, unsubstantiated promises. Paltry miracles.'

Pel thinks carefully before speaking. No Keeper in the records has dealt successfully with a god. There are limits. Diplomacy reigns in this subterranean hell.

'My Lord, I understand your frustration. I do my best, but the church is popular. The world is changing whether we like it or not. There will come a time when you have no more souls offered to you. Already it is a fight each time a person comes to me and asks to be buried with the old words. Sons and daughters often want them buried at the chapel. But releasing your monsters will not help. The piskies and spriggans help at the harvest, the brownies in our homes. That is how you will keep the faithful. Sending your monsters will only bring death, and it will drive them away.'

His piece spoken, Pel retreats into silence. And the King stands. His horns scrape the mural on the ceiling, flakes of paint showering the old god's shoulders.

'Death?' The god's laugh is short, cynical, the sound of a cave sealed shut with a boulder. 'What death? I sent my children above with instructions not to kill. And they haven't.'

Pel starts to speak but is silenced by a raised hand, fingers branching, telling him to stop.

'I am not counting livestock, Lord Hunt. A little mischief, some worrying of the edges, but nothing fatal. A reminder, that is all. Of the world below. Of the fate any might find themselves with if lost out in the bog. Faithful or not. The deaths have been entirely one sided. Enough of this false modesty, Keeper. Admit to your crimes.'

From either side of the throne, two pale and translucent ghosts emerge. Not in the form Pel had known them, but as they were in life. One gold, one blue.

'Hello, Pel,' they speak in unison. The gold figure a tattooed man, face twisted and cruel and dressed in furs and mail, an axe in both hands. Cutty Soames. Bluecap smiles besides him. A young woman, her tunic scorched, her skin blistered. The God of the Mire puts an arm around each.

'You know these two, do you not Lord Hunt? Both killed. By you.'

'Bluecap was not dead when I left her. Cutty still roamed.'

'She does not have the protections you hold. You cannot

goad a bear dressed in armour and hope your companion in rags survives. She is dead, Pel. Her spirit returned. As for Cutty, I asked if you had come about recent breaches. I gave you a chance to come clean. I opened the doors to let some creatures out. I want to discuss the one that broke in.'

Pel stands silent. He had known this was coming. Had known in his heart he was, in part, to blame. That Cleaver, that Nancy, was right.

'It was Callum, then. He made it. He was here.'

'Yes, Lord Hunt. He was. Indulge me if you will. You are concerned with balance, are you not? I, too. There is a reason my followers adhere to me. A reward. When they arrive here, my subjects are ghosts, riders without a horse. Like our friends here.'

Cutty and Blue flicker at their inclusion, like light passing through woodsmoke.

'As their bodies decay in the mire above, that which made them is preserved. I keep it safe and in time I return it, in a form of my choosing. A spriggan, a pisky. Something else. Cutty here was known as a butcher amongst the Danes. His gods would not have him. I saw his potential. I made him anew as an agent of my will on earth, and he razed the moorland under his curlew claws. Until your predecessor sent him back in chains. Blue here set fire after fire in her village and her village burnt her for it. Her body, laid in the mud, weighted with stones, was black and blistered, but I took her in. Changed her too, into the engulfing flame. Do you recall, Lord Hunt, why she came to your attention, the first time?'

Pel shakes his head. He knows when to hold his tongue.

'No one had made payment at the harvest. No offerings laid on the stones. And I had helped the crop grow into a strong one. Not a word of thanks to me or my gentler children. Blue burnt those fields to the ground, some farm hands too. A message sent and received, and garlands laid on the granite. When the world was a little younger, and I took these things more personally.' At his side Bluecap sniggers. She remembers the fires; they are burnt into her mind.

'You returned her to me whole that time. Just as your masters had returned Soames. Because the materials of my gift are finite, Lord Hunt. There is little spare. A body dissolves and I take the dust. If there is no body then I am forced, if needed, to compromise.'

Raising his arms, the God of the Mire whispers something to the shadows and on either side of his throne the Huntsmen, his guards, begin to shake. Loosed from their leashes, the two wish hounds run yelping from the chamber. Pel can hear their worried whines echoing down the hill. The shaking figures smoulder and smoke and it is like a thread has been pulled. They unravel, their matter and form spooling at their feet in a cloud of shining dust, and in moments both are gone. Nothing left but pulsating masses where they stood. Moving his arms like a puppeteer, the God gestures and shakes his hands and the piles of matter rise and coalesce in front of the ghosts of Cutty Soames and Bluecap. First into a glowing network of veins and nerves, brains blooming like flowers on spine-stems and then bones appear. There is a hum and a metallic taste to the air and Pel has to check he has not bitten his cheek, for his mouth feels like it is filling with blood. Around the skeletons, still hanging there, flesh creeps and folds, a dreadful envelope of skin. One bulges with muscles that whip and bind their way under the taut new flesh. The other writhes as she struggles her way back into her form. Like a hand in a new inflexible glove. With a howl, the creatures are reborn. From the fingertips on Cutty's hands, scythe-claws tear from the skin and with the familiar pop of catching gas Bluecap is ablaze again.

'Do you see, Lord Hunt? How it works? How without proper procedures there are decisions to be made?'

Pel nods. He had thought he understood the process, had not thought of the brutality of it. Something to be considered later.

'When Callum arrived here, using books that you had allowed him to take!' The god's voice rises to a shout here and Pel closes his eye against it. He stands in the floral tempest until the storm abates.

'When he arrived, he was eager to change. Eager to please. I would find him speaking to the giants, to the sisters bobbing in their pool. He would pester me to give him form. He thought himself special. But I explained to him, as I have to you. Until his body decayed, he would exist formless, a ghost. And the idiot boy had taken tinctures, draughts. The same I suspect you have taken, though he mixed them poorly. He did not prevent his death, only his decay. I could feel it, hanging above us, his husk. I knew it would be an aeon before his matter was available to me.'

Pel hangs his head now. He has never failed like this before, made so grave a mistake.

'He found a way to cause others here harm, found creatures desperate enough to help him. Spirits were found dead. Each morning, when I woke, I would find him preening over a kill like a proud cat with a bird, the poor creature's soul hanging above their corpse. I ignored him every time. I will not be forced, Lord Hunt. He should have known his place. It was a mistake. What did you do to him? To make him that way?'

At this, fury flashes in Pel's eye and he forgets himself.

'I did nothing! The boy was stolen, broken by the spriggans, and destroyed by his father's stubbornness. I did everything I could for him!'

Silence, and then the god continues as if nobody has spoken.

'He came for me whilst I slept. Tore at me and raged at the injustice he felt. His hands... I do not know where he had found his power. I had tolerated his mutilations of the lesser beings. Had not thought it important enough to investigate. He was a trophy. A victory over both you and that upstart god. I underestimated him, Lord Hunt. Do not do the same. The Underfolk he killed were practice, trial runs.'

Reaching up with a thorny arm, the God of the Mire unhooks his mask from the crown. Beneath the gold and the bone, an old and awful face stares out from under the silver birch. Pel gasps in horror and falls to his knees. The face looks mummified and drawn, yet Pel can see deep marks carved into the skin, interlocking circles within circles, knotwork and boughs of trees above a mouth filled with the teeth of a dog. The god's eyes shine from their sockets like diamonds, rimmed with a coal-dust shadow that glistens with fragments of tin.

A jagged hole rips through the old god's forehead. Pel can see the magic leaking from it, a blue flame flickering in a cranial sconce.

'He did this, Lord Hunt. He tore my flesh from me. He took a little of my power. He left me unmade. I am a God, Keeper. I cannot repair myself with the bodies of spirits and the dead. You do not repair gold with lead. He broke me, then tore through the Undermoor. You've seen what he did, the decay he's wrought. He is a cancer. He must be cut out. I know he is above, I felt him return to his body, though I do not know how he left the mire. He ought not to have had the power for that, even with what he took. And now he kills my followers and leaves them broken in the mud. Drives the rest into his father's arms.' The old god stands again. His voice cracking with anger. 'I am a King! Lord Hunt. A God. I will not end my days a pawn in another man's game. You came here to ask me to cease hostilities. I ask you this in return: end whatever monster he has become, and I will return to the status quo, I will sink gently into the mire just as I have been destined to from the start, with dignity. But fail, Pel, or refuse, and I will send these two back along with every horror that dwells here, I will transmute each harmless brownie into a howling torment of blades and fire, and I will raze the moor and any I meet to ash. Let their new god face me then.'

Pel stands with this new information, this task. But he still has questions. He can feel them crawl over him like ants.

'What is he doing? Why is he killing those people?'

The God of the Mire, King of the Undermoor smiles, and the orchid breath blows past shining teeth.

'I do not care. The affairs of men are nothing to me any longer. You know my terms. If you need any further motivation, I suggest you turn around.'

'Pel...'

At the voice, every part of Pel stills. His ears fill with the echo of a change in pressure, time stops. He finds himself turning, though he does not want to, does not want to look towards the door. He can hear the god's laugh behind, Cutty and Bluecap with him. There she stands, looking just like the girl he knew all those years ago, lost and alone and looking to him for the answers. From his one eye tears stream and his mouth shakes as he answers her.

'Oh Nancy, my darling girl. I'm sorry.'

FURZE

PEL CAN TASTE his tears. She looks so like the child he took in, stood there in the doorway. Her life comes rushing before him. The connection he had felt when he had saved her. The promise in her. The power. That beautiful, infuriating girl is here before him. Her form the same half-flickering ghost that Cutty was, and Blue. She looks so sad, he thinks. Pel moves slowly towards her, his hand raised then left to fall, there are no shapes left to make. No spells he can cast. Some things are beyond him.

'I'm sorry, Pel... ' Her voice is thin, distant, hoarse. She holds one hand to her throat and Pel sees her feel about in surprise. He moves close to her now and reaches out to brush the hair from her face, but his hand passes through her, and she shimmers, ripples like a reflection in a pool when a kingfisher dives in. *Even in death she shines*, he thinks, *still catches the light.*

'Why, love? What can you be sorry for? I failed you, I left you and... ' he cannot finish that thought, it sits in his mind and eats the light, tears strips from inside his skull.

'I didn't stop anything, Pel, I didn't stop him. Callum. It was Callum. He's the one who killed them all.'

'I know, my dear, I know.'

Nancy lowers her hand and Pel sees the livid red mark, the wide splayed handprint on her neck where Callum burnt the life from her before he broke her neck.

She cannot be dead.

How can he stand here, this man who has survived, how dare he survive this? Tears still streaming he turns from her, looks back towards the god on his throne. The old and creaking figure still has a smile on his lips, below the smoking hole in his forehead. Pel can feel the knot inside him tighten, and then as swiftly as it had happened, when he had seen her standing there, it goes. He sees the solution so clearly; it is the easiest thing in the world.

'Take me.'

The god stops smiling. At his sides Cutty Soames and Bluecap chatter wildly, excited at these new developments. Long and ancient arms bat them away like flies and they sit silent in the shadows behind the fires.

'She is dead, Keeper. That is final. You know that.'

Pel is undeterred. He does not turn around. He'll not look to her 'til he's struck this deal, but he can hear her at his back, 'Pel, no, please.'

Mouth set, Pel walks towards the god and for a moment dwarfs him, the Keeper filling the room with his presence. For the first time in eternity, the god steps back. Pel's voice pinning him in place.

'You've shown me what you can do, Lord. I know your power. Think of what you could do with me out of the way. Better still, think what you could do with me here.'

The old god closes his eyes. Thinks. Magic still seeps from the wound in his skull, Pel can see the vapour as it evaporates.

'Her body remains intact. What would you have me build with?'

'With me. I give her my body. Whatever remains is yours to keep, repair yourself if you think it fine enough.'

Nancy gasps. She knows what this means. The implications

of a life below alone, with no hope of transmutation. He would be a ghost for eternity.

'Very well, Keeper. State your terms.'

Nancy rushes forth now, gliding across the old stone to the Keeper's side. Every particle of her soul desperate to hold him. She does not want him to save her. Does not want him to leave.

'Please don't do this, Pel, please. Leave me here, go back, save them.'

Pel looks at her, finally, at her face. Nancy brushes black hair from tear-stained eyes. She might be dead, but even ghosts cry.

'Daughter.' The first time he has used the word aloud. A lifetime spent afraid of the cost. 'When you were young, you used to ask how old I was. Do you remember?'

Nancy smiles, her green eyes shining, she does.

'You used to tell me, "old enough," I'd get so angry at you Pel.'

'Well, it was true. It still is. I am old enough, Nance. I'm through. I was through when we met and you brought me back, for a while. My time is done. It's your turn now, you'll be the moor's Keeper. I believe in you.'

'I can't, Pel, I tried, I did. It didn't work.'

'You'll try again. You've learnt a lesson. You'll go back. You'll stop him.'

Nancy shakes her head, but the old Keeper is firm. Standing, he approaches the throne, still straight backed and upright, his good eye burning through the darkness.

'You asked my terms. You will return my daughter to her body, repaired and whole. You will call back every fiend you released. You will give her time to put my mistakes right, to end Callum, to return what he has taken. In return I will remain here, I will not argue or dissent. I will let you be.'

The silence fills the room, dancing with the firelight. Nancy can feel the weight of it. The old god bows his horned head in thought. In the quiet there comes a noise like wind through willow leaves, a sigh that rakes through a divine throat.

'Very well. I accept. I will return her; I will make her anew with your body. And I will recall *some* of my subjects from the moor. If she's to be Keeper, then let her work for it. She can send back the rest, and the Hunt stay.'

Pel bridles at this.

He looks to Nancy, and she nods.

The thundering cavalclade of hooves and howls that had passed him when he arrived here.

'You released them? Why? Our agreement not withstanding—'

'Did you not hear them as you arrived? The Hunt was replaced by the Keepers, Lord Hunt. You are the Keeper, you left. I had no choice. There were transgressions that I could not tolerate.'

'You could not have sent them for the boy?'

The King slams a fist into the arm of his chair.

'You think if I could he would still live? No. The power he took shields him from them. They sense me within him. They are there for others. They are there for a particular purpose and they will return when it is done. But mark this, Lord Hunt. I do want the boy. She will return him to me with the gifts he stole and any who abetted him. Meet these demands and the balance is restruck.'

Pel looks back at Nancy and smiles. She is still shaking her head, still mouthing 'no' at him, but he wants this, wants to give this to her. It's all he has left to give.

'A moment, Lord, with my daughter.' He feels the words in his mouth, regrets not using it more. She is his daughter; he is her father. More by a league than her own was. He walks to Nancy and gestures her outside.

The puddle moon still hangs above, its cratered surface shining under the watery sky. In this perpetual twilight the Undermoor glistens, darting beads of light marking the passing of the spirits. In the distance Gow's great head lumbers onwards with his cattle and the air is filled with moths, their wings beating dust in the moonlight. They sit, this pair, on a ledge overlooking the valley, amongst the coloured grass, and for a moment sit quiet.

It is Nancy who breaks the spell.

'How long have you known it was Callum?'

Pel bows his head in the moonlight.

'Long enough. I'm sorry Nancy, I didn't… I thought I could fix it.'

Nancy stares out across the Undermoor, tears streaming but mouth fixed.

'Is that why you stopped letting me help? Stopped training me? Have you been waiting for this, the whole time? Dammit, Pel. We could have avoided this. You know that don't you? You bloody old fool.'

Pel does not respond. He wants to place a hand over hers, wrap his arms around her. There aren't any words to fill that gap.

'I thought I could still save you. I wasn't easy on you, Nancy, growing up. I had told myself I needed to train you. When I saw what I had done to him… I couldn't undo all I had done, what I had already made you into, but I thought that if I stopped teaching you, perhaps you would find your way out.'

'That wasn't your decision, Pel. He should never have been able to attempt what he did. All he's done, all this,' Nancy gestures to the decaying landscape, 'could have been stopped.'

Nancy laughs, it is a broken bell. 'All those eyes and not one saw him die. I can't imagine how alone he must have been.'

At her side, Pel shifts uncomfortably and Nancy tips her head.

'What is it, Pel? Tell me.'

'The night he went to the mire, he threatened you. Said he would take what you owed it. After he left, I went to your cottage, kept watch. They came to tell me what he had done, was trying to do, later that night.'

'Who? Who told you, Pel?'

'I've seen a lot, Nancy. Fought monsters, ghosts. Have prided myself on my courage. The thought of him hurting you, though? I hadn't known I could be so scared. I had lied to myself, all those years, tricked myself into believing I'd found a ward and not a daughter. The piskies told me he had made a mistake, that he was dying. Told me where to find him, that I should hurry.'

'You—'

'I still remember that sunrise. It was the most beautiful morning.'

They sit together, father and daughter, on the edge of an underworld. For the moment, alone. The temple behind them, the moors in front, nothing now. Empty space. Pel reaches across, lays his hand so it falls through Nancy's, and she does not move it away. He sobs, a great heaving cry, and she smiles through tears of her own. Cried out, he turns to face her.

'I made my choice. The same I make now. I have made many mistakes, Nancy, saving you has never been one of them. You will be the most marvellous Keeper. I'm just sorry it's the life I have left you.'

'What will I do, Pel? How can I be a Keeper? I'm not grouchy enough.' She sees his smile from the corner of her eye. 'Are there others down here? The other Keepers? They can't have chosen the chapel yard to lie in.'

Pel's smile fades.

'No, Nance. There are no others here like me. A Keeper is balance. We can't take sides. We are supposed to burn when we die. Become ash on the wind. But don't worry. It will be fine, in the end. I'll be safe here.'

The silence flows into the gaps of conversation, like the sea at low tide catching on rockpools.

'Will I see you again? Is there any way out?'

'I don't know, Nancy. Maybe. There are spirits here I owe a favour, perhaps I could owe them another. They have no bodies. I'll speak with them, see how things are done. They are trouble, those two. But these are problems for me to deal with, alone. You have work ahead of you girl. Did you learn anything, before you died?' The last word catches, trips into a sob and he wipes away tears as she answers.

'I read the ink; someone has taken body parts from the dead. You remember Hocken Darrow? His spleen was gone. And Caleb's heart, Jenkins' liver. They are in Callum; I could see them beating.'

Silence again. Pel thinking in the midst of it.

'And Cleaver let you raise them, to check?'

'No,' Nancy is wary now. Like a child unsure if they've done wrong. 'Spirits raised Jenkins. The others I raised alone.'

Pel starts at this, his head whipping round to face her. 'You used magic in the chapelyard? Impossible. The place is immune. What spell did you cast?'

'I cast no spell. It came from me.'

Nancy sits nervously in front of her father. She sees his one eye lost in thought, brows knitted.

'Pel? It just happened, I needed answers and it happened.'

Pel is gone, for a moment, lost in thought.

'Do not dwell on it. Focus on Callum. If he holds the old god's magic, he will be hard to stop, but the organs, the replacements, a man did that. Find out who, find out why.'

'Cleaver is working with Callum, Pel. At least I believe so. He has Harry Pascoe's silver acorn on his mantlepiece. Other charms too, and he was there, on the moor when Callum came. He fled.' Pel looks haunted, eyes wide and mouth clenched tight.

'No, it is not him. He would not do this. He couldn't.' He shakes his head as he speaks.

'I saw his books, Pel. You have them too. Why not him? It is his son, after all. You of all people know the lengths to which a father might go.'

Pel closes his eye, pictures his once-friend. The nights sat by fires arguing, drinking in the hidden bar at the Nest. He looks at Nancy, wraith besides him, knows she's right.

'Talk to him. Please.' Pel's mouth trembles, his hands shake. 'If there is reason left there, I would see him survive this, even now. But you will need to prepare yourself for a fight, ward yourself.'

Nancy frowns. But the light in her father's eye is hopeful, and she'll not cut this tether to his salvation.

'I'll try, Pel. I will.' Her father smiles in relief. 'What of the Hunt?'

Pel's face grows graver than she's seen it before.

'Leave them be, Nancy. Whoever He has set them on are gone, whether they are dead yet or not. Do not stand between them, promise me?' His eye twitches with panic as he speaks, and she nods.

'I promise, Pel. I will leave them.' Nancy pauses as Pel's

shoulders drop, his mouth moves into an uneasy smile. She returns it before continuing. 'There was one other thing, I was reading your books, the insert, from your home.'

'You translated it?' A flicker of pride quickly subsumed by the worry that follows.

'"*Left on the dark shore, let black water or white light take you, to torment or to rest.*" What does it mean to you?'

Pel grimaces. He knots his hands in his lap, his uppermost thumb rubbing nervously at the one below.

'It is a rite, from the church I was raised in. A benediction of sorts. But a warning, too. Why?'

Nancy shifts on the ledge so she is facing him, looking him in the eyes. She forgets for the briefest moment that this conversation has a terrible end and loses herself in telling her father what she has learnt. If she is to lose him, she wants him to know she has a chance to stop Callum. That he taught her well.

'Could Cleaver have made a translation? Before I died, I saw him. He was praying, I only caught the end but... '

Pel stares out across the Undermoor. Curses the island that birthed him. He turns anguished eyes to his daughter and ignores the question.

'Nancy, be very careful when you return. My home, Eythin, there is a reason I have not spoken about it. That prayer, it is dangerous. If it has a part in this, if Cleaver is so far gone as to have invoked it... '

Nancy smiles at her father.

'I'm already dead. Can it be worse than this?' Nancy almost laughs at the thought.

'Just be careful. Please. Now, there's work to be done.' Pel's voice hardens as he speaks, the old mask, shattered at her death, gradually piecing itself back together.

Pulling up his shirtsleeve Pel bares his arms, the spider-work lines and symbols. Volumes of text inscribed shorthand on his skin.

Nancy steels herself against sobs, and the pair rise and walk back inside. The God of the Mire, his mask hooked back on his crown, sits impassively on his throne.

Pel walks towards him and gestures a hand towards the King.

'A knife.'

Reaching into the folds of his robes, the remaining diamond stars glittering in the firelight, the King of the Undermire pulls out a shining curved blade. The hilt, jutting out of a stamped leather sheath, glistens. Its golden inlay shining with knotted beasts, a coiled and sleeping viper on the pommel. Picked out in amethyst and diamond are tiny shining crocuses that run the length of the grip. Holding it carefully, the King removes the sheath, its dark and bloodstained surface pitted with patterns, with deer leaping amongst grass. As it slides from its housing, the blade is revealed, long and tapering in an echo of Cutty Soames's claws, of a curlew bill. The metal shining blue black in the half-light, a single thin vein of gold running through. It has a name, this knife. It is called "Saffron Death."

Pel takes it by the hilt, feels its weight, and removes his shirt. Stood bare chested, his age shows clearly, as do the patterns and shapes he's kept hidden, the anchor cross, the three-tined spear. Deftly, Pel draws a line gently through a mark on his arm with the blade and stifles a jolt. He can feel the cut much deeper than his skin. The god looks on, leaning forward eagerly as with three more cuts, Pel severs the cords of the rope that binds him. Only one thread remains.

'My Lord. I would ask another boon of you before this is final.'

Having leant so far as to almost fall in anticipation, the god shifts back in his seat. The great horned head nods.

'I have a gift for my daughter. See that she gets it.'

The head nods again and satisfied, Pel brings the knife up for the final time. With a firm stroke, Pel slices through the anchor cross in its place above his heart and sinks to his knees. Behind him, Nancy gasps and claps ghostly hands to her mouth. It is done. High above, from its stasis in peat and mire Pel's body jerks. Molecules that have for decades, centuries, held each other close release their grip and the magic that bound them together decays. There is a speed to it that is unusual; without magic to sustain it the centuries old body turns rapidly to dust, to peat. As it rots Pel's form in the Undermoor dims, he begins to fade. Begins a journey from man to shade, and soon enough stands spectral in that stygian court.

'It is done, then.'

The god's voice booms through the room, echoing with the clatter of the knife as it falls to the floor. Motioning to Cutty to retrieve it, the God of the Mire stands and gestures towards his crown. There is a fizz like molten metal cooling, and the God removes his mask again. His face now whole, a shining gold spreading across his brows like a birthmark and his two eyes glimmering.

'I keep my word, Keeper.'

It is with a shock Nancy realises he is addressing her. Raising his arms, the old King looks upwards and concentrates on a spot high above, where, tossed in the mire by a bitter son, Nancy's corpse drifts. Sifting through the mud, the God of the Mire takes the matter released from Pel and draws it into the girl. He feels for the break, for the severed spine, and the molecules and particles that were bound to her father wrap like ivy around Nancy's neck, spreading through her body, seeking out necrosis, the dying and burnt flesh. Replacing it with something new, something beautiful and strange. When the work is almost done, the King pauses.

'If you have goodbyes to make, make them now.'

Rushing to each other, both ghosts, Nancy and Pel embrace. Father and daughter.

'I love you, Nancy.'

'I love you too, Dad.'

And high above magic and matter ignite a spark in a renovated brain, and Nancy's ghost is gone. Just a dead Keeper and a god in a cold subterranean tomb.

THE MUD IN the Fellmire bubbles and boils in the midnight cold. Late night travellers, passing by, pause then scurry on. Badgers and owls that know when to stay well away. There is no frost tonight. Instead, the world is slick and wet from a storm just passed. The hilt of Pel's pocketknife still stuck into its stump shines under the moonlight. The Fellmire steams. There is always a heat to it. Above, an inversion of its brother below, a waxing moon looms large in the sky, white and pale as though the face within it has leant forwards for a closer look.

From the bubbles, a shape emerges. Rising up from the depths is Nancy Bligh, reborn. She rises with arms outstretched like Venus from the waves, dripping with thick black mulch, with mire and rot. Buoyed by the old god's magic, she stands barefoot on the water and pauses, feels the cold air on her new-born skin.

She coughs and splutters out a lungful of leaf mould and peat, and her breath fogs in the damp air around her. She shivers. Treading carefully, she walks on the surface tension of the water to the bank and turns to watch the bubbles die down, for the Fellmire to regain its mirrored edge. Looking down, she sees the tattered remnants of trousers and shirt, sticking wetly to her, clumps of mud sliding off. Discarding them on the mire-bank, she steps onto the wet grass and heather and begins the walk home, her dark muddied body blocking out the stars.

PART THREE

"Saint Francis and Saint Benedight,
Bless this house from Wicked wight,
From the nightmare and the goblin
That is hight Good Fellow Robin.
Keep it from all evil spirits,
Fairies, weasels, rats, and ferrets.
From curfew time
To the next prime."
—Traditional

SPEAR THISTLE

NANCY DOES NOT go to the boat. She can't face it yet. She skirts low beneath the village, the world laid out in monochrome and her shadow leading the way. There are no lights burning in the village. She is the only one awake.

She wonders how long she has been gone. Enough time for the search to finish; no torches dance on the moor and there is no shouting. Her head feels thick and dulled, as if she has woken from a fitful sleep. She looks down at her mud-streaked body. She was not at the Fellmire when she died. She knows that. Callum must have taken her there. Did he know where Pel was? Was she sent as a message? No space in her head for thoughts like these. She sees her house, her cottage, rising from the moor ahead of her and pushes the heavy oak door open gratefully. It is as she left it, sparse and neat, her bed made. She falls into it and is asleep in a moment. No dreams disturb her. The moon sets, and Nancy sleeps through the sunrise.

She wakes to the smell of camomile and lavender and foxglove. In front of a burning fire her old tin bath is full and steaming, a milky, herbal brew infusing the water. It smells like the mire to her. Still only half awake, Nancy moves awkwardly from bed to bath, her head still foggy from its revival. The water helps, despite the imagined stench. The steam clears her knitted brow, tries to allow her muscles to relax. The dark mud gives up its hold on her skin and stains the water black.

Sitting there in the clouds of steam, Nancy cries. Great sobs that rack her body, sobs that seem to never end. The ache inside her is a visceral beast. Carving out its home where her heart once sat and dragging its nails around the inside of her chest. Each time she closes her eyes a series of images play out. Like slides from a magic lantern show. Pel, staring at her in that place below. The sadness in his eyes at her failure. She failed. She knows it is true, he trusted her to keep things going above and she died. Tried to do things alone and was killed for it. His face as it turned from man to ghost will startle her awake until the day she dies again. She knows that. It doesn't matter that he told her not to worry, that it was not her fault. Her father has died, and she killed him.

Between each slide of him is another. The same picture painted in thick red paint. Callum. His face close to hers and the hand on her neck burning. She raises her hand to the scar as she does every few minutes. Feels the raised welt. She will never forget that feeling. The strength of his hand. The hate in his eyes. When it happened. When his hand closed, when her neck broke. She had heard the crack. Felt it. Felt it judder like the body of a bird that has flown into glass, a single jolt then nothing. A nothing that subsumed the terror she felt at *him*. A terror that subsumed all. Nancy had felt her body disappear. In the moment before she died, she was nothing but thoughts and a strange, crackling feeling. As though her whole body had fallen asleep but try as she might, she couldn't move to wake it up. It had felt as though her legs, her arms, were curled tight, hunched into her body. But she knew that wasn't right. She knew she hung limply from that burning hand. The last thing she had seen was Callum smile. A wretched cut of a thing that rang with the sound of a corpse, laughing.

This is the show that plays on the backs of her eyes every

time she closes them. Her father, her death, and the man who killed her. The creature in her chest that presses grief into her ribcage pushes a rage there too. Pel knew. He knew it was Callum. Had suspected from the start, and the arrogant old bastard said nothing. Did nothing. He should be here now. It could all have been avoided.

She stays in the water with these rolling thoughts and dreadful images until the bath is cold then, encouraged by the smell of coffee brewing, steps out onto the boards.

'Thank you.' She can't see their faces, so she talks into the corners, but she knows the little brownies are close by. Taking the towel that they have laid out across the bed, she dries herself and pulls on a white smock dress she finds at the back of her wardrobe. She takes a seat in front of the mirror at the dressing table, her hair hanging wet across her shoulders.

'Look at you, girl.'

Lifting her chin, she again raises a hand to her throat. There is a bruise where her neck broke, the livid stain of Callum's hand. But it is already fading. In its place, a fractal scar, a lightning strike of damaged tissue that she traces with her fingers. She can feel the raised skin where she has been repaired. It winds like ivy around her throat. She can feel him.

'I'm sorry, Pel.'

There is a scuffle behind her, and she turns. On the bed, her muddy sheets replaced with new and fragrant linens, is a small velvet pouch. She sees them now, her brownies. Their faces peering above the bed, curiosity drawing them out. Nancy reaches and unfolds the fabric, tipping the bag out onto the bed. On a long silver chain is Pel's seal-tooth pendant, the red of the polished coral shining from its engraved mount. Pel's final gift to her. She's never seen him without it. It feels heavier than she expected. The chain coiling around itself like a snake. She closes her palm over it and stands for a moment, quiet in the morning light, then places it back in its bag.

'I can't do it yet, Pel. I can't.'

She places the bag in a drawer by the bed and sighs. All she wants is sleep, to be left alone for a while, but she knows she can't. He has trusted the moor to her, and she won't turn her back on that.

'What would he do?' She thinks, then discards the thought. She knows what Pel would do: he would bury himself in books then head back onto the moor. Pel's way has brought them far enough down the wrong path already. From now on, she would do things her own way. She'd need to visit the boat, to collect some things. She'd need Pel's book. But first, she must go to Mirecoombe. She'll not make the mistakes her father did.

Turning back to her room, Nancy opens the wardrobe. Discarding the smock, she dresses instead in riding trousers, a white shirt, and a jacket she can move freely in. She pins her hair up, tucking a wayward lock behind her ear, and faces herself again in the mirror. At the scar striking upwards from her collar to her chin. She sets her jaw and steps outside. The air is cold and there are clouds on the horizon. There is a fluttering deep inside her that threatens to overwhelm. A black ball of feathers and anxiety. Grief bound tight. Even as she does, Nancy knows she ought not ignore it. But there are things to do. Monsters to stop. She has no time to feel sorry for herself. No time to feel anything at all. She lets the wind rake across her face, lets it tuck her problems back down inside and calls into the open moor.

'Who's about?'

She asks her question loudly, keeping the wavering from it. She doesn't know who the old god left here, who he called back. Bracing herself for trouble, she is relieved to see a pisky poke their head from behind a gorse bush.

'Hello. I don't know you.'

The pisky does not look at Nancy, instead making a strange hopping movement that Nancy realises with surprise is an attempt at a curtsey.

'Bower, Miss Bligh. My name is Bower.'

Nancy motions for the spirit to stand up.

'What on earth are you doing?'

'I'm the first you've spoken to, Miss Bligh, since you became Keeper, I mean. Everyone's talking about it, I just wanted to acknowledge it.'

Nancy stiffens a little, swallows a sob.

'Thank you, Bower, but I'm not a Keeper quite yet.'

Nancy looks away and takes a deep breath, feels in her pocket for the hag stones she keeps to comfort herself. Little stones with holes running through. As she rubs her fingers along their smooth sides she calms, steadies her breathing. Tries to ignore the images that flick across her mind.

'Regardless, I need some help. I need my horse, Selkie. Have you seen her?'

Nancy hasn't seen horse or dog since she died, and she's going to need both. But Patroclus, no fool he, would have looked after himself. She worries for her horse though. Bower pauses, anthracite eyes scrunched up in thought. Her wings flutter a little as she thinks.

'No, I've not. But I'll find her.' And the pisky is gone, back into the landscape leaving Nancy alone again. She turns into the wind and heads to Mirecoombe. It is not far from her cottage and Nancy approaches the village from the south, at the boundary closest to the Nest. She looks at the bridge with dismay. The rough granite slab holds firm, but the cross, that has weathered three centuries, has cracked in two leaving a narrow run of stone to cross on. Reaching the other side, she lifts her head. The air is wrong. There is no sound coming from the village. No clang from the smith, no hooves in mud. No children laughing. Staying close to the walls of the Mare's Nest Inn, she moves slowly into the village. The roofs of the nearby houses are missing slates, Nancy can see the wooden batons of the roof in the gaps. The corner of the forge has fallen through, the lime mortar binding it crumbled to dust. The village nicked with a hundred little cuts. Fallen stones and broken windows. Carts whose wheels have fallen off. Pel's little protections, woven into the very fabric of the village and maintained by the Underfolk are failing, one by one.

As she makes her way to the yard side door Nancy casts her eyes about, but no other gaze meets hers. The village deserted. She knocks on the door and waits for an age. It is not so early in the day that the Nest would be shut. Madge always opened early. Nancy knocks again and the door opens a crack, Madge's eyes glistening from the gap. There is a gasp, and the door opens fully, and Madge grabs Nancy in an engulfing hug as tears stream down her face.

'Oh, my dear, my dear, you're alive! Come in, come out of the mud.'

Nancy is bundled into the Nest and the door is shut and bolted behind her. She allows Madge to sweep her into the small bar she had interrogated Kenwyn Gunner in before.

'Madge,' Nancy pushes her friend away so she can look her in the eye, 'What is it? What's wrong?'

Madge's face looks tired, her eyes dark and ringed and red with tears. Nancy sees that the landlady's hands, clasped in her lap, are shaking. When she speaks, Madge's words are soft, shaking.

'Nancy, where have you been? Nobody has seen you since the night they found Harry, you or Pel. I thought you were dead! And the rest of them, well. They thought something else.'

Reflexively Nancy reaches up and places a hand on her neck and Madge draws a breath sharply when she sees the scar. Callum's handprint is fading but it still shows red, and Madge reaches towards it protectively.

'Nancy, what is this? Where's Pel?'

It hits Nancy like a flood, and the whole tale comes pouring out. Madge sits back and listens, ashen faced, and takes it in. When Nancy is done, there is a silence that neither woman knows how to break. In the end it is Nancy who speaks. Sharing her story has cleared some space and she can think a little straighter now.

'Madge, what's happening here? Why is the village deserted?'

The older woman sighs, stands, and pours herself a drink, placing another glass on the table for Nancy.

'That night, the night you disappeared. None of us knew what to expect. That mist! It was Remfry Doble who found Harry. He must have been lying there since the fire, that old fool. Half in and half out of the stream. He wasn't in a good way, half eaten by crows. But he had the mark on him, just like you do.'

Madge pauses to take a drink and Nancy does too.

'It was a tipping point. Between finding Harry, and the destruction at the churchyard.' Nancy chokes a little on the liquor. 'They went looking for Pel, for you. All of them charging about the valley. They went to the boat, I think, though I can't imagine they managed to do much. Cleaver was howling his usual rubbish; he had pulled a charm from

Harry's pocket just like all the rest and was screaming about the hypocrisies of this and that. Do you know Nancy, he wouldn't have Harry in the churchyard? Harry who sat there every Sunday. Said he'd had enough, there would be no more picking and choosing. "Black water or white light," he said, the choice would be made for us. Just as it was for Harry. Anyway. It wasn't enough. The search and the speech had riled them all up, those stupid, stupid men. They went looking for a scapegoat and they found Billy. He'd come to talk about an order for the brewery, come to see me. They grabbed him as he came out of the fog and pushed him down. I tried to stop them Nance, I did!'

Madge is crying now, and Nancy lays a hand on her friend's arm as she stands.

'I know, Madge, I know you did. What happened, where is Billy?'

Madge swallows hard and continues, eyes downcast.

'They needed someone to blame. Cleaver has them all turned inwards, Billy didn't fit. Always asking questions, nosing about. Those stupid charms he buys, like the ones on the dead. He's in the cold room, Nance. They want him to hang.'

'Where was Cleaver in all this?'

She lifts her head, the old woman's eyes clear of tears, and she fixes Nancy with a stare.

'Cleaver? He was there. To his credit, he did try to stop them, hold them back. Kept mouthing on about the proper way to do things. He didn't, doesn't, see his place in this. You can't set the hounds off baying and deny them a kill. Nobody's seen much of him since then, he's the look of a man that's overreached if you ask me. Nancy, you've a look in your eyes I've seen before. You'll do no good with that rage, that anger. They'll kill you too if you stand in their way.'

'Anger?' Nancy laughs mirthlessly, 'I'm not angry, Madge. I am furious. At Cleaver, at them, at Pel. He spends a lifetime refusing to train me properly, then falls on his bloody sword and expects me to step up? No. I will not sit here and do nothing, and I will not mourn whilst there is a good man about to hang. I have the responsibility of a Keeper now. Nobody else is coming. This is the burden Pel has left me. Besides, I've died once this week, even I can't be unlucky enough to suffer it twice.'

Nancy strides out of the pub and into the streets. A fine rain falls, thin and cold, and Nancy makes her way through the houses. She shakes with fury. With guilt and rage. Turning the corner and into the centre of Mirecoombe, Nancy sees that though the village is quiet, it is not empty. Sat around at the entrance of the long house are the men of the village, Luk Calder at their head, his brothers in the shadows. They are surprised to see her. Nancy can tell, it is written clear across their faces. She sees fear there too. As she crosses the space between them, the men rise and form a barrier in front of the heavy, locked door.

'Stay where you are, Miss Bligh. You're not getting through. Where's Pel?'

Luk Calder's voice shakes as he speaks, but Nancy ignores him and keeps moving forwards.

'Pel's dead, Luk. Get out of my way.' It is the second time today she's delivered that news but the first time she's felt it, truly. She is furious at Pel. She is angry he left, angry with what he has left her, what he made her do. But she misses him with every fibre of her being and saying it out loud has made the ball of lead in her stomach swell. She simmers with it, this stew of emotion and she can feel rage building from deep within her. She draws level with Luk Calder, the other men fallen away and watching from a distance. She is not as tall as he is, but he still avoids her gaze, shifts uncomfortably on his feet.

'Unlock the door, Luk. Billy is coming with me.'

Though he pauses, the farmer's son stands his ground. Still not meeting her eyes, he straightens, puffs out his chest. Nancy had not brought much with her in the way of charms. She has no pockets full of tricks this time. Curling the fingers of her left hand, bending her wrist upwards, she places her right hand on Luk Calder's chest. He might not have taught her everything she would have hoped for, but Pel taught her a lot, and she can make up the remainder herself. She readies the spell in her mind when Luk reaches for her neck. Her whole body stiffens, and she struggles to stifle a scream. Callum flashes before her, it feels as though her throat burns again. Luk's eyes widen. He can feel it just as she can. The Murmur leaps to her defence. She couldn't stop it if she tried, but why would she? She is tired, so tired and she will not worry about protecting men who don't deserve it.

She steps aside and lets the Murmur fly. Luk stumbles as the village begins to shake. Cracks appear in the ground and from the roofs the slates fall, some breaking as they hit the floor, some slicing into it, standing bolt upright in the earth. The vibrations increase, and Nancy begins to wonder if perhaps this was the better way all along. No waiting, no spells. None of Pel's intricacies and charms. As long as the moor shakes, she doesn't feel anything at all. She walks towards Luk arms outstretched and demands again to be let inside.

'Witch!' Luk howls the accusation at her even as he backs away towards the cold store, but she cannot hear him. He can't hurt her now, nobody can. She breathes deeply and, on the exhale, pushes the Murmur out again, rattling windows loose from their frames, splitting the granite horse trough outside the Nest in two. She hears nothing but the blood pounding in her ears, a roiling sea of rage. Does not hear the screaming, the crying. Does not see as women and men flee inside, huddle beneath tables with children held tight. When she draws level with Luk, Nancy does not speak. She summons all of her anger, her rage her disappointment and pushes him hard against the door, which shakes as he hits it. She strikes him, hard, across the face. First with one hand, then the other, and then both, pounding her fists into his face and shoulders. Stunned, the man covers his head, hands her the key even as he buckles to the floor. But she can't stop, won't stop hitting him and the Murmur's tremors increase in their severity. Chimney stacks fall and there is a scream.

Nancy stops. The tremors cease. There is silence, then the creep of birdsong. She takes a step back and turns in a dazed circle. Stares at the terrified faces of her friends, her neighbours. Nancy and Pel had rarely used magic in front of people, let alone on them. It was easier to hand out charms, to work indirectly. They had never seen anything like this. With the scream continuing and the sight of the carnage, the ball of guilt returns. The creature in her chest wakes again.

'No!' Nancy is facing the source of the scream now. Madge Gould lies quiet beneath a stack of stone. Nancy runs to her side, the onlookers silent, unmoving.

'Madge,' Nancy shakes the landlady's shoulder. Her arm trapped beneath the largest stone. 'Madge please.'

'I'll live, Nancy, go to Billy, get him free.'

Nancy kneels over her friend, moves to lift the stone.

'Go Nancy, please. I'll be okay.' Others are already running to help, glancing in terror at Nancy who stands cautiously, then turns back to the cold store. Luk has recovered a little of his senses, hauling himself to his feet with the doorframe, and seems ready to put up a fight. It goes out of him when Nancy calls the Murmur forth again, feels her guilt dim. It is Madge that stops it. Her voice thin, but urgent enough to be heard.

'Enough Nancy, you've made your point. If you're the new Keeper, then be that. But don't forget what he taught you.'

Slowly Nancy releases her fists, the ground stops its shaking and the men in the village flee. Luk remains, struggling to stand after his beating. Her breath comes fast, her cheeks flushed, and tears fall from her eyes.

'You witch, I'll tell everyone about this. I'll tell Dad, and the Reverend. It's not right!'

'Move aside, Luk.'

Luk staggers past Nancy, and with one last look over his shoulder is off and gone with the rest. Nancy heads to the long house and opens the door, the grey daylight falling on the haggard face of Billy Askell in the corner.

'Not been a good week for either of us, hey, Billy?' Nancy's voice is quiet, shaking. 'Come on, let's get you out of here.' She helps the man up and leads him out into the rain.

'Thanks,' Billy smiles from a bruised and bloodied face, 'but how are we managing that?'

Nancy smiles, though her eyes aren't in it, and hopes the sound she can hear is what she thinks it is.

'I've a friend on the way, come on now.' Nancy turns back to where Madge had been laying, but someone has helped her free, the stones lie alone. Nancy takes a step back as Selkie comes galloping onto the trackway, Bower clinging onto her mane.

'Thank you, Bower.'

The pisky smiles, nods, and dismounts, handing the reigns to Nancy. Billy stands confused at Nancy thanking the air.

Nancy climbs up and pulls Billy Askell on behind her, and the two are away. As they ride, the heavens open. They stay in silence until they reach the end of the track to Mirecoombe, where it joins with the road. Billy climbs down but Nancy stays astride her horse.

'I'm sorry to leave you, Billy, but I've got to get to the boat. There are things I need. You head away from here, don't come back for a little while, hey? I'm sorry for how it's gone. You didn't deserve that.'

She pauses. Billy's face has fallen, and he stands sheepishly, soaked through, eyes down. Nancy stifles a tut, the world hangs heavily on her, she's no time to stand in the rain.

'What is it, Billy?'

'It's the boat, Nance. The men were laughing about it, as they tied me up. They burnt it.'

Nancy pulls on the reigns wordlessly and turns Selkie into the wind. With a shout she sends them galloping across the moor and towards Pel's home, Billy Askell drenched and shaking, facing a long walk home.

BACK IN THE village the streets have cleared. There is an emptiness that goes beyond the absence of people; something has been torn from Mirecoombe today. Something hard to replace. The sign of the Mare's Nest Inn rocks in a breeze that picks up without warning. Inside their homes, shutters are closed. Families draw close to fires that have suddenly burnt low, and though not a person knows why, nobody looks to the windows or doors. The dark sky seems to scrape the slates, merging with the mist that rises and eddies in the wind so the whole village looks like a charcoal sketch being gradually erased.

Into the silence comes the sound of hooves.

The Hunt rides slowly through the streets. The wish hounds walking at their masters' sides. Their heads twist at every sound, every nervous cough or shifted seat. The horses, their heavy black feet striking sparks from cobblestones, move slowly. No faster than a walk. The leather and steel of the Huntsmen's uniforms creak and scrape as they ride. The dogs sniff at doorways, but none hold the person they seek. The dogs raise their heads, sniff the air and bay into the mist, then turn with the horses and gallop away.

Nobody sees them, but everyone hears the dogs howl.

FORGET-ME-NOT

SELKIE MOVES QUICKLY across the wet grass. Nancy spurring her on, urging her to move fast enough that she can outrun the thoughts that bite at her heels. The boat couldn't be damaged. The boat was always fine, always. There had been issues before, Pel upsetting somebody he'd promised to help, Calder's sons rabble rousing after a night at the Nest. But not once did they dent the wood, break a window. Pel had bound enough charms in that place as to make it unsinkable. Hadn't he?

Nancy can see the boat rise in the distance, a comforting whale back arching out of the moor. It looks fine. It looks how it always has. It is only as she draws closer that she can make out the scorch marks. Great swathes of black that cover half of the stern, the diamond panes of the windows warped and cracked. The lead has melted away in places, dropping the glass panes to the ground. The grass around the base is blackened too, although already there are flowers growing, little ember glows of heather in the ash.

Nancy slides from the saddle to her knees. The weight in her chest heavier than ever. *Another loss. Another failure.* She cannot still the thoughts, cannot close her eyes for fear of the terrors that wait there, her father's ghost and Callum's hand joined by Madge beneath the chimney. She cannot move. The boat makes it real. The twisted bow proof he's dead. Not gone. Not absent. Dead. No power left to protect his home, no way to keep her safe. Eyes wide, mouth open, Nancy sits like a boxer who's losing the match, ears ringing with each successive blow. *Twenty-one. I am twenty-one. How am I supposed to do this.*

There are times in life when help is needed. A person just needs to ask.

'What am I supposed to do, Pel? I've ruined it. I killed you.' Selkie pushes her velvet nose against Nancy's cheek, and she takes it in her hand. There is a sound coming from the darkness of the stables. Nancy lifts her head, steels herself for whatever new horror waits there for her.

She stands and feels weaker than she ever has before. More alone. *Perhaps it's better this all ends here. I can't do it.* She feels the weight, the creature in her chest settle in, waiting to be fed. As she rounds the corner she is struck by the shadows. The day is overcast but it isn't this dark. She can't make out the end stall, Eponina's stall. She can see Selkie's though. The empty bay still filled with straw but there, at the back, movement. Nancy tenses and begins to form a spell with her hand, though it is half hearted. Thin. She moves closer towards the shifting straw, and she is almost on it before she sees it for what it is.

'Patroclus!' With a shout Nancy pulls the straw away, revealing the old dog cowering beneath. He turns to look at her and his eyes light up, his old legs straighten, and he bounds into her arms and pushes his nose hard against her.

'It's all right boy, I'm here, I'm here.' The weight inside her lightens and though it doesn't leave she shakes with joy, tears falling fast but soaking the old dog's coat with happiness. She strokes his head, and she can feel the dog's muscles relax, though there is still a tension there. She buries her face in him, he licks the salt from her cheeks. They sit for a moment, then

Nancy stands and begins to walk outside, Pat at her heels. As they leave the stall, head for the open side of the byre, Nancy turns again to the darkness at the far end, listens for the scuff of Eponina's hooves. Nothing.

'Stay, Pat.' Nancy raises a hand to press her point, but when the old dog sees where she is heading his ears prick up, and he begins to whine softly. Nancy ignores him and continues towards the shadows, her confidence returning with her friend. The voice stops her in her tracks just before she reaches Eponina's stall.

'He's dead then.' The voice has an accent that Nancy can't place but she can smell the salt on it.

'He is, he's gone.' Nancy tries to hold her ground but can't stop herself from taking a step back as the owner of the voice steps from the gloom, leading Pel's horse by its gilt bridle. They are small, dressed in some gown or tunic in green and gold brocade, the fabric held closed at the waist by a sash. Barefoot, Nancy sees that their toes are clawed and that their ankles and wrists are ringed with bangles and torcs. Fine-featured, their face is hard to parse, and though the half-light does not help Nancy suspects that is not the only reason— because every time the creature turns away, she forgets what they look like.

'Where are you taking her?' Nancy gestures towards the horse, surprised her hands aren't making any signs. Somehow, she knows she shouldn't stop this.

'She was a gift, freely given. But to him, not to you.'

'He'd want me to take care of her.' Nancy's voice falters. Eponina is a part of Pel. She finds it hard to see the horse without her father in the saddle.

'He might. But he's dead, has no say in this. She'll be safe with us, she's coming home. Maybe one day you'll earn her back.' The creature pushes past Nancy and out into the rain, as the horse and its leader step outside the shower increases to a deluge and they are both lost in the rain. The two stand, girl, and dog, until whatever magic they've witnessed passes and washes into the earth.

'Come on, Pat, let's go inside.' The old dog pants a smile, happy to have someone back, though he still looks past Nancy, searching for Pel. They cross the small patch of ground between the stable and the burnt boat and the pair are soon at the door. It hangs on its hinges, and the old iron that has held it in place since Pel arrived God knows how long ago is buckled and snapped. As Nancy pushes it inwards, Patroclus drops his ears and growls.

It is a wreck. Papers and books torn and scattered across the floor, Pel's maps torn and trampled. The ink stain on the table is still there, but the butterfly cases are shattered, and their iridescent dust covers every surface, giving the destruction a cast of magic that the scene does not deserve. Nancy lifts a hand to her mouth at the sight of it and bends to search the table for the book she came for, Pel's book. So engrossed is she in her search that for a moment she cannot hear that the dog is still growling. Patroclus is pointing to the furthest corner and baring his teeth. Sat on a chair, in the eddies of Pel's life, is the Reverend Jacob Cleaver, as white as a sheet and staring at a ghost.

'You died.' His voice is thin and quiet, but Nancy still starts at it. She takes a breath and turns, kneels to fuss at Patroclus, then stands and lifts a broken vase from the table. The flowers in it dead and dried. She crushes a rose head between her fingers.

'I was killed,' she spits the words at him. 'I'm feeling better.' The Murmur rises within her and there is a roll of thunder outside. The ground shakes and Cleaver leaps from his chair, eyes darting, and looking frailer than he's done before. Nancy stills a flare of panic. *It comes unbidden now, then.* She does not know how to stem the flow, so she distracts herself.

'Pel doesn't believe me, doesn't think you have it in you, but I know it was you who brought him back.'

The tremors subsiding, the Reverend sits again, a cloud of butterfly dust rising as he does so. Patroclus has not let up his growl and Nancy lays a hand on his head to quiet him. Stepping through the papers and broken bottles, Nancy drags a chair across the floor and sits opposite Cleaver. She can see him more clearly now; the priest looks haunted. The steel is still there, though, in the ice of his eyes. So she presses her advantage.

'You aren't looking well, Cleaver.'

The old man sits and fiddles with his hands, his eyes darting occasionally to the open moor, visible through the broken windows, searching for someone.

'You might find this hard to believe, Nancy, but I am pleased to see you. Is Pel back too?'

Nancy stiffens.

'No, Cleaver. Pel is dead.' The panic again. The weight in the pit of her stomach. For a moment the Reverend looks genuinely sad. It passes.

'Hm. I suspected. The rabble that did this beat on the door for hours and then it simply opened, let them in. You can live too long, you know, Nancy. Life catches up with a person in the end. And a father shouldn't outlive his child.'

Nancy feels the rage spread like the gorse fire through her body. The Murmur rocks the boat. She can barely contain herself and it takes all her will to quiet the forces building inside of her. But she does, she lets the old man speak.

'He was only doing what he thought best, Callum. He is a good boy. You would have tried to stop him from doing our work. You would have desecrated our mission as you did the graves at the chapel.' He turns to her then and she recoils, his blue eyes filled with tears, but wide open and shining with madness.

'God gave him back to me. Gave him the grace to forgive me. Gave me the tools to bring him back. You see that, don't you?' His eyes search Nancy for assent but she gives him none.

'God? God did nothing, Cleaver. I don't fully understand how you brought that thing to life, but it isn't holy, and it isn't Callum.'

'But it is, Nancy. It is. He is changed, it's true. But he has been shaped into the sword of God. He has been sent back to me, to help me, to ensure no other father suffers as I have. To ensure that our valley is safe from the evil Pel has spread across it.'

'What are you talking about, Cleaver? The people Callum killed were good, they were kind!'

'They were hypocrites! They made a mockery of God.' Cleaver twists to his feet, his lithe frame suddenly powerful and in the debris of the boat he looks like a wraith. 'They sat every Sunday and listened to me preach. Nodded along. And then went home and left gifts for devils they think live on the moor. Bronwen, before she died. She asked me to pray for her sister. You recall she was ill. But then, of course you do, because is it not true that she came to you and Pel to ask for a charm? A charm you gladly sold her?'

Nancy is up now too and jabbing a finger into the old priest's chest.

'And why is that so wrong, Cleaver? For a worried woman to hedge her bets? What damage does it do to you, to anyone?'

Cleaver stands firm against her accusations and looks around the detritus of Pel's life.

'What damage? You of all people should know the damage it does. What kind of life have you had, working for him? I remember you, Nancy Bligh. You were such a happy girl, before Lord Hunt involved himself in your life. Is this the life your mother would have chosen for you, had she lived? You should be married. A mother yourself! I only wish I had spoken up. Told her not to indulge him. But that was before… before I knew the damage he did. Can you not see him, girl, for the poison he is?'

Nancy ignores the priest and, walking to Pel's desk, begins searching for Pel's book. His flowers. She will need it now he's gone, and the looking distracts her from Cleaver's babbling.

'Was Pel helping your mother, with her illness? Was it him who provided her medicine?'

She continues her search; she will not be drawn. Not like this, not by him. It's only now she remembers the book was with her when Callum—when she died. The thought engulfs her, and Cleaver's words come as though underwater. Still, they make it through.

'No healthy woman dies so quick. Think about it. It's how he worked. Callum was fine until he got involved. Until he began pouring poison into his ear about piskies and magic.'

Nancy grits her teeth and turns.

'My mother was sick, Cleaver. She was sick and she died and Pel did everything he could to help. I understand you are angry, upset. But do not press this. Callum was sick too. And he died. Pel did his best for both. He wasn't perfect. But he did his best. Now leave, I need to collect some things and you are not welcome here.'

She turns back to the desk and waits for the sound of

Cleaver leaving. It does not come. The priest stays exactly where he is.

'It was Pel who gave me the idea.'

Nancy pauses.

'He sent me a translation of the Christian rites of his home. Years ago, when we still shared our beliefs with each other. It made very interesting reading.'

She faces the old preacher.

'Left on the dark shore, let black water or white light take you.' Nancy shivers every time she reads it.

'To torment or to rest. Yes, Nancy, that's it. Did he speak much about how he was raised? An interesting outlook, the church of his home. It gave its adherents a choice. You can worship inside the chapel walls, or outside of them. But you had to make a choice. Or it would be made for you. It did not register at the time, another of Pel's stories, but after Callum died... we all must live by something, Nancy, do you see? We should all be willing to die for what we believe. Callum was. Callum did.'

Nancy listens quietly. She doesn't interrupt. Cleaver has moved to stare out of the wrecked window.

'I tried. Nancy. After I saw the damage Pel's teachings cause—after my son died—week after week I tried to explain, to show the dangers. Some came to me willingly. Calder and his sons, Cusk too. Then more. You know it's true, Pel hadn't been their Keeper—in any sense—for years. He didn't seek out those that needed help. He sat and waited for them to come to him, or he sent you out in his place. Why would they come to me? Why work, why give themselves to Him, body and soul, why repent and strive to be better when the two of you offered solutions tied up with string? I could have helped them, Nancy. I could have. Not with trinkets or salves but with a listening ear and a thoughtful word. Those that turned to me knew it. They sat and listened and chose the white light of the Lord, put aside this belief in creatures of the moor. My congregation grew, steadily. There were always going to be those I'd not reach, like you and Madge. You chose too. And that was fine. I can live with that, not all can be saved, and you were firm in your faith. I respect that. It was the rest. The uncertain, the ones that wanted it all. That I couldn't abide, Nancy. I just couldn't. You probably think I'm mad, but this was the last resort. Truly it was. I was at my wits end, lying awake at night knowing Pel was sat here. A rusted nail in a wound, preventing it from healing. It's funny, really, that he provided my answer. I found Pel's translation again by chance, it fell out when I was rearranging papers and suddenly, it slipped into place. A key in a lock. I gave them a choice. Me or the moor.'

'And Callum?'

'We are given tests, in this life, Nancy. As Job was tested, so was I. Elizabeth... you did not know my wife, did you?' Turning from the window, Cleaver's lip shakes as he talks. 'She was the rose in this tangle of thorn.' His gaze is distant, fixed on a ghost. 'Callum has her eyes.' The Reverend lifts a broken frame from the wreckage, the pressed flowers it held turning to dust between his fingers. 'God sent the Devil to Job. He sent me Pel. That man took everything from me, and I watched as he did it. He took my family then he took my parish. Can you imagine it, Nancy? The loneliness of a church with no congregation? Of an empty, loveless home?' There is a crack from the rear of the boat as a rafter falls, the sound of breaking glass. Nancy does not answer, and Cleaver's sermon goes on.

'Sometimes, Nancy, when we have lost all hope, God shows

us a way. I came close, yes, but I never turned away from Him and as my reward my son was given back to me. I was lying awake, staring at his gorse wood cross, and he knocked on my door. Even as he now is, when I opened it, I knew my boy. Weak, yes, but returned. He helped me. Showed me which of the books I should use. Showed me what he needed to be strong again, to stand at my side, to help me as he was always meant to do.'

'It was you who cut apart those poor men?'

A flash of fire in the Reverend's eyes.

'God meant it to be so. Three men, dead that past month. An unusually high number. It was a sign.'

Nancy scoffs.

'It was a wet and dangerous month.'

Cleaver ignores her and she sees in the old man's eyes that he believes himself to be speaking the truth.

'The books were clear. A liver for blood, a heart to pump it. A spleen to regulate his bile. Once they had been sewn into him, he was reborn. My darling boy. God's avenging angel given to me.'

'Callum is no gift, Cleaver. You just finished building a monster you raised. Callum stole his power from a different god; there is nothing holy in him. His hand is marsh fire, it's from below not above. He is not here to help you. He's here for vengeance, yes, but it is his own he's seeking.'

'You felt it, did you not, his hand?' Cleaver's eyes shine as he speaks.

Nancy nods.

'It is the Lord's own, Nancy. Vengeful and old. God had seen my strife, seen my effort to repair this place, and let him in. Seen how I had been thwarted by a godless man. Callum was his gift to me. It is as Milton promised. "*Should intermitted vengeance arm again his red right hand.*" He sought them out, my son, the hypocrites, the unbelievers. I had always planned for him to be at my side, shepherding our flock. Death has merely sharpened his righteousness. I hold the crook; he sniffs out the wolves.'

Nancy shakes the image free from her head.

'And the charms, Cleaver? Those clumsy keys and bags of bones. What of them? I saw your collection. Why replace good charms with bad?' The Reverend's face breaks into a worried frown and Nancy sees. 'You were scared they might work, weren't you? Might stop you somehow? You staged charms you knew held no power.'

'Those trinkets were the devil's work. As an agent of good it was my duty to remove them. I needed the village to see, though, had to show them proof. So I made trinkets of my own.'

'What does it matter? Billy Aksell almost hanged for his trinkets!'

She has lost him. Nancy can see it in his vacant, enraptured eyes. He has not heard a word and when he speaks, though his voice is distant, there is an edge to it.

'Callum brought it to me, Nancy. His spell book.'

'I... what do you mean, Cleaver?'

Cleaver smiles, a cruel and thin smear that spreads across his face.

'Pel's spell book. Callum brought it to me. I burnt it. The night you left. To prevent his infection from spreading further.'

This is too much. Nancy leaps at the old man, grabbing the lapels of his black coat and hurling him backwards, over the chair and leaving him splayed on the floor of the boat. He weighs almost nothing. Standing over him, she can feel the Murmur rise, and above anyone, he deserves to feel it. But Madge, crushed beneath the stone, flashes in front of her eyes and she holds it in place, a quiver in her chest. Barely contained. As it pulses and rocks the boat, books fly from the few remaining shelves. As before, in the village, at the chapel yard, the air is thick with the scent of an oncoming storm.

'You did *what*?' If the air is the storm, then Nancy's voice is the lightning. Cleaver pulls back from it, flinches from her words. 'You had no right to that book, Cleaver! None!' Though she is furious, devastated, Nancy uses every nerve to stop herself from crying. That book was Pel's life. It was his aide. She couldn't picture the Keeper without it. His coat and stick were just props, the book though, the book was him. Still sprawled in front of her, Cleaver holds her gaze. If he is aware of the magic that she is barely holding back, then he does not show it.

'I destroyed it as I would any evil. As I took the charms. I have a purpose again, Nancy. Callum has given me that and neither Pel nor his nonsense has any place in it.'

Clenching her fists, Nancy takes a step towards the priest still lying on the floor. As she moves, she steadies her breathing, focusing her attention on the man at her feet. Everything in the boat hums now. At the back of the mind, she recalls the ink-reading, the shaking and confusion she had blamed on her inexperience. But she recognises it now. It was her. It was the Murmur, and she needs it under control. She'll do this, level-headed, with pinprick carefulness. Cleaver holds his son's leash. She can't risk letting Callum run free. She scans the room for something, anything to ground her and her eyes rest on a framed row of pressed flowers. Orchids. She stares at them until the Murmur fades then breathes deep and extends a hand to the sprawled priest.

'Get up, Cleaver. I'll not ask again. But I'll say this. If your son is back as some divine retribution, as some great balancer, why kill me? I'm not one of your hypocrites. I don't believe a word you say. Why did Callum kill me that day? Why were you so scared of him?'

For a second Cleaver's expression falters and something close to doubt passes across it. Then it is gone, the clouds clear, and the cold blue of his eyes shines again. Without speaking the old priest struggles to his feet and collects himself. It seems for a moment that he will talk to her, that he has something to say, but this too passes, and without a word, he leaves.

Nancy watches him go, and once the door closes, she sinks to her knees. The energy she had been generating stops and dissipates like blood in water. Patroclus stops growling and nuzzles his head into her side. Reaching out an arm, Nancy strokes him and looks around for other friends. There is movement, under the desk, in the darkness with the torn books.

'You can come out, darlings. He's gone.' Her voice stutters with a grief that's barely held.

From the shadows the otter-faces of the brownies emerge, and they clamour around Nancy, wrapping arms around her legs, climbing on Patroclus' back to reach her better. She lets them fuss, takes the comfort they offer.

'How did this happen then?' She motions to the mess, to the decay. The brownies look at each other nervously, and Nancy gives them a reassuring smile. She knows how this happened. Pel died. After the fire, she supposes; that's why it didn't take as fully as it could have. They must have come back recently to finish the job. The door just a door; no magic to hold it shut. The fact that nothing seemed damaged, just strewn about, was a testament to her friends.

'I'm taking some things, but then I'm going home. Will you come?' The brownies shake their heads sadly, and one points to the threshold. It takes a moment for their meaning to reveal itself to Nancy, but she gasps when it does. 'You can't leave?' The brownies shake their heads. Nancy remembers Pel telling her about them, the first time she came home with him, after her mother had died. He had said that they were bound to a place, until they weren't needed any longer.

'He's gone, loves. Pel isn't coming back. Come with me.' The brownies retreat to the shadows and Nancy thinks she can almost make out their whispering. When they return, the one who had gestured before comes to the front, nods. Nancy smiles and begins to collect what she needs. She lifts broken-spined from the floor the books Pel had so neatly stored and places them into a bag. She takes Pel's maps, too, carefully rolling them into tubes. His souvenirs, his ostrich eggs, and giant's bones she leaves; they aren't her memories. She opens each drawer in every cabinet and carefully lifts out the bottles and jars within, placing them gently in trunks and cases. It takes three trips, back and forth—Selkie's saddlebags filled, and a cart found in the stable—before she has all she needs. Looking about the boat she smiles. There are three things still to pack. Pel's coat still hangs on the door, heavy and still smelling of him, his ghost still haunting the threads. She takes the slate axe too, that Pel had used to split his logs, with its soot-blackened blade and handle worn smooth by use. Finally, and with trepidation she picks up the cane with its brass-snout handle.

'Closest I'll get to you now, Pel. I'll keep it safe.' And turning, she's gone and out onto the moor. Sitting astride Selkie, cane at her side, coat spread across the horse's flanks, she takes a last look at the boat. The brownies, crowded in the doorway, spill out onto the grass and ring the boat. Nancy realises that the birds have stopped singing, the wind has fallen still. She cannot hear the chant, but she feels it, first in the back of her skull and then up through Selkie's hooves as the moorland itself begins to shake. Tears stream down her face as she watches Pel's home lift from its moorings, the wood splintering and buckling in the middle as the whole structure is swallowed by a newly emerged quaking bog that swallows it down like a hungry whale. When it is over, the brownies climb into Selkie's mane and there is nothing to see but bubbles breaking blackly on the peat-stained water. Nancy doesn't move, doesn't make any sign. But her horse knows her mistress and begins the quiet walk home.

HONEYSUCKLE

NANCY SPENDS THE next night in silence. As Pel's rehomed brownies fight with Nancy's for space beneath the floors, Patroclus growling now and then to keep the peace, Nancy lies on her bed and stares at the ceiling. The bags of Pel's belongings lay still packed in piles on the floor. She can't face going through them yet. The sinking of the boat is another nail in her father's coffin. The loss of the book cuts deep. She's not sure she can summon magic without it, not the safe kind. Her own magic, the Murmur, that keeps breaking out—that is an entirely different problem. Madge beneath the chimney stack. That was her. That is her fault. Her heart flaps in her chest like a butterfly under a glass. Pel's book was a cabinet, each drawer locked. The flowers the keys. She needs that focus. She is dangerous without it.

She drifts off to sleep dreaming of a garden.

As she opens her eyes the next morning, Nancy squints against the bright gloom of the day. The sky is grey, but bright with it, and through the window she can see a cloud of starlings pulse across the clouds. She feels the Murmur respond to its namesake. *Quiet*. She doesn't think it hears her, but it stops, nonetheless. Groaning, she turns to face the room. On the table, fussing over a pot of coffee, are Pel's brownies and hers, slapping hands away from the sugar bowl, tripping over mugs.

'Good morning.' Nancy forces out a smile and they stop their quarrelling. Swinging her feet from beneath the sheets, Nancy yawns. From the corner, the thump, thump of Patroclus's tail beats out. The old dog is happy to see her rise. She passes to the table and sits quickly, avoiding the mirror on the wall. Though she can't bring herself to look again, her hand is feeling the scar, tracing the scarred tangle of roots from her neck to her collarbone. She shrugs it off and drinks her coffee. 'What'll we do then, loves? Who's to be first?'

She makes a list in her head. Cleaver, the Underfolk, the wish hounds, the Hunt. Callum. It is a list that sits very heavy indeed, each task clamouring to be the first completed. As she thinks, a brownie pushes a plate of fried kidneys, pungent with mustard and ground spices, under her nose and for the briefest moment she is free from worry. She eats, eyes closed, and enjoys her meal. When done, she stands and goes to the dresser. She pauses, and instead rummages in a box, pulling another pair of striped regimental trousers from it, brought with her from the boat before it sank. She had enjoyed the freedom they had given her, and they reminded her of him. She draws them tight about her waist with a stamped leather belt. She takes a new shirt, white with rowan leaves embroidered on the collar, puts it on over her chemise and tucks them both into the waistband of the trousers. Next are her riding boots, polished and shining black, the heels tall enough to grip a stirrup. She ties her hair back with a red ribbon and then turns to face the ghost in the room. Pel's coat hangs over the kitchen door, lifeless. She pulls it down and holds it for a moment before swinging the heavy cloth around her shoulders. It feels different now that he's gone. Picking up the brass head cane on the way, Nancy walks to the mirror—the full-length wood framed one in the bedroom—and confronts herself in the polished glass. The coat sags, several sizes too large, and where she once found comfort, she now only sees the space he's left behind.

'This won't do,' she sighs. 'This will not do.'

Patroclus noses open the bedroom door and stands next to his mistress. The sight of herself, the baggy silhouette next to the old dog, cane in hand, teases a smile from the corner of her mouth. The first green leaf on a tree after winter. But the joy stops there.

'Quite the Keeper, hey, old man?' and she's not sure if she's talking to Pel or the dog. She paces around her small cottage, picking at the cuffs of the coat, shrugging at the heavy fabric. Eventually she stops. Gives a short sharp nod to the shadows. She takes off the coat, leans the cane by the door, and reaching under the bed draws out a wicker basket with a quilted top. Her grandmother's sewing box. Then her mother's, now hers. She lays it in front of her like there is a ferret trapped within. Opens it gingerly so nothing escapes. She takes the coat and lays it on the table. Takes out a pair of long bladed scissors.

'Sorry, Pel.' Nancy takes the scissors in her hands and sets to work. After carefully unpicking the seams, she cuts deep slashes through the thick wool of the overcoat's back. She folds the fabric, trims it, and darts the old coat at the waist, drawing it in. She takes apart the collar too. Pairing back the wide lapels and turning it up, so it will hug her neck when cold. Into the hem she sews lead weights, so it flares as she turns. It is mid-afternoon before she is close to finishing, and when she is done, she pulls it back on, watches it fall and settle across her shoulders. Her thoughts from the boat return. The coat is a prop. Though one that reminds her of him. Smells of him. Without the book, she is half a Keeper. Aside from Pel's magic, the spells and wards she's yet to learn, without something to focus her, the Murmur will engulf her. She knows it.

The rest is just a masquerade. Nancy takes off the coat, her boots. She walks to the chair by the fire, lit in anticipation by the brownies. Patroclus had beaten her to it and is already asleep by the hearth. The clock on the mantle ticks loudly.

'Stop your tutting,' Nancy has her eyes closed. 'I know I should be out there.' She closes her eyes and tries to picture the book. Each time she thinks of it there is a tremble as her rage sets the Murmur to stirring.

She breathes. Steadies herself. Pictures a daisy and twists her hand into the shape of the spell. Nothing. She can't get a hold of it. Can't keep the daisy in mind. Cleaver's gloating face keeps drifting through her brain. She clenches her jaw and tries again. The spell is simple, it is the first she learnt. Daisy. Hand. Cleaver.

'Blast it!' She shouts and kicks the small table next to the chair. Screams out to a man she knows can't hear her. 'How am I supposed to do this? A century of practice and you still needed that bloody book. Gods Pel!' Eyes closed she tries again, and again and each time the same.

Daisy. Hand. Cleaver.

Daisy. Hand. Cleaver.

Daisy. Hand. Cleaver.

'Gods!' She tries again and this time Cleaver is joined by a brutal host. The Hunt, Cutty, and Bluecap, and she screams in frustration as Callum looms before her, his burning hand reaching for her neck. She kicks the table again, stands, turns, and glowers at Pel's overcoat. The coat stares back reproachfully from its chair. It knows she's the reason it needed altering. *And I still don't fit.*

Sitting back down, she lets the monsters subside. Once they have gone, she closes her eyes and thinks again of flowers. Thinks of the garden she dreamt before. The orchids trapped behind smoke-glazed glass. She is exhausted, and without the spell to complicate things, it finally works: sleep finds her in the thicket she's created, and she falls asleep with the setting of the sun.

IN THE DREAM Pel is sitting away from her. Guarding her, seated on a grass hummock, back turned. She shouts, but he cannot hear her, focused on a receding storm, lost on the horizon. She takes a step, feet sinking into the moorland, the sky a shadow of itself and the ground a black scar of burnt grass. She feels the Murmur shake itself awake inside her, feels it rattle the earth. She tries to stop it, but she cannot. Yells for her father but still he does not turn. It splits the peat, black water oozing from the fractal scar like ichor from a foetid wound and she is sinking. The black, sucking water pulls her under, fills her lungs. After an eternity drowning, she rises again. Raised up on climbing vines. They wrap around her, locking her arms at her sides. A tendril wrapped around each finger and like the breaking of twigs each joint snaps, knuckles pop, her hands remade into claws. Nancy screams but another vine snakes around her throat. She can feel it itch, like a nettle sting at first, but it blisters and boils, the skin tearing, the pus running down her neck, and when the pain is greatest, when every twist of the vine is agony its grip tightens, it snaps her neck just as before. Her head hangs limply, her body too, both held aloft by the vines released by the Murmur. When the vines have had their fill, her broken body is pulled back into the mire, and the vine around her own neck grows taut. As it cracks her neck back into place she can feel the vertebrae of her spine realign, feels the bone scrape against bone. The vines tighten then blossom with thorns that mix her blood with the peated water. Red swirling with the black. The vine retreats, and Nancy steps back up onto the moor. She raises her hands and closes the earth beneath her, the Murmur hers to control.

Finally, Pel turns. Face fixed in a smile. Then he's blown to dust by the beating of the Murmur's wings. She sees herself, as though from afar. Alive. Floating ten feet above the ground with eyes that boil with black tar. Beneath her, on the newly made ground a patch of ragwort rises and blooms. In the distance a woman laughs.

NANCY WAKES WHEN she hears the horse arrive, her head clouded with the fog of a too-brief sleep, sweat drying cold on her brow. Heavy hooves on compacted earth and the jingle of bells. Patroclus lifts his head and cocks an ear towards the sound, but Nancy raises a hand to still him. She's called for no guest.

Standing, she walks to the front pulling the newly fitted coat across her shoulders, slipping her feet into the leather boots. Her hand reaches for the cane, but it feels clumsy, so she replaces it by the door. Instead, she pockets three glass vials from the shelf. She is about to open the door when she sees the brownies have gathered around. She'd never seen them this eager to greet a guest.

'Who is it that's come, dearies?' The brownies raise their faces, there's anticipation in their eyes. Nancy realises she has her hand at her neck. Stroking the welt that rises around it. She pushes her hand into her pocket and stands straight. Feels for one of the vials and opens the door. She'll meet whoever this is head on.

It is a girl, about nineteen, or twenty perhaps, and she rides an old draft horse. Nancy cannot tell the breed, but it reminds her of a French breed she saw in one of Pel's books. A Trait Breton? It is flaxen chestnut and its blonde locks blow in the breeze tied with bright ribbon and silver bells. Its tail the same. There is no tack. No saddle. Not even a simple bridle and reins. The girl herself wears a long riding cape, the hem muddied after a long journey, and the hood is down. Bare feet hanging from beneath it. It could have been red, once, but has faded to a russet brown and it blends with the bronze coat of the horse. Her freckled face shines in the cold twilight air and she smiles under a tangle of auburn hair that sits like a nest on her head. You can almost hear the birds singing from it.

'Good morning,' Nancy steps off the step to greet her guest who is swinging herself from the horse's back. She is carrying a leather case that she must have held in her lap as she rode; it clinks as she carries it.

'And to you, Nancy.' The girl's voice has a lilt to it, an echo of the sea, it reminds Nancy of the creature that took Pel's horse. 'I'm sorry about Pel.' Nancy stops. Her body stiffens against the grief. She pushes the thought back and reaches out a hand in greeting.

'You have me at a disadvantage, Miss—?' The girl does not respond, just clutches her bag close, as if scared that Nancy will take it, and steps past her into the house. She smells like almonds, like the blossom on hawthorn. Nancy does not move to stop her, the reason why that might be no more than a leaf passing on the breeze, she follows her inside.

'More pleasant than that old boat, isn't it?' The stranger talks as if the two are friends. She talks as though they are mid-conversation. 'And old friends, I see!' The brownies swarm from the shadows, Pel's ones pushing past Nancy's to preen at the visitor's feet. She kneels to greet them before moving to the table, discarding her cloak on the way to reveal a loose smock beneath. Plain linen embroidered with bright red thread in crosses and flowers. The stitches pulling the fabric into elaborate pleated patterns around the yoke and cuffs. Nancy finds she is smiling but banishes it beneath what she hopes is a professional frown.

'I'm sorry, who are you? Why are you here?' The girl does not answer. She opens her case then, a scowl furrowing her brows, moves around the cottage. It's a little unsettling, watching her move through the house. She opens drawers as if she lives there, always finding what she's seeking, never making a mistake. Cloth and bowls to fill with water, tinctures, and ingredients—Nancy's eyes widen—for pain relief. The brownies still gather round her, and Nancy can see Patroclus, sleeping in the corner. It's fine, she reassures herself. If they trust her, then it is fine. But still, a worry lingers. After what seems like an hour, the girl takes a seat and motions Nancy to join her. On the table is a bottle of black ink. Next to it a series of intricately carved wooden sticks, each topped with a binding of savage looking needles. Nancy swallows hard at the sight of them.

'Sit down, Nancy.' Nancy does. 'Forgive me, but there is a way of doing things and I'm as bound by it as you are.' The girl clears her throat. 'Nancy Bligh. You have been nominated by Lord Pelagius Hunt, last holder of the post—currently deceased—to succeed him as Keeper of the High Moor. Do you accept?'

Nancy nods, against her better judgement; she has a *lot* of questions.

'Excellent. Then, as is my duty, agreed by all parties living, dead, and eternal, I come to make the marks.'

The girl raises her right hand and moves it in a pattern

Nancy struggles to follow. A daisywheel perhaps. A hexafoil. Once she's done, the visitor visibly relaxes. Laughs.

'Sorry my love, always awkward that bit. Pel looked just like you do when it was his turn. Well, not quite like you.' She laughs again at Nancy's dazed expression, winks. 'I've walked the moor a good deal longer than you'd think to look at me, longer than you'd ever imagine I'd wager.' Nancy, still speechless, looks at the table of needles and inks and the smallest corner of this puzzle makes sense.

'You're a tattooist?'

'I'm *the* Tattooist. Yes. Amongst other things.'

'Pel never mentioned you, I'm sorry I didn't catch your name...'

'My name is not important. And no, of course he didn't.' She gives Nancy a smirk, raises her eyebrows and despite her confusion Nancy laughs in return. The first real laugh since she returned from the Undermoor.

'Don't worry,' says the girl. 'You are far from the first Keeper to bear my marks. There are some signs that I must make, they go with the job, but the rest is up to you. I remember Pel's design; I can do that if you w—'

'No,' Nancy stops her. 'Not the same as Pel.'

Nancy closes her eyes, she can feel a thought tickling at the back of her skull, taking root. Her eyes open and she smiles.

It comes to her fully formed.

Nancy talks the girl through her idea, her act of remembrance. Her solution. When she is done, the girl smiles and motions to the bed.

'Are you sure you want this? I know Pel's named you as his successor, but you could decline the task. It's not official until I'm through.' Nancy shakes her head, her mouth set hard. The visitor nods. 'Well then, I shan't argue. Not often I have cause to use these.' She goes back to her case and besides the vial of black she withdraws row after row of bottles. A rainbow of inks within. She pulls the table over to the bed and perches on the edge.

'Undress,' Nancy doesn't question it. She removes her clothes and lies on the bed. 'Here,' the girl passes her a bottle the shape of a teardrop, 'it will help.' It tastes of angelica. The tattooist dips the head of one of the needles into the black ink and without further warning, begins. When the first needle pierces the skin of her shoulder, she braces against the heat of it. The room slips. The draught starts working. The roof fades to black and tendrilled plants curl from the shadows. Blocking out everything but the bed, the room hidden behind the shifting blues and greens of a forest. The girl's needles find a rhythm, and Nancy finds her breathing mimicking it. Breathe in, then out as the needles slide in. The girl's hands rocking on her skin, the pressure of her palms easing aching muscles. The draught is not perfect, it has only lessened the pain, but the little left-behind is the sweetest part.

As she works, the Tattooist talks softly, though Nancy can't make out the words, and she places each mark carefully. She moves Nancy's body with care, lifting her arms, gently moving her legs as the needle runs up her thigh. The girl leans close and Nancy's head spins with the scent of almonds. She trails her hands across Nancy's body, mapping her marks the way an astronomer maps the stars. Her splayed fingers a set of callipers. The spinning room an astrolabe. The Tattooist traces the line of Nancy's collarbones with her fingertips, pausing at the notch where they meet before moving her hands down, between Nancy's breasts, across the muscles of her stomach. Nancy lies ragdoll beneath her; the room fills with sparks of light. There is a moment, as the needle passes over her hip where the bone and skin come closest to touching, that causes Nancy to wince, her eyes to water. The breath juddering out of her as she relaxes back into the pain.

'Good girl.' The words a whisper but they still Nancy's breath. She hangs in ecstatic silence until the next press of needled ink, and Nancy's body shakes under the weight of it. Nancy exhales, and then her breath comes deep and steady as she licks blood from her lips; she hadn't known she'd been biting them. The Tattooist reaches for Nancy's neck, traces the mark left there and Nancy tenses, but the girl's touch feels safe, and it passes. Still, as the needles meet the scar there is a shudder that runs through the cottage as the Murmur pushes against the pain. Nancy lets it out, then takes it in, and hears the strange girl's breath catch as she does it. The Tattooist works throughout the night, and when she is done, there is not an inch of skin she has not tended to, that has not felt the brush of her fingertips, the bite of the needle. Nancy's body aches, it is hot to the touch. Each time she shifts on the bed there is a new thrill of pain. The girl lifts Nancy. Holds her tight to her as she wraps her body in clean white bandages. Removes the bloodied bedsheets and lays a blanket down in their place. She lays Nancy back down tenderly, as though unwilling to let her go. Nancy smiles at her, she feels the kindness even through the haze of the draught, its tendrils now receding, the room returning to view. The moon shimmers back into existence through the rear window. She passes out into sleep and hopes the pain cuts through to her dreams.

THE SCREECH OF an owl wakes her. The savage, human cry of a barn owl, and Nancy sits upright at the sound in a panic, heart racing and her head filled with wish hounds and Huntsmen and Callum Cleaver's hand. Of Mirecoombe on fire. Madge crushed beneath a stone.

The cottage sinks in darkness. Hard to tell what time it is. Looking out of the window, she sees only black clouds drawn tight across the starlight, blocking out the setting moon. She slows her breathing, *it's okay,* she holds the thought firm to calm her *you've only been sleeping for a few hours.* It's only once the shock of waking so suddenly has worn off that Nancy feels the tattoos. Her entire body aches, every nerve ending throbbing. There's no point in trying to return to sleep.

Careful not to wake Patroclus, who still sleeps soundly, or the brownies who have earnt their rest, Nancy crosses to the desk and lights the oil lamp. In the warm circle of light, she looks down at the wraps that hug her body. She can feel them sticking to her skin in places, can see the pinpricks of blood seeping through. She smiles at the memory.

Nancy looks about, a blush of hope across her chest at the thought that the girl might have stayed, though she knows she hasn't. The smell of hawthorn fading already. She sees it then, the folded paper on the table leant across an object wrapped in cloth, and smiles, her cheeks reddening. She runs to it, only slightly embarrassed at her excitement at the gift. Across the front is her name, written in an elegant and curling hand. The back sealed with black wax, a three-tined spear pressed into it. She pops the seal open with a satisfying crack and reads.

Nancy,

   I hope you like it. It will hurt like hell, for a while, but I've left something that will help. Leave the bandages

until the morning then remove them, carefully. I've taken
my payment. You'll not miss them. I'll treat them well.
  Be safe.
  C x
  P.S I've left you two gifts. Pel and I were friends, or the
closest either of us had to one. He'd have wanted you to
keep it. The other is from me.

Nancy holds the paper for a moment, lingers on the initial, on the kiss. Her eyes still catching on it as she turns back to the payment. What could she have taken? She notices the quiet then. Her stomach drops and she calls out into the darkness.

'Hello, are you there? My loves?' Bleary-eyed brownies shuffle out into the light. She recognises those that lived with her, but Pel's are gone. Panicking, she calls again, but no more spirits appear. She can feel the loss, as though a hand has a grip on her heart, one of the cottage's attendants steps forwards, places a small hand on her leg. Nancy looks down into large eyes and kneels to meet them.

'They've gone?' The brownie nods. 'Will they be safe?' They nod again and turn and vanish back into the shadows with the rest. Distraught, Nancy sits at the desk, ignoring the pain it causes. She knew they would not all stay, but she'd have liked to wish them goodbye.

Patroclus, who has up to now remained sleeping, raises his old body up and pads over to where she sits before slumping heavily to the floor. Nancy looks to the moon. She had thought to go back so sleep but her body is alive with pain, her heartbeat quickens at the thought of all she has to do, and though she won't face what's coming in the darkness, there'll be no sleeping now. Her fingers drum on the surface of the table. Turning back to the roll of fabric on the desk, Nancy draws it towards her and opens it carefully. It is well wrapped, and she can feel the shape of multiple items trapped within its folds. It reminds her of a party game she played long ago.

The first object to emerge is a stoppered vial. Removing the cap, she inhales deeply and coughs at the mixture of scented oils stored within. Instructions for its use written on the label. Placing it carefully to one side, Nancy continues to unroll the present. Next to emerge is a hair pin. Each of the two tines are sharp and capped with a spray of varnished blackthorn, thorns intact, that glisten blackly in the morning light. Smiling, Nancy presses her fingertips to its needle points, dares herself to draw blood. A chill runs down her spine, not unpleasantly, and Nancy places the pin next to the bottle.

There is only one thing left in the bundle and as she gets closer, Nancy feels a tingle of familiarity. As the last layer is folded away, she gasps. It looks like Pel's stick. She looks back into the room to check, but it is not where she left it, leant against the range. It is his. The original. But the visitor has changed it. The brass-nosed creature still shines at the top, the snarl of its lips just as it ever was. But the shaft of the cane is shorter now, barely a foot long, and capped with a folded strap of brown leather held in place with iron bands. It is a riding crop, and it is perfect. Holding the crop in her hands Nancy twists the brass head, as she has seen Pel do countless times and withdraws the wave-ripple blade that hides within. She draws it steadily through the air in front of her. Marks the change. Holding it, now, she feels something close to confidence creep back into her body. Though the tide of panic still laps inside she can see a time when it will recede. A time, even, that she could turn it back. The moon is almost gone now, it will not be long before the morning rises. She lets the worry and anxiety of her duty in. Holds it. Pushes the blade back into the sheath.

'Come on, girl. Work to do.' She speaks to her own shadow, then turns to run a bath. When its copper sides are filled, the water warmed with kettles from the stove, Nancy pours the contents of the stoppered bottle into the bath. Swirls the liquid through the water with her hand and the room fills with heady, intoxicating scents. Nancy steps in, submerging herself in the cloudy water and closing her eyes. She can feel the water seeping into the bandages, loosening them. Clotted blood, where the needles cut deepest, falls away, turning the white water pink. Carefully, Nancy peels the sodden bandages off, dropping them out of the side of the bath into a soggy heap by its claw feet. She lets the tincture from the bottle work, can feel her skin heal, feels the ache dull until it is barely there. She reaches for the table, picking up the thorny hair pin she left there and uses it to hold her washed hair in place, out of her eyes. Standing, she lets the water drip from her and crosses to the mirror, picking an item from the desk on the way.

She stands in front of her reflection, and, for a moment, her breath catches in her throat. Every inch of her body is covered in flowers, colourful and vivid as life. Delicately painted, just as they had looked pressed in Pel's book. As though someone has taken a meadow and pressed it so hard against her skin that each petal had left a coloured bruise. She cries to see them, foxglove and tormentil and eyebright, all finding their place on her skin. She turns her hips, twists to see each mark on her. At her neck, the scar of her resurrection has been transformed into the creep of ivy it so closely resembled. Emerald, three pointed leaves winding around her throat. Here and there, between the petals, are sigils that she recognises from Pel. The signs she must bear to hold the title of Keeper. And across her heart, where Pel had his, the anchor cross of Eythin, the badge of Pel's home. She raises a hand to touch it, traces the creep of yellow rattle that winds around it, the spray of meadowsweet. Her flowers. Her magic. Always to hand. Or so she hopes. Until she tests her theory, they are just pretty pictures.

She turns her wrist and stares at the daisy she has tattooed there. Smiles. Focuses on the shape of it, the colour. The sting of its engraving. She lets it in until her head is nothing but white petals and yellow stamen, and lets her fingers curl of their own accord. Above them, hanging like a firefly, is a little orb of flickering green fire. She flicks her wrist, and the fire goes out.

She giggles.

Tries another.

Foxglove now, and the air around her shimmers, hardens into a shield. She races through them, rattle, rue, thrift, gorse. She's laughing at the flow of it. The air fills with flame and light and rippling shapes. Each time it is easier, and she knows with the first bit of confidence since she returned that her idea has worked. She keeps reaching for her face to check her smile's still there, fixed in a grin at the joy of this. She looks at herself in the mirror again. Straightens her back and reaches to the mantle for the pouch she placed there. She inhales deeply and then, nervously, hangs Pel's necklace around her neck, the red coral tooth shining, the silver chain cool on her chest. She can feel it connect to her, become a part of her, and she knows in that moment it will be around her neck until the day she dies. And now that it is on, there is no telling how long her life may be.

Drying herself, Nancy dresses. Her boots, her trousers with their red stripe, and her shirt. The newly fitted coat sweeps majestically across the floor, and when she stands in front of the mirror, she smiles. At her cuffs and throat the tattooed flowers seep out. She clutches the crop tightly with her right hand. She is ready. Rapping the leather cap of the crop against her thigh she looks at Patroclus.

'Come on then, Pat. Let's get to it again.'

RUSH GRASS

THE RAIN BEATS down, and as she rides singing to the tor, Nancy worries. She has never held a meeting without him, and she is not sure who, if any, will come. The words feel heavy in her mouth, and she considers going back for Pel's horn when she remembers it sank with his house.

'Damn.' The realisation stops her song, and she begins again. She leans down to pat Selkie on the neck, comforted by the mare's shaggy winter coat. Patroclus follows at their heels, looking about every now and again, and breaking Nancy's heart.

'It's just us, Pat. Pel's gone.' The old dog looks sadly at her, and the three carry on. The downpour is heavy, and they are almost on Echo Tor before they see the rocks loom out of the rain. 'Here we go, then.' Nancy rides into the circle and dismounts. She looks about for the Hunt, though she does not really expect to see them. They aren't tied to this place, to her. They have no reason to attend this meeting. She looks about for friendlier faces. She does not see them. Row after row of spriggan, of pisky, friends, mouths set in hard lines. There are other creatures too, drawn by the gravity of a new Keeper to leave their haunts and holloways and creep out into the day. The lantern men, the goblins. There are spirits too who have no place here. Buccas, still foaming with long-left waves with seaweed hair and black shark's eyes. Knockers, their copper skin tarnished green and carrying pickaxes, their faces ground deep with rock dust and sparkling tin. All here with heads cocked to hear Nancy speak. To be present at the birth of a new Keeper. It has been many, many years since this last happened. Nancy can feel their expectation. It weighs heavily on her. She coughs, clears her throat, and as she does the thunder rumbles overhead.

'Friends. And I do hope you will be that. Thank you for coming. My name is Nancy Bligh and I take my place as Keeper of the High Moor.' A lightning crack and from a row further back, a voice.

'And who named you as such?'

Nancy scowls. She cannot see the speaker. 'Lord Pelagius Hunt, who transferred the post to me.'

'Where is Pel?' There is a clamour of voices as those that know of Pel's death tell the others. The racket grows. 'Killed him, did you? To take his magic?' Nancy shakes as she tries to stand fast but the accusations rain down. The spirits friendly to her try to quell the rancour, but there is trouble on the way. She clenches her fists, but she can feel it rising again, the Murmur. *You're bound by these flowers too.*

Raising her left hand, she feels beneath her shirt, along her collarbone, for the red poppy tattooed there and her stomach flips with the newness of it. This access to magic, always to hand. She stills herself, feels for the Murmur, for the writhing form of it. Holds it with poppy roots. She will not lose control here, not today. She finds the voice, still laughing, and holds it in her mind alongside the sting of the nettle tattooed on her back. She forms the shape with her left hand, her right still holding the crop, and in the crowd, the voice that started the trouble stops.

'Come forward.' Through the crowd pushes a panicked looking bucca. Mouth gasping like a fish out of water. The ranks of spirits quieten down and wait to see how it ends. What kind of Keeper will she be? When the bucca stands in front of Nancy, she kneels to speak.

'I will give you your voice back, little one. But you will not speak until I ask you to. Do you understand?' The bucca nods. 'Good.' With a wave of her hand, Nancy releases the creature from the spell, but it stands there mute, eyes fixed on hers. 'You are a very long way from home. You oughtn't be drawing my attention to you. You definitely shouldn't be making me cross. Why are you here, causing trouble?'

The bucca does not speak, it waits until Nancy waves her hand impatiently for it to begin.

'Dead Keeper. New Keeper. Times have changed. The edges fray.'

Nancy scowls.

'The edges are just where they've always been, little bucca. And they are just as sharp.' She holds the gaze of the bucca, lets a closed poppy head uncurl in her mind, and the ground beneath the creatures shakes. She struggles to keep composed, to not let on how tired this makes her, and as soon as the creature looks scared enough, she snaps the poppy shut. Pushes the Murmur back down. It takes all she has to keep her breathing steady, and she hopes that in the rain nothing sees the sweat on her brow.

'Go.' The sea spirit whimpers, races down the hill and out of sight, and the remaining faces turn to each other in silence. 'I am not Pel. But he trusts me to continue his legacy, and I will. I will not let any one of you undo the peace he has brokered. Those of you who live on this moor know me. You know I am fair, that I will help, that I will keep you safe. But do not mistake that for weakness. I've been through hell for this,' she pulls her sleeve back to show the waiting spirits the black marks nestled amongst the flowers, 'and my patience is thin. Those of you who are here to gawp from mines and coasts you know I hold no jurisdiction over, go home. If I see you here again, I will be very interested to know your reasons.'

The buccas and knockers shuffle out of their seats and slope off down the hill. They are a different Keeper's problem.

'There are faces here I have not seen in a long, long time. Welcome. I am glad to see you well.' The creatures she addresses do not smile back. A pisky—Nancy knows her, her name is Kist—breaks rank and walks nervously towards her, hands open to show she comes unarmed.

'With respect,' the voice trembles, and Nancy wonders just how short a straw it drew, 'the marks are one thing. The moor is another. Are you to protect them,' the spirit gestures towards Mirecoombe, nestled in the valley, 'or us as well?' In response a howl goes up from all sides. The wish hounds keen ears tuned and listening. Nancy stands straight and speaks to the crowd.

'I understand, I do. I'm here to help everyone,' heartbeat skipping at the weight of that answer, 'and I know I need to prove it. I said before, I am not Pel. I will not, cannot, do this alone. So tonight, if you will not give me your endorsement, then at least give me your trust. Trust that I will earn this position. That I will protect those that need it against those that would do them harm. Do not mistake that kindness for laxity, or softness, but know I will listen if you talk. The hounds, the Hunt. They go back below tonight. That, I promise. The moor will be set right.' Nancy breathes a little faster at the promise she's made, at the one she's breaking. *Sorry, Pel. I know it's what you'd do.*

There is a hubbub rising from the crowd, but one by one

each face turns and nods. Kist slowly reaches behind herself, draws a flower from a bag, and lays it at Nancy's feet. Nancy recognises it from drawings in one of Pel's books. This hasn't grown on the moor for two hundred years. It is a gift from below.

The pisky bows and leaves, and then the tide begins. The creatures come to her all bearing little gifts. A spray of gorse, lumps of stone burnished smooth by moorland streams. One leaves a lump of bog-oak carved with intricate and astounding patterns. When the Underfolk are done, Nancy stands again at their centre.

'Thank you, friends. I will be the Keeper you deserve.'

The faces in the circle all nod solemnly. This is a vow they take seriously. Nancy bows to them then, to the Underfolk. To the moor she now serves.

'Thank you. I'll need you all, soon. But now, tonight, I have work to do.'

WHEN SHE HAS gone, and the spirits and creatures have left, a figure slips from their hiding place between the rocks. Stepping out, Callum Cleaver turns about in the hollow crown of the rock, the rain beating on his leather skin like a drum. He kneels amongst the gifts left for Nancy. The coloured stones and buzzard feathers. With calloused fingers, he turns each gift over in his hands. The carved bog-oak distracts him most. He seems to know the piece is special, how long it took to make. Gripping it tightly between his hands, the creature twists the wood, digging into the grain and working it back and forth. The oak is old and hard, and almost black with age, but it breaks in the end. Shattering into thousands of mire-dark splinters that pierce Callum's hardened skin, though no blood gushes from the wound. There is no blood at all.

Callum's eyes burn with pain and searching anger, and he howls into the rain and the thunder and the light. Standing, he kicks at the pile of gifts, scattering them into the wind and water, treading stones into the earth until the rock hollow is muddy with it. When he is done, he climbs to the highest of the stacks, where Cutty Soames once sat, and balances on the top. His body hangs unnaturally on his frame. The time spent in the water has warped his bones, and though he tries to stand upright, he is unsuccessful. Instead, with his chest puffed out, shoulders back, he screams away the last of his humanity into the blackening, bruising sky.

FOX SEDGE

MADGE SITS BEHIND the bar. Her left arm a scaffold of wood and pins set unceremoniously by the local cooper, under Madge's strained direction. She has no great hope it will heal, but the bones are at least set back in place. Though she feels the broken edges grate every time she moves, and it stops her mid-breath every time. Calder and Cusk sit where they always do, and the bar buzzes as if nothing has happened. As if not a day before they had tried to hang a man for nothing.

'Another please, Delen,' says Cusk, and raising his empty cup, shakes it at his friend who nods, 'and one for him.' Delen Rowe, who has come to help, takes both cups wordlessly and refills them. Madge makes a sound, a disgusted tut, and though Cusk seems not to notice, Calder's eyes fix on the landlady with a bleary, drunken scowl.

'What, Madge? Our business not welcome, is it?' He doesn't wait for a reply. 'Askell got lucky. That girl attacking my boys and taking him off is proof enough for me. Two killers loose now. Mark my words, none are safe.' Cusk grunts noncommittally. 'Look at what that witch did to you. Or are you with them? Eh?' A hush has fallen across the rest of the room as drinkers listen in. They each played a part in Billy's arrest, they're keen to hear how they've come out of it. Madge will not be baited though. Not today. Not by Calder. She keeps her thoughts to herself.

'Aye. Thought as much. We'll be needing another after this. Something stronger maybe. Give us some of the stuff you kept for Pel. I hear he'll not be needing it.'

Turning his head, Calder spits a glob of saliva onto the floor. 'Good riddance I say.'

Wordlessly, Madge points Delen to a dusty bottle on the shelf and the girl pours out a measure. At a look from Madge, she pours the landlady one, too. Madge lifts the glass with her good arm and downs it smoothly. Calder reaches for his, throws it back and falls coughing to the floor.

'Jesus, woman, what is that?' Gasping for breath, he reaches for his ale and tries to put out the fire in his throat. Madge tilts her head at Delen, who pours her another, and drinks it as the bar erupts into laughter.

'Get out, Calder, go drink at home. You too, Cusk. Everyone. The Nest is closed.'

Silence. Not one amongst them can remember the Nest shutting. If they can't drink here, then they'll have to face home, and there's few amongst them that want that. It has been a kind of spell, these last few days. The hunt for poor Harry, the detention of Billy Askell, the adrenaline thrill of potential death and each man's hand in it. With Billy gone, they have had time to think about it and nobody is as sure as they were it was the right thing to do. So, they've been here. Drinking. Waiting to be told what to do. Even Calder, bold as he is, needs directions from above, and not a soul in the village has seen Cleaver in days. They all look back to the bar, but Madge is pointedly showing Delen how to clean the pewterware and will not meet anybody's gaze. There's nothing else for them to do. Calder stands.

'Fine.' His voice still rasps from spluttering and his whole face is red. 'Come on, the lot of you. I'll open my cellar.

Come on up to the farm.' And he's out through the door with a sad trail of faces following. Hugh Dell is amongst them. He played his part in rounding up Billy, landed a few good kicks. It had calmed him, a little. But even that evening when Billy Askell seemed sure to die locked up in the longhouse, his grief and anger had returned. He has nowhere left to put it, and it eats away inside. He lingers, at the back of the queue, and after the man in front is gone, he closes the door. Alone with Madge and Delen, who shifts uneasily behind the bar.

'You too, Hugh Dell. I saw you that night. I know you're grieving, but you know Billy didn't kill Salan.'

Hugh Dell stands with fists at his side and takes a step towards the landlady.

'Be careful, Hugh. Think about this.'

Hugh Dell does stop; there is something in Madge's voice that calls for respect, there always has been. But some things run stronger.

'You can't keep defending them, Madge. Not Pel or Billy, not Nancy. None of it. They found charms on Billy, in his pockets. More than one man should have.'

'As you'd find them in mine. In Sal's. They'd have found them in yours not too long ago. Billy is a boy with more notion than he's meant for. You know how he played at magic. He bought them in town.'

'They killed my son! Those bloody charms were a beacon, Cleaver says it's so! Yes, I carried my share of them. Once. But he changed, Madge. You've not been to the chapel; you've not heard him tell it, but Cleaver knows. He tried to stop him, but Pel grew greedy, angry we were moving on without him, to the church. He killed our friends, my Sal, for power. To scare us back to him.'

Madge looks sadly at Hugh, her eyes full of tears and sympathy. Delen Rowe edges to the rear of the bar and reaches for something stowed there.

'Pel wasn't evil, Hugh. He wasn't always right, but he was never bad. Cleaver is as full of grief as you are. He's angry.'

'No. No, Madge. I'm sorry, but you're wrong. You'll have to see it sooner or later. Or you'll have to go.'

Madge waits as Hugh Dell leaves, and relaxes; Delen returns the pistol she's been clutching to its hiding place behind the bar. Madge smiles at the girl.

'Get on, Delen. I'm closing the Nest. For a while, I think. Thank you.' Delen moves to speak, but Madge raises her hand to stop her. 'Pour me another and get home. That's a good girl.' Delen does as she's asked, and steps into the fresh air with palpable relief, leaving Madge alone in the stillness of the bar. The silence does not last long.

'He's right, Madge.' Cleaver emerges from the shadows, startling her. He must have been waiting in the back bar. Creeping up on her through a memory.

'How long have you been back there, Jacob? I'd have told Delen to pour you a glass if I'd known.'

Cleaver does not answer. Instead he moves slowly towards the window, stands in the pane of light that ripples with the rain, and sighs. The hem of his cassock is muddy, wet, and beneath it, Madge can see his boots are caked in peat. He has not been here since the night of the fire.

'Do you remember those evenings, Madge? The three of us? Before all of this.' He waves a hand towards the rain, towards the line of trudging drinkers heading up towards Calder's farm. Madge nods. 'I trusted him. Madge. I trusted Pel. I trusted you.'

'Jacob, what happened? I know Callum dying hurt. It hurt

us all. But it wasn't Pel. You must realise that? He tried to help the boy, once he was returned.'

Cleaver turns, and in the cold light his features are more grave-like than ever, his blue eyes piercing the gloom with a jackdaw gaze. When they pass over her broken arm, they soften.

'Returned? For goodness' sake, Madge. Callum never went anywhere. It was a lie, to keep Pel's legend alive! And now he's... Never mind. It doesn't matter now. Pel is dead. Madge, tell me, would you have done things differently?'

'Than what, Jacob?'

'Than I have. This valley needed a guiding hand. That is all I have given it.'

The Reverend walks and takes a seat next to Madge. She places a hand on the cold, black cloth of his sleeve and squeezes his arm. He does not stop her. The pair sit together, backs against the settle, and watch the rain run down the window. Madge speaks first.

'There is room for you both, for you and Nancy. You don't need to make them choose.'

Cleaver sits for a moment before responding, and when he does, his voice has lost its assertiveness, its certainty.

'I do. It is for their own good. I can't let anyone else be lost to the moor. Not the way Callum was. If there was a way forward, a path wide enough for both of us, it was Pel who narrowed it, not I.'

'The things they helped us with have not gone. We need her still.'

Cleaver's eyes are still distant, but the strength is returning to his voice.

'The things they claimed to stop do not exist, Madge. They are not spirits or devils, only words. Superstition. But words can get too powerful. They can take a son. A friend. They hurt.'

Glancing at Madges arm, Cleaver's eyes cloud with tears, and he looks as old as he is. Frail.

'I miss my friend, Madge.' He lowers his head, and Madge puts her arm around his shoulder, lets him cry. She does not say anything. Sunlight breaks through the clouds and illuminates the last of the rain. A shadow moves past the window, the same window Salan Dell looked through the night he died. Cleaver sits up straighter, dries his tears. There is fear in his eyes.

'Thank you, Madge. But I should go. It is almost over, and he needs me.'

'Who needs you, Cleaver?' Looking again at this man who was once her friend, Madge can see this last vulnerability dissipate. In its place lies a steely-eyed determination.

'They are the better for it. I did what I had to do.'

'Jacob, what did you do?'

Cleaver turns to her, distracted, with a smile that does not reach his eyes, and places a hand on her shoulder.

'He's waiting.' The shadow passes across the window again, and Madge catches the faintest glimpse of a figure moving swiftly between the houses.

'Who is that?' The priest, still smiling, turns to leave, and Madge's stomach feels heavy and sick. 'It can't be. He's gone, Cleaver. Jacob... '

'Shh, Madge. I don't want to lose you. Rest. It will be over soon. I am sorry about the way it has gone, but it was necessary. Stay here. He can be indiscriminate, but it is not his fault. He works with God's will. And His motives are not always clear to us.' Cleaver stands and moves towards the door, and for a moment, Madge's friend is with her again, the kindness so long absent back in his eyes. 'Please Madge. Please, just stay inside.'

She struggles to find it, but she puts on a smile, and the old priest seems reassured.

'Thank you, Madge. Thank you.' And he drifts through the front door of the inn, his black cassock absorbing the sunlight and the rain in equal measure.

A shadow passes across the window again. Madge stumbles to the door and bolts it, fast.

BLACK BRYONY

THE QUEEN'S ROCKS rise like a cresting wave above the moor. The scattered stones at its peak catch the sun, shining like surf. The day is ending. The sun burns the last threads of gold from the horizon away; the stones wait patiently for the moon.

Nancy waits, too. The moor rolling out from the hem of her coat like a wedding train, the flowers picked out like embroidery on the grass. Her body still aches from the tattooist's needles and the pain works in lockstep with the cold wind, sharpening her senses. Selkie, grazing on rush grass growing from a spring, raises her head. She feels what Nancy feels, the keen anticipation of the hunt. Nancy has replaced Selkie's simple tack with the ornate and burnished set that Eponina wore. She has polished the brasses, and they hang around Selkie's neck like a golden charm bracelet. Nancy has fixed the entire set to her horse. Even the plated armour, a polished tusk set into the faceplate, covering Selkie's face. Tonight, Nancy is at war. And she's come dressed for it. Placing a booted foot into a stirrup, Nancy is astride her horse and with a swift whisk of her brass-topped crop she's away cantering, sure-footed down the hillside. This horse was born and raised on the moor. Her iron-clad hooves never miss their mark.

'Good girl.' Nancy leans forward to speak into the horse's ear, feels their canter roll into a gallop, Selkie buoyed by the praise. Here, in the foothills that ring Nancy's home there is little sign of their quarry. Nothing but friendly faces smile back at them from the stone-pitted scrub. The night sky is clear and bright, though there is a darkness coming. To the west, a rising tide of cloud is erasing the stars. A storm. Nancy can hear the thunder, and every now and then a lightning flash bursts from deep within the sky, lighting up the clouds from the inside. The Hunt is out.

She has done her research. Read all she can of them. Read and reread Pel's notes, scrawled in between the words of the Hunt's entry in the book of folktales, searched every book she saved from the boat. In between stories of chained men, of witches and wild beasts, the Hunt rode. A snippet here and there. Black horses and wild dogs. Found the account of the last time they were free. Put back by a Keeper who killed himself the next day muttering about horses that bore like ticks into the ground. She has pieced together a fragile story and hopes at least some of it is true.

One thing was constant, in all the stories: the Hunt only left when it had brought down its quarry.

Nancy shivers. She did not think they would attack within Mirecoombe. Even if they could ride there, and she suspects they can, the protections Pel has woven over the years should prevent out and out murder. Their master had dispatched them to bring someone below. She'll not let them find their victim today, whoever it may be, regardless of whether they deserve it.

She looks down at her coat, her ink coated skin. *A test,* she thinks, *before Callum.* One monster at a time. There is a single road leading into the village. The villagers, with stone to sell, fenceposts scarred with the grooves of iron spikes, drive their carts along it to the main highways. Drovers used it too, herding livestock to market. Nancy hopes that is where the Hunt is waiting. Before spurring Selkie on towards the road, Nancy pats the pockets of Pel's coat. She has prepared carefully for tonight. She couldn't afford to face the Hunt if she'd forgotten something. But no, Pel's lessons have stuck: she can feel the stoppered bottle in the right-hand pocket, feel the bundle of twine-tied totems in her left. Feels too the comforting presence of Pel's pendant hanging at her breast.

'No use dallying, Selk. Let's away.'

Following the curve of the road as it leaves the village, Nancy scans the horizon for her prey. The road follows a brook, a stream, fed from the hills and tors and lined with twisting trees whose branches bridge the water. Heaps, too, of discarded spoil long grown over with grass – the remains of ancient tin works. The clutter of the treeline makes it hard to see far ahead and Nancy strains to see through the thicket of branches.

'Where are you?' The wind takes her words and spreads them along the route. There is a rustle, starlings take flight, and Selkie rears as a creature drops from a branch onto her mane. It looks like a pisky, though not one that Nancy is familiar with. And unlike most, it has no wings. Its body, too, is different, covered in lichen and oak moss that hangs heavy over its brow, covering its eyes.

'Miss Bligh?' The creature bobs in curtsey, wobbling slightly on the horse's neck. Nancy studies it before replying.

'Yes, little one, what is it?' She is polite. She knows well enough it never pays to be rude. But she also knows not to trust a stranger, especially one that falls from the sky.

'You're looking for the Hunt, yes?' Nancy nods and the creature continues, its head darting about. 'They are ahead.

Past the bend.' Nancy nods and Selkie stamps impatiently on the bankside.

'Thank you, little one, that is very good to know.' And it is, they would have ridden straight into the Hunt without the warning. 'Tell me, what's your name? I don't think I've seen you before.' The creature shifts, and Nancy can't be certain, but it seems uncomfortable with the question. Still, the creature answers.

'Knot, Miss Bligh, my name is Knot. Someone's watching out for you, remember that.'

And with that, they are gone, diving from the neck of the horse into the brook, and swept away with the current. Nancy doesn't like it, but she can't turn away the help. She dismounts, nudging Selkie off the road and under the leafless canopy of the trees.

'Stay here, girl. I'll call when I need you.' Nancy pats the horse on her neck and pulls Pel's coat close about her. It isn't just that she wants him near. The russet brown of the coat blends with the winter grass, keeps her hidden. She moves silently through the root-lined path along the riverbank, the greedy water swallowing any extra sound as it rushes to keep pace.

She sees them soon enough. As the pisky said, just around the bend. They gallop in a circle twenty feet above the ground, the clash of hooves striking air, the horses rearing and falling, the riders whipping their mounts into a frenzy. A line of stone falls between her and the Hunt, Nancy can't see what they're circling from where she is. Tentatively, she leaves the cover of the trees and creeps across the track to where the moorland climbs away. Scrambling quietly up the hill, she moves to a vantage point above them, a granite rock her perch, and stiffens. She can see what it is they circle now. There, on the road, is a cart, one wheel lying in splinters on the road and the axle broken. Bending under the immobile vehicle is a figure Nancy knows: Yestin Calder's broad shoulders heave as he tries to right the cart. Leaning against a rock nearby, his brother Jan.

Nancy sighs, of course it is them. A part of her would keep her promise to Pel, leave the Hunt to it. She knows though that were her father here, he would try to save them. If only to crow about it.

Nancy is Keeper now; she has a job to do, besides, she had dropped the beetle into Jan's pocket. She'll not be responsible for this. Sloggett's children's tale had left out exactly how they killed, but the group are speeding up, the frenzy of the horses increasing, and Nancy knows, as sure as the pit that's forming in her stomach, that she does not have much time. Leaping from her rock she lands heavily, startling the farmer's sons. The Hunt does not change their behaviour, does not stop their advance. Once he has regained his composure, Jan Calder snarls at Nancy. Yestin hovering behind him. There is a wildness in both men's eyes. *They know something's up.*

'You? What do you want, Miss Bligh? I'm busy. If you're not going to help, then be on your way. I've no time for your nonsense. Go save another criminal.'

Nancy chews the inside of her cheek as she approaches, the only thing stopping her face descending into a scowl. The brothers show no such restraint, their faces twisting into a grimace and as she walks towards them Nancy makes a decision. Jan Calder turns his back and, pushing down on rising bile, Nancy ignores him and walks up to Yestin, leans close. Whispers urgently into his ear.

'Listen, you oaf, I need you to be sensible. I know you're not a thug like your brothers. I am helping. When the time comes,

I want you to take Jan and run, fast, back to the village. You are three steps from death, Yestin Calder, and I'll not have it on my watch.' She drops a small clay figure wrapped in twine into his pocket, then pushes him away. As she does, she moves her finger, just a little. Deep within the folds of Yestin's clothing, the bad-luck beetle folds in on itself and dies. Ignoring the stream of curses coming from her back, she faces the Hunt, who are a blur above them. One of the riders moves out ahead of the rest, their horse stamping at the air. It is a signal, and the Hunt rise up like a mourning ribbon before crashing down to earth. As each horse lands there is a shower of sparks where horseshoe strikes granite. They move so they ring the two brothers and Nancy completely. Then silence.

'Nancy—' She turns. Yestin and Jan Calder are white. Their eyes wide.

'You see them?' She turns back to the Hunt. 'They see you?' The foremost bends forwards from his saddle, and Nancy recoils as the bloody stump of a neck draws level with her eyes. For what seems like an age the rider examines her, the scent of his rotting flesh filling her nose. Then he straightens, turns back to the group, and raises an arm. His gloved hand pointing at the brothers. Nancy does not move.

'Yestin.' She speaks fast and low. 'Listen to me, we're beyond running now—that has passed. Do you understand?' There is silence from behind her. 'Now, listen. These creatures, they do not come without reason. What did you do?'

Silence again.

Nancy grits her teeth. No time for secrecy or unspoken words now. 'I know what Cleaver has done. Did you help him?' The horses stamp again, snort impatiently. 'Yestin, tell me what you did.' When Yestin speaks, his voice is soft, questioning. Like a child seeking reassurance that they haven't done wrong.

'Cleaver said it was right. That we were help—' There is a sharp shush from Jan, but the older man is too afraid to speak, and Nancy pushes her advantage.

'What was right? Yestin, what did you do to help?' But the younger man stays silent. She directs her attention to the Huntsman before her. 'My—' she's cut off before she has a chance to try her plan. The horses rear and the Hunt ploughs forwards. They encircle the brothers and Nancy, pushing in until the horses stand flank to flank. Nancy reaches for the Murmur but stops, the image of Madge, crushed beneath the stone, flashing before her, and in that moment of indecision, Jan is lost. Time slows.

The man rises, head bent back, until he hangs a foot from the ground. Yestin is screaming, she sees that, but all she hears is the beating of her heart in her ears. Jan's eyes are wide with terror, he clutches at his face. The Hunt raise their hands in unison, reach for him, close their fists in one movement, and Jan Calder's jaw is torn from his skull. It peels down his front, tearing a strip of skin with it leaving the man's tongue flapping like an eel. His upper teeth bared and blood pouring from his throat. The noise comes back and Nancy closes her eyes against the sound the man is making. Anguished, he struggles to form words as he chokes on his own blood. The Hunt's hands raise again, and this time Jan's chest tears. It bulges and rattles, there is a crack as his ribcage splits and his belly writhes as though invisible hands rummage through it. Organs are raised and discarded, the man's lungs and heart torn out and thrown on the grass besides him. Through some arcane method, Jan is still alive. His eyes darting between the Hunt, his brother and Nancy, and his own disembowelment. It appears there will be no end and then, rising steadily and held aloft, still linked by viscera to its home is Jan's spleen. Nancy's trance breaks as she finally understands.

'Hocken Darrow. *You* raised him?' Nance stares at the man beside her and Yestin nods, though he can't wrench his eyes from his brother.

'We raised all three—Nancy, what—'

'They don't care about the other two, the chapel yard is the Reverend's God's domain. Hocken was buried on the moor; he belongs to something else. Damn you, Cleaver. Damn you.' The spleen hangs there for a moment, then the veins and arteries that hold it rupture and the organ burns to ash in the sky. As the last ember dies, what little horrid peace there was fractures. Nancy turns and screams at Yestin.

'Run!' The man is in shock, but she is loud enough to reach him, and he listens, turns to flee. One of the riders reaches towards him, their horse prancing and stamping the ground as she bends low to take him. As their hand touches his coat, there is the crackle of gunpowder taking. The rider bursts into flame and Yestin twists free. The air fills with the scent of a corpse burning. The charm Nancy slipped into Yestin's pocket burning the rider back. Eyes mad, he reels at the heat of it and Nancy shoves him through the gap in the hunters. As she does so, a sword glances off her temple, cutting a gash across her forehead, blood pouring over her left eye and one side of her face. She draws the curved knife from the crop and raises it, ready to deflect the next blow.

'Run you idiot, now!' Yestin turns and Nancy forces herself to focus, wipes the blood away. She reaches into her pockets with her free hand, pulls out the vials she stashed there and hurls them at the riders, fire flashes across their flanks and three horses throw their riders in the panic, landing with a crack on the ground. She had hoped to carry out her plan with care, she should have known it would be like this. *They can be forced back below the earth.* That's what Pel had written between the lines of his book. He'd told her how to do this. She can hear him. *Even a lion can be put back into its cage. It just takes a little more power.*

'Power, is it? Well now, you bastards, power I have.'

Nancy thinks of poppies, tries to steady the Murmur as it rises but it cracks from her like a carriage spring and rips a hole in the earth. The riderless horses and two of the hunters fall through, and just as with Joan, the ground snaps back. It traps one hunter halfway through and they scream, the sound emitting from the stump of their neck like a ringing in the ears after a knock to the head. It takes resolve not to fall and cover her ears, but Nancy stays standing. Stays standing and whistles loudly, so it cuts through the wind. The noise from the Hunt is louder, deafening. She barely hears her horse's hooves as Selkie comes rocketing towards her down the road. Nancy does not know what the horse can see, but if she is aware of the Hunt, it does not show. She is through them with no loss of speed and Nancy hauls herself up and onto the horse's back. She curses herself, one day a Keeper and a man already dead, she'll not fail again, she won't. She shakes her head to clear it. Still. She promised herself she would do this her own way. Monsters or not, she'll give them a chance. Those that are left, at least.

'Huntsmen!' She screams over the howls of the fallen rider still trapped between the worlds. The other hunters turn their horses to her. Their cloaks and armour smouldering, their horses wild, veins bulging across shimmering black flanks. She has their attention.

'I address you as new Keeper of the High Moor. This moor no longer recognises your jurisdiction over it. It is mine, and I hereby claim the right to your bounty. I claim Yestin Calder as my responsibility. I withdraw his warrant and I ask your Lord to call you home.'

Nothing. Nancy holds her gaze. The Huntsmen that remain turn as one, galloping towards Mirecoombe and the lonely figure of Yestin Calder who stumbles too slowly towards the light of home. Nancy closes her eyes. Holds the poppy in mind and draws up the Murmur to shake the moor. The walls at either side of the road shake and fall, another rider slips from their saddle and crashes to the floor, rolling into the crack that has appeared there and then gone below. Every part of her aches, her mind a cloud of screeching birds. She does not know if she can do that again. Breathless, she calls the Murmur home and the ground settles. The stacks of stone stop shaking. Nancy lets out a ragged, breathless pant and shouts to a god she hopes is listening.

'Well? Have I not proven myself? I will send them back one by one, but if you want Callum stopped, then see sense! I can't do both!'

Thunder rolls under the moor. For a second, the ground ripples, then all is still. The remaining Huntsmen leap, rise high into the air and then, just as the Keeper in the stories had described, burrow into the earth like bloated ticks, and are gone.

Silence.

She waits long enough to be sure the pit has closed, that the moor has returned to a merely terrestrial danger, and sinks in the saddle. Holds a hand to her bleeding face and closes her eyes against the dull thud of the pain. She finds herself laughing, tears rolling down her face, diluting the blood. Her whole body aches, she is shivering in the wind as the sweat dries on her skin, and the monstrous task to come seems ridiculous now. The pain and the chaos of the last few days washes over her. She licks the salted blood from her lips and crows at the sky, revelling in the catharsis of the moment.

'Damn you all! I am Nancy bloody Bligh, Keeper of the High Moor!' At her side Patroclus lifts his head and sets to baying, a joyous modulating howl. Selkie rears, whinnies and stamps at the ground. She laughs at them too, pats Selkies neck.

'There, boy, there my girl. We did it. Sent back a horror story Pel only ever heard told.' She breathes out great lungfuls of pain and lets go of her shame. *It's not my fault, Pel. Not yours either, entirely. But not mine.* Her rage still lingers, but she feels it fading. She slides from the saddle and walks to the stream, kneels, and washes the blood and sweat from her face. Rubs the fresh water across her neck and chest. Drinks it from cupped hands. She lets out a final sigh and stands. Kicks at the earth that swallowed the Hunt and climbs back onto Selkie.

Satisfied this job, at least, is done with, she turns towards the rolling grassland that hangs like a hammock between the tors, behind the village. The Hunt control the hounds. That's the way of it. So where are the dogs? Without their masters they are directionless, wild beasts looking to be fed. Nancy knows Calder's cattle are grazing in the valley, easy targets for masterless dogs, so it is towards the pastures she turns and rides.

Something is wrong as she approaches. She can smell it in the air. She finds the cattle easily enough, they huddle in a terrified mass in the stone corral, untouched. The hounds are only slightly further on. Each is torn apart, bloodied entrails linking piece to piece. The empty sockets of their eyes still smouldering.

Dismounting, Nancy places a hand against one's chest. It is still warm. There is only one creature that could have done this. Callum has sent her a message, she thinks. *I can defeat monsters too.* She is exhausted but draws on enough of the Murmur to return the bodies of the dogs to the Undermoor, then rides for home. Callum will take everything she has. She needs to rest.

MILES DEEP, WHERE the bletting landscape of the Undermoor rots under its puddle moon, rain falls. Nancy's magic easing the return of the dead. As hoof and limb and claw pass through the rippling sky they transmute into the glittering stardust they came from and form in drifts against the trunks of trees, settle between blades of grass until needed again.

DOG VIOLET

NANCY TREATS THE preparation as a ritual. A poor night's sleep has left her fitful and restless for the fight to come. She had laughed when she'd thrown back the curtains, the sky a quilt of gold and grey as rain clouds fought with the sunshine. Somebody, above or below, has a sense of humour. She has an idea of the things she might need to put an end to Callum, to what he's become. But she needs to prepare against those who might defend him. Against Locryn Calder and his remaining sons, against the villagers. Against Cleaver.

It takes much of the day, this ritual. She packs carefully stoppered bottles into pockets, bottles that when broken could put a houseful of people to sleep. She packs the skulls of animals bound tight with string and pins that can stop a person in their tracks. She could do all of this with spells of course, or even risk using her magic, but she will need those for Callum. And she needs to face him alone, far from bystanders, from friends. The vials and objects she can cast without thought. She'll need her mind focused on him. She stands in front of the mirror again when she's done.

The blackthorn pin left by the Tattooist holds her hair above her head, and she clutches the crop tightly in her right hand. There is a red line where the sword cut, a night packed with a poultice has cleaned it, and a little magic helped by the yarrow tattooed on her ankle has closed the edges. But it stings. She's proud of it though, her first scar as Keeper. On the lapel of her coat, she has pinned Pel's regimental badge, the anchor cross garlanded with rowan. Her fingers are heavy with rings. Some she took from Pel's cabinets before the boat sank, some she has collected herself. Not all have magic in them, though many do, and her favourite is a band left to her by her mother. Her grandmother's ring, wide and fretted into a knot of silver ragwort stems. Pel's coral tooth hangs comfortably at her breast, and she has added other necklaces and torcs to her neck. The brownies have polished her riding boots and they gleam in the late afternoon sun, catching the reflection of the stripe of her trousers. Patroclus sits solemnly at her side. He knows what's coming.

'You don't have to come, Pat. I don't mind,' she lies. But Patroclus continues to sit. He takes his role seriously. Nancy smiles at him. She knows he felt Pel's death as keenly as she did. Since his master's been gone, he's lived up to his name. 'Let's go and say goodbye, properly. Just in case… ' she leaves the rest unsaid. She needs her confidence intact. Leaving the cottage, locking the door behind them, and waving to the brownies pressing faces to the glass, the girl, her horse, and her dog turn away from home and head towards the Fellmire.

The journey there passes without incident, she's too distracted to notice anything anyway. Still, as they approach the mire, Nancy shivers. This place of rebirth and death still holds Pel's bones. She kneels at the water's edge, by the hawthorn stump with Pel's knife still stuck into it.

'It's time Pel. We're off to slay the monster. Just like you used to do. I'm sorry it ended like this. That you could not find peace before the end.' The love she feels has a partner, a rage she had thought she'd let go of, but it pushes up and past her heart. Her anger at her father. 'But Pel, we could have avoided this, you see that, don't you? If you'd listened…

I've been a Keeper for a day and already people have died.' Nancy's voice catches, 'But I don't need you. I'll work this out alone.'

There is a sound from the water, a discharge of gas that erupts in a boiling black mass and for a moment Nancy thinks he might return to her. But he does not. The mire's bubbling stops, and the pool is a mirror again. Nancy smiles as she's joined in her reflection.

'You thought he'd be back too, then, did you?' Madge stands in the fine rain that gleams in the sunlight, alongside the grey in her hair. Her arm hanging awkwardly at her side. Nancy smiles at Madge, rainbowed in the mizzle, and feels a chamber of her heart fill at the sight of her.

It's a rare sight indeed, Madge Gould untethered from the Nest and roaming free. 'You're a treat to see, Madge, truly. I—' Madge looks to her arm, sighs.

'I know, Nancy. Don't worry. Look at you, dressed up in your finery. His coat fits you better than it did him. You look the part, girl.' The landlady doesn't wait for an invitation, sitting herself down next to Nancy, not minding the wet grass. She raises an eyebrow at Nancy's scar, Nancy nods to her arm and both women smile. They sit in silence for a while, these two. One has known the other all her life. It is Madge that speaks.

'Cleaver told me to stay inside. Know anything about that?' Nancy stiffens.

'I do. And it's a rare thing but I agree with him. You shouldn't be out.'

'And I'll not be told why? By either of you?'

'See how it shakes out, Madge. If this can end quietly, it would be better for it. I'll tell you once it's done, regardless.'

'Fine. You've got a fair amount of the old man in you. Pel

never liked to share a plan either. But remember, Nancy, look at me, I meant what I said before.' Madge stares into her friend's eyes. 'Pel is not all you are. You are more than him. I saw you rescue Billy. I saw what you did.'

Nancy turns away with hair blowing around her face, a little ashamed of the smile that's broken free. She bites it back.

'I see what I did too; I should have done it Pel's way. I shouldn't have panicked.'

'The things you've survived, Nancy? It's no wonder. My arm will heal. Most things do. You did it your way. And that's how it needs to be. Pel wasn't often flustered because he didn't allow himself to feel things. You do. You are Nancy Bligh. There's strength in that name. Magic, too.'

'Since Pel left, died, whatever he did—since he has been gone, I've been giving in to it, to the Murmur. I promised him, Madge. I told him I wouldn't. Nothing comes for free, that's what he said, there would be a price for the gift the piskies gave me and –'

'A gift? Is that what he told you?'

Nancy is looking at Madge again, cheeks flushed with shame, bracing herself to be chastised.

'He said that I was given it when I was taken, as a favour, to be repaid.'

Madge is not smiling now, her eyes fixed firm and hard on Nancy's.

'One day, Nancy. I will tell you about Pel. How he got to be our Keeper. What he did, who he hurt to get here. But stories won't help you now, so I'll save it, 'til you're done.' Madge touches her good hand to her breast, to a pendant hanging there, eyes brimming with bittersweet memory. 'But this you need to know. Pel was a different man, before you came, spent, used up. He had stopped listening. He wasn't from here, had no connection to the moor other than a drive to be best. Beat back the monsters. But he'd done that, had become bored, restless. Distant. It was you, Nancy, you brough him back.'

Nancy sits, chews her lip. Her chest a ball of anger and longing for a father who keeps moving further away.

'I remember the day he saved you; he came to the Nest.' Madge pauses, Nancy sees something flicker in her eyes, but it is gone in an instant. 'Pel saw something in you, Nancy. That's why he stayed, helped your mother. Why he took you in when she died.'

'What does this have to do with my gift, Madge? There is trouble coming, you said it yourself I don't need distractions now. Tell me this story when it's through.' Nancy rises to leave but the landlady stays her with a hand.

'Sit down, Nancy. Please. My point is that Pel is not from here. Not from this moor. He did his job as Keeper for the glory, out of pride. You know it's true. He could be a callous old bugger if he was slighted. That's why were in this mess, isn't it?'

Nancy nods.

'He was training you from the moment he brought you home. I could see it, we all could. And I was glad of it, Nancy. I knew you'd be what we needed when the time came. You were born here, on this moor, in this village. You have a stake in this. You never met your grandmother, did you?'

Nancy shakes her head.

'No. I did, that is, I met her once, when I was a girl. Her name was Meliora, and she was a witch.'

Nancy starts at this. Her mother had rarely spoken of her own, and when she had it was at a distance. They had not been close.

'What are you saying?'

'There have always been women, Nancy, born on the moor, who had a little more at their fingertips than the rest of us. Sometimes these things skip a generation.'

Silence. Neither woman speaks, and the dog holds his tongue. The only sound is the rain falling on grass and water like the distant sound of gunfire. Nancy is the first to break from cover.

'What happened to her?' Madge turns away, rubs her broken arm.

'She died, Nancy. But that's not a story I can tell. I don't know the truth of it, but you'll find out, soon enough. I'm sure of it. What matters today, here, is that your gift, is nothing of the sort. The Murmur is your birthright, Nancy. Use it.'

The older woman stands and turns, pausing only briefly before she walks away. She's said what she had come to say. Nancy does not move, does not say goodbye. She sits in the rain, staring into the black pool of the Fellmire with a head on fire. News like this takes time to process. It is an awful lot to take in, and it is hours before Nancy stirs. She lifts her head, looks to the horizon to the tors and rock stacks, and to the moor rolling out around her, and Nancy Bligh, new Keeper of the High Moor, smiles.

DEEP BELOW, BENEATH the wreckage of his home now lost to the Undermoor, Pel looks up, sadly, and sighs.

'Good luck, Nancy. Good luck.'

'Hard to hear a child lose respect for a parent.' The grating voice of the seated god echoes from his chamber. Pel has grown used to this, since their joining. Each never without the other.

'Quiet. It was for her own good. I did what was best for her.'

The old god slumps back into silence and leaves Pel with his thoughts. He watches piskies and spriggans chasing each other in circles on the plains, scattering Gow's cattle as they go. The old giant swatting at them with his staff. Since their reunion, Gogmagog has sat on top of the Queen's Rocks, reshaping the tor a rock at a time. A throne half-built now perched on top. Reminiscing, their memories returned, about the life they led. Every now and then their laughter rolls through the Undermoor and shakes the rocks.

Pel has his eye on them.

There is some sense of repair to the Undermoor, now Pel has stabilised the crown. Though the beast still stalks its dark arena, the witches' heads still hang from the tree. He felt the Hunt, the wish hounds' bodies returning to mulch in the ground above, can feel too the thrum of energy that emanates from Callum as he stalks about the moor. He looks at the hollow-headed god and frowns.

'She'll understand one day, you wait, she'll thank me.'

MUSK MALLOW

Nancy Bligh rides head high into Mirecoombe. The sun is starting to fade, setting slowly behind waterlogged hills. The village is busy. The men who have spent the afternoon draining Calder's cellars stand in clusters, faces flushed with alcohol and outrage. The air is a cider press wound too tight. It will make the world bleed. Madge sees Nancy approach, sees her jump Selkie over the boundary ditch and land splashing in the square and smiles. A cloud of starlings beats in the sky and all eyes turn to face her. Every man watching takes two steps back. But they hold their fists clenched tight at their sides.

Nancy does not make eye contact with the villagers, rides on by, towards the chapel, eyes fixed on her goal. *Yestin reached the village then.* The thought rises, falls. She feels the pressure building but she's no time for it now. Hugh Dell staggers out from the crowd and starts to follow her up the hill, his wife rushing from their cottage to join him. The news of Jan's death spreads. And one by one, the villagers join the throng. Calder has appeared, and Cusk, who grasps the sleeve of a passing man and confers in hurried bursts before the man pulls free. Cusk's face goes white with the task as he passes the news to his friend. Calder turns with a face of fury and sorrow to Nancy, still slowly riding away.

'Where is my son!' Nancy rides on, calling to Patroclus to ignore the farmer. 'Where is Jan, you witch!' The old man bends down, overtaken by the crowd who can't bring themselves to wait. Standing, he lifts a lump of quartz taken from the pile that marks the path, and hurls it towards Nancy. There was little force to the throw, Calder's best days long behind him, but it strikes Selkie on the rump and causes her to kick. Her hoof catches a man just below the shoulder and he spins to the ground, groaning and clutching his arm.

It is the spark the mob needed. Noise erupts and Nancy shields her head against the volley of stones, shoots a glance to the chapel. Turns to the mob that is growing in number and rage, the mob that has caught up with her and crowds now around her and Selkie. She digs her heels into Selkie's side and spurs the horse upwards towards the graveyard wall. It is slow going, the bodies pressing against the horse are not people she wants to hurt. She turns her head, amongst the crowd she sees Madge, calling out for order in the chaos despite her arm. Delen too is doing her best. To Nancy's surprise she sees Seren Dell amongst the villagers shouting for peace, and a gap appears in the crowd.

Nancy takes her chance. She flicks the crop across Selkie's back and the horse picks up her pace, the nervous trot rises to a canter up the narrow coffin road to the chapel. She takes the wall in a leap, rear hooves cleaving a stone from the top as they pass. Patroclus takes the lych gate and hops carefully over the coffin stone to join Nancy on the other side. The crowd are still following, fighting their way up the hill. For a moment, Nancy has space to think. The chapel yard shines in the sunset. Large squares of white cloth draped over the graves she disturbed all those nights ago. She regrets that. There are lights on in the chapel and she can hear voices.

The first of the villagers reach the lych gate, removing any choice of what comes next. Nancy calls to Pat, and the old dog races to the chapel door that stands a little ajar. Leaping up, he pushes against it with his two front legs and races inside. Nancy follows, still astride Selkie and just squeezes through the wide old doorway, her head scraping slightly on the lintel. She skids to a halt on the large slate flagstones, just shy of the altar, where Cleaver sits grimly trying to talk to Yestin Calder who sits insensate on the floor. Burbling his brother's name, Nancy's too. A moment later the villagers burst in through the door and form a dense crescent around the mounted Keeper, the old priest, and the dog.

'Miss Bligh,' Cleaver speaks first. It is his house, after all. 'What on earth do you think you are doing? This is a place of God.'

Yestin Calder stands and runs frightened to his father, he can't speak, his eyes are wild, he buries his face in his father's chest and Locryn hugs him tight.

'Yestin, I—'

Cleaver interrupts as he stands.

'What damage have you done now, Miss Bligh? The boy is half out of his wits. Where is his brother?'

'His brother is dead.'

Calder lets out a howl and clutches his youngest son more tightly to his chest. Luk has appeared too now, pushing through the crowd.

Nancy tries to focus on her breathing, to keep herself calm.

'He's lying to you. To all of you. He killed your friends. Hugh, he killed Salan!' She turns to Hugh Dell who looks dazed and unsure of himself. 'You claim Pel practiced witchcraft. You, accuse me of the same. Suspect me now of killing Jan. I see it! But ask Cleaver to show you his drawer of charms. His secret books. Calder, ask Yestin why his brother died. What Cleaver had him do.'

'She's lying! She lies. You know this. I have explained this to you all.' Cleaver's mouth remains in a patronising smile, but Nancy sees his eyes. Panic creeps across them. 'She's peddling the same stories that Lord Hunt did, the same nonsense about fairies to keep you all in check. There is nothing on that moor but stone and grass.'

Nancy scowls down at Cleaver from Selkie's back.

'You know full well there is more in this world than that, Jacob Cleaver. Is it not time to be honest with them? If you expect them to follow you to salvation, should they not see the bones they walk on?' Cleaver remains silent, chest heaving with rage.

'Look about you, all of you. See for yourself.' Nancy begins to sing, the song she always uses to call them but changed, just a little:

'Come gather, small children and beasts of the moor,

up the hill in the village through the old wooden door, the door, the old wooden door.

Come sit in the rafters, 'til the whole roof might burst,

and show them your faces, sweet folk of the earth, the earth, sweet folk of the earth.'

The villagers look around, look up to the eaves at the carved faces in the ceiling. Cleaver looks too. Nancy sees the faces in between as one by one, like stars in the evening sky, the Underfolk lean out of the shadows. Piskies and spriggans, their faces smiling down at these people they've lived alongside for so long. They've never been inside the church before. But Nancy's assault on the graveyard has breached the walls, left a gap for a different kind of spirit to pour through.

Nancy smiles. There are more than she could have dreamt of. Faces she knows, many she doesn't, but they all came for her. They all came to help. Comfortable, even here in this previously forbidden place, as long as Nancy is with them. Throughout the chapel, hairs stand on end. Skin prickles. Though they cannot see the Underfolk, a quiet descends on the villagers, on the chapel. Everyone present can feel that there is less space inside than before. That there are others in the church alongside them. Nancy breaks the peace.

'I am not a liar, Cleaver. Nor was Pel.' She turns to the villagers, to the farmers and stonemasons, to the weavers. 'These are your friends that you feel; these are the creatures who help you work the moor. You, Davy, when you feared the granite would not split? It was the spriggans who helped your spike find the vein. Delen, it was these piskies that helped your mother home when she wandered lost on the moor. They are not here to hurt you; they are not devils. But mark me, those creatures do exist,' she pauses, Yestin Calder's face still pressed into his father's shirt. Nancy's voice falters briefly at the sight of him, 'and I can keep you safe from them. The only thing I can't protect you from is him.' She extends an accusatory finger at Cleaver, still gawping at the rafters.

Nancy studies him. His eyes darting between carved faces, impish smiles of stone. And she's sure he can see them; she is sure he can see all of the things he's denied. Nancy looks at the Underfolk, every face turned to Cleaver. They pulse in the shadows like the shine on a raven's wing, teasing the old priest with colours in the darkness. If anyone but the Reverend can see them, they do not show it. Most of those congregated in the chapel have their eyes closed now, content to sit with the peace Nancy has brought. Madge's eyes are open though, and she's walking to Selkie, smiling up at her friend.

'Thank you darling, for sharing them with us.' Nancy smiles back. Others, too, voice their thanks. Some even mutter apologies. Only Calder remains staunchly unconvinced, charging up to the Reverend and shaking him from his stupor.

'Speak, dammit! There is nothing up there but wood and stone and if you think there is anything in what that witch has said then they are devils plain and clear, exorcise them! Banish them! Cleaver!'

There is a flicker of recognition on the old priest's face, but it does not last long. He folds it into the frown that furrows his brow, clenches his jaw. There is muttering at the back of the crowd and the sea of people parts, leaving the centre aisle of the church clear.

Stood in the doorway, body twisted and knotted like a lightning-struck tree, is Callum Cleaver.

He ignores the creatures in the rafters. His attention is focused on Nancy, sat atop her horse. At her feet, Patroclus growls.

'Cleaver, what is this?' Calder shakes the priest again, hoping to rattle the answers loose. The old priest smiles, relief unknots his face and his blue eyes fill with tears.

'It is my son, Locryn. It is Callum.'

Calder steps back in disbelief as Callum creaks his way towards them. Nancy slides from the saddle, looping the reins back and out of the way. She can feel her heartbeat rattle at her ribcage, so hard she worries her teeth might chatter as she talks.

'See? He lied to you, not me. Here are my friends, there stands his. There too is your killer. Cleaver did this, not me.' Nancy forces herself not to take a step back as Callum approaches, the memory of the torn hounds fresh in her mind.

'Is this true, Jacob?' Madge looks searchingly towards the Reverend. 'Did you do this? All of it?'

Cleaver turns at the question, eyebrows raised at the landlady. Astonished she has to ask.

'God returned him, Madge. I was just his instrument. We have been sinful, in this valley. God sent Callum to cleanse our souls. This is not how I would have shown you, but it is all His design.'

Silence. Looks are shared. Then, the stillness breaks as Hugh Dell strides out from the crowd and swings a drunken arm at the priest. Callum lunges towards him, arms outstretched but Cleaver shouts him down.

'Enough! Callum, stop! All of you, leave him be! Yes, he took Salan, the others too, but you must understand—it was needed. That the dead wood needed removing so we could grow and put this heathen nonsense behind us.' Cleaver is manic, preaching a sermon that has left everyone behind. He does not notice. Waving a hand towards the rafters, Cleaver warms to his theme. Piety or madness, it fills him up. 'The deaths were regrettable. But Callum has only hurt those who made a mockery of the Church. You are all safe here, I promise you.'

Hugh Dell will not be mollified. He charges again at the priest and there is a gasp as Callum plucks him out of his stride, holds him aloft. Callum's hand, hard around Hugh's neck, begins to burn, pops into flame. The room runs cold at the heat of it. Callum uses his free hand to hold firm on the grieving man's shoulders as Hugh's skull blisters. As the skin on his cheeks turns red then black. The chapel fills with the scent of cooking meat. Hugh begins to scream, but it seems Callum doesn't like it and as the first howl emerges the creature pulls up, and Hugh's head peels from his neck as though Callum was tearing apart an overripe pear.

No longer interested in it, Callum drops Hugh's body to the ground where it twitches sporadically, blood pumping fitfully through the parts of the neck not cauterised by the fire. Hugh's skull still smoulders, his eyes liquifying and dripping down his cheeks with a sizzle in a foul imitation of tears, flames licking from the vacated sockets. When the fire is at its peak and the skull is black, Callum tips his head to the side, like a cat playing with a bird, unsure of why its toy has stopped moving, and closes his fist. Hugh Dell's skull evaporating in a cloud of sparks and ash.

Silence. Then the screaming begins.

'Please!' Cleaver has broken, blind to what is happening, and deaf to the screams of his congregation, he prattles on as though his son has been caught misbehaving at school, hitting another child. 'Leave him, Callum, please, this is not what you were returned for, He did not bring you back for this!' Callum ranges about the church, dead eyes darting from one person to the next, tearing at the backs of the village as it flees. Opening his mouth to add his own curdled shriek to the screams.

A mass of bodies meets the doorway full-force and crushes between the stone. Men and women fall beneath their neighbours' feet, between the panicked sobs Nancy hears ribs breaking, Callum snapping at their backs like a rabid collie. At the sight of him, even those trampled manage to haul broken bodies up and over the stone step to freedom. Madge, broken arm preventing escape, sticks close to Nancy, pressing into Selkie's flanks. Nancy since Callum's attack has stood frozen, her hand at her neck. Nancy who remembers how it felt when it broke.

'Nancy!' The landlady's shouts cut through. She has misjudged. Had not expected Cleaver's hold on his son to be so fragile. *Pel would do something. Would have already done it.* Her mind skitters from one option to the next, then reaches for the Murmur, but the sight of Madge's broken arm, the memory of her failure with the Hunt, stops her. She reaches into her pocket for a small vial of iridescent glass and uncorks it, careful not to ingest the vapour from its contents. She hurls it towards Callum, and the glass shatters on his mummified skin.

The effect is almost instant. A green moss creeps across his body, its microscopic roots finding their way into every crack, the weight of the green shag slowing him down. He tears at it frenziedly, his skin ripping as the roots pull free.

The only people left are Cleaver, frozen now, eyes wild with confusion, Madge still huddled against Selkie's flanks, and Locryn Calder. The crowd had rushed around him, the last support of a bridge washed away, and he stands stranded in the church immobile, eyes glazed, as his eldest son shouts fruitlessly from the doorway.

'Dad!' Luk is screaming at his father. 'Dad please, come on now, we need to get home!' Callum is tearing away at the green blanket covering him, howling all the while. And in lieu of other prey has his eyes fixed on the farmer in the centre of the church. Yestin, still white as a sheet but the old shock buried under the adrenaline of the new, tries to push his way past his brother, reach his father, but Luk holds him back. He is old enough to know their father wouldn't want to be the death of them.

'Dad, please.' They are quieter now, it seems inevitable. Callum lurches towards Calder. There is no time to focus, to breathe. Her eyes dart to Madge, and she races to push her friend behind Selkie. The horse stamps and bridles in a show of protection, horned faceplate lowered to protect her charge.

Nancy feels for the flowers she needs. Petals of pink and white, and holding them in mind she throws an open hand out, towards Callum, the air around him bursting into crystals of ice. Blinded, Callum stumbles into the far wall, cracking the plaster. He screams and smacks his fist into the wall, a crack running up the side of the chapel, across the ceiling, the arched wagon roof creaking under the strain. The sound of wood splintering.

'Calder, move!' Nancy is running over the pews to the old farmer. When she reaches him, his eyes are scared, distant.

'Devils, they're all devils.' The old man mouths the words, but Nancy does not stop, she grabs him round the waist and pulls him aside just as a roof beam crashes to the spot where he'd been standing.

'Come now, Locryn, your sons are waiting.' Nancy places a hand at his back and pulls him towards the door. Callum is lifting himself from the floor, batting away frost, plaster falling in white showers from his shoulder, and his attention is turning again to the farmer, to Nancy.

'Cleaver, for God's sake! This is not right!' Nancy screams at the Reverend, but he does not move. This needs to stop. After a glance to check that Selkie still shields Madge, she forces her breath to calm, purses her lips and forces the air out in steady, measured gasps. Holds the image of wildflowers in her mind. It feels as though she holds the leash of a giant, the Murmur is straining to be free, but she tries to hold it tight. Binds it with flowers. Nancy breathes out and, though she has it chained, the Murmur still shakes the church. The columns supporting the roof slip and their carved capitals slide with a crash to the floor. A ledger stone beneath Callum's feet breaks and he falls through to his waist, howling as he scrabbles at the stone. She can hear his feet scrape for purchase on crumbling bones.

Nancy gasps as she brings the Murmur to heel. She can feel it resist, feel it lash round the chapel shaking the hill, tipping over pews, and ringing the iron bell with its vibration. The Underfolk in the rafters have fled. Their help only extends so far, and they know when they're outmatched. Invisible, they follow the villagers back to their homes, see them safe inside, sit watch at their gates. The sun is almost gone now, the valley cast in gold, the chapel burning black against the sunset. Pushing the insensate Locryn Calder the final few steps to the door, Nancy releases him into the grip of his sons who bundle the old man out and down the hill, still mouthing 'devils' to all he passes.

'Madge, go!' Nancy screams at her friend, but the landlady still clutches Selkie's mane. Callum is almost free of the grave, and, the farmer lost to him, he is turning his attention to Madge. This, finally, seems to wake the priest.

'Callum, no! She is a friend, son. Please.' It is not a command, it is a plea, and it is going unheard. Callum hauls himself free and stalks towards the horse and the woman in the centre of the church. Selkie thrashes her head at him, the horn raking through the air. The Reverend Jacob Cleaver does not move from the spot, instead he raises his eyes and begins to pray.

'I am well pleased that the Lord hath heard the voice of my prayer,

That he hath inclined his ear unto me, therefore I will call upon him as long as I live—'

'Cleaver!' Nancy shouts to the man, 'This isn't God's work, it's *yours*. He can't undo your mess, stop wasting time and help!' But Cleaver continues to pray, even as Callum draws closer to Madge. Selkie's horn connects and tears a gash down the side of Callum's face, the white bone of his skull showing through. He screams and rips the faceplate from the horse's head, the buckles and ties snapping free as he whirls in a head-ringing daze. Selkie staggers back and only by ducking beneath her is Madge saved from being crushed. It is exhausting using the Murmur, but Nancy runs to the landlady, shoulders her onto the horse.

'Madge, get on Selkie, now!' In a stupor the old woman pulls herself clumsily into the saddle. Selkie, already half wild, needs little encouragement. She turns and makes for the door, Callum in a sprint behind them. Cleaver's voice still rising above all, as though volume was what prevented his god hearing his prayers.

'The snares of death compass me round about, and the pains of Hell have hold upon me,

I shall find trouble and heaviness, and I shall call upon the name of the Lord.'

Around them, the church is in disarray. The pews lie tipped and out of line, everything covered in a fine dust. Selkie struggles, picking her way over broken wood, discarded hymnals. Callum moves swiftly. More swiftly than the horse. Nancy hurls another handful of vials at him. They break in clouds around him, moulds growing over pew and column, oozing puddles spreading over the flagstone. One hits directly, shattering across Callum's back and boiling and bubbling at the skin but it does not slow him. He shrieks as he claws at the horse's tail. Selkie kicks out and clouts Callum across the face.

Cleaver is still praying, and Nancy is out of options.

'Cleaver, if you won't help then get out of the way. Now.' The priest stays kneeled.

'O Lord. I beseech thee. Deliver my soul.' His head turning slowly, Cleaver nods, hesitantly, then runs out through the back of the chapel.

Selkie has broken free of the wood, eyes bulging in fear, and is almost at the door, Callum close at her hooves, turns at the sound of the back door closing. He scans the room, looks straight past Nancy, and stands aimless for a moment, in the centre of the floor. His torn, dry lips peel back, and he forces out a word.

'Da?'

With Callum distracted, Selkie takes her chance, tearing through the doorway and hauling Madge to safety. Shaking free of his reverie, Callum turns and walks steadily towards Nancy, bathed in gold and red and blue, the sunset piercing the stained glass of the chapel.

'Stop, Callum. This can stop. He's gone, he's left you. You should be at rest. Please.'

Callum does not stop. They are alone, now. No one to hurt she doesn't mean to. So, with a heavy sigh Nancy raises her hand, releases the Murmur, her mind a riot of overgrown flowers, and brings the ceiling of the nave down on them both.

PURGING FLAX

Nancy flickers in and out of consciousness. Her head a tangle of water and weeds.

There is a face. Her mother's, or close to it, but with blonde hair not black, that waves in a current, like bladderwrack. The sound of chains dragging across a seabed. The sound of sailors drowning. She tastes salt on her lips and blood on her tongue and her head shifts with the pull of the tides. An eel the length of a man wraps round her and sings her awake.

It is night when Nancy opens her eyes. She flinches at the pain shooting down her side, but she is safe enough. Nothing broken, nothing damaged beyond repair. The interior of the chapel is bright with moonlight, streaming from the hole in the roof. Groaning, Nancy pushes herself to her feet, dusts herself off. Much of the rubble lies heaped in the centre of the room. Pews stick out of it, a pincushion of stone and wood, but there is no sign of the monster beneath.

'I'm sorry, Callum.' Nancy moves towards the debris, searching for the body. But there is no sign. No limb askew, sticking out from beneath a rock. Nothing. There is a whine from the doorway and Patroclus steps into the church.

'Hello, boy. Thank you, have you been keeping them safe?'

The old dog pads across the floor to Nancy and wags his

tail at her side. He has spent the night walking around the village, keeping an eye.

'Pat, is he dead? Is Callum here?'

Patroclus presses his nose to the floor, walks around the heap of stone. He pushes his snout into every crack, every crevice. He pauses at the body of Hugh Dell, half covered in broken masonry, but there's nothing more anyone can do for him. Satisfied he has searched every corner, Patroclus stops and sniffs the air. He turns, following a scent leading out towards a broken back window, the shattered form of Reagan, Mirecoombe's patron saint, pointing the way. Patroclus stands on the lintel and barks, twice. Nancy sags, exhausted.

'Of course, he survived. Of course, he did.' She moves to the dog in the window, stares out across the moor. She can see it, the Fellmire. Can see the starlight shining off the patches of black mirror water.

'He's trying again.' Her pockets are empty of vials, and the charms and talismans are useless in the fight to come. She still has her crop, held tight in her hand. And she can feel the flowers blooming on her skin.

'It ends tonight, Pat. It must.' She steps out into the night. Grass crunching underfoot, Nancy walks across the moor, Patroclus at her heels and moonlight in her hair. She has only walked a hundred metres when she hears the hoof fall behind her. She hauls herself thankfully into Selkie's saddle, pats the horse's neck.

The ride to the Fellmire is silent. Nancy's face set grim against the dark, Patroclus padding quietly alongside the horse. There are few clouds, and a huge moon shines down on the moorland, casting long shadows from every squat rock. When she reaches it, this border crossing, Callum is standing with his back to her, staring into the water. The moon is so bright she can pick out his every detail, can see his emaciated form. She can see, too, the lines of stiches that mark Cleaver's handiwork. The stitches that hold him together.

'You're tired, aren't you? That magic you stole is fading and your father did his best, but he didn't understand; there's more to making magic than following a text.'

Callum turns slowly, teeth bared between thin lips. Nancy dismounts, walks towards him in the moonlight and motions Patroclus to stay. She needs to do this alone.

Panic rises as she approaches. The last time they met like this, he killed her. But she is ready for him now. She looks at him, this husk. His chest does not rise and fall, no breath comes from his mouth. The rotting, stolen heart, the liver, the spleen taken from other bodies pulse unnaturally under his taut leather skin, pushing against the cat gut stitches holding them in place.

'Stop now, Callum. Let it end. I know your life was not what you wanted, or what you deserved. I'm sorry for my part in that. But this can stop quietly if you let it. You can rest.'

Callum stands, swaying slightly, in front of Nancy. And then, with a hideous rasp he pushes air across a petrified larynx.

'No,' and he lunges.

Nancy is ready for him, jumping backwards she pulls the shining knife from the crop and slices the air in front of her. It nicks Callum as he moves towards her, across the top of his chest but no blood issues forth, and he bears down on her still. Nancy smiles. What was a risk in the chapel is safer here, there is little to damage. For the first time in her life, she can give in completely to the restless power inside her. Can see what it is capable of. Free from the fear of it. She had worried she was spent, but from the second her feet had touched the moor she had felt her strength returning. Felt the Murmur rise to feed. She remembers her childhood games.

Throwing both arms down at her sides she pulls at the earth, raises her arms, and works a stone loose from the earth, just as she used to raise quartz and coins. As it draws close to the surface, she lets the Murmur loose in a jolt that runs through her and ripples the earth, forcing the stone free like a spat cherry pip. Wrong footed by the shifting earth, he doesn't see it coming. It crashes through him, tearing an arm from its socket and burying it deep, a howl tearing through the dead man's lips. Whilst he is distracted, Nancy strikes, dragging her blade through the stitches in his side, at the left, and as the last pops open the slick black clump of rotten liver falls flatly to the earth. Callum turns his skin-taut skull towards her, slamming his remaining fist hard into her shoulder. She buckles. She had not forgotten how strong he was, her neck still testament to it, but nor had she been prepared for the blow, and it sends her sprawling. Nancy throws an arm up in defence, and an arc of black mud rakes across Callum's face, the slick peat blinding him and pausing him in his advance. She takes her chance and sweeps the knife again, but it only nicks at the thread on his back. Callum leaps on her, biting and pummelling her back. Scrunching her eyes tight Nancy yells, but before she can summon the Murmur, Callum is gone. Patroclus rolls heavily away, the wind knocked out of him in the leap, but he rights himself and squares up to Callum who howls in fury at the old dog. He leaps, Patroclus still growling, no thought now, just reflexive rage and Nancy screams the moor into submission. The ground splits and roils, Callum struggling to stay upright on the bone shaken earth.

'Pat, go! Thank you but go!' Patroclus shoots a worried look, but he does as he's told—he knows he hasn't much strength left in him and he's a good dog at heart—but he runs with his head turned until the fray is out of view.

Before Callum can right himself, Nancy nicks through the rest of the stiches, and drives her hand into the wound. She pulls the rancid spleen out through clenched fingers and hurls it into the mire. Only the heart remains.

Beating.

Nancy allows herself a moment to gloat, the earth singing its support. But she's not done yet, and life loves a reminder. Heaving his corpse up off the floor, Callum swings in a scarecrow arc, smacking Nancy hard across the face with his remaining arm. It sends the Keeper sprawling, dazed on the ground. Worse, the knife with its bright-eyed hilt and polished serpentine blade flies spinning off behind her, lodging in the mud. Callum looms over her, blotting out the stars and the gathering storm with his shadow.

Time slows. Nancy is keenly aware of the damp grass cushioning her head, of the seeds and roots beneath. She can smell the mulch, the peat. Aeons of death, decay, and rebirth. Though the stars are gone, the clouds begin to pulse with lightning and thunder rolls the earth beneath like the rind of a fruit, releasing its oils and filling the air with the scent of rain.

Is this it then? Lulled into peace on this grassy bed, Nancy searches for an escape. Above her, Callum is lit by a flash of lightning, and she sighs. His face drawn in pain and rage, but there is sadness there in the hollow of his cheeks, in the sunken pits of his eyes.

'They let us both down, didn't they? I'm sorry Callum, truly.' Nancy braces herself for the blow but instead, in the next flash of light, watches as the curved steel of her blade bursts through the front of Callum's chest, slicing the remaining stiches that held Callum's life in place. The dead, rotting heart, slips free from its cage of leather wrapped ribs and lands wetly on the earth besides her head. He grabs at it, tries to stuff it back inside, but the rancid flesh seeps through the gaps in his fingers, drips like black treacle onto the earth. Nancy watches him stagger back, turn, gaze with hurt into the eyes of his father. Cleaver drops the knife, it clatters on exposed granite, and he catches his son as he falls.

'My boy... I'm so sorry Callum, I should never have done this. I should never have done any of it.'

Nancy keeps quiet, what is there to say? She watches as the old Reverend and his long dead son touch their heads together. Watches as Cleaver stands with his son in his arms and walks back into the Fellmire, treading unsteadily on the bedsheet grass, the water roiling below.

'Cleaver... ' Nancy starts but the priest stops her with a look. There are tears streaming down his face.

'I should have believed him, Nancy. I should have listened to my son.'

Nancy stands, walks towards the edge of the water. Callum still lingers, the light in his body not quite gone, but fading fast.

'Cleaver, listen, you need to come back, away from the water. Please.'

'No, Nancy. I don't. I can't go back. I can't face them.' Cleaver turns his eyes skyward, 'Will you tell them—please— that I did my best? I tried.'

Nancy reaches for him, clutches at the black of his cassock, but the old priest takes a step back, his feet sinking in the water a little more with every step.

The ground makes no noise as it tears under his feet. Nancy watches mutely as the Fellmire swallows both priest and son, lost to the moor. A gasp escapes from her, and then the tears begin. Patroclus pushes under her arm and lays there with his mistress as they cry for those lost, and high above in electric clouds, a bolt tears a hole in the sky for the rain.

MEADOWSWEET

SPRING BREAKS ACROSS the moor with a raft of colour. Vetch and stitchwort breaking through the green, the flowers finding their way back to the light. It has been three months since that night. In Mirecoombe there is a sense of waking, of breaking free of a dream. The chapel still stands ruined on its hilltop, the hole in its roof unrepaired. Inside, where the rain can reach, a blanket of moss has spread across the stone, little white flowers like pinheads in the leaves. Below, in the village, Madge serves all in the Mare's Nest Inn—though it will take some time for her arm to heal—and across the valley people get ready for the season's work. Farmhands drive sheep and cattle up to summer pastures; in the small gardens, the mud is worked into rows of produce and the green shoots of summer break their heads above the ground. The buildings of the village have been repaired, even the cross across the boundary has been fixed. The two halves clamped together in an iron truss. Old protections strengthened; new ones applied.

Hugh Dell is buried next to his son, and Seren watches the graves. A host of piskies now roam free in the churchyard. Caleb, Hocken, and Jenkins have had what Cleaver took from them returned, and complete at last, Hocken can drift happily into the Undermoor. Who knows what waits for the others.

There has been talk (of course there has), of the night

389

the chapel fell. Of what each person saw, of what they felt. Certainly, the small shrines long since forgotten have seen a bloom of use, of charms and stones left on freshly swept granite. The work in the fields is easier, as small unseen hands help more fully with the work, a little gratitude going a long way. And though these old ways, these lost rituals, have found a footing once again, they are not alone. In the cracks of stone that make up her house, Delen Rowe has put back each charm her mother removed, but over the stove in her smoke-blackened kitchen a gorse cross hangs in the firelight. Because though some found comfort that night in the chapel, plenty more found fear. Once seen, some things cannot be forgotten, and they do not sit easily with everyone.

For some, like Calder and his remaining sons, like Cusk, though they have not forgiven Cleaver's actions, they still find comfort in his words. They sit each Sunday in a ruined church and close their eyes against the world they know now is full of devils. Even if it was their own Reverend that created them. Word is that Cleaver's replacement has already been found and is riding his way towards them. Which is all right and proper.

There must be balance.

Nancy Bligh sits on a blanket by the Fellmire, Selkie grazing close at hand and Patroclus sleeping in the fresh spring sun. The mire has been changed ever since that night. The ground is firmer, and flowers grow around the edge of the pool. Foxgloves sway in the breeze, and the heather and violets that grow at the edge fall smoothly into the water. The stump of hawthorn, Pel's knife still stuck trunk deep, and long thought dead, is blossoming again. Green shoots wrap around the handle of the blade and threaten to bury it in new wood, and the air is full of the almond scent of its starry white blossom.

Nancy has spent the season working. There is a new appetite

for help, from both the Underfolk and from Mirecoombe, and she has been busy. Her scar has faded to white on her forehead. In the time left each day she has practiced her craft, honed her skills. She has read Pel's books, the journals she saved from the boat. She has found some answers there. But the Murmur still worries her. Still threatens to carry her away even knowing its provenance. She has tried to find out what she can about her grandmother but can find no record. As though someone has removed all trace.

She has spent a long time too thinking of Callum. Why had he done it? Any of it? The only explanation, that after a life of rejection he just wanted to burn it all, his father's teaching and Pel's, destroy both their worlds, did not sit happily with Nancy. Not least of all because to believe that is to acknowledge her place in it. Even if she had been a child. Instead, she chooses to believe that Callum was searching for the truth of it. He had suffered, died, had tested Pel's stories, had pushed at the edges of the Undermoor and found them wanting. Then, reborn, had done the same in the service of his father. Tested another god. Both had come up short. Every answer spawning two questions, a hydra-headed puzzle. Nancy is thinking it all over for the millionth time when Patroclus wakes with a start and his tail begins to wag furiously. Nancy startles. It is unlike him to exert this much energy, and she looks about for the cause. She sees it soon enough: the black water of the Fellmire is bubbling again. A sick feeling hits her gut. He can't be alive, can he? She saw him die. Standing she takes the knife from its crop and braces herself for what comes next. She is not prepared for what does, the knife falls clattering from her hand. In front of her, shining in the morning sun which refracts as it passes through him is the ghost of her father, Pel.

'Hello, Nancy.'

'Pel… '

The shade smiles under sad eyes and lifts a hand to stop Nancy rushing to him.

'I'm not here, Nancy, not really. But I had power enough to see you, just this once. The God of the Mire and I have decided to share duties.' Pel pauses here, smiles, unable to hide his pride. 'I need to tell you something, but first, I wanted you to know, Cleaver is here. Callum too. It will take time, I think, for them to reconcile, but they will find peace in the end. Jacob and I have been talking again, too. Who would have thought it?'

Nancy clamps a hand to her mouth, tears streaming down her face.

'Pel, I've got so many things to ask you… ' Pel shakes his head.

'No, Nancy. No. I don't have long, and I need you to hear this. There is murmuring, chattering, here in the Undermoor. I don't know what they mean and that in itself is a concern. I need you to be ready.'

Nancy looks at him in confusion, in anger.

'What are you talking about? Not a word of thanks?'

The ghost shimmers in the daylight and Nancy cannot make out the expression on her father's face.

'You lied to me. About my magic. About the things I could do. You made me scared of it, you took away my history, Pel.'

Pel's ghost shifts.

'And I am sorry for it. I had always meant to tell you when you were ready. I—'

'No,' Nancy closes her eyes, turns away. 'Don't you dare pretend it was some grand plan, admit it. Admit you were scared.'

The ghost of Pel thinks, the black water beneath him not reflecting his form, for several moments in the spring light.

'I was, yes. I was scared. But not of you. Never of you. Nancy, I had no idea how to teach you to control it. I was scared I would break you, cause you to lose control... I could only teach you what I knew. After Callum died, after I saw what my help did, I couldn't bear losing you. You were, you are, far more capable, more powerful than he was. I couldn't risk it.'

'And you knew nobody who might have helped me? Not Madge, or another Keeper, not that girl who drew your tattoos?'

'You're right. I knew others too.'

'You arrogant old bastard.' She gives a watery laugh. 'You damned Callum because you knew what was best for him, and you came close to damning me. And now, what? You're trying to control a god! Dammit, Pel. Because you thought you had the answers, you left me and I died and before you say a single word, I know you brought me back. I know you gave your life but that isn't the point. Is it?'

For the first time in life or death, Pel has nothing to say.

'I love you. You are my father and I love you so much that seeing you again is tearing me apart. And I love you for what you've given me. I will be a good Keeper, Pel. I will be good. But I'll not be you.'

Lord Pelagius Hunt smiles in the sunlight.

'I know, Nancy. I know.'

Nancy's face softens. It's three months since he left her and though she's not forgiven him yet, she loves him. She can see beneath his smile he's still itching to tell her his news.

'Well then, out with it. What must I fight now? What have you let out?'

The ghost's shoulders sag and when it speaks it does so sadly.

'This is not my doing. Not directly, at least. Something is coming, something powerful and old and I don't know how to stop it. The King can't, I can barely keep him in check, and I don't have much magic left.

'I only have a name, Nancy. Every spirit knows it, it seems, and they are scared. All of them keep repeating the same thing.' There is a cold gust of wind, and the ghost of her father is gone, leaving only an echo behind. An echo that tastes of the sea.

'The Mother, Nancy. The Mother is coming.'

DEAD NETTLE

Deep below, in the Undermoor, Pel sits quietly in the hall of the god. Since Nancy left, the pair have been in silence. Neither knowing quite what to say to the other. It is Pel who breaks the silence.

'Did you think about my suggestion?'

The old god turns his masked head towards Pel, but he does not speak. Since Nancy left, Pel has watched him, the King of the Undermoor. Studied him.

'Your Grace.' The god's voice rumbles around the chamber.

'Pardon?'

'You will address me properly, Lord Hunt. As I do you. Out of a courtesy I do not have to maintain.'

Pel thinks for a moment, sucks his teeth.

'Very well, your Grace.' He even bows, just a little, then walks to the centre of the chamber and looks the ageing god in the eye.

'How does it feel, the matter of my being knitting that hole in your skull together?'

There is a rumble from behind the mask, the disgruntled acknowledgement of the old Keeper's help.

'It hurts.'

'Yes, I'm sorry, it will.' Pel walks closer and lays a ghostly hand on the arm of the monarch. 'I can't trust you; you see. You're broken. You can't rule this—' Pel gestures out towards the balcony, across the Undermoor— 'broken. You've made some bad decisions. I know it was Callum, but I can't leave you in charge. You need help.' The crack in the old god's skull is almost closed now, synapse firing to synapse beneath it.

'What have you done, Keeper?'

'Your friend Bluecap told me how things stood. She didn't tell you that, did she? She's scared of you. They all are. They call you mad. Even Cutty was surprised you let him out, let alone the Hunt. So, I prepared before I arrived here: I bound some parts of myself more tightly to my core. Just in case.'

Pel's voice breaks here, the old Keeper's confidence shaken. 'Nancy dying changed things. It clarified some things for me. I bear my part in this mess, my Lord, but so do you. You and I were each other's fail safes. I can't afford for you to be Nancy's, only to fail again.' Pel flicks the wrist of this left hand, forms the spells just as he did in life. There is a spark behind the old god's eyes, and then a stillness. 'You'll still rule, but so will I. We will be here for Nancy, together. There is a little of me in that head of yours now. You will listen to me. The Undermoor needs stabilising.' Releasing his fingers, Pel finishes the spell he has been working. It has drained him. Most of his essence inside the god, the ghost that remains is dim. 'Do you understand?' The old god squirms on his throne, a battle rages behind his eyes, but he nods.

'Now, my suggestion. These two... ' Pel gestures towards two lights that have floated into the chamber. His aides, the spirits that helped him on his journey through the Undermoor. 'Re-join them, give them their form. You've not used their matter, have you?' The old god shakes his head.

'You know it was those two that helped the boy.' The God of the Mire's face is grim.

'I do,' says Pel, 'but they helped me too, and I gave them my word. Besides, we have enough power yet to dismantle them if they're foolish enough to give us cause to.'

'Very well. I have not touched their matter. It lies where they fell.' Raising his arms, the god closes his eyes, and thunder cracks overhead. Rushing to the balcony once again, Pel watches the two lights dance out and into the space beyond. A stream of black, like coal dust, begins to fall from the sky and coalesce around them. Just as Cutty and Blue were rebuilt, so too is Gogmagog reborn.

The skeleton that forms is colossal; far across the Undermoor, the giant Gow cowers at the sight. Two heads blossom from a single neck, and as the skin folds down the giant's frame, laughter collides with the lightning. Once it is done, there is silence. The giant Gogmagog raises their hands, turning them over and inspecting them from each angle. In unison they turn their heads, tears falling like waterfalls from their eyes, gouging plunge-pools in the rocks at their feet. As they meet each other's gaze the two heads merge, as if a face has been pushed into a mirror, and when it is over, they speak as one.

'*Thank you, Lord Hunt. Thank you.*'

And turning, they are gone, long striding over the Undermoor and chatting away to themselves. King and Keeper lapse back into silence. It is the King that breaks it.

'Will you tell her?' Body or not, Pel's spirit bristles, tenses at the question. 'I felt it, as I remade her, where she comes from. Who her blood is. She does not know, does she?'

'She does not.'

The god laughs.

'So full of righteousness, Keeper. What contradictions fester within! She will learn it with or without you, you know that.' Pel sits for a moment, then sighs. Looks up to the rippling moon.

'I do. Forgive me, Nancy, I do.'

ACKNOWLEDGMENTS

I WANT TO thank my partner, Bex, for her unwavering support and belief in a creative career that has taken a little longer to get off the ground than I may have led her to believe. She has listened to fragments, scraps of ideas and nonsense whenever I've needed her to, and I can't wait for her to read this (when it arrives in audio format).

I couldn't have done this without the support of my family. My dad and my brother, but especially my mum. Who's early readings, edits and suggestions made a huge difference to the first drafts and who despite ending every call and email with "feel free to ignore everything" had a huge impact on me and my writing.

To my friends, who listened with apparent enthusiasm to my sudden but complete pivot to writing, thank you. Particularly those who read the book early on and offered thoughts, support, and advice. Helen, Julie, Hannah, and Neil, I am so grateful for your help.

To my agents, John and Julie who have been, from the day I sent them my query, the most enthusiastic champions of my writing. I'm so glad to have you both in my corner, your ideas and edits have made *Gorse* blossom. Thank you for helping me put a little more blood and starlight into its pages. I can't wait to start work on all the other projects I both have and haven't told you about yet.

To Amy, my editor, whose feedback and incisive notes showed me *Gorse* in a whole new light and made its needles and flowers shine brighter for it.

To the team at Solaris, to everyone who has helped this book on its journey, thank you.

Finally, thanks to Cornwall, to trees bent sideways by the wind, and to the moors and mires I've fallen into. I found Pel and Nancy caught on your rocks, and I'll never forget it.

FIND US ONLINE!

www.rebellionpublishing.com

/solarisbooks /solarisbks /solarisbooks

SIGN UP TO OUR NEWSLETTER!

rebellionpublishing.com/newsletter

YOUR REVIEWS MATTER!

Enjoy this book? Got something to say?

Leave a review on Amazon, GoodReads or with your
favourite bookseller and let the world know!